29/2 ... A ... 5 B

GW01325946

About the Author

At eighteen, I undertook a nine years' stretch in the Royal Navy (Submarine Service) as I was bored with the English lifestyle. On leaving the navy at the age of twenty-eight, I decided to follow the sun, and went to South Africa; there I found out what living was really about and spent forty-three years of pure contentment. Due to the loss of my wife, and the problems that were growing there on a daily basis, I decided to return to the UK to have my book published, as the synopsis of my story was over here.

Not In My Backyard

Keith Hardy

Not In My Backyard

Olympia Publishers
London

www.olympiapublishers.com
OLYMPIA PAPERBACK EDITION

Copyright © Keith Hardy 2018

The right of Keith Hardy to be identified as author of
this work has been asserted in accordance with sections 77 and 78 of the
Copyright, Designs and Patents Act 1988.

All Rights Reserved

No reproduction, copy or transmission of this publication
may be made without written permission.
No paragraph of this publication may be reproduced,
copied or transmitted save with the written permission of the publisher, or
in accordance with the provisions
of the Copyright Act 1956 (as amended).

Any person who commits any unauthorised act in relation to
this publication may be liable to criminal
prosecution and civil claims for damage.

A CIP catalogue record for this title is
available from the British Library.

ISBN: 978-1-78830-068-1

This is a work of fiction.
Names, characters, places and incidents originate from the writer's
imagination. Any resemblance to actual persons, living or dead, is purely
coincidental.

First Published in 2018

Olympia Publishers
60 Cannon Street
London
EC4N 6NP

Printed in Great Britain

Dedication

I would like to make a dedication to Karen Corradi, who helped me keep my commitment to finishing this book during a very low period of my life

Preface

This story is completely fictional, and all characters and incidents depicted herein, are of my own imagination and have no authentic relation, in any way, to any other person whatsoever.

I am writing this book for two reasons; firstly, I want to enlighten all the innocent people around the world to the dangerous times that, although invisible to us, surround us on a daily basis. Also, I would like to implant in their minds a stronger awareness to be watchful as to what is happening around them during their normal daily routines. We do not need to be reminded of what happened in the United States of America on 9/11, and in the United Kingdom on 7/7, not forgetting the many other countries such as Spain, Bali, Kenya, Israel, Nigeria, Russia and Indonesia and so many other countries throughout the world that have been put through these horrendous and murderous attacks for reasons totally unknown to the people of the western world other than the perpetrators hate for our own beliefs, their own religious beliefs being of a very different interpretation to the normal western world's beliefs.

In these attacks, many innocent people have been killed or maimed: yes, hundreds of thousands of innocent men women and children. I am also writing this book knowing that the story line that I have interpreted in this book is a very real predicament that could happen, and will one day almost certainly take place, somewhere, sometime, in any one of the many countries throughout the world. I hope that reading this book will invigorate and enhance a greater awareness in people's minds of these very dangerous times that we are all having to live with. Yes, folks: times have changed immeasurably over the past twenty-five to thirty years, and, unfortunately, every person, no matter what your religion, race, creed or doctrine is, will have to live with it, probably throughout the duration of your life span and, most regrettably, probably well into your children's and, maybe, for all we know, even your grandchildren's life span.

The second reason that I am also writing this book is in honour of a man who, over a number of years, I came to revere; as time went by, he became my best friend and mentor. I met him at the very young age of eighteen, while I was serving in the British Royal Navy's Submarine Service. At that time he was serving with the British SAS (Special Air Service).

Never having known my father, I was, maybe, on reflection, I suppose unknowingly, looking for that very special someone to look up to, to respect and, to some extent, probably, admire. We kept in contact over a number of years, to the extent of a night on the town in London, a meal at a restaurant, or a few drinks in a bar, and even, one time, a football match in Portsmouth. All these unpromulgated meetings meant so much in my life, and, I am sure, meant just as much to him in his life. In those days I could never really work out why we were so close, but in later life it all came together.

Alas, I lost contact with him, due to both of us serving our time in the British armed forces; he was moving regularly to different parts of the world, doing what the SAS had to do, and I myself was being drafted to other submarines from time to time, and also to various parts of the world, so it was not really possible to keep in close contact; and I suppose I should have known that total loss of contact was an inevitability over such a long period of time, as, in those days, there were no internet sites or mobiles. In fact not many of us had even telephones at home, or even a car for that matter.

On leaving the Royal Navy in 1968, I immigrated into sunny South Africa, and started to build a new life around my family; then, out of the blue, two years into my time in South Africa, a miracle occurred, in an unforeseen meeting at a restaurant with a business associate. I found that the man whom I had grown to respect and admire all those years ago was living in South Africa, not in Johannesburg, but down on the south east coast of Natal, in Richards Bay. It was a great sensation to know that we were once again going to get together.

Our first meeting was a great sensation to both of us, but due to the fact that we had both grown up, so to speak, and obviously matured over the interim years, there was still that very special bond that I always knew would never be broken.

Even though we were living in different parts of South Africa, we always kept in very close contact; and although both of us were now married, and I myself had two young children, we spent many wonderful hours of intrigue and subterfuge together; plus, we had a very, very close kind of family / friendship relationship, but without living in each other's pockets.

Over the years in South Africa I spent a great deal of time in his company, where he related to me all the electrifying times that he had had during his time in the SAS, and later with MI6. It made my time in Submarine Service with the Royal Navy seem like a walk in the park on Sunday afternoon.

Because of my monumental admiration for both him personally, and his attitude and diversity to everything and everyone around him, it gave me the mental strength and, probably, above all, the character to put pen to paper, so to speak, in his honour.

Sadly he died on the 27th of February 2010. The Naughty Boys will always remember and miss you. WE SALUTE YOU!

Chapter One

My name is Steve Taylor, ex-SAS, and Special Services, commonly referred to as "THE REGIMENT".

I have served my Queen and country in the armed forces since I was a young immature lad of seventeen, when I joined the parachute regiment, looking for excitement, and a chance to have a look at the other interesting parts of the world. I served in a few western-bloc countries, and also in Ireland. Then, on reaching the rank of Lieutenant in the parachute regiment, which was about three years into my service, I came across those extremely powerful words: "Who Dares Wins." I made a few enquiries, and within a matter of six months or so, my whole life had been changed completely.

To me, it was something that I could not, as a virile young man looking for a life on the edge, resist. I applied for a transfer to the SAS immediately, and was put on a three-week acceptance course at the Brecon Beacon's, the SAS training grounds in Wales. The area around Brecon Beacon's is mountainous and just about the roughest terrain that you could ever find in the UK, and I must say the acceptance course was the most intensive, rigorous, demanding, mind-blowing and sometimes, even, totally humiliating experience that any man could ever want to go through.

During the four or five weeks I was there, we only had approximately four hours sleep a night; and many of the men, and they were exactly that, men, either pulled out, finding it far too overbearing, or they were rejected by their principals, and sent back to their initial regiments. There were only seven out of the fifty-nine recruits who had started the course who were accepted, and, very proudly, I was one of them.

After completing the course, I was ceremonially accepted, and was initially seconded into the counter-terrorist unit; this was just about the highlight of my life. I was just twenty-three years of age, and, serving with the very best of the best, the initial sensation inside me was totally electrifying and mind-blowing.

In my first couple of years with the SAS, I was in Ireland a couple of times for short periods on covert operations, then I served in a couple of eastern-bloc countries, Northern Africa and various parts of the Middle East. Throughout my time with the SAS, I obviously came into contact with M.I.6 and M.I.5 personnel, and liaised with them quite frequently on covert and counter-terrorism operations; so my being contacted by them was not an uncommon occurrence at all, and I took it as a normal day at the office. I was now a Captain in the SAS, which meant that I had a very high security clearance, and was very much fully involved in all SAS counter-terrorism operations; and obviously, from time to time, we were very closely involved, with both MI5 and MI6 or S.I.S (Secret Intelligence Service), as it is known in some circles.

I was asked to attend a meeting in Century House in Lambeth; that was then their H.Q. at the time. I was very much under the impression that this was in connection with some of the goings on in Ireland or Croatia. I had no idea that my whole life was once again going to experience another extraordinary transformation, of unbelievable proportions.

My meeting was with a Mr. D. Franks, about whom, although I had never met him, I had heard; and I had seen many memos from him from time to time. He was very high up in MI6, and was revered for his work in Ireland and the eastern-bloc countries, over a twelve to fourteen year period.

At the initiation of the meeting, we discussed certain areas where our paths had crossed over the years, especially in Ireland and Croatia. He was very detailed and explicit when co-ordinating what I had been involved in. I was very surprised at some of his knowledge; it even extended well into my private life. In fact, this guy knew more about me than any other person I knew, and he wasn't reading anything from my file; this was all emerging from right out of his head.

A full two hours into our discussions, I was asking myself what the hell this was all about. There didn't seem to be any point to the meeting at all; we were just reminiscing about the past. It was like two old school mates meeting after having been apart for a number of years, and assessing the whys and wherefores of what we had achieved in life.

Then two other people, a man and a woman, were ushered into the office. They seemed very plain, run-of-the-mill people, whom you would expect to have as neighbours in your middle-class quiet suburban street. After the formal introductions, and a few arbitrary questions that seemed to be leading absolutely nowhere, the mood of the meeting took an unexpected turn, and I was told that they were looking for trained recruits from the SAS, to be seconded into the Secret Intelligence Service (MI6); and seemingly I, Captain Steve Taylor, was right at the very top of their list.

Being confronted with this information, I was quite shocked to say the least; but all of a sudden, things were starting to make more sense. They were very strong in their resolutions, and spoke about me as if I was the best thing since sliced bread. Listening to all this lavish chatter in relation to myself and my years with the SAS made me feel like a genuine hero. In hindsight, I now realise that this was all bullshit, to whet my very youthful appetite.

After all the ins and outs had been paraded, all the 'I's dotted and the 'T's crossed, I sat totally mesmerised at the whole situation. I could not believe that I, Steve Taylor, was going to be a James Bond. I would have to practise: 'Taylor, Steve Taylor'; 'shaken not stirred'. But no matter how many times I said it, it just didn't sound anything like "Bond, James Bond". What, stupidly, did cross my mind was what my number would be, perhaps 0077?

At the end of the very long-drawn-out meeting, three and a half hours to be precise, I was told to take a couple of days to think things through thoroughly, and, as a result, I would then have a thorough and first-rate understanding of just what would be expected of me, and also, of course, what I could expect of them, if I accepted the position. I sat there in total and utter disbelief, as to what was being implied. I wanted to pinch myself, to see if I wasn't dreaming. It even crossed my mind that maybe this was all a joke.

I was ordered, in no uncertain terms, not to mention this meeting to anyone, not even my mother. It seemed kind of funny, really; it was all so captivating to me, and I knew that I was going to accept the position before the meeting was even over. You must understand that I was a young mature man, who had lived on adrenalin for the last five or six years; there was no chance that I was going to turn the position down, and the agony of having to spend two whole days before I could say yes was totally mind blowing. I was like a four-year-old child, counting the days before Father Christmas would come and give me my presents.

On my acceptance of the position, which was well within the forty-eight hour period they had given me in the meeting (I just couldn't wait the last forty-eight hours to open my presents when I was a child, and I guess I haven't changed), to put it bluntly, I was in total trepidation now as to what my future was going to bring, at the outset of a very new and exciting career.

I was ushered once again into Century House HQ for my indoctrination, which was basically a short introduction to a few bigwigs, and then a mound of very authoritative documents that I had to read, internally digest, and then, of course, sign, one of which was, obviously, the Official Secrets Act.

On my first day at the office, so to speak, I was put in an office with an older man. He went by the name of Charles Pierce, and he very quickly made it quite clear to me that he was Charles and not Charlie. I was told that he had been with MI6 forever, and some people inferred that he had been there since 1909, when MI6 was first formally established; but of course, that was a total exaggeration.

Over time, Charles became my mentor, so to speak, and, over the next few years, we became very good friends both in and out of the field. I admired his sumptuous lust for exactness, both in his work at HQ, and also in his home environment. It was this that gave me a momentous advantage when I was in the field, just knowing that I had Charles Pierce back there at Century House, backing me up to the hilt.

Charles's wife had died of ovarian cancer seven years before I came on the scene, and, since then, I was told, he had put his head down, and lived for his work. He was the most meticulous guy one could ever meet, in every way, even in his dress. In his work, all the 'I's had to be dotted and the 'T's had to be crossed; it was either perfection or nothing at all with Charles. To have a man like that behind you when you were in the field was a godsend, make no mistake about it; he made me feel very secure in every way, and that, I can tell you, is very important when you are in the field and your life is on the line.

Over the next few years I spent quite a lot of my time in Pakistan, the Punjab (in Northern India), Israel, Yemen and Libya; and Charles was always there watching my back from Century

House HQ in London. This took away any excessive pressures from me, and made my assignment, although still very dangerous, much less worrying.

Alas, as the years went by I had come to the conclusion that there must be better ways of making a living. I was tired of living on my wits, I wanted a taste of the real life; I wanted to meet with my friends for a drink on Friday evening, and go with them to watch the Arsenal wipe the floor with the other first-division football clubs; but most of all, I wanted to be able to tell my friends what my job really was, instead of lying all the time. They all thought I was into imports and exports.

When I resigned from the SAS the first time – and, let me tell you, if you are an MI6 agent it is not easy to resign – I then resolutely looked around for something that would satisfy me both physically, mentally and, most importantly, emotionally; and, knowing the type of person I was, it wasn't going to be a walk in the park to find that, that I can tell you.

Around eighteen months into my retirement from MI6, I was doing some private investigation work with Vee, my now partner, and pride and joy. We had a small private investigation company up and running, and we did a lot of work for large commercial and industrial companies in and around the London area, covering all aspects of company security. Funnily enough, because of my security clearance in MI6, we even did quite a lot of work for various governmental departments. It was all very interesting work, especially with the awesome speed and growth in and around the computerisation infrastructure that was coming into the business sector at a very fast pace, and the growth in technology, that seemed to be moving faster than the speed of light. Then, of course, mobile phones suddenly burst on to the scene. All this brought a dynamic change for everyone in all walks of life, especially in the security business, as the bad guys were always even with, and, I've got to say, sometimes ahead of, the good guys. My business grew very quickly, helped by all the modernisation of the communications infrastructure. I have to admit that it was also a very lucrative business, and I must acknowledge that both Vee and I gladly enjoyed it very much.

Vee and I were an item by this time. We had met in the Punjab in India some three years earlier. She was working at the time for the Indian intelligence agency, and was stationed on the border between India and Pakistan. We were now living in Greater London, in a nice house with a back garden, a barbecue, a white Scottie dog, namely, Basil, and, yes, I had to admit that my life was really coming together now – or so I thought.

It was at about this time that I was more or less blackmailed into going back to MI6 to do some investigations into the Lockerbie aircraft bombing in Scotland. I had to leave Vee to run the company, and I spent about ten months running around Libya in the Middle East trying to put two and two together and always coming up with three or five. I can tell you that it took me about a year to get the sand out of my shoes and eyes.

I didn't realise it then, but I know now that governmental politics was the prime evil that was making me always come up with three or five as the answer all the time. I have never understood politics or politicians; they are voted in by the masses, and then they spend as long as possible lying to the masses, so that they can stay in power longer, only so that they can lie to the masses even more. I just cannot get my head around all this governmental crap. I always knew them as public servants: now they are gods. Are they clever, or are we, the masses, bloody stupid? It makes you think, doesn't it?

In the midst of my time in Libya working on the Lockerbie incident, I was picked up from my hotel room in Tripoli by a gang of armed militia. After being beaten into a state of semiconsciousness I was handcuffed, blindfolded, thrown into the boot of a car and driven for over four hours through the very rough terrain of the Libyan Desert. In the searing heat of the day, I can tell you that it wasn't much fun at all. I was taken to a small, run-down compound, deep in a very mountainous region, where I was questioned and beaten routinely on a daily basis for about six weeks; and, had it not been for my training and experience over the years with the SAS, I don't think I would have come through that experience alive.

I was freed from there with the help of eight SAS soldiers, who willingly put their lives on the line for me. It was very much touch and go for me, as I was in very bad shape, both mentally and physically, when they came and extricated me. Also, it was quite devastating to all involved in my extrication, as Corporal John Hamer, a well-liked and distinctive soldier, was killed in the fire fight that ensued in securing my release.

It took me nearly a year before I was back in the driving seat, so to speak, and I then vowed "never, never again," but I had said that a few years ago, hadn't I?

It was August now, and Vee's thirty second birthday, and to celebrate it we were going on our own to our favourite French restaurant that was situated smack in the centre of London. We were both looking forward to an evening of good palatable French food and wonderful French wine, and also, last but not least, the best company any man could wish for.

We were ushered to our table by a very French and very, very gay waiter; he sat us down at a table, making an enormous fuss over Vee. I must admit, though, she looked absolutely stunning in her black wet look dress, and she could probably make any gay man think about his sexual preferences. We ordered our wine, which was uncorked and poured with all the dramatisation you could imagine from a French gay man.

We ordered our meal. It was asparagus and lentil soup to start with, followed by a fish main course; and, as always, with Vee's favourite, a crème de menthe sweet that would embellish and complete a most memorable and wonderful evening.

We chatted and laughed, and I must have told her I loved her twenty times or more. We held hands across the table for the entire first course. When we had finished our soup, and had been served with our main course, the lights had been turned down and the candle light from the table flickered across both our smiling faces. Vee's olive skin exaggerated her sparkling white teeth and her eyes twinkled wildly in the candle light; her long thick black hair played with the shimmering of light from the candle to give her something of a halo. This evening was going to be the most memorable time that we had ever spent together; or, at least, that was what I thought at that moment.

Chapter Two

The enormous force and sound of the blast ricocheted throughout the building with a shocking and thunderous crashing sound. Windows shattered, chairs and tables flew through the air, and I am sure that the sheer power of the blast must have lifted the roof from its structural locations and fallen back into position again. My ears were ringing with a very dull Bow Bell ring; my eyes were not focusing too well, but I suppose that that was because of the shocking power and the blinding flash that came from the explosion.

I was laid flat on my back on the floor where I had landed. I was completely disorientated and unsure what had happened. The room was obviously now in darkness, and when something like that happens, no matter who or what you are, it's hard to convey the reality of the situation; one minute I was eating beautiful French cuisine with an even more beautiful dinner partner, then, the next minute, I was hurtling through the air like a paper tissue in a force ten gale. As I looked over at the devastation that was in my view from the floor I asked myself the inevitable questions that always come to mind at a time like this. Was I still alive, or was I dead? And the other question of course: what the fuck had happened?

As my mind and eyes started to focus a little better, my SAS military instinct took over. I started to go through all my body parts and limbs. Everything seemed to be there. I could hear someone moaning close by, and intermittent whimperings coming from various quarters of the restaurant; there were female voices screaming hysterically and painfully from just about every direction in the room. The restaurant was now pitch black, the air was full of dust, smoke and debris, and my body was crying in pain just about everywhere.

All of a sudden, I was taken back some ten or so years; a smell came across my nostrils. It was the very strong pungent smell of marzipan. I then knew that this explosion was from semtex or, as most people know it, C4. This could only be a terrorist attack. Don't tell me the bloody Irish had started up all over again.

I lifted my head and tried to roll on to my side. My heart sank; dread rushed through my mind, as I could not move one of my legs. I tried to focus my eyes on my lower torso, dreading what I was about to see. As my eyes adjusted, I saw the body of a man sprawled across the lower part of my left leg. It was the gentleman who had been sitting to my right with the old lady, probably his mother. It definitely wasn't him doing the screaming; his right arm and shoulder were missing, as was the back of his head. I remembered that he had been wearing light blue trousers and a white cashmere sweater. The trousers were shredded now, and the cashmere sweater was adorned with a mixture of blood and brains.

I prised my legs from beneath him and in doing so I nearly lost my left shoe. Having looked at the guy in the cashmere sweater, I could count myself bloody lucky to be still in one piece.

The police, fire and ambulance services' sirens were wailing loudly out in the street, and uniformed men and women were rushing into the deluge, going from person to person trying to help and give comfort to the lucky ones who were still alive...

I got to my feet very gingerly, giddiness came over me and I stumbled forward. Someone grabbed hold of me from behind with very firm yet very gentle hands. He lowered me back to the ground.

It was a fireman in all his regalia; his mouth was covered with a sort of surgical mask and he was wiping my face with a table cloth. I could see blood all over it, and knew that the blood could only have been mine.

"Are you OK?" he said, shining his torch into my face,

"Yes, sure," I lied, "What the hell happened."

His reply was muffled by the frightening sound of police and ambulance sirens; he wiped my face again, then moved away to help other people around me. I once again staggered to my feet, and tried to move myself through the debris. My eyes were scanning the floor; where the hell was Vee?

Dust and smoke was burning my eyes, and a sharp acidic smell burned in my nose and throat. I could still make out the marzipan smell of the C4 explosive. My eyes felt like two gravel pits. I reached up to rub them; my hand felt wet and sticky. I glanced down and saw that my hands were covered in blood and a thick mixture of dust.

At that moment I caught sight of Vee's spread-eagled body. She was laid flat on her back with one arm across her face, and her black wet look dress was up around her waist. As I clambered over towards her my foot slipped. I tried to grab at an overturned table, misjudged it and fell prone on my face. I felt nausea coming over me as I tried to get Vee back into my sights again; then I must have blacked out.

I am not sure whether I lost consciousness at this point; but the next thing I saw was a police officer kneeling over me. He also had a surgical mask over his mouth. I could see a great deal of sympathy in his eyes above the mask.

"Take it easy, sir, take it easy," he said. "There's help on the way."

I moved my head to my left; the policeman followed my gaze to Vee's naked legs as I tried to reach out to her with my right arm.

"Take it easy, sir, I'll check her out for you," he said. I watched as he went and knelt beside her. I could see him checking her pulse at her throat, and wiping away the dust and debris that was on her sprawled, forlorn body. As he finished, he pulled Vee's dress down below her knees, probably to preserve her dignity. A nurse took over from him, and the officer came trundling back through the debris towards me.

"I'm pretty sure she's OK, sir, just unconscious with a few light cuts and abrasions; and, looking around at the bloody mess in here, you can both be very thankful mate." He was wiping my face with a cloth of some kind while he spoke to me. "Lie still now sir, we'll have you both out of here and in good hands in no time at all." Then I must have blacked out again.

Chapter Three

The next thing I remember was waking up in a bed of either very heavily starched, or canvas sheets. My body was sore, and my head was booming like a bass drum. Also, I was struggling to focus my eyes; it was like looking through a cloud or mist of cotton wool. My body ached in just about every muscle and joint, and I felt like I was going to throw up.

When people on the movies wake up in hospital, and I was only presuming that I was in a hospital, because it smelt as a hospital normally smells, there are always family or a beautiful nurse standing by the bed. Not in my case: I got no one, and I was in a stark white tiled room with a plain pearl globe hanging from the ceiling. Welcome to the real world, Steve Taylor…

I guess I must have lost consciousness again. My head felt as if it was about to explode, or had just exploded. I opened my eyes slowly, and looked about the room and, to my amazement, the room had a dull red glow. I swung my head to the right, and saw one red globe burning on the wall. This place looks like a bloody morgue to me, maybe they think I'm dead, or, even worse, maybe I am.

To my relief, the door burst open and in came a nurse, a dragon of all dragons. In my next life I want to come back as a bloody film star; then someone else can have the dragons.

"Oh, we're awake, are we?" She said in a very business-like tone, but with a broad cockney accent that seemed to vibrate in the bare tiled room. She pressed a switch on the wall; the red light on the wall went out, and the pearl globe hanging from the ceiling burst into life. The nurse was built like a London bus, and her round face was the same colour. She was dressed in a white nurse's uniform, with large flat black shoes, and yet, considering her size, she walked silently across the tiled floor.

"How are we feeling today, ducky?" she said, in a heavy voice that emulated a growl. She had already pulled a thermometer from nowhere, and had made it disappear into my mouth. It's funny, you know: all doctors, dentists and nurses always stick something in your mouth and then ask you a question; maybe they are scared of what your answer will be.

"Where the hell am I?" I questioned, mumbling around the thermometer, "Why am I here? What the bloody hell is going on?"

"You're at St. Christopher's Maternity Hospital, ducky," she growled. She keeps calling me ducky; do dragons eat ducks? "Don't worry, love, you are not pregnant," She was grinning down at me.

"Sorry about the decor, but when sixty-three people are injured and fourteen dead in the same incident, there isn't much time to think about five-star comforts. We put you in here because it was the only bed left, unless you wanted to be in a room with forty or fifty two-day old babies, crying and screaming twenty-four-seven."

"Fourteen dead and sixty-three injured?" I blurted, as she whipped out the thermometer with deadly accuracy.

"Yes, ducky, sixty-three injured, and fourteen dead. I don't know what this world's coming to, all this terrorism crap. You can count yourself very lucky that you were just about the least injured: a few cuts and abrasions around your face, some bruising on your upper and lower body, and a very bad case of concussion. Other than that you are in pretty good shape." With that she took out the largest syringe I had ever seen.

"What in hell's name are you going to do with that?" I blurted, wide eyed at the size of the thing.

"If you're a good boy and roll over, I'm going to inject you in the meaty part of that lovely bottom of yours; if not, I'll just have to find a nice bony part, and listen to you howl."

Her eyes stared at me questioningly. I could see she wasn't playing games, so I slowly turned on my side, facing the white tiled wall.

"How do you know anything about my lovely bottom?" I groaned, as I slowly and painfully turned again, back on to my stomach.

I swear that she must have had the hands of an angel. I never felt the needle at all, just a slight burning sensation as she ejaculated the fluid into me; in fact the little slap on backside she gave me as she extracted the needle was all I felt.

She looked at me, and I think I saw a crease of a smile, as she said, "I was on duty two days ago when you were brought in, let me tell you, you have no secrets from me, ducky, no secrets at all." As she said it, she was waving her little pinkie in the air, and now she had a big grin across her face, and didn't look at all like the dragon of a few minutes ago.

"Two days ago," I gasped, turning trying to sit up, "Have I been here two days?"

"Yes ducky, two whole days."

"That's it," she said, as she checked the bandage around my face and wrists. "I'll come and change your dressing in a little while, and maybe a cup of soup would go down well, what do you think?" Her eyebrows rose up at least an inch making her last words into a question.

"Yes, maybe that would be nice, nurse, thank you," I said, smiling at her.

Just then the door burst open, and in walked a doctor; at least, I presumed he was a doctor, his white coat open and furling behind him, stethoscope around his neck, with a look on his face that said 'Trust me'!

"Ha! conscious at last, I see," he said, in a typical doctorly tone. He pounced on me, shining a light first into my left eye, then my right. "Mmm," he said. "You still have quite a bad concussion, sir. How's the head feeling?" he said, looking at what I presume was my file.

"It feels like a war zone in an atomic attack," I said, very seriously.

"Yes, I bet it does; you were very lucky Mr..." He paused and glanced down at my file. "Taylor, you were very lucky indeed; a few cuts and bruises that shouldn't leave any scars. Although the concussion will take a little time to rehabilitate, but then you should be back to square one I'm sure.

"I'm Doctor Burns, by the way; I've been looking after you for the last couple of days," he held out his hand, which I gripped firmly.

"It's good to see you back in the land of the living" he said, smiling down at me. "As I said, there doesn't seem to be any complications at all; however, let's just give you a quick once over," he put his stethoscope into his ears, and I got the cold end against my chest. "Breathe nice and deep! Good. OK, roll over. Breathe nice and deep again, excellent."

He was writing on a pad when I had turned over on to my back.

"Any pain in your ears?" he asked.

"No pain, Doc, just a hell of a whistling." I put my thumb and index finger to my nose, squeezed, and blew hard, but to no avail.

"You don't worry about the whistling; it will go away given time."

During these procedures, I had been trying to put what had been said into some kind of logic. Somehow nothing was making sense.

"Doctor Burns, isn't it?" I asked.

"Yes," he replied, looking into my ears with another cold instrument.

"Doctor – just how long have I been here? And how long have I been unconscious?"

"Two days since the explosion; it happened late on Friday night, and you were brought here in the early hours of Saturday morning around twelve thirty. You've had a very bad concussion, and have been comatose up to now, and it's now Monday, and the time is," he looked down at his watch, "five forty five."

"Day or night?" I asked.

"Oh, yes, there are no windows down here, sorry; yes, its five forty five in the evening," he said, smiling down at me, in his best bedside manner.

"What caused the explosion, Doc?" I asked. "The nurse," I looked around the room but she had gone, "said it was a terrorist bomb."

"Yes, it was a terrorist bomb, or at least that's what the papers say. No one has yet claimed responsibility for it, though," he replied, not lifting his head from writing in the folder he had lifted from the foot of my bed. "You can thank your lucky stars it wasn't a nail bomb, I dread to think of the devastation that would have been caused in the restaurant."

"Doc," I asked, "I was with a friend that night, a lady: dark hair, olive skin, in a black wet look dress, and I was wondering if you knew how she was. Her name is Kaveeta Ashenda, we call her Vee for short."

"No, sorry," he said looking at his notes, "But it was such a mess that night, we didn't have any time to take much notice of anything. Our aim was to save lives and look after the injured. With regard to remembering any single person, that would be impossible. Also, most of the injured were sent to different hospitals. You can imagine: sixty-three people injured, there isn't a hospital in greater London which would be able to fit even twenty very badly wounded people in at such short notice."

The dragon pranced into the room again, with a tray of stainless steel torture equipment, and a mug that definitely smelt like chicken soup. She put the torture equipment down on the table at the foot of the bed, put another two pillows behind my head, and helped me up to a sitting position, then she handed me the mug of soup. I took a sip, it tasted like the nectar of life.

"Nurse," said Doc Burns, turning to face her. "Can you try to find out the whereabouts of this gentleman's" – gentleman, that's a first, let me tell you – "young lady. Her name is Kaveeta Ashenda, Vee for short." He looked at me over his glasses for confirmation. "Correct?" he said. I nodded in acknowledgement, and then he turned back to the nurse and said, "Have a look in the computer; maybe you can track her down and find out her whereabouts."

Doctor Burns watched, as she left the room, then walked over and closed the door behind her; he turned back towards me, with a very analytical look on his face.

"Mr. Taylor," he had a questioning look on his face. "May I call you Steve?" It wasn't a questioning look any more; it was a worried look.

"Sure, Doctor, I've been called a lot worse in my time," I replied.

"Steve, after the explosion, the police spent a lot of time interviewing the people who could be interviewed, and going through the personal effects of people who, like yourself, could not be interviewed, for obvious reasons."

He glanced briefly down at the floor then back to me.

"I was subsequently ordered to put you in a private ward. I explained that we didn't have a private ward empty; but they insisted that you be moved to a private ward immediately."

His eyes were looking straight into mine, and I could see something was worrying him.

I was," he went on, "at this point in time, very unsure of your physical state; so I couldn't take a chance in moving you to another hospital. Thus we put a bed in here and moved you in." He smiled down at me. "This, by the way, is our morgue; it doesn't get used very often, as this is a maternity hospital, and you can understand that we don't have much need for a morgue."

Doctor Burns walked from the door where he had been standing, and perched one cheek on the bed.

"Steve, quite a few people had a direct interest in your medical prognosis." Looking at the Doctor I noticed that the worried look on his face was getting stronger. I felt my body go rigid; I was sure I knew what was coming next. Why me, O Lord?

"After we moved you in here," he went on, "a man came to see me, a Mr. Donald Franks."

With that I just wanted to be sick.

"He said he was with MI6; he seemed to know you very well. He said you were both old friends in fact, and had worked together for a number of years so I have to presume you are also MI6."

So bloody Frankenstein had found me. My body was shaking, and if the dragon were to take my temperature now, it would read below freezing. Every time this individual comes into my life, my whole world gets turned upside down.

"I wouldn't say old friends, doc. But our paths have crossed from time to time; and I can assure you that I am not MI6, well, not any more, anyway." I rubbed my eyes to try to get the blurred vision away, and said, "Christ, what a bloody over-statement. Old friends we were definitely not, Doctor Burns."

"Steve," he said adjusting my pillows. "Since Mr. Franks left, he has had a policeman standing outside the door in the corridor, twenty-four hours a day. Only Nurse Davidson, whom you have met, and Sister Richardson, who has never seen you awake, and myself, obviously, have been allowed into this room. I have been given strict instructions to inform Mr. Franks as soon as you regained consciousness again."

"To be frank, please excuse the pun, Steve, I take great exception to people with Mr. Frank's arrogance and intolerance towards others. He seems to take great pleasure in belittling people and in showing an attitude of authority, or, even more so, a bull-in-a-china-shop attitude, towards both myself and my staff."

Doctor Burns looked towards the door then back at me.

"Steve," he said, "I can hold him off for a couple of days; I can tell him you are too sick for visitors, or still comatose. It's entirely up to you."

He got up from the bed, crossed his arms in front of himself, and walked towards the door.

"What do you think, Steve? Do you want to see him now, or would you like me to hold the son of a bitch off for a couple of days?"

I emptied the last drop of chicken soup down my throat; I must admit, it was great.

"Thanks, Doc." I said in reply. "Thanks, but no one, as you put it, holds Donald Franks off for a couple of days. The cops outside would have seen the chicken soup come in, and I can assure you that he will have already contacted Franks and told him I'm conscious; and you can bet your bottom dollar that he will be high-tailing it here at this very moment."

I started to feel dizzy at the thought of it, and the single light globe started to get blurred. I am not sure whether it was the concussion's effect, or the thought of Frankenstein walking through the door at any moment.

Then it suddenly struck me that maybe Franks might have some information as to the whereabouts of Vee. I have got to admit it though, I hoped that he didn't, really, because Frankenstein was Frankenstein, and if he had information, it would definitely cost me an arm and a leg to get it.

"Well, Steve, I want you to sleep a little now," the Doc said, in his quiet but strong doctorly tone. Your eyes are still a little cloudy, and, as from now, only good rest and a little nutritional food can bring you back to normal health."

With that, he turned and walked from the room, his open white coat furling behind him.

I don't know how long I had been sleeping, but the noise of some kind of instrument being dropped into a stainless steel bowl or tray caught my attention. I opened my eyes, and into my view came an angel in a nurse's uniform. She had short reddish blonde hair with her little white cap perched on top of her head. Her mouth was one of those mouths that seem to have twice the teeth a mouth is supposed to have; and her face had a sort of sparkle. Putting the whole situation together, I suppose she was the one who was always there when James Bond woke up in hospital.

"Good afternoon, Mr. Taylor," she said in a beautiful Irish lilt. I was feeling better already. I could feel the concussion disappearing, and my eye sight was getting better by the second.

"I just want to give you your injection; can you roll on your side. It won't hurt, I can assure you," she lilted.

Roll on my side? I would roll round the globe for her if she asked me.

"There you are, all done. How are you feeling? Would you like me to get you something to drink? Or maybe you are ready for some food?" I didn't reply; I couldn't reply. I had only just noticed those dark, dark green eyes.

"Are you OK, Mr. Taylor"? she asked.

Suddenly, I came back to reality

"Yes, yes; I'm fine, Nurse," I stammered. "I would love a drink, but I don't think you will have my brand in the hospital."

"Sister will do fine, thank you," she said, correcting me in a business-like manner. Then she checked the dressings on my face and arms. "Well, we are getting better aren't we?" she smiled.

When she talked, she sang. This girl could win the Eurovision song contest just talking.

I was starving all of a sudden, but I was scared that if I told her, she would go away and never come back. Standing in front of me was the best cure for anything, and I had discovered her.

"Yes Nurse, sorry, I mean Sister," I said, reluctantly. "Some food would be great, thank you."

"Let me see what I can rustle up for you." With that she turned and showed me the rear view of heaven, as she walked from the room.

I turned over to face the wall, and snuggled under the sheets to await my angel's return with my food. Maybe I had dozed off again, I don't know, but I heard her return. I turned on to my back and opened my eyes. It was the worst sight I had seen in three bloody years.

"Well, Taylor, you're looking much better now."

It was Frankenstein in the flesh – no, belay that, I don't think he has any flesh. This guy just isn't human. He hates humans, in fact; and I don't think he likes anything or anyone.

"Why did I know you would be here before long, Franks?" I glared at him, "When the bad penny shows up, everyone can always count on you to come and steal it," I retorted.

"Don't be like that, Taylor! I've saved your arse so many times, I've lost count. I was sure I saw a slight smile on his lips as he spoke.

"Then fuck off and save someone else's arse. I have learned to save my own arse over the past few years and I find it much more satisfying."

The door opened and the light from the hallway spread across the floor and in walked my Irish angel with a tray of food held in her two hands.

"And who might you be, sir?" My angle spat placing the tray on the table at the foot of the bed. "Mr. Taylor is still not up to visitors yet."

"Franks, Donald Franks is my name, MI6," he retorted flashing his identification wallet. "I would appreciate it if you would leave us alone for a while. I have some questions I would like to ask Mr. Taylor."

"I don't care if you are the King of bloody England, Mr. Franks. I want you out of my ward now." Where had my angel gone to? She didn't sing those words, they came out like venom from a rattle snake. "Go, out, now," she ordered, pointing to the door, "Do you think I'm talking to the bloody leprechauns? Go, out, now," she repeated, pointing her index finger towards the door.

I was staggered: Frankenstein turned and walked out of the door. Either he had had a change of heart over the last few years or he had just met his match. I think it was the latter. Franks went scampering through the door without a murmur, and I started to giggle like a child; I had never seen anyone get the better of Franks before, and it was a pleasure to watch.

"Come, now, Mr Taylor; let's get some sustenance into that body of yours." The angel was back, and she was singing again. It was as if I had dreamt of Frankenstein being here.

Doctor Burns entered the room. He had a grin from ear to ear on his face.

"I saw our Mr. Franks just now," he said, with a gleam in his eyes. "Why do I think that he has just felt the venom of my favourite nursing sister?"

Her eyes glanced up from the tray that she was settling on my lap. She just looked straight into my eyes, not saying a word; but those eyes, those beautiful dark green eyes and the grin on her mouth said everything that needed to be said.

"There you are, Mr. Taylor, it's not much," she said, apologetically, "but it's the best I could get at this time of day. Eat as much as you can. I'll be back in a couple of minutes to change your dressings, and then settle you in for the night. A good night's sleep, and I think you will be as right as rain. What do you think, Doctor Burns?" And with that and a few flaps of her wings, my angel was gone again.

"I think your Mr Donald Franks has just met our own MI6. What do you think, Steve?" The doctor said with a very tenuous smile on his face.

I had a mouthful of food, but I was grinning from ear to ear and nodding my head.

"Sorry, Steve," he said, "There's still no word on Miss Kaveeta Ashenda, but we are still trying to trace her. I will let you know instantly, as soon as we have even the slightest information at all."

"Thanks a lot, Doctor Burns; I really do appreciate it."

With that, Doctor Burns turned and walked out of the ward.

A couple of minutes later the door opened again and in fluttered my angel. She picked up the tray from the table at the bottom of the bed, and started to change my dressings.

"Your wounds are healing very quickly," she sang, "and I'm sure they are not going to leave any scar tissue at all. You were very lucky, Mr Taylor."

After a couple of minutes of straightening up my bed and putting the old bandages into a plastic bag, she turned to walk out of the door, as she got to the door she looked back at me, and for a second I could only see one beautiful green eye, and I realised she had just winked at me.

Chapter Four

I awoke feeling like a different person. I think it must have been because the angel had tucked me in. I had a grin on my face second to none, reliving the sight of Frankenstein meeting his master. My head was now very clear, and my eyesight was nearly back to normal. A good shower, or, better still, a bed bath by the angel, and I would be as right as rain.

The door opened, and in walked the dragon. I must have got better: she didn't look at all like a dragon any more, and she was smiling broadly, with a clear air of serenity in her eyes.

"Good morning, Mr. Taylor, how are we this morning?" she chirped. "I'm going to give you a bed bath and then a nice breakfast before the Doctor comes to see you." She put the bowl of warm water on the table next to me, and was undressing me as if I was her one-year-old baby. I felt a little embarrassed during the procedure, but I must admit she was very competent, and totally business-like.

After I had finished my breakfast, I felt that I was getting back to normal. The food was great: cheese and tomato omelette, and a couple of slices of toast. Not what you would expect for hospital food; or maybe it was because I was hungry, and needed the sustenance.

I took my watch from the side table, and was surprised to see that it was only five a.m., I never thought there was a five a.m. in a morning. I took the magazine that had been left on my side table, and started to browse through it, not reading, just looking at the pictures.

I never heard anyone enter the room; I just saw the shadow across the bed. It was Doctor Burns.

"Good morning, Steve, how are we feeling this morning?" he asked, in a real Doctor's bedside manner.

"Great, thanks, Doctor Burns," I replied. "I think I'm as close to normal as I'm going to get. My vision seems to be coming right, and the whistling in my ears is down to a very low hum."

He walked over to my bedside and proceeded to do the usual doctorly activities, checking my eyes, nose, ears, throat, glands, heart and lungs, back and front; it was never ending. He never uttered a word. so I presumed that he was of the same opinion as I was.

"OK, Doc?" I enquired, as he started making notes on my chart at the foot of the bed.

"Yes," he replied, "you must keep yourself in very good condition, Steve; your recovery has been quite remarkable. Now let's have a look at your blood pressure." He lifted my right arm, and did what he had to do, "Yes, good," he said, scribbling on my chart again," I think you should be out of here in within a couple of days."

"A couple of days, Doc, you must be joking!" I retorted. "I can't lie here for two days, Doc. I need to find Vee, please Doc!" I put on my best pleading voice. "I've got to get out of here today: she's very important to me."

He stood looking down on me, hands on hips, with a wily grin on his face. "If I let you go today, you must promise me you will take things very easy and I mean very easy. Rest is what you require; there is always the unknown with these types of injuries, Steve, and I strongly advise that you must be very, very careful in the next two or three days. No running or any over-exertion at all."

"I just need to find Vee, Doc. Then I will rest for a year if you like," I pleaded.

"OK," he said with some resolution, "Let's see what I can organise for you." With that, he turned, and left the room as quietly as he had entered.

I was laid on my back, hands behind my head, feeling good that I was about to be released into the real world. It was then that my real world disintegrated. In trudged Frankenstein. He stood at the foot of the bed with a sort of gloating look on his face that said 'got you'.

"Shit!" I exclaimed. "The bad penny again, what the hell do you want, Franks? I really thought I had seen the last of you three years ago."

Franks walked back to the door and closed it, then turning towards me, still having that gloating look on his face, he walked back over to the bed. He was dressed in his usual dark trench coat, the shoulders of which, and his hair, were really wet, so I had to presume that it was raining outside.

"How can you be so bloody rude, Taylor? I am only interested in your well-being. I must admit you got out of it very well, the angels were looking after you on Friday night."

"Don't bullshit me Franks," I retorted, "You have never had any one else's interests at heart. You don't even have a heart: you're MI6 and only MI6, and you always will be, you have never ever had even your family's interests at heart. I bet when you go to church and the preacher talks of God, you think he is talking about you. Now get the fuck out of here, before I call the wrath of Ireland to throw you out again."

He just stood gazing down at me. His face was totally emotionless; and his dark brown eyes were staring at me as if he could see inside my mind.

"If you are really interested in my well-being," I went on – I was on a roll now – "why don't you use the powers that be in your bloody MI6 to try to find out which hospital Vee, my dinner date, was sent to, or fuck off and leave me in peace."

My temper was rising fast. If the Doc had to take my blood pressure now, he would keep me here for at least ten years.

"Calm down, Taylor. Vee is one of the reasons I'm here. She's fine, but for a few bumps and bruises." His face was still totally expressionless.

"What the hell are you talking about, Franks? Do you know where she is?" I retorted. I had now sat up in bed and, probably because of the concussion, my temper and my blood pressure rising, I became quite dizzy. I could feel the sweat on my forehead start to run into my eyes, and my vision was getting blurred.

"Where the fuck is Vee, Franks?" I was shouting at the top of my voice. "I need to know where she is, and now."

Franks walked to the end of the room, picked up the chair that was standing behind the door and placed it next to the bed with the back of the chair towards me. He straddled it and placed his arms across the top, his eyes still totally expressionless.

"I got word when I was on my way over here," he said. "They didn't say where she was, just that she was safe and well. As soon as I get back I will find out where she is and let you know immediately."

He put both arms across the back of the chair; he was staring down at me, and his eyes and face had gone back to his normal dark sombre MI6 way of thinking.

"Taylor." Just the way he said it made my hair stand on end. "Remember, in 1975, you did us a big favour. You were sent into Ireland under cover to get information on the IRA guys that did the Birmingham bombing. Do you remember that, Steve?"

"Stop right there, Franks," I said. My temperature was now really rising. "Number one, I didn't do you a favour, you blackmailed me into doing it; and number two, I do not do favours for the fucking MI6. It took me two years to lose the Irish accent I had to manufacture, and at least another two years to get the mud off my boots. Franks, you can be assured that there is no way I am going back there or anywhere else for that matter. Get it into your thick skull that I'm not the idiot I used to be. All that for Queen and country crap is for the birds and your up-and-coming James Bonds you've got there."

Franks just stared back at me with his benign, wily smirk. "Steve, please hear me out." He got up from the chair, walked over to the door, opened it, and looked out into the passageway. He closed the door again, then turned to face me, leaning with his back against the door, and arms crossed in front of him.

"Steve, my boy, where you got Ireland from I do not know. Let me explain a few things, then we can discuss it with a full deck of cards, and both reading from the same page."

He moved from the door, and perched himself back on the chair. His face was about two feet from mine, and it gave me a very uncomfortable feeling.

"The bomb that exploded on Friday night in the restaurant you were unlucky enough to be in," he stopped, put his hand to his mouth, and coughed twice, "was not placed by the IRA or the new IRA. It was Muslim Islamic extremists who perpetrated it; although we have had no one owning up to it, we can say with a ninety nine per cent guarantee that it was done by home grown fundamental extremists, who are growing daily in the United Kingdom."

"Just answer me two questions, Franks," I retorted.

Franks put his hand up to stop me. "Steve I will answer all your questions when I have finished; all I am asking is for you to hear me out."

He put his hand inside his jacket and took out a pen; he rolled it vigorously between the fingers of both hands.

"Taylor," he said, shifting his eyes back towards me. "September the 11th was a day that the world will never forget, almost three thousand people were murdered in cold blood by Muslim extremists. If they had put some thought into it, and the timing had been two or maybe three hours later, it could have been as many as ten thousand innocent people murdered."

He coughed again into his hand. His eyes went up to the singular pearl light bulb hanging from the ceiling, he stared at it for a good fifteen seconds, then he looked back to me. I had never before seen emotion in Frank's eyes, and as he spoke, even more surprisingly, there was emotion in his voice also.

"Nobody could have predicted that that would happen, Steve; and, to be very honest, no one could have stopped it happening either."

His voice and temperament had changed. He stood up and began to pace the tiled floor.

"For the simple reason," he went on, "that no human being could or would ever expect another human being to implement such a catastrophic, murderous attack on innocent civilians. But this is now a new world, Steve, with very different rules, very different rules indeed, full of people with very wide-ranging political and religious ambitions with varying views."

I had never seen this side of Franks before, he was talking like a human being with a heart, and he was also calling me Steve. This was too much to grasp; I couldn't get my head around it, and I knew that there was something coming that was going to screw up my life again.

"Steve," he said, "what is going on in the world today is very serious, very serious indeed. We now have to look at things in a very different light. We have got a bunch of fanatics out there who have a religion that is far stronger than they themselves, and even their minds. The entire world over, there are millions of Muslim people; they are growing in numbers by the bloody hour and they can only see, because of their strong religious beliefs, what they are told to see." He came over and straddled the chair again.

"They are a people that state that they are peace loving, and yet in ninety percent of the countries that they populate, there is bloodshed in the name of Allah. Take Kosovo, Chechnya, Afghanistan, Pakistan, India, Iraq, Iran, Palestine, Malaysia, Indonesia. Even in Africa: Mali, Nigeria, Somalia. Look, Steve, I could go on forever." He was slapping the back of the chair with the palm of his right hand.

"These are a people," he went on, "who will kill, maim, and even massacre innocent people, men, women, and children; and because it is in the name of Allah then it is right in their eyes. They are total utter fanatics, who make Black September and the IRA look like children playing in a local park." He hit his right fist into his palm again. It made a sharp crack that resounded around the bare tiled room.

"Just a little information for you," he went on. "Did you know that one hundred and seventy British females born and bred in the United Kingdom, some British for over twenty generations, are marrying Muslim men and changing to the Muslim religion every year? This raises the question: will these females turn on their own in time to come? It makes you think, doesn't it? You can be very sure that some, if not all of them, will."

"In a lot of Islamic States," he went on, "we, as Christians, are not allowed to take a Bible or a crucifix into their countries, never mind teach Christianity; and yet they are spreading throughout Europe and the western world, in all walks of life, spreading their religion, building Mosques, and, because of our naivety in some cases, because of human rights in many others, the Western World as we know it is allowing it to happen openly; and I've got to add that our naivety and human rights is being shown as the foremost reason, but it is all really governmental, and mostly in the name of bloody oil."

He turned and walked towards the door. I jumped, as a loud crack rang out. Franks turned towards me; his knuckles were bleeding. He had hit the door with his clenched fist. I was quite surprised to see him bleed. I hadn't thought he had any blood in his veins.

The door burst open, and two police officers ran into the room, both were wide-eyed, and somewhat in a crouch position. "Everything OK, sir?" the Sergeant questioned glancing quickly around the room, and looking rather a little stupid.

"OK, Sergeant," Franks stammered. "Everything's fine, thank you." He waved his hand, as if playing cricket and bowling an underarm; and both officers quickly went out of the room, with embarrassed looks on their faces, Franks closed the door behind them and looked down at his damaged fist.

He turned and leant with his back against the closed door, took a handkerchief out of his pocket, and wrapped it around his hand. He looked across at me. At first I thought it was rage that I saw in his eyes; but, surprisingly, I realised it was fear. This was not the bombastic Franks that I had known over the years; this was definitely a new more meaningful Franks.

"Steve," he said in almost a whisper, "These bastards have got to be stopped, or the world as we know it will change to a world of adversity, where all men, women and children will live in fear, every day of their lives.

"They put bombs on planes, and destroy innocent people; they indoctrinate young men and women and send them out as suicide bombers, destroying themselves and all the people around them, even their own Muslim people, and they do it in the name of Allah, so that makes it right in their eyes. They tell their people that, if they die in the name of Allah, they will become martyrs, and for this they will go to paradise and be given seventy virgins; and the worst thing is that these people really believe it. That is why I say that their religion is far stronger than their minds. A Muslim is a Muslim, Steve, and you know as I know that there is definitely no sliding scale."

He stared at the wall for a while, as if he was trying to calm himself down; he wiped his forehead on the handkerchief that was wrapped around his fist.

"At the moment, Saddam Hussein, so we are told by CIA intelligence, is manufacturing a wide range of chemical weapons that can be used for mass destruction. He poisoned one hundred and forty thousands of his own people with nerve gas in the north of Iraq because they did not agree with him and were of a different sect from his own beliefs; it is thought that he could also, probably have nuclear weapons, or be well on his way to developing them. All we know and can be sure of is that he has the capability to manufacture them. Can you believe it? You can get all the information from the bloody internet for the manufacture of nuclear bombs. Christ!" He put his hands over his face. "What a fucking world we are living in."

His eyes were now focused back on the wall. I have got to say I was quite shocked at his outburst of iterations; this was a brand new Franks, a Franks that I had never seen before. Or maybe it was just one of his crafty manoeuvres that he subjected people to.

His eyes came back to me and he straddled the chair once again. There was a look of devastation, deep down in his eyes. I had never seen this side of Franks before, and I still cannot, under any circumstances, believe that he has any feelings whatsoever.

He looked down at me, rubbing his nose with one finger, and said, "At this very moment, we have the SAS and American Special forces inside Iraq, working with the resistance there. We are going full out to topple Saddam Hussein from power. This is a very delicate operation, as you can well understand. I myself don't think it will succeed; I feel that the west should start to fight fire with fire, forget the rules of engagement, and just eliminate all the regimes that are proliferating this bloody condemnation throughout the world with such impunity."

"Steve," he looked down at me questioningly. "If two boxers get into a ring to fight, and one boxer has to fight to the Queensbury rules, while the other can do his own thing, it doesn't take a rocket scientist to know that, if you stick to the rules, you are going to be the loser. These people are fighting a war against the Christian society throughout the world in such a brutal way, by way of murdering and maiming unarmed civilians, men, women and children, where they know they have little chance of failure or capture. It has gone on for nearly two and a half decades now, and, in that time, tens of thousands of innocent people have been brutally murdered and maimed. These people, Steve, are total cowards, and humanity cannot in any way allow it to go on."

Franks closed his eyes, and once again wiped the sweat from his forehead. He was looking at the wall again, and I've got to say that I really thought that he was being serious.

"Steve, remember in Libya a few years ago. You were looking into the Lockerbie bombing for us; you had spent weeks to get four guys into a house together. You gave us all the coordinates so that the Yanks could blow them to hell and gone, and it didn't happen. It didn't happen, Steve, because two teenaged Muslim boys arrived in a car with the last two men. When you radioed this in, we detonated the rocket in the air, at a cost of five million dollars, rather than kill those two, maybe innocent, teenaged youngsters. We never gave it a second thought; and yet those teenagers could now be the next generation of suicide bombers."

"Steve," he went on. "That is why we are not winning this war against terrorism, we are fighting to the Queensbury rules, called rules of engagement, and both you and I know that the Muslim extremists are definitely not."

He looked down at his hands for a second or two, then straight into my eyes.

"Steve, I want you to know that these are very much my own personal beliefs, but I am sure that if all the governments around Europe were not trying so hard to be politically correct, and being pushed by the human rights people, we would see that they are of the same mind as we are." He stood up, and started to pace up and down the room; he was looking at his shoes. As he came towards the bed, his eyes came up to look directly at me again.

"If you look at the war in Afghanistan, as the cities were taken and surrounded, the Afghan elders always went in first to negotiate, or so they said. When our guys got in there, all the Taliban or Al-Qaida of any position of authority were gone. Nobody saw hide nor hair of Osama Bin Laden, and you can bet your life he was moving around the country freely. If it had been Hitler or Myra Hindley we were looking for, someone would have collected the twenty-five million dollars reward before the ground troops had gone in. But I must reiterate again: these people are fanatics to a religion that means more to them than any country or even life itself. Always remember, a Muslim is a Muslim, and I say again there is definitely no sliding scale."

He unravelled the handkerchief from his hand, looked at his broken skin, and carefully wrapped it back around his fist again.

"Look at the western world today, Steve" he went on. "They are all living in fear, yes, fear, wondering when it is going to happen here, and, even more so, whether they themselves will be on the receiving end. Look at the Middle Eastern countries. They claim to be peace-loving people, and yet they are wreaking terror throughout the world. They are blackmailing the western world with terrorisation, and it's got to be stopped."

I was laid flat on my back now, looking in amazement at Franks. This was a very different Franks to the one I had known for the last eight or nine years. He was showing concern, he was showing feelings, even fear. He was staring at me with a look of perplexity on his face. I squeezed my right thigh just to make sure that this wasn't all a dream.

Franks walked over to my bed, and perched one cheek on it. "Sorry, Steve," he almost whispered. "Sorry."

I sat up on the bed and started to clap a slow handclap.

"Franks," I said, "That was a great performance. But I am an ex-and, I repeat, ex-SAS officer, and I am also an ex-MI6 operative, and I am definitely not the head of the performing arts. If you are going to go into acting, you got the wrong address to do your performance." He just kept staring at the floor. "I don't know what this has got to do with me, if the whole of the western world can't solve it, what in God's name are you, or I for that matter, as individuals, going to do about it?"

He never answered; his eyes were still glued to the floor.

"Franks for fuck sake get out of here and leave me alone," I blurted.

The door burst open and in marched my Irish devil. She was looking over her shoulder, and spewing Irish venom at the two policemen in the passageway.

"You don't tell me what to do until you have got your doctorate," she retorted to them. I could see the two burly policemen standing outside in the passageway with very red faces. I presume that they had tried to stop the Irish devil from entering, and had got the brunt of her Irish temper.

I smiled to myself, because I was sure I knew what was coming. I glanced at Franks. He had now stood up, plunging both his hands deep into his trench coat pockets. He stood there looking like a fourteen-year-old schoolboy who had just been caught with his hands in the cookie jar, and I could see that he knew that he was going to get the wrath of the Irish spurned upon him.

My Irish guardian stood, legs apart, her left hand holding the door open. "Out!" she spat, waving her right arm, and pointing towards the passageway. "Out now!"

Franks now really looked like a schoolboy caught in the act with his hand in the cookie jar, even down to the blood-red face.

"Out!" she spat again. "Now."

Franks walked towards the door. At the door, he stopped, turned facing towards me and said in a very low and surly but humiliated tone, "Steve, think about what I have said. I'll contact you in a few days' time, or as soon as I get more information on Vee's whereabouts." With that, he turned and left the room.

The Irish devil closed the door behind him, and turned to face me. All of a sudden she had that sexy smile on her face, and her eyes were sparkling like the morning dew.

"How are we feeling today, Mr Taylor?" her voice was that of an angel again.

"Fine, Nurse," I said.

"Sister, will do fine, Mr Taylor; or you could call me Sam, short for Samantha, and let's keep the rank and file for MI6 and Mr Franks."

"Fine, Sam," I iterated. "And you can call me Steve."

"OK, Steve," she lilted, picking up her stethoscope. She did all the usual things with the cold end.

Doctor Burns walked into the room, stethoscope round his neck, and his white coat opened at the front and furling behind him. "How are you feeling today, Steve?" he asked, in his very doctoral voice.

"Fantastic, Doctor," I lied. "When do I get my clothes back, and get out of here?"

"I've already organised that. Your clothes will be here in a few minutes; we have also had them cleaned for you," he said, flashing his torch into my one eye then the other. "Let's have another look at those drums," he said, poking something into one ear and then the other. "Mmm," he murmured.

The door opened, and in walked the dragon, with a brown paper parcel in her arms that she placed on the foot of the bed.

"I've organised to clean all the wounds and change all the dressings for Mr Taylor, Doctor." The dragon wasn't a dragon any more. "Just bleep me when you are ready." With that, she disappeared through the door.

"Steve," the Doc said, as he was feeling the glands under my chin. "I've got some good news and some bad news. The bad news is, we cannot trace Vee anywhere. The good news is that a policeman, and a DI Jeffries came in just now delivering your car, a Mini Cooper, I believe?" He turned and looked at me questioningly. I nodded in response.

"It's parked in the parking lot out front, and here are your keys, wallet and a few other things we had locked up for you when you came in." He handed me a large A4 brown envelope.

"Thanks, Doc," I said, taking the envelope from him. "Did DI Jeffries say anything else?"

"Yes, he asked for you to contact him as soon as you were out and about. He said that you would know where to get hold of him."

"Thanks Doc; yes, I do."

He held out his hand. It was a very firm grip, "You are a very lucky man, Steve. You are only walking out of here because you were in such a good physical condition when it happened, but Steve; please don't take any chances. Should you get any spells at all of dizziness, headaches, or blurred vision, give me a call right away."

"Thanks, Doc, I'll do that," I lied, looking straight in his eyes and shaking his hand.

It took me about two hours to get bathed, dressed and have the dressings changed, and then give my heartfelt thanks to my dragon and my little Irish angel.

Chapter Five

I found my car in the hospital parking area. It was raining a bit, but not very hard. I jumped in the car and left the hospital grounds heading into town. I didn't have a phone, as Vee had my mobile in her handbag. I just drove around for about an hour or so, trying to get my head around what had happened since Friday night. I took a left at the lights and headed for Chelmsford; a friend of old had a business there. Funny, you know, I must have known him for more than fifteen years or so, but I didn't know what his business was. All I know is that it must have been a very lucrative one, as he lived far better than I did.

I pulled up outside his office. As I got out of the car, I noticed that the rain had stopped, but the sky was still very grey, with a promise of more tears shortly.

I walked into the reception. Carol was sitting behind her desk working on her computer. She had long dark auburn hair, with a green ribbon tying it back in a pony tail. She looked up to see who had entered, and a naughty smile crossed her face.

"Well I'll be damned," she shouted. "Look at what the devil has brought in!" With that, she ran to the door at the back of her desk.

"Charles, it's going to snow tonight for sure; look who's just walked in."

Charles appeared in the doorway. He was a man in his early sixties with a full head of very grey curly hair, and one of the fastest minds that I had come across in a long time, and his body that was holding everything together was that of a fifty-year-old.

"Jesus, come in, come in Steve." His eyes smiled with glee. He turned to Carol. "Carol: coffee, black, plenty of it, and I'm out even if the bloody Queen comes."

He grabbed me by the shoulder with a very strong grip for his age and ushered me through the door into his office at the back.

"Sit, man, sit. Jesus, Steve, how long has it been? Three, four years?" he questioned, with that big beautiful toothy grin across his face.

"Nearer five, Charles," I said. "It was when I came back from the Middle East that I last saw you. You had then bailed out on the bloody government and retreated into retirement."

"Dare I ask?" Charles said, pointing at my face, "What the hell have you done to your bloody face, Steve?"

"All in good time Charles, all in good time," I replied, grinning back at him.

We sat on two easy wingback chairs, an oval mahogany coffee table separating us. Charles's office was always tidy, never a piece of paper out of place. The walls were covered in a deep rich mahogany wood, and adorned with rows and rows of books and pictures of world war two airplanes, with the Spitfire taking the central and dominating position.

Carol brought in a tray with coffee and a few chocolate digestive biscuits on it, and vanished out of the room without a sound.

We drank coffee by the gallon, and talked of old times for a good hour; it had started raining again outside. I could see the rain running down the window facing me.

"Steve," Charles said "This is not just a visit to get the best and cheapest coffee in town. Let's get down to the nitty gritty, why are you here?"

I glanced up at him with a smirk on my face. "I've got a small problem, Charles and I need a bit of help, maybe; but, overall, I just need someone to bounce my problem off and maybe get a different angle on things, if you know what I mean."

"You've never, as long as I've known you, had a small problem, Steve, and if it was a small problem, you wouldn't be here now: you would be out there sorting it out. Now settle down, and bend my ears."

He stood up, picked up his coffee, and walked over to stand at the window.

I gave Charles the rundown on what had happened over the last four or five days, leaving out my meeting with Franks.

"Well, I'll be damned" he retorted. "I was wondering about all the dressings and things. I thought maybe you had married, and the wife had given you a going over." He giggled, and went to pour more coffee, but the jug was empty.

"Yes, Steve, I read all about it; fourteen killed and sixty-odd bloody injured, I think it said. Christ, Steve! You still have the luck of the devil with you."

The door opened and Carol popped her head in, "More coffee, guys?"

"Coffee? Not on your life, Carol! Two glasses, ice and a bottle of Chivas. It's three p.m., and time to whet our whistles."

"You're the boss, Charles. Coming up!" and with that, she disappeared.

As the door closed, I said, "Charles: I need to use Carol for a couple of hours. As I said, I lost Vee, a female friend of mine, in the bombing, and I need to know where she is and if she is OK. Also, I need to get hold of a DI Dave Jeffries from New Scotland Yard; I told you that he had my car delivered to the hospital, and I feel he might have some idea of Vee's location."

"Anything you want Steve, anything. Both Carol and I are fully at your disposal for as long as it takes."

Carol came back, adorned with a third of a bottle of eighteen year old Chivas, two Chrystal glasses and a bowl of ice. As she left, Charles followed her out into the outer office, and closed the door behind him.

I poured myself a very stiff Chivas and dropped in a couple of ice cubes; it looked very inviting. I rolled the glass around, and listened to the ice tinkle against the Chrystal glass as I watched the rain run down the window pane. I was definitely feeling my real self now, as if I had found a comfort zone here with Charles.

Charles walked back into the room, closing the door behind him. He poured himself a drink similar to the one I had poured myself, and sat in the chair opposite me. He looked straight into my eyes, and, holding his glass of Chivas high in the air, said, "It's great to see you again Steve, you just made my year."

Charles sipped his drink, held it up to his eyes and shook it lightly, listening to the ice tinkle in the glass. "Steve, how long have we known each other?" he said, smiling across at me.

"Something like fifteen years," I replied. "Why do you ask?"

"Well, in all that time we have learned to understand each other very well; and although we've been chatting for the last hour or so, I am sure you have more inside your head than you have told me. Something's wrong Steve, are you feeling OK after the blast? Or is there something deeper that you haven't told me?"

"Well, Charles," I said "I was very well looked after in hospital, and was given a clean bill of health on leaving," I lied. "I'm just worried about Vee; no one seems to know where she is."

"Let me get Carol on to that right away." He went over to his desk and called Carol on the intercom, and within seconds she was standing in the doorway.

"What the hell do you want now?" she said, with a cheeky smile on her face." Don't tell me you've drunk the bottle already."

"Carol," Charles said, grinning, "Dump the Prior file for the time being, there's no real rush there; I want you to do Steve a favour. He was in the restaurant explosion on Friday night with Vee, his lady friend."

"You were in the explosion?" she blurted, putting her hand over her mouth. "I saw the plasters and stitches on your face, but I thought you had been in one of your usual bar fights or something. Where's Vee? Is she all right?"

"Yes, Carol she's OK," I said, with my fingers firmly crossed. "Or at least, I think she is; the problem is that I don't know where she is, and the hospital that I was in couldn't trace where she had been taken after the explosion. Would you be so kind as to get on the phone and see whether you can track her down? Her full name is Kaveeta Ashenda. Please do not contact the police; just ring all the hospitals in the close vicinity to the explosion."

"I'll get on it right away, Steve," and with that she closed the door and was gone.

Charles was staring at me as if I was a naughty boy. He wiggled his index finger at me, and had that fatherly look on his face.

"Steve, I think it's time you gave me the whole story. You're not in the right state of mind just now to think coherently. Give me the gist of the story, and let's see what we can work out. You know, as I do, that two brains are far better than one."

I sat twirling my Chivas Regal; the ice tinkling on my glass was the only sound in the room. I was very reluctant to give Charles the whole story on Franks, but I needed someone to bounce the story off, maybe to get a different angle on the whole scenario, and maybe another perspective on what was happening.

I sat for perhaps a couple of minutes. I looked up to see Charles, with a very fatherly look on his face. His warm brown eyes cast across in my direction; he raised his eyebrows, as if to say "Well?"

"OK, Charles," I said. "I will give you the whole story, just as it happened, but you must understand that this is between you, me, and the Chivas. Also, you must understand that I am looking for your advice, not your help."

Charles just stared without blinking. He nodded at me very slightly, and said, "Steve my boy, at my age, advice is all that I can give, let me just ensure that we have peace for a while."

With that Charles ambled out of the room, and closed the door behind him. On his return he slid into the chair opposite, looked at me once again with that fatherly look and said, "OK, Steve the floor's yours, let's have it."

I rambled on for about an hour and a half, explaining who Vee was, how we had met, and some information on her passed. Charles just focussed his eye on me, never wavering, other than refilling our glasses.

"Vee and I," I went on "have been together now for almost four years, we met in the Punjab Province in the north of India about six years ago. She was there heading up the Indian Intelligence Service and working closely with the CIA endeavour that was looking into the influx of Al-Quaeda and the Taliban into Northern India from South Eastern Pakistan. As you know, I was with MI6, liaising with a group from Special Forces who were searching for a group of Muslim fanatics that were causing a few disruptions in the Kashmir area."

I had a sip of my Chivas, put the glass back on the table, and leaned back in my chair.

"Vee was there, Charles, because she was Indian by birth and had grown up in the Punjab; also, she had a very good knowledge of the people and their culture, and was totally familiar with the terrain within that area. She was also fluent in both the Indian and the Pakistani languages, and was very efficient in their different dialects."

I gave Charles a rundown on what I remembered about the explosion, the hospital, and the meeting with Franks. I left nothing out, as I wanted him to have a full perspective; then he would be more able to advise me on what he thought was going on.

When I got to the part about the Irish Angel throwing Franks out of the ward twice, he burst into a fit of laughter; he laughed so much, he went into a coughing fit. I was a bit worried that he was going to have a bloody heart attack. Slowly he got his breath back; his face was as red as a bloody beetroot. He pointed at me with the index finger of the hand he was holding his empty glass in, coughing into the other hand, and said, "we should have got her into MI6 fucking years ago, it's about time someone showed that prick where to get off! Boy oh boy! I would give my right arm to have been there. Well, maybe not my right arm."

He reached over the coffee table, and poured another two very large Chivas, dropped a couple of ice cubes into each glass, sat back into his chair, had a sip of his drink, twirled the glass around, looked across at me, and said, "Well, well, well, that's a very interesting story Steve, yes very interesting indeed."

At that moment there was a knock on the door, and Carol popped her head in.

"I have found Vee," she said proudly, "or should I say I have found where she was, seemingly," she went on. "She was taken from the St Thomas hospital yesterday by three men; one was a doctor. I enquired where she had been taken to, but to no avail. Nobody seems to know where she was taken to, sorry," she said, shrugging her shoulders. "I'll keep trying, though, maybe someone at the hospital will know."

"Look Carol," Charles said, "take a ride over to the hospital. It's no good using the phone. Get over there and waggle your arse at a couple of the doctors and maybe the security officers. Someone there must know where she was taken to, and who took her."

"Carol," I said, turning my head towards her, "at the hospital I was in, there was an Irish nursing sister called Samantha; I don't know her surname, but St Christopher's Maternity hospital is only small. You won't have trouble running her down, and I'm sure she will help. Ask her to go with you, she will know the run of the mill around hospitals, and know the right people to ask. Also," I said with a little snigger, "no one will ever bullshit her, that's for bloody sure."

"OK, consider it done," she said, smiling broadly; and with that, the door closed quietly.

"It's fucking Franks, I know it is," I shouted. "What the fuck is he playing at? One of these days, Charles, I'll kill that bastard, I know I will."

"Calm down, Steve," Charles said with some sympathy in his tone. "We don't know anything at all yet, and after the incident in the restaurant, you are in no condition to think straight at the moment. Let's go through what we know, and see what we can come up with."

I stood up and walked over to the window. It was still raining. I watched as the rain trickled down the window panes. I saw my car parked on the street; it was looking rather grubby, and needed a good valet. All the paintwork was dull, and I knew that the interior was like a pigsty.

As I glanced across the road, I saw a black Rover with dark windows parked diagonally across the road from my Cooper. The windows were tinted, so I could easily see that the driver's window was partially opened, and cigarette smoke was flowing through the opening.

"Charles," I said. "Come and look at this."

"Look at what?" Charles said, striding across the office towards me.

"That black Rover over the road with tinted windows: there's someone inside smoking. See?" I said. "You can see so much smoke coming out of the driver's open window that it looks like a steam train."

"Yes you are right, Steve. Can you read the number plates? My eyes are fucked these days," he said with something of a giggle.

I read the number out to him, and Charles walked over to his telephone and dialled a number. "Hi, Dave," he said, "How are you doing?" There was a short conversation of preliminaries, and then Charles said, "I need a favour, Dave. Can you do a trace on a number plate for me, I need it quickly?" Charles repeated the number to him and put the phone down.

"Let's see what he comes up with," he mumbled, picking up his drink. "Come over here, sit down and let's consider your story of the last couple of days,"

I sat down, picked up my drink, crossed my legs, and looked across the room, as Charles lowered his frame into his chair. He was rubbing his chin and looking very thoughtful. He took his pen from his shirt pocket, twiddled it in his fingers and pointed it at me.

"You know, Steve, you always were the best in the business," Charles said thoughtfully, "The very best; and things have changed in the world, Steve. All the other stuff was pea knuckle compared with what the world is facing now; and I am sure that they are thinking that the best is what is required, and they are looking to recruit you once again."

"Sorry, Charles," I interrupted. "You got it wrong. Maybe I was the best, 'was' being the operative word, but I have finished with all that shit now. I'm thirty-seven years old, have never been married, and now I want a piece of the real world. I am at the moment trying to make a living being Mr. Steve Taylor, civilian, looking at marriage, children, a mortgage, and nice garden to sit in. I don't want to live on the edge any more, Charles; I want to be a real wholesome run-of-the-mill civilian type of guy."

Charles smiled broadly, running his fingers through his silver curly hair.

"Steve," he said. "Not even five years ago, I remember that your saying was 'if you are not living on the edge then you are taking up too much space.'" He raised both hands in front of him, palms up. "Well, what's changed, Steve, what's bloody changed?"

"Yes, Charles," I interrupted, "But that was years ago. Since then, I have been stabbed, shot, not to mention taken prisoner in the Middle East and tortured for days on end. No Charles, it's over, enough is enough. A man can only take so much."

Charles smiled and sipped his drink, "I know you mean what you are saying, Steve; but you know and I know that you are not ready to sit there in the garden of your mortgaged home, reading the Sunday newspapers, with nappies on the washing line, blowing in the wind. No, Steve; you know the real world is not in the newspapers. The real world is in your heart, and always will be."

Just then the telephone rang. Charles uncurled himself from the chair. "Could be Carol," he suggested.

He lifted the handset. "Pierce," he said, into the mouthpiece. He listened for a while, nodding his head. "Dave, I'm going to put this call on open line, I have someone here who is also interested." With that, he pressed a switch in the phone. "OK, Dave, you said you had no luck with the number."

"Yes, none whatsoever," Dave replied. "It could be a stolen car with a false number plate, either that or maybe a government car.

I've got to say, I expect it to be the latter but I cannot be sure on that, Charles."

"OK," Charles said. "I'll get back to you, Dave. Thanks a stack: I owe you one." With that, he switched off the button on the phone, and walked over to the window.

"Government, eh?" he mumbled, then, turning to me, "Who did you say had brought your car to the hospital, Steve?"

"DI Jeffries; he's with New Scotland Yard," I replied.

"Do you know him well? Could he now be with MI6?" he said, looking over to me with his eyebrows raised.

"I don't know him. I have just heard of him; in fact, I don't think that we ever met, but the Doc said that he had given him my car keys, and said he was with New Scotland Yard and I would know how to contact him."

Charles walked over to his desk, dialled a number, and stood with a brooding look on his face. "Good day," he said. "Can you put me through to DI Jeffries please?" He put on his brooding face while he was waiting to be put through. "No, don't bother. I'll phone again later: what time do you think he will be back? OK, thanks a stack." With that he cradled the phone and stood by the desk, tapping the phone with his index finger; then, looking across me, he muttered, "He will be back in about an hour Steve; something's not right."

He walked around from his desk, sat down in the wing-backed chair, and poured another generous Chivas Regal into my glass.

"Questions, Steve, questions," he said as I sat down across from him. "How the fuck did Jeffries get your car? That place would have been crawling with MI5 and MI6 within fifteen minutes of the explosion. Nobody from New Scotland Yard would have got within half a mile of the place. It would have been in total bloody lock down. Where was your car parked?" he asked.

"We parked at the back in the parking area. We always park there; they book you a parking space when you book your table, if you are a regular." Then I started to understand Charles's thinking. "Yes, Charles you are damn right; that area would have been in total lockdown and it probably still is, even now. We need to find out how Jeffries got my car and who had it before him. Also, how did he get the car keys? They were in my pocket when I was in the restaurant. This doesn't make any sense at all, Charles. Something is going on, and I know Franks is at the bottom of it."

Charles stood up and walked to the window, looking out at the Rover. "Did you come straight here from the hospital?" he asked.

"No," I said. "I drove around for an hour or so, to try to clear my thoughts."

"Do you think you could have been followed here?"

"Not a chance," I said. "It's automatic with me, I would have spotted a tail."

"Then your car's bloody bugged, Steve," he said, tapping his index finger on the window. "There's this black Rover parked across the street that's got spooks written all over it; so either they followed you here, or your car is bugged for sure, that's the only explanation as to how they could know where you are. How low can MI6 bloody go? they have the audacity to bug your car, then pass it along to New Scotland Yard to deliver it back to you. Things certainly have changed from our days, Steve, but they are leaving out the fact that you were not born yesterday, and you are far from stupid."

"You know, I think you could be right, Charles; they could have put it in my car, and then given the car over to New Scotland Yard, to be returned to me at the hospital. That would alleviate any connection with MI6. The bastards! But what the fuck is going on, Charles? What the fuck is going on?"

Charles and I sat for maybe an hour, discussing the probabilities of what was going on, but couldn't come to any conceivable conclusions whatsoever, other than what we had come up with.

"Well," said Charles, sinking the last of his Chivas, "let's give them a run for their money. We are going to switch off the lights, and I'm going to get in my car. It's in the garage; they won't be able to see how many people are in the car, so they will assume it's you and I, as they must have seen Carol leave earlier."

He was smiling with a very broad grin, and I could see he was really enjoying this. "I'll give them a run for their money for half an hour or so; well, that's if they can keep up with me."

He walked over to his desk, then, glancing back to me, he showed me his cheeky grinning face. "Just like old times Steve, eh?"

He was opening a drawer in his desk. "When they pull out to follow me, you will have plenty of time to find the bug and scarper. You can then get to where you're going without a tail, and I suggest you put the bug on another car, just to give them a bit more soup on their ties. Oh, I'm really enjoying this."

He clapped his hands, and rubbed both palms up and down on his face. I could see that he was loving every minute of it. This was the old Charles that I had known and trusted for all those years, and I am sure he was reliving the life he had had with MI6.

"Here" he said throwing a very neat little bug detector over to me. "You'll find it quicker with this, and here: take this mobile phone, then you are in touch with the world. Both mine and Carol's numbers are in there, so we will always be in contact with each other."

As Charles was about to switch off the lights, I said, "Thanks, Charles; I owe you one."

He looked at me, grinning. "You owe me ten, my boy, not one. Oh, and a half bottle of Chivas." He pointed to the empty bottle still standing on the oval table.

"Cheers, Steve," he said, and, with that magnificent smile on his face, then he disappeared out through the door and was gone.

I sat in the dark in the wingback chair, waiting to hear movement outside. It wasn't long before I heard wheels burning up rubber, as Charles tore off in what looked like an MG Sports. I could imagine the spooks in the Rover panicking to get on our tail. It took them about thirty seconds to throw their cigarette butts out of both windows, start the car, and tear off down the road in hot pursuit. I smiled a cynical grin and said to myself, "Have a nice day, gentlemen."

I gave them a minute or so to get out of sight, then, opening the door, I stepped out into the cool night air; it had stopped raining, but the streets were still wet, and glistened from the street lights. It took me a couple of minutes to find the bug; it was under the rear bumper. I was going to stamp on it, but I realised that Charles's idea was good. It would send them on another wild goose chase, after they had seen that I wasn't in the car with Charles.

I jumped into the Cooper, and tore off down the road like a teenager after two hours of happy hour. I took a hard right at the end of the street, and the bug detector that Charles had given me shot off the seat and hit the passenger door, it started bleeping and the little red light was flashing. "Shit! Those crafty bastards! There must be another bug on the car."

I stopped the car about a mile down the road and rummaged around. It didn't take long to find it, it was under the dash on the passenger side. I was laughing at the stupidity of the spooks, when a large overnight euro truck stopped at the traffic lights. I walked over to the truck, and put both bugs under the tarpaulin cover on the back. I noticed that the truck had Spanish number plates. So that would really give them a run for their money. I hoped they had their passports with them. As the truck drove off, I smiled and gave the bugs a little wave. I hope the spooks enjoy the sunshine in Spain, I thought.

I had to move quickly now, as the spooks would know that the Cooper was on the move. I headed down towards Millbank as quickly as possible, yet keeping as close to the speed limit as I could, and, in the Cooper that was very hard to do. I felt quite safe now, as the spooks would take at least an hour to catch up with the truck and find that they had been spooked. I grinned to myself, as a few spots of rain started to hit my windscreen. I switched on the radio. There was a John Lennon song playing, 'Hey Jude'. I sank down in my seat, took my foot off the accelerator an inch or two and sang along with him.

There was a pub come hotel down in Millbank, not exactly the Ritz, but it would serve my purpose well for the time being. I needed some sleep and some time to get my mind into gear. The whisky Charles and I had consumed was now starting to take its toll, so a meal would be a dire necessity.

I pulled into the parking area at the rear of the hotel; there were a few cars parked there, but plenty of room for the Cooper. The rain was coming down hard now, so I had to run across the car park to the rear door of the building. As I pushed open the door, the sound of music came to my ears and the smell of stale beer and cigarettes rushed up my nose. The place was quite dingy, to say the least. I walked down the passage towards the bar; as I entered I saw Tudor leaning across the bar, listening to some big-breasted blonde. I stood waiting for him to look my way, but I knew it was going to take a lot to get his gaze away from her cleavage.

I caught the eye of Erica. She was a very small girl, about five foot and a matchstick, with an unbelievable figure and a more than fantastic personality. She had worked as a barmaid and waitress here for at least three years. I think she told me one time she came from Cape Town in South Africa. She was here studying at university and earning her living managing Tudor's place. She always said that she loved the London lifestyle, and would probably stay here when her studies had come to fruition. When she saw me, she ran down behind the bar, stood on a beer keg and lunged herself across the bar to give me a big heart-warming hug and a kiss on the cheek.

"Wow, it's great to see you Steve!" she shouted above the music. "It must be a year since you were here. Where have you been hiding, big guy?" She looked over my shoulder, and asked, "Where's Vee? And what's all that bloody camouflage on your face?" And, without waiting for an answer, "Oh you've just made my day!" She jumped up, put her arms around my neck, and gave me another big cuddle. With Erica, you always knew that whatever she said she meant, and you could see it, deep down in her steel blue eyes.

Tudor had managed to prise his eyes away from the cleavage of the big blonde, and he glanced down towards Erica and me at the end of the bar. A big smile came across his face, and he lumbered down towards me, banging the palm of his hand against his forehead. "Stevie!" he shouted above the music, burying my hand in his in a powerful handshake. "Great to see you again, what's with the bandages? Did Vee give you a hiding?" he questioned, pulling a pint for the big-breasted blonde woman. "What can I get for you?"

I just smiled ruefully, and shook my head, knowing that the Chivas Regal I had had with Charles, was now really taking its toll.

"No, nothing at all, Tudor," I replied. "I've had plenty tonight, all I need is a room for a night or so, and maybe some food up in the room, not down here in this bloody den of iniquity you run."

"OK, fixed up my boy. Erica will sort you out with the room, and I'll get the kitchen to rustle up something special for you.

Maybe we can have a chat and play catch-up later, when it's not so busy?" With that, he walked back up the bar, and started pulling a couple of pints for one of the clients at the bar.

Tudor was a great big mountain of a man, aged around fifty-six, or so I should think, bald as a badger and about six foot three tall, weighing at least two hundred and fifty pounds. His biceps were about the size of my thighs, and yet, surprisingly, he had such a very calm personality, with a lovely placid attitude. I'd known him since I was fifteen. He had once caught me drinking in his bar when I was underage, and had thrown me out; then, about two or so years later, when I was old enough to drink, I came back, and he gave me my first drink on the house. At the time I was very surprised that he even remembered me, but now that I know him better, I realise that that is the type of person he is.

Erica came alongside of me, put her arm in my arm and gazed up into my face. "Let's go, Steve. First the room, then I'll go and get your food, you big handsome brute," she laughed, hanging on my arm and flashing her big beautiful steel blue eyes up at me.

Erica took me to a room at the front on the fourth floor. She said it was away from the noise, and it was the best room they had; it had all the basics, a bed with clean bedding, a shower, and that was all that I would need tonight. I walked across the room and pulled aside the curtains. The view was tremendous. A smile came onto my face as, in the distance, and about a kilometre or so away, was eighty-five, Vauxhall Cross, the home of MI6's Secret Intelligence Agency. There is no way they are going to look for me right under their noses, that's for sure; and I know Charles will die laughing when he knows where I am.

"Where's your bag, Steve?" Erica asked coming over and standing beside me.

"Haven't got one," I replied, turning from the window, "Can you fix me up with a toothbrush and tooth paste, also if it's possible at this time of night, could you go and get me some clean underclothes, and maybe a pair of socks?" I put fifty quid down the front of her 'T' shirt, "I think that should be enough, Erica, you can keep the change."

"No problem Steve," she said then with a sheepish grin, "You can use my undies if you like, I'll even put them on for you."

"Get out of here, smart arse," I said, laughing.

With that, she turned and shot out the door and closing it quietly behind her.

I lay on the bed for a while, wondering where the hell Vee could be. I was tired, and my mind wasn't really up to it; and I suppose the Chivas I'd drunk was now really taking its toll.

I must have fallen asleep, as I heard Erica calling down a long tunnel. "Come on, big guy. You need to get some food in you. I've got you some fried chicken with some chips and vegetables. I've put some soap, towel, toothbrush and tooth paste in the bathroom. There's a couple of pairs of undies and a couple of T shirts and socks on the dresser with your change. I'll collect the plates tomorrow, get a good night's sleep. I'll see you are not disturbed." And with that she was gone.

I had a shower, and took off my camouflage, as Erica called it. I couldn't shave with all the cuts and abrasions around my face, but at least I felt a little fresher.

I ate most of the chicken and the chips with my fingers, gobbling it down, then I climbed into bed, the first time I had a real bed for a while. The sheets were nice winter sheets, all fluffy, not like the starched sheets at the hospital. I've got to admit that my body was feeling a little sore, and bruised in places, probably from the explosion; a good night's sleep and I was sure I would be feeling a little more human.

I thought of phoning Charles, but decided against it, I would get him first thing in the morning. I switched off the light at the side of the bed, turned on my side and, at that moment, I think I died.

Chapter Six

I woke with that feeling: 'where the hell am I?' There was classical music coming from somewhere in the room. I threw my legs over the side of the bed. I could see my half-eaten dinner on the coffee table. It didn't look half as good as it had last night. I followed the sound of the music to my trouser pocket, on the chair in the corner. It was the mobile that Charles had given to me yesterday. I clicked the answer button and said "Hi" into the speaker, with a little apprehension, as I wasn't sure who would be on the other end.

Charles's voice sounded very excited. "Hi,Steve, good morning to you! It's Charles here. Where are you?"

"I'm at Tudor's place," I said, walking over to the window. The rain had stopped, but the streets and roofs were still wet, and the low grey clouds were promising more rain in the very near future. "I'm looking out of the window, and you will never guess what my view is, it's the majestic building of MI6, would you believe? I thought I would get myself right under their noses; they would never think of looking for me here."

"That's great, Steve." I heard him taking a puff of his cigarette. "Tudor's a good man, and a man you can really rely on when the chips are down."

I heard Charles take a swig of his early morning coffee, and a couple of frog-in-the-throat coughs.

"Well Steve I've got good news and bad news for you. First, the good news. Carol picked up your angel from the maternity hospital, and they started their trek around all the local hospitals, and, as luck would have it – third time lucky – they were told that a Doctor and two very official guys in suits with documentation had taken Vee from the hospital in an ambulance early on Monday morning; but no one knew where they had taken her. They were told that she was in a much better state than you were, mainly just a few cuts and bruises and a slight laceration on her left shoulder; and, of course, as you had, a slight concussion."

I heard Charles take another swig of his coffee and a puff on his cigarette.

"The next bit of luck you are not going to believe," Charles went on. "When the girls got down to the car the bloody car wouldn't start, but a knight in shining armour came to their rescue, in the name of Doctor Lionel Turner, and, get this, he was the doctor who was treating Vee in the hospital. Can you believe their luck?"

I heard Charles take another swig of his coffee, and another puff on his cigarette.

"Your angel started to ask questions about who had taken her, and where they had taken her, but got nowhere, except that he said that the doctor who came with the suits was a student at university with him, and his name was Doctor Philip Downs. I checked up in the medical journals and registers, and found that he had his own practice as a neurosurgeon in Greater London."

Once again I heard Charles take a swig of his coffee, and another pull on his cigarette.

"Steve, I hope you don't mind," he went on, "but I got him on the phone early this morning; and get this. Seemingly he had been asked by MI6 to assist and oversee in her removal from the hospital to another institution. He himself thought that it was because she had been in an explosion, and concussed, that they were just playing it safe, getting a neurosurgeon to accompany her."

I heard him take another sip of his coffee, and a pull at his cigarette.

"Now listen to this, Steve. Doctor Philip Downs said he was very surprised when they reached their destination, because the destination was, now, wait for this Steve, you're not going to believe it: it was MI5 at Thames House on the Millbank road. He said he asked a lot of questions, as he did not think the whole thing was kosher and above board, but, as you can guess, he got a lot of long winded replies from them that had no substance or clarity."

"Shit, Charles! What the fuck is Franks playing at? And what has MI5 got to do with everything?"

Now my mind was spinning. "Did you ask the Doctor how she was?" I asked.

"Yes Steve, but his diagnosis was the same as Doctor Philip Turner's: slight concussion, cuts and bruises and a slight laceration to her left shoulder. In fact, he said he could not understand why they needed a neurologist to be there to move her. Just goes to show how careful they were being with her, Steve."

I looked across the roof tops, and I could see the MI6 Buildings, wet and misty, and also somewhat mysterious; and now, for some reason or other, Vee wasn't in there. I was very pleased. In a way, at least I now knew where she was; and, to top it all, I knew she would be in very good hands and being well looked after, and in no danger at all.

"I still can't work out what Franks is up to, though, Charles," I whispered into the mobile.

"I know exactly what he's up to, Steve," said Charles "And so would you if your mind was clearer. I have always told you, Steve, that you are the best of the best. I know it, but, I'm afraid, so does Franks. He knows he can't get near you, because you would always be one step ahead of him all the time, but he knows exactly where you are the most vulnerable, and he is using that vulnerability to draw you into his lair. My father used to call it fishing. He's using Vee because he knows she's the best bait around for the type of fish he wants, or should I say needs, to catch. All I can say, Steve, is that you're bloody well and truly hooked if you will excuse the pun."

"It's OK you talking that way, Charles," I said, musing on the situation through my now very befuddled mind. "But it still leaves the question, why? And what is going through his mind, Charles? I finished with his shit years ago and the stink still sits in my nostrils. The worrying thing, though, is it looks to me like he has something that has to be done, something for Queen and Country, and it seems he needs me to do it for him. I'm too old for these typical MI6 games Charles. I now have a real life in the real world, and, also, a mind of my own; and, to put it bluntly, I am really enjoying that life."

"Steve," I heard him take another pull on his cigarette, "If he wants you to do something, then it's top priority, and you can be assured it's going to be bloody dangerous. Maybe they have got Vee at Thames house because they have better facilities; or maybe, just maybe, it's a local situation that MI6 and MI5 have to alleviate and they are pooling together to work on it. I suppose that in this day and age, with all this terrorism shit, they are maybe forced into having to work as a team, or they would find themselves like the Yanks, with the FBI screwing the CIA and visa versa."

"Look, Steve" he went on. "We can talk about this until the cows come home, and we could be completely barking up the wrong tree. I suggest you get a shower and a change of clothes, then we can analyse the whole scenario together and plan our next move over breakfast at Daniel's place. How does that sound?"

Daniel's is a small coffee shop on the banks of the Thames, and serves the very best coffee in town and a breakfast of unrivalled excellence.

"OK, Charles," I replied. "That sounds good. See you at Daniel's at about ten thirty, and thanks, Charles, for standing up with me, you're a great friend." Then, as an after thought, "Charles: can we make it Daniel's at twelve. There are a few things I need to do first."

"That's fine with me, Steve," he said. "See you there at twelve," and the line went dead.

I quickly got dressed, put all my belongings together, and headed downstairs to find Tudor. He was in the back, shouting and screaming at a couple of the staff about how they were stacking some empty beer crates.

"Morning, Tudor," I said.

He looked around with that great big grin on his face.

"You're looking much better, Steve, nothing like a good night's sleep is there?" He gave me a big cuddle, and when you get a cuddle from a guy that size it really is a big cuddle. We walked over towards his office, shoulder to shoulder.

"Coffee, Steve? Or maybe something a little stronger perhaps?" he said, looking at me across the desk and rolling his eyes.

"Coffee will be fine Tudor, black and strong with one sugar," I replied, taking a seat in Tudor's office.

I sat in Tudor's tiny office and gave him some bullshit story about a problem that I had had. I knew he didn't believe me, and I knew he would never ask any questions of me.

"Tudor, I need a favour." I was looking out at the mist, and knew it was going to rain soon. In the UK it rains twice a week: once for three days and once for four days.

"Anything you want, Steve, anything you want, all you have to do is ask," he said without a flinch.

"I need your car for the day, I will leave the Cooper here just in case you should need some transport yourself."

He looked over at me and burst out laughing, "Steve I wouldn't be able to fit in that little Cooper powerhouse of yours, never mind drive it, and, if I did get in it, I think your suspension would be stuffed within the first two miles." His eyes went over to the corner of the room. "The keys are hanging on the hook by the safe. The car's in good shape as always and parked in the garage next to the stores. I suggest you put your car in the garage, out of sight." He winked at me as if to say he knew I was not being fully upfront with him.

"I can live with that, Tudor," I said, grabbing the keys hanging by the safe.

Tudor looked out of the window, then turned to look directly at me.

"Steve," he said in a very serious tone. "If you need any help, any help whatsoever, you know where I am."

With that he walked out of the office, speaking in earnest over his shoulder, "See you later, Steve," and then as an afterthought. "Be careful Steve, be very careful." With that, he disappeared out into the passageway.

I drove Tudor's car out of his garage and replaced it with the Cooper. Tudor's car was a big six cylinder Ford, with six gears and tinted windows. It took me under thirty minutes to get to my place. It was still raining, but very little, and not enough to cause any problems in the traffic. As I turned the corner into my street, as I had already predicted, there was a black Sedan parked about thirty yards down from my place. The thought went through my head, thanks for the darkened windows. I parked two doors up from my house. Grabbing a newspaper from the back seat, I jumped out of the car with the newspaper over my head, blocking their view of me, and ran into the alcove of my neighbour's house, two houses down from me.

I knocked on the door twice and waited. Anne came to the door in her dressing gown. She was a stunning woman in her early thirties, with long blonde hair, usually done up in a pony tail. She was short, probably about five foot five, with a very nice figure. I've got to say that the dressing gown she wore didn't do her any justice whatsoever; but then she worked from home, writing children's books, so she could dress casually most of the time. That's why I knew she would be at home.

"Steve" she said in surprise "What the hell have you done to your face? Come in out of the rain, shit you look terrible. You haven't even shaved in days. What the bloody hell's going on?"

I brushed past her and walked down the hallway and into the lounge.

"Can I get you some coffee or something Steve?" she asked.

"No, Anne, I'm fine. I just need your help. I was in the restaurant bombing with Vee the other day, and I have been laid up in hospital since then. Before you ask," I went on, "Vee is fine. I cannot explain the whole issue to you, but I need to get into my house, and I only have the back door key," I lied. "Can I use your back door and climb over the two fences to get to my place?"

"Of course you can, my love," she said with a look of horror on her face.

"OK, will you leave the door open? I will come back the same way."

"Steve what the bloody hell is going on? I know your back door and front door have the same keys." She had a kind of worried look on her face.

"Don't worry, Anne," I replied. "I can't explain just now. I'm a little short of time, and if I had the time I wouldn't be able to explain, as I'm a little unsure what's going on myself. All I can tell you is that both Vee and myself are fine, and you mustn't worry."

With that, I ducked out of the back door, and into the rain again. I jumped over the first wall, very Olympiad-like, into my neighbour's garden, and took a run for the next wall, hoping that Mr. and Mrs. Smith would not be looking out of the window. On clearing the next wall into my garden, I ran to the back door and let myself in.

I quickly showered and changed my clothes, got out our medical kit, and redid what my angel had done at the hospital. It was nowhere near as neat but it would do for now.

As I dressed, I looked at my watch. It was only eleven thirty. I still had time to get to Daniel's well before twelve, and all I had to do was to get into my car without being spotted by the bloody spooks.

I ran into Anne's place, she was standing in the kitchen with a cup of coffee in her hand, and fully dressed this time. I could see her eyes were full of questions as she looked at me.

"I feel great now, clean as a sixpence," I said, smiling at her, and rubbing my fingers on her cheek. "I owe you one, Anne," I giving her a kiss on the cheek, "I'll let you know more when I know more, but please, don't worry; I can assure you everything is fine with both Vee and myself."

I picked up the newspaper I had left on the back of the settee, and headed for the front door. Putting the newspaper over my head, I ran to Tudor's car. I pulled out and drove the car straight toward the spooks, knowing that they could not see into my car. Their windows were slightly open on their car, with cigarette smoke curling out of the gap. I noticed at least ten cigarette butts alongside the car, so they must have been there the whole night. I grinned as I put my foot down, leaving unobserved, and headed over to Daniel's place to meet Charles.

I was lucky that I got parking right outside Daniel's, and I could see Charles's car parked across the road by the telephone booth. As

I entered Daniel's, I was hit by the strong smell of roasted coffee beans and bacon, and then I realised that I was very hungry indeed. Charles was sitting at the back in a four-seater booth. The place was quite full as usual, mainly businessmen and women, just having coffee, or maybe business breakfasts. Daniel waved at me, as he sorted out the bill for a young couple standing at the counter. I waved back, and made my way towards Charles.

I slid into the seat across from Charles. "I expected you to be late, Steve. I have ordered the usual, hope that's OK. I told Daniel to wait until you arrived, so it should be here in a few minutes."

"That's great, Charles, let me tell you I'm bloody starving; and to top it all I'm feeling great, after a nice shower and a change of clothes, I must be coming right now," I said with a smile.

A waitress walked up with a mug of hot steaming coffee for me, then she topped up Charles's mug from the coffee pot she had in her other hand. We both gave her a thankful nod, and off she went into the background.

"Steve," Charles said, lifting his eyes from his coffee and on to me. "Let's cut to the chase, shall we? We know where Vee is now, but we don't know why. Steve, you are good; but I don't think you're good enough to get her out of there," a smirk came over his face, and his eyes glistened. Then he said as an afterthought, and pointing his index finger at me, "Or are you?"

We both laughed heartily out loud, but both our eyes weren't laughing. We knew it would be impossible to get her out of there without doing it the political way.

"It's not like it used to be, Steve," Charles went on. "Now it's full of know-it-all little shits with top of the range computers, who spend most of their time running around spying on each other rather than spying on the enemy. No, Steve I have thought long and hard about it, the best thing you can do is go in to MI5, and see just what the bloody hell is going on. They can't keep Vee there as a prisoner.

If you don't like what they have to say, tell them to go and get fucked, walk out of the door with Vee, and shazam! The whole palaver is over and done with. See, it's easy if you look at it from a basic analogy."

Just then, Daniel came over to the table with two plates crammed full of eggs, bacon, sausage, tomato, baked beans and a side plate of whole wheat toast. It looked great. And it made me realise that it had been over four days since I had eaten a good, wholesome meal.

"Well, well, the two naughty boys again. How are you both doing these days?" Daniel asked in his very quiet but strong London accent. "I haven't seen you two together for a long, long time. It makes me think that something is brewing, besides my coffee."

"We're both fine, Daniel, and also both very hungry, and what you have put in front of us is perfection," Charles replied, with a grin on his face.

We both shook hands with Daniel, and we all passed around the normal greetings. Daniel wiped his hands on his apron and said "Enjoy, enjoy, absolutely wonderful to see both of you again, and I hope to see you both again in the near future. Oh, and next time, bring that pretty partner of yours. She's much easier on the eye than Charles." And with that, he turned away, and went back to the counter, laughing.

We both got stuck into our breakfast, and not a word was spoken until we had both cleaned our plates.

"More coffee, please," Charles said to a passing waitress. She filled our mugs, winked at Charles, and disappeared down the aisle.

Just then Charles's mobile rang. "OK. Yes, he's here. OK, thanks."

He switched off and looked across at me. "I suppose you can guess that that was Carol. Seemingly Franks, or Frankenstein as you prefer to call him, is trying to contact you. He's called me at the office twice. Apparently he wants you to go in and pick up Vee at Thames House. He says she is in the best of health and has had the best of medical care that any one could have, and she is missing you very much."

"Thames House," I said, having a sip of my coffee. "Why, Charles? Why is she with MI5? I don't understand it, Charles, the whole bloody thing doesn't seem kosher to me. MI5 and MI6 have been at war with each other for the last thirty years. Why, all of a sudden, are they trying to mix oil and water?"

I put some sugar in my coffee, and stirred it gently, staring out of the window. The clouds were quite heavy, but the rain had stopped now, and I could see that it was brightening up a bit.

"Why does that bastard always think that everyone but him is bloody stupid?" I said angrily. "What a pathetic disgrace he is for a human being. Have you ever looked closely at him, Charles, with his tall forehead, closely cropped hair and his sneaky eyes? You know, if you put a bolt through his neck, he could well be the perfect image of Hollywood's Frankenstein."

I took a swig of my coffee, and looked around the restaurant, trying to control my anger.

"Calm down, Steve," Charles said, reaching over and squeezing my wrist tightly.

"Look, Steve" he said, leaning forward and staring straight into my eyes. "The best thing you can do at this moment is just walk in there unannounced, and ask them what the fuck is going on. Listen to what they have to say. Then, and only then, will you know what's going on. It's no good trying to second guess them. They are far too devious and manipulative for anyone even to try to surmise what they are up to."

Yes, I knew Charles was right; but it was ripping me to pieces inside, thinking that I had to kowtow to this conniving bastard. I drummed my fingers on the table, staring down at my coffee.

"You know, Charles, you're right; but I'm fed up of being manipulated and used by these people, and I think the only thing to get them out of my hair is to leave the country. Look out there: it just rains and rains and rains again, day in, day out, in this country. I'm going in there, getting Vee out, then I'm going to look at going to South Africa or Australia or some other country that has better weather. Vee and I have discussed it many times, but nothing ever came to fruition. Maybe Franks has done me a favour, you know, given me the big push that I needed to make the move? Yes. I think that would be good for both Vee and myself; and to top it all, I would be out of reach from these conniving bastards and out in the sunshine, out where the weather is congenial for humans, it doesn't matter where. In South Africa, although it's a third world country, it's developing at a fast rate, and I'm sure that I could fit in well there."

I sat, still drumming my fingers on the table again, and staring out of the window.

"Yes, Charles I think you're right. I must go over and see Franks, tell him to go get fucked, then thank him for helping me in making up my mind,"

Charles was grinning. "That's the Steve I used to know. Go give them hell, my boy."

The waitress came, and started to clear the plates away from the table. "Anything else I can do for you guys?" She said smiling. "Did you enjoy your breakfasts?" She asked, looking from one to the other of us.

"Yes, sweetheart, it was great. We won't have to eat for a week, now," Charles said, looking up at her, "Could you please get the bill ready for me? My friend here has got a couple of urgent things he has to do." He looked across at me and winked.

We left Daniel's together. On the pavement, we shook hands; but Charles still had that mischievous look on his face.

"Go get them, Steve," he said, walking away; then, as an afterthought: "And please keep me in the loop." With that, he turned and walked towards the telephone booth where his car was parked.

I watched him for a moment, negotiating his way through the oncoming traffic, as he crossed the road. Then I turned, and made my way over to Tudor's car. I sat in the car for a while, trying to get my mind together, and wondering what the hell this would be all about.

Chapter Seven

I drove the few miles from Daniel's to Thames House. It's a very impressive building, standing there, dominant, and majestically overlooking the river Thames. I drove down into the underground parking area. Albert, the guy on the gate, gave me a wave. "Good to see you again, Mr. Taylor. Long time no see," he said, opening the gates for me. He must have been about seventy years of age, and he had worked there for as long as I could remember. While I was signing the book, I asked him if Franks was there.

"Yes, Mr Franks came in about an hour ago. He said you were coming to see him, and that I must let you through. Have a nice day Mr. Taylor, nice seeing you again," he said, taking the book from me, lifting the boom and waving me through.

Have a nice day, you bet I will Albert, I thought to myself. That was a dreadful understatement of how I envisaged my day was going to be.

I found parking, and made my way over to the lift. As the doors closed, I pressed the button for reception. As I stepped out of the lift into the reception, it was a large airy room with very high ceilings, and behind the security barriers were two curved spiral staircases, ascending upwards, left and right, to a large double door on the first floor. There was a mull of people moving from one side to the other, all dressed in suits, some carrying briefcases, others just moving from A to B with papers or folders in their hands, and still others walking with mobiles jammed in their ears. I walked over to the reception desk. The receptionist was just putting the phone down.

"Good afternoon, sir," she said, very politely, looking up at me. "How can I help you, sir?" The sir was just good manners, as I must have looked like a bloody plumber.

"Good afternoon, Claire," I said. I knew her name was Claire, as she had a security card tagged on to her navy-blue jacket. "My name is Steve Taylor, and I'm here to see Mr Franks, Mr. Donald Franks."

"Do you have an appointment, Sir?" she asked politely, but she was looking me up and down as if I was from the homeless crowd.

"No, I'm sorry, I don't," I replied. It was only then that I remembered that I had plasters all over my face; and, to top it all, I hadn't shaved for nearly a week. Thinking about this, I knew I would have to be quite forceful to get by her.

"I'm afraid Mr. Franks is in a meeting, and does not want to be disturbed," she said quite assertively. "Also, I'm afraid an appointment is a necessity to see Mr. Franks."

I leaned forward, putting both of my hands on the edge of her solid oak desk and looked straight into her big brown eyes, gave her a big smile and said, "I don't care if he is having lunch with the bloody Queen, Claire. You tell him Steve Taylor is here, and I can assure you that he will bow out of his meeting immediately and be down here within in thirty seconds."

"Sorry, Mr Taylor; I have strict instructions not to disturb him. He has a government minister and Deputy Minister of security with him, and he cannot be disturbed under any circumstances," she said, even more assertively.

I leaned further forward, took the smile off my face and asked, "How long have you worked here, Claire?"

"Four years, Mr Taylor," she replied, with a look of astonishment on her face.

"If you like your job, Claire, I would do as I say, because if you let me walk out of here, both Franks and the ministers will not be too impressed, I can assure you. Now, please make that call."

I pointed to the phone on her desk with my index finger. Claire looked very perplexed, and looked down at the telephone in front of her, and then back to me. She saw that my finger was still pointing at the phone, and I was looking straight into her eyes.

"Do it," I said. "Now." The "now" was said very loudly, and my voice echoed around the walls of the reception.

Claire picked up the telephone with great reluctance and punched in a number, not looking up.

"Mary," she said into the receiver, "I have a Mr Taylor here to see Mr. Franks, and he is insisting that he sees him immediately. Yes, that's right, Mary, Mr Steve Taylor." Claire glanced up at me while listening on the phone. "Yes, OK, I will, immediately," she looking quite shocked.

Claire stood up, straightening her jacket, "Mr Franks will be right down, Mr. Taylor, I'm so sorry that I messed you about, but I have been given very strict instructions," she said it very apologetically, and looking straight into my eyes.

I stood away from the desk, and looked towards the door at the top of the two spiral staircases, "20, 21, 22, 23, 24, 25, 26, 27, 28," I counted out loud. With that, the door burst open, and Frankenstein was peering over the balcony down into the lobby.

I smiled at Claire and winked "I was wrong, Claire," I said "It only took him twenty-eight seconds."

Claire giggled into her hand, and had a very sheepish but relieved grin on her face, as we both watched Franks rushing down the spiral staircase, his leather-soled shoes clattering loudly on the marble steps, and echoing loudly around the walls.

"Steve, Steve, my friend, good to see you." He put his arms apart as if to hug me. I took a step back, and put the heel of my hand firmly into his chest.

"Cut the crap, Franks; where is Vee?" I growled.

"She's fine, Steve; she has just had lunch and she's dying to see you. Come upstairs; I'll take you to see her." He had a very embarrassed look on his face which I had only seen once before, when he had locked horns with my little Irish devil at the hospital; so I knew that I had him where I wanted him, and where I was going to keep him.

As we walked towards the security barrier, I looked back over my shoulder towards Claire, with a young boy's grin on my face, and waving my fingers at her. She was still covering her grin with her hand.

Franks got me fixed up with a security card, and ushered me through the stile and past the security guards. We both proceeded up the staircase to the first floor. As we entered through the doors, we were in a large hallway with deep maroon carpets, There were offices left and right. Some had windows, with vertical blinds also in the same deep maroon colour. Every door we passed was closed, and every door had a security keypad for password entry. At the end of the passage, we came to a lift on the right. Franks thumbed the lift button time and time again, which assured me that I had unnerved him, and had him just where I wanted him.

The lift arrived; Franks stood well back, and waved me into the lift with his right hand. I entered and moved to the rear of the lift. Franks stood just inside the door, and pressed the button for the seventh floor; the doors closed and he stood looking up, as the numerals changed as we passed each floor. He never looked back at me, and never uttered a word.

We exited the lift, and turned left, and then sharp right. I noticed that everything had changed from the deep maroon to a nice shade of fawn. Franks stopped at a door with a security key pad on the wall to his right; he pumped some numbers in very quickly so that I would not be able to see them: 7,9,3,7,7and 4. He underestimated me, I smiled to myself. This was the guy high up in MI6. The first lesson you are taught when you are interned as a spook is: never ever underestimate anyone.

Franks opened the door and turned to me, saying, "I'll leave you alone for half an hour or so, while I finish off my meeting, then we need to have a chat with both yourself and Vee. I do hope that you will both give us the courtesy of say two hours of your time, as we have a few things that we would like to run past you."

I just nodded, and looked at him blankly. What he didn't know was that I had the security pad numbers for the door, and I knew that I could just walk out of here with Vee, any time I wanted to.

He could see that I wasn't interested in anything that he had to say, but he carried on. "Steve, just give us two hours, that's all we request: just two hours, and then, if you are of the same mind, we can shake hands, and the both of you will be left alone. That's a promise." He held up his right hand with three fingers upright. "Scout's honour!" To top it all, he bloody smiled at me.

I didn't reply, nor did I look at him, I just pushed the door open, entered the room and let the door slowly close automatically behind me.

Vee was laid on a leather settee and fast asleep. She had clothes on that I had never seen before, so I knew that someone had bought clothes for her. I knelt beside the settee, and rubbed my index finger very lightly across her forehead. She was such a beautiful woman. I remembered how I had laid awake so many hours, just watching her in her sleep.

Her eyelids flickered slightly, then they abruptly opened, and I saw those beautiful dark brown eyes staring back at me. She gave a

90

low cry of surprise, and both her arms were quickly wrapped tightly around my neck.

She was sobbing slightly as she said, "Oh Steve, Steve! I've been so worried; they kept saying you were fine, but I was very reluctant to believe them." She squeezed harder, and we both lost balance and finished up sprawled on the floor together, by now we were both laughing and smiling, I think more from the relief of finding each other than anything else.

We climbed back upon the settee, giggling like schoolkids. We just sat holding hands, looking into each other's eyes. God, she was so beautiful.

"Vee," I said, squeezing her hands firmly, "We don't have much time, I'm afraid; Franks will be here shortly, and I need to give you a rundown on what is going on, or should I say what I think is going on." I rubbed my hands down the side of her face. She put her hand on my hand, and moved it to her lips, kissing the fingers on one hand and then the other, and looking deeply into my eyes.

"They told me that they moved me here for my safety, and I was scared," she said quietly. "I couldn't understand why, and no one would give me any details, except to say that as soon as you arrived, everything would be explained."

"Did they look after you, sweetheart?" I asked. "I can see that someone bought you new clothes."

"Yes, Steve, and I've had my own bathroom." She nodded to a door by a desk. "And the room service has been five star, to say the least. I have had a lovely lady, Judy, to chat to from time to time, magazines to read, and even television to watch." She nodded towards a television by the wall across the room. "Also, a Doctor has been in a couple of times a day to give me a once over and change my dressings; yes, Steve, everything's been fine, except that you were not here, and I didn't know where you were. That was my only worry."

She pulled the shoulder strap of her dress and showed me quite a large dressing on her shoulder.

"Vee, I'm not sure what the bloody hell is going on; I'm only guessing, but I think they need me for something. I don't know what it is, but I do know that I'm not interested whatever it is. I've done enough for Queen and country, and enough is enough. They will be coming down any time now to take us into a meeting; so we can wait and see what they have got in mind, or we can walk out of here now if you like."

"No, we can't, Steve; the door has a security lock, and is always locked. I have tried it."

"Vee, I was with MI6, remember? The security numbers are 7,9,3,7,7,4 and, as I said, we can walk out of here right now if you like."

Vee was running her fingers over the dressings on my face. "Look at you, you haven't shaved for days," she said laughing, "Go into the bathroom. There are some ladies razors above the sink. You look like a street bum," she laughed, and it was so nice to see that her eyes were sparkling once again.

I walked into the bathroom, it had everything: bath, shower, douche, the works. I ran the water while Vee took the dressing from my face. I would have to use soap to shave, but that wouldn't bother me; I'd had to shave with a lot less in my time.

The door in the lounge opened and a voice asked "Steve, its Paul, Paul Lawson. Can I come in?"

We both walked out to the lounge, and there stood Paul Lawson. Paul and I had known each other for quite a few years in the Bosnian conflict. He had been in charge of liaison between the UK and the guys with their feet on the ground. We had worked very closely on quite a few assignments; he was always great to work with, very meticulous and efficient, and always leading from the front. We shook hands and greeted each other with an old long-lost-friend enthusiasm.

"Come into the bathroom, Paul," I said, standing there with soap suds all over my face. "I just want to have a shave and clean up a bit," I said, pointing towards the bathroom door.

"Sorry, Steve; no time for shaving; they're all waiting for you downstairs. The whole bloody family. I don't know what's going on, but from the little I have heard, it sounds very serious, as it's being kept very hush, hush, if you know what I mean."

"Everything is bloody hush, hush inside these walls Paul; even the toilets flush silently," I said, grinning broadly at him.

He grabbed the towel from around my neck, and pushed it into my well lathered face, laughing. "Come on, go and swill that soap off your bloody face!" Then, as an afterthought, he walked over to Vee, who was standing by the bathroom door. "Hi, Vee!" he said, shaking her hand. "We haven't met but I've heard a lot about you when you were in the Punjab. I was liaising with Steve quite a lot during that period."

I swilled the soap lather from my face, and dried myself off. I took a look in the mirror at myself. "Shit, I look more like a homeless person who's just been mugged." I threw the towel on to the edge of the bath, and walked out into the lounge.

Paul was standing by the door with Vee. He stepped to his right to hide the security pad from my sight. I said out loud "7,9,3,7,7,4".

Paul looked back over his shoulder with a wide grin on his face; I just looked back at him with a very nonchalant look on my face. I just wanted to relay to Paul that I was still as good as I was way back when.

As we walked towards the lift, Paul looked back at me over his shoulder, with a knowing grin across his face. "You haven't lost your touch, Steve; you never miss a thing, do you?"

I looked at Paul, still with that nonchalant look on my face, and muttered "Not when I'm dealing with MI6 or MI5, Paul, that's for sure; and probably, not missing a thing is what kept me alive all those years in the field."

We took a left and followed Paul to the lift. The doors were open, as if they were waiting for us. Paul pressed a button, the doors closed and we started to descend. Paul stood in front of us, watching the numbers change, until the doors opened. We came into a passageway that had navy blue carpeting. There were doors from the passageway, but no windows.

Paul stopped outside a large solid oak double door with large brass handles; he knocked on the door and turned to me with a sort of sheepish grin on his face. He shook my hand with a very firm grip. "Hope to see you both again Steve," he said very genuinely, then he turned to Vee, and gave her a sort of bow with his head.

Melvin White opened the door and stepped out into the passageway. Melvin was very high up in MI6, but he was a first-class person with a great sense of reality. I was very pleased to see that he was there; at least there was someone who could see both sides of any situation.

He shook hands with me, while his left hand was squeezing my right shoulder. "Good to see you again, Steve, as always," he said, and I could see in his eyes that he meant every word he said. This made me feel a little easier, but I was still very perplexed as to the overall situation.

"Not so sure it's good to see you, Mel," I said, smiling back, "Remember, I'm the one that doesn't know what the hell is going on, aren't I?"

"All will be revealed soon, Steve," he said. "And I want to say a special thank you to both yourself and Vee for giving us this audience," he smiled and nodded his head towards Vee, in a manner of respect. "I only regret how the whole thing was done, but I can assure you that that was not of my doing."

Mel ushered us into the room. As I stepped in, I glanced around, looking for familiar faces. Behind me, I could hear Melvin greeting Vee. There were only seven people in the room, not including Vee and myself. I only knew three of them. Franks was one, and I truly wish I had never known him; the other one was Margaret Pewter, who was in charge of the Anti-terrorism Unit for MI5. She was a very meticulous woman, who always had her T's crossed and I's dotted, and I always found her to be very exact and to the point, and, overall, a very down-to-earth, genuine person. Then there was Mel, for whom I always carried a great deal of respect. The other two guys I had never met, but they were obviously MI5 or MI6; and then there were another two, who seemed to be from the government, mainly because they didn't seem to fit in with the rest of the group at all.

Margaret Pewter stepped forward, holding out her hand. She had a very firm hand shake, and looked straight into my eyes.

"Good to see you again, Steve" she said. "It's been a long time. Ha! And this must be Vee," she said switching her eyes from me to Vee, "Very nice to meet you at last Vee, you are even more beautiful than I was told," she said. "I wanted to come up and meet with you but I'm afraid that everything is moving so fast at the moment that I didn't get a chance; but I knew that, with Judy looking after you, you would not be wanting for anything."

Vee smiled, and nodded. "Yes, I was well looked after and I thank you for that."

"Come in, both of you. Thank you, Paul," she said, closing the door, with Paul on the outside.

We were personally introduced to everyone in the room. Franks was standing in the corner of the room staring out of the window with a cup of coffee in his hand. If I hadn't known Franks better I

95

would think that he was a very worried man; this side of him, I had never seen before. The two odd guys in the room were introduced to us and were, as I thought, government men from the Home Office. They spoke with mouths full of silver spoons. The other two in the room were introduced to us as MI5 anti-terrorism operatives; this I found quite peculiar, as there was only Franks and Melvin from MI6. Things were getting more and more mysterious; everything seemed to be out of sync with the reality that I had known in all the years that I was with the SIS.

We all took seats at the solid oak oval table. I was seated at the head of the table with Vee on my right hand side. Vee moved her left hand to rest on my right hand, as soon as she did that I knew she was worried. I glanced at her, and gave her a great big "don't worry" smile, and a wink that was supposed to tell her that I was in charge here. But I've got to admit I was getting a little worried myself; nothing seemed as it should be, for some reason or other.

Margaret Pewter sat directly across from me at the other end of the rectangular table; this told me straight away that she was taking charge of the meeting, and yet she was MI5. Questions, questions and more questions.

The two MI5 delegates sat in the two chairs on from Vee, and the two silver spoons sat on my left hand side. No one had any files or paperwork, not even a pen in front of them. There were plastic bottles of water, glasses and a small bouquet of flowers in the middle the table. On my right, there was an oak bookcase, with shelves carrying various books, and two cupboards that were both closed. On my left were two large windows, both with a heavy anti-terrorism shielding on the glass, making it look quite dark outside.

I rubbed my hand across my unshaven face. I had not had a beard this long since I had last been in theatre, some eight years ago.

Margaret stood and looked around the table. Everyone seemed to turn their heads towards her at the same time.

"Well, gentlemen," she spoke, with a very business-like voice, "let's get down to the nitty gritty of why we are all here." She walked over to the cupboards, and sort of leant against them.

"Firstly I must reiterate that everything said or heard here in this room is a matter of National Security and must never be discussed with anyone outside this room, even between yourselves."

"Steve," she said directing her eyes towards me, "I know that both you and Vee are civilians, but I'm afraid that you must both come under the National Secrets Act with everything discussed in this room today." Both Vee and I nodded in unison.

She smiled at Vee and I, then held out her left arm, with her palm uppermost towards Mel, who immediately got off his chair, lifting a leather folder from a briefcase at his feet. He came around, and stood directly behind Vee and I.

"Sorry Steve, but both Vee and yourself will have to sign the Official Secrets Act." He coughed into his hand nervously, and placed the papers on the table in front of us. He gave Vee his gold Cross pen, saying, "Vee, please would you initial each page, and a full signature, date, time and place, on the last page?"

Vee looked at me questioningly; I nodded back to her, and she quickly signed without reading what was on the pages, and handed the pages back to Mel and the pen to me for me to sign.

I quickly signed my papers, and handed them and the pen back to Mel.

"Thank you both," he said with appreciation, taking both of our sets of papers, crossing the room, and taking his seat again next to Margaret.

"Wow, Vee, you trust them far more than I do, you never even read it!" I said smiling at her.

Everyone in the room burst out laughing.

As Mel took his seat, all eyes went back to Margaret, "Thank you Vee; thank you, Steve. I know just how you are both feeling, as I've been in the deep end once or twice myself when I couldn't swim, and I know that it can be quite intimidating." She was smiling at Vee with, surprisingly, quite a motherly smile.

"Firstly, I would like to apologise to both of you for the way you have been treated but I can assure you that it was to some extent a necessity, although very crudely done." She glanced down towards Franks, shaking her head.

"Over the next hour or so," Margaret said, taking her seat again, "You will come to realise the importance of you both being here in this meeting."

Margaret took a sip of water from her glass, replaced it on the table, and then looked around at all in attendance, with a sort of instigating look.

"As we all know, we are having an immense problem in the United Kingdom, and the whole of Europe for that matter, with home grown terrorist cells, who are being incited into terrorism by Al-Qaida's radical fundamentalists from inside Pakistan. At this moment, we have as many as three thousand of them, all around the country. We have doubled our complement of agents over the last two years, to try to keep a tighter control over the most serious ones. But I am not reticent to admit that we all feel that we could never, with all of our modern up-to-date security systems and analysis data, come anywhere near to saying that we are in control. And, as you no doubt fully understand, the ramifications of getting behind in this race are to a large extent too incomprehensible even to understand."

It was not hard to realise that Margaret was relating all this directly to Vee and I.

"Our biggest problem at the moment, funnily enough," Margaret went on, "is that the home grown terrorist is not a sophisticated person, but a very fundamental person, who is working with basic tools to deliver death and mayhem on the unsuspecting public on the streets of our cities, here, in Europe, in the United States and also in many other countries around the world."

Margaret moved from the cupboards, and stood behind her chair.

"Steve, Vee," Margaret was still looking directly at both of us. "I suppose you are wondering what all this has got to do with both of you, and I don't, for one minute, blame you."

I had to admit she was right, but what the hell had all this got to do with both of us?

"Margaret," I said scratching my bearded face. "You're damn right there; I left MI6 a number of years ago, I've settled down to a normal life with a house and a business, we even have a dog. Vee and I and Basil our dog are very happy. We are making a good living, and we are not interested at all in either MI6's or MI5's troubles, and I can tell you right now that I will never, under any circumstances, let either Vee or myself be seconded into any of your problems. You just said that you had doubled your agents over the last two years, so you should have enough field agents to call on night and day. I'm sorry, but I've got to ask: why me, Lord?"

I was staring at her, and I could definitely see a glint of embarrassment on her face.

"Margaret, please try to understand that it is not some lackey off the streets to whom you are talking. I was a field officer for years with full honours in theatre; but now, Margaret, I am an ex-, and, I repeat, ex-MI6 agent." I stood up and moved, so that I was behind Vee, sitting in her chair. I placed both my hands firmly on her shoulders.

"Margaret," I said. "I know and you know, as does everyone around this table, that you have a fully equipped MI6 and MI5 anti-

99

terrorist Infiltration Unit which is there only for one use, covertly to infiltrate their agents into situations of this nature and get relevant, and let's not forget even the irrelevant, information, back to HQ, so that every move made by the bad boys is summarised, analysed and programmed for use in all relevant departments." I lifted my arms outright. "So I ask again, Margaret. Why have you gone to all this bloody trouble to get Vee and myself in here? I for one, and I am sure that Vee also, cannot see any significance in this that could justify both of us sitting around this table."

Margaret looked at both Vee and myself with a kind of motherly look. She held her palm up toward us, and gave us a sort of surreal smile.

"I understand your attitude to the situation thoroughly, Steve," she said, "and I am very sure that you know that the home grown terrorist cells are very closely knit family units, and near enough impossible for our infiltration units to penetrate into their groups. But only now, in fact, only two weeks ago, something inconceivable happened that gave us the edge that we have been looking for, for years."

She crossed both her hands across her chest and went on. "But please, Steve, all we are asking is for you to listen to our predicament, and then you will understand why you yourself and Vee are sitting with us around this table. Steve should you then be of the same mind, both yourself and Vee are free to leave here with your heads held high. That is my promise to you both."

The look on her face was open and honest, and I felt that I must at least give them the time and place fully to explain the more intricate details. I supposed that that was the least I could do.

"Steve," she went on. "Everyone around this table has the greatest respect for you, as a person and as a field officer. You have done more for Queen and country than anyone I know; but all we are asking for is for you both to listen, nothing more, Steve, nothing more."

She looked over to Mel, sitting on her right, and then back to me.

"Please, Steve; we are, at the moment, only asking for your time. Only your time, that is all; please, please take your seat again."

Margaret had a very serious look in her eyes, but I could see that she was being very down-to-earth with me.

"OK, Margaret," I said, taking up my seat again. "I'm prepared to listen, and, if necessary, give advice, but no more than that; no promises, and definitely, absolutely definitely, no field work."

"Thank you Steve, we all appreciate that," she replied, with a very obvious look of relief on her face. "I, or should I say, all of us around this table really appreciate your *raison d'être* so far as the implications of this meeting are concerned, and we fully understand your position. But now let me hand you over to Melvin, as he is the one who instigated this meeting, and who has got everyone here today."

Margaret glanced towards Mel, on her right hand side, "Please take the floor, Melvin."

Mel stood up, walked towards the oak cupboards, and opened two of the doors, revealing a forty-two-inch flat screen television. He picked up the remote, and walked back to his seat. I could see that he was nervous, and this was not like Mel at all; so, I knew that this was going to be the coup-de-grace of the meeting. He cleared his throat with a nervous cough, looked around at everyone sitting at the table, gave another slight cough, picked up the television remote, and went back to his chair.

"Two weeks ago," he said, speaking in a very serious and authoritative manner. "We received some information from the CIA in Pakistan. It's a weekly disclosure that gives us a lot of relevant information regarding the irregular movements of certain Muslims, who are well known to us, and have clear connections with Al-Qaida throughout the world. In this report, we were quite shocked to see that a Muslim who is known as Salim Riaz, who is a very deftly and respected Al-Qaida commander, was second in command in the bombing of the American embassy in Africa. So we looked into it, and found that he is arriving in the United Kingdom in eight weeks time. This obviously set alarm bells ringing all around MI6 and MI5; at first we were going to have his visa revoked, but then we thought that he might be coming here to implement or oversee some kind of terrorist act. We thought that if he was, and if we kept close tabs on him, maybe, just maybe, he could lead us to someone or some group who are home-grown terrorists over here. These people would also definitely be held in quite high esteem by Al-Qaida In Pakistan.

Mel took a drink from his glass, and replaced it. Once again, he looked at everyone around the table.

"Having time on our side," Mel went on, "we then decided to look into Salim Riaz a little deeper before making any decisions. Whereupon, we dug out as much information and intelligence as was available on him; and thanks to the CIA, we got photographs of both him and his wife, as recently as last week."

He glanced down the table towards Vee and I, gave another nervous cough, and carried on.

"When the photographs came across my desk, I was somewhat shocked, because I somehow recognised him; but I could not put my finger on the reason why I should recognise someone who lived in another world, and whom I knew I had never, ever met."

Once again, he looked down the table towards Vee and I, this time looking even more nervous.

"Donald," he said, lifting his hand and pointing to Franks. "Came into my office while we were scrutinising the photographs.

He made a joke about Salim Riaz. I think he said something like. "That's the limit, has Steve Taylor turned bloody Muslim."

With that statement everyone around the table sort of laughed a nervous laugh into their hands.

Mel gave another nervous glance down the table towards Vee and I, then went on, "I got the surprise of my life, Steve. It could have been you with a beard and Muslim garb in the photograph."

Hearing that made me rub my beard and remember how Paul had stopped me from shaving earlier.

"Wow, I know exactly where this is going," I retorted, getting to my feet again, "and I also know where I'm going, home. My dog Basil needs feeding and some loving, he hasn't seen much of us over the last week or so; thank you, gentlemen. Vee," I glanced down at her, and put my hand on her shoulder, she was looking up at me with a very perplexed sort of look on her face.

"Come on Vee," I said, standing up. "Let's get out of this bloody den of iniquity, I've finished being used and abused by these bastards."

Vee stood up next to me, and put her left arm in my arm while squeezing my upper arm with her right hand; she still had that perplexed look on her face, that was starting to look like embarrassment.

Mel and Franks had their heads in their hands, and elbows on the table.

"Gentlemen," Margaret had now risen to her feet.

"Please, Steve," she moved both her hands indicating for us to sit down, "Take your seat, please, I'm begging you; just give us a chance to elaborate a little as to what we are trying to propose. As I said before, when all is revealed you can walk out of here, there will be absolutely no pressure put on either of you, but please, please just hear us out first; then you can make your judgement."

Because she was such a down to earth person, you could see in her face that she was not ordering me, but pleading with me, to listen to the end.

"OK," I said getting back down in my seat. "But I want you all to fully understand that no matter what you are proposing my answer is 'No'. Now, is there anyone around this table that doesn't understand the word, or any part of the word 'No'?"

I looked at everyone individually as I spoke, making sure that everyone understood what I had just interpreted.

Mel looked at me with relief on his face. "Steve, I'm very sorry that this is upsetting you, and Vee, as well. I also understand your position; and, as you know I have always admired you as an SAS Officer, and as an MI6 agent; and for that matter, even in your personal capacity, I have nothing but reverence, and the greatest of respect for you. Please, please I'm begging you to hear us out."

Mel was looking directly at me, with a look of determination and resilience on his face.

"As you know Steve," Mel went on, "the world is at war. We are not fighting an enemy that we can see. We cannot even recognise who our enemies are, nowadays; they don't wear uniforms, and they don't have any respect, not even for their own fellow Muslims. Islam is supposedly a religion of peace and tranquillity, although I've got to say that I myself am a little unconvinced on this, but it seems that the vast majority of Muslims want just that, to live in peace and harmony. Although this assertion may be true, it is entirely irrelevant and meaningless fluff, meant to make us feel better, and intended to somehow diminish the spectre of fanatics rampaging across the globe in the name of Islam and Jihad. The fact is that these minority fanatics rule Islam at this moment in time. It is the fanatics who are waging at least fifty wars worldwide at this very moment. It is the fanatics who systematically slaughtered Christians, and even Muslim tribal groups who didn't interpret the Quran according to their understanding; this transpired all across the continent of Asia and Africa, gradually aiming to take over entire continents, in an Islamic wave of Jihad. It is the fanatics who bomb, murder and honour-kill. It is the fanatics who take over mosque after mosque so that they can preach Jihad to the peace-loving Muslims. It's the fanatics who zealously spread the stoning and hanging of rape victims and homosexuals. It's the fanatics who teach their young to kill, and become suicide bombers. The hard, quantifiable fact is that the peaceful majority are the 'silent majority' so to speak, who are classed as pathetic and extraneous individuals by the fanatics."

Mel was using his hands in sometimes, you could say, very violent gestures, as he leaned forward in his chair, speaking directly to Vee and I.

"For all our powers of reasoning," he went on. "We often miss the most basic and uncomplicated points, such as the fact that the peace-loving Muslims that have been made irrelevant by their silence. Peace-loving Muslims will also become our enemies if they don't learn to speak up; they will awaken one day to find that the fanatics own them, and the end of their peace-loving world will have begun. Many others throughout the world have died because the peaceful majority did not speak up until it was too late. And the same will be true of us, we who are watching all this unfold, we who never paid enough attention to the only groups that count, the fanatics that threaten the Western World's way of life."

I was very surprised that Mel had made such a speech. He was never a speech sort of person, a realist maybe, but never had I heard him talk with so much emotion and venom.

He looked around the table with a kind of embarrassed look on his face. "Sorry about that folks, it's been some time since I ever ran off at the mouth like that." He was rubbing his hands together with great vigour.

"Now folks, let's get down to what we are here for," Mel said. "Let's get down to the nitty gritty."

Mel stood up with the remote in his hand; he glanced around the table at everyone individually, then he lifted the remote and started the video.

Franks stood up, took the remote from Mel and walked around to the television screen; he stood there motionless, just staring at the blank screen.

"Well, folks," Franks spoke very slowly, picking his words with his usual precision. "First of all, we have a few recent and very clear photographs of Salim and Sharma Rias, his wife, in Pakistan. They were taken last week by a CIA agent, so we have no need to question their authenticity; plus, Salim is also carrying a newspaper, where the date can be clearly seen on enhancement."

Franks clicked on the remote and up came a picture of Salim's wife, dressed in Muslim regalia, I was shocked at the resemblance the photograph had to Vee, it was incredible; they could have been sisters, or even twins.

I felt Vee's left hand tighten on my right hand. Her right hand went up to her mouth, and she said, under her breath, "Oh my God, Steve, that could be me or my twin sister; she even dresses as I would dress, back in India."

Vee turned to me; she still had her hand up to her mouth, and everyone around the table could see that she was utterly shocked at what she had just seen. Margaret looked straight down the table at both Vee and I; she had also recognised the shock on Vee's face.

"I can see that you are both as shocked as we were," Margaret cut in. "Vee, you are the spitting image of Salim's wife; or you could say that she's the spitting image of you. Whichever way you put it you could be, as you suggested, identical twins."

We all sat staring at the television screen. No one uttered a word, and there was a stunning silence throughout the room. All you could hear was the low hum from the air conditioners.

"Let's go to the next one," Franks said, breaking the silence, and bringing everyone back to reality.

"This," he said, "is Salim Rias himself, with his wife Sharma, outside a Hotel in Northern Pakistan. I'm afraid we are unsure who the other person is in the picture, but the CIA are looking into it at this very moment."

Up came a photograph of three people, Salim Rias, his wife Sharma and another man. Salim and the unknown man were shaking hands; both were smiling broadly, and, to my surprise, Salim was, although wearing a full beard, very much the image of myself.

"We have fifteen photographs and three videos of both Salim and his wife, Sharma," Franks went on, "all from different views and varied angles; and, with enhancement, we are able to see all the relevant features. For instance, Salim has a scar over his right eye, and a sort of wart on the right side of his nose. With Salim's wife, Sharma, there are no relevant features, but," he turned towards us with a great big smile on his face, "we do know that she is two and a half months pregnant. But I'm afraid we don't know the gender of the child." Franks smiled and glanced at everyone around the table, as if he was waiting for applause at his joke.

I've got to admit I think I have only seen Franks smile four or five times in the last ten or eleven years; today I'd seen him smile twice. Maybe he was also starting to get hot flushes.

Well, now I knew what had been going on behind the scenes in MI6 and MI5; and I also knew how Vee and I were going to fit in, or, should I say, where they wanted us to fit in. I had to admit this was a phenomenal acquisition that the CIA had come up with. It was unbelievable seeing the likeness of the photographs to Vee and

I; and I also very well understood their way of thinking. But I had no plans to help them in realising their intentions, not in this life, anyway.

I got up from my chair, and stood directly behind Vee, with both hands massaging her shoulders. I could feel the tension in the muscles around her neck. She moved her head backwards and sideways, and looked up into my eyes; she looked a little bit shocked, but deep in her eyes I could see fear.

"Ladies and Gentlemen," I spoke loudly with a touch of venom in my voice. "I have listened to every word that has been discussed in this room, but I am afraid my answer is still and always will be a definite 'No'. I would never ever allow you people to entrap me into anything ever again. It's not only me, now, but you are trying to implicate Vee, my partner, into your world of anti-terrorism. Under no circumstances whatsoever could I allow that to happen. I cannot believe it! She doesn't even have a British passport, and, if she applied for one tomorrow, it would be refused, and yet you are asking her to serve Queen and country, and put her life on the line."

I looked around the room at each person individually, and just shook my head. "Let's go, Vee, I think we have heard enough for today."

"Steve." It was the Minister of security who spoke. He had a look of anguish on his face. "We are not, and I repeat, not, sending you into theatre; all we require of you both is to take the place of those two individuals, and lead us to whomever they are going to rendezvous with. Once that has been achieved, your side of the operation will have been completed. From there, both MI5 and MI6 will take over the inner workings and we hope that it will save hundreds, if not thousands of lives, and these home-grown Islamic extremists will be put behind bars, where they should be for the rest of their lives."

"Steve," He went on. "We cannot do this without your help. You have seen the pictures of Salim and his wife; they not only look like you, they are of the same build and virtually the same skin colouring. For the first time in our lives, we have a chance of getting someone on the inside of a Muslim cell, and, most importantly, right at the top, the whole set-up is so unbelievably perfect that it will take only a couple of days for both yourself and Vee to go in. Do your bit, then hand it over. Just a couple of days, Steve, that is all we are asking; just think about the amount of lives you are going to save. For all we know, this could be a nuclear attack, and there could be millions of lives at stake."

I looked over at Mel, who was looking very seriously at Vee and I.

"Yes, Steve," he spoke very sternly, "maybe even Vee and yourself could be affected with this whole scenario; maybe it could be your friends or family." He looked around the table, with a very solemn face then back towards Vee and I. "Just a few days, Steve, that's all; just a few days, that's all we are asking." His voice was very low, down to almost a whisper. "Think about it, Vee. Think about it, Steve. Hundreds, thousands, maybe even millions of lives could be saved, or lost, depending on your answer."

The room was deathly silent; the air conditioner seemed very, very loud now. Mel stared down the table towards Vee and I.

I sat staring directly at the Minister; I could feel my temper rising to a crescendo and I felt I had to let my feelings be known.

"Minister, you are asking Vee and I to get you out of a predicament that has come about by governmental incompetence and that was incurred probably without any discernment towards the people of Great Britain over the past thirty-five or forty years. If we go back over those years, it was the governments who have been in power who allowed these Muslims into the country in their hordes; it was the governments who allowed them to build their mosques and take over vast areas of cities, almost like the apartheid system that is in South Africa, and that I must say you were very much against in South Africa; and yet this is being allowed by all the governments throughout Europe, probably because, unlike the South African government they do not put a name to it."

"Let no one fool you about Islam being a religion. Sure, it has a God, and a hereafter, and seventy-two virgins, and all that crap; but in its essence, Islam is a political ideology. It is a system that lays down detailed rules for society, and the life of every person. Islam wants to dictate every aspect of life throughout the world. Islam means 'submission'. Islam is not compatible with freedom and democracy, because what it strives for is Shariah law, all around the western world. If you want to compare Islam to anything, compare it to communism or National Socialism; these are all totalitarian ideologies.

I stopped and looked down at Vee. She had a look on her face that really did show fear. "Support Israel, firstly because it is the Jewish homeland, after two thousand years of exile up to and including Auschwitz; secondly, because it's a democracy; and thirdly, because Israel is our first line of defence. This tiny country is situated on the fault line of Jihad, frustrating Islam's territorial advance. Israel is facing the front lines of Jihad, like Kashmir, Kosovo, the Philippines, Southern Thailand, and Darfur in Sudan, Lebanon, and Aceh in Indonesia. Israel is simply in the way, in the same way that the West Berlin wall was, during the Cold War."

I took a drink of water, and put the glass down on the table with a sharp crack. "Gentlemen, the war against Israel is not just a war against Israel. It is a war against the West. It is total Jihad. Israel is simply receiving the blows that are meant for all of us. If there had been no Israel, Islamic imperialism would have found other venues on which to release its energy and its desire for conquest. It's thanks to the Israeli parents who send their children to the army, and lie awake at nights, worrying about their sons and daughters, fighting in theatre, that parents in Europe and America are sleeping well, and dreaming of a wonderful tomorrow, totally unaware of the dangers that are looming around them. Many in Europe argue in favour of abandoning Israel, in order to address the grievances of our Muslim minorities. But if Israel were, God forbid, to go down, it would not bring any solace to the predicament; it would enhance everything towards the end of Christianity, and also democracy."

The Minister put his hand up to stop my lethal utterances, that were pointed directly towards the governments of Great Britain and probably all of the governments of Europe and the western world. But before he could say a word, I put up my hand up and stopped him.

"Mr. Minister, this is not the time to implement excuses for governments, this is the time to shoot from the hip or turn away, and I can see this government doing the latter. In the last few months you blocked Geert Wilders, the leader of the second most popular political party in Holland from entering the country, because he is anti-Muslim, and yet he was allowed into the United States, and gave political speeches in various venues throughout America. One thing he said that stuck in my mind was that in a generation or so the United States of America will ask itself 'Who Lost Europe?' It makes you think, doesn't it, Minister?"

There was silence again in the room, and the air conditioning was all you could hear. Everyone was in utter disbelief at what I had said, but I didn't give a damn. I wanted them all to realise just where I stood on this whole situation.

"Now, Mr Minister, let us look at a country like Switzerland," I went on. "Switzerland is a country that looks after its own; when the build-up of Muslims came into their country their government utilised common sense. When the Muslim people asked if they could build mosques for their people to pray to Allah, the government said, 'Yes, you can build your mosques, but only on condition that we can go to your country, and build churches and teach Christianity.' Mr Minister, let me tell you: there are very few Muslims in Switzerland, and definitely no Mosques. You people, as the government, have allowed these people to do anything they like; they are multiplying yearly, and taking over vast parts of the country, in Leeds, Manchester, Birmingham, Nottingham, Bury. There is a small town in Lancashire, called Brierfield, where the population percentage of Muslims is at a record high of ninety per cent. And now – and you must have knowledge of this – Shariah law has been incorporated into British law in Birmingham, and I am sure that it is being negotiated vigorously by many Muslim clerics in many other cities throughout the United Kingdom."

I could see on the Minister's face that he would have no answers to what I was saying, as he knew it was all accurate, and there for anyone to see, if they took the time and showed the interest.

"I very much understand your predicament, Minister, but I also understand the cause. To get right down to basics, Minister, you people have fucked up to an horrendous extent; and it's not that you do not have the will to rectify it, but that you cannot rectify it, because the whole scenario has gone much too far to be rectified. And to top it all, you people, as the government, now need other people to put their lives on the line, to sort out individual happenings that are erupting around the country, that any competent person understands will never stop as long as we are kow-towing to the Muslim people, not only in Great Britain but throughout the bloody world."

I stopped and took a drink of water, but nobody in the room stirred.

The whole room went electrifyingly silent again. Everyone was looking at everyone else to come back with some common sense that would break the silence.

Mel gave a nervous cough, and looked directly towards me, with a look of concern on his face.

"Steve, remember about 1988 in Libya. You were captured and tortured for days on end. As soon as we found where you were held I personally went to the SAS and organised for eight volunteers to go in there and get you out. All thirty men who were not in theatre at the time stepped forward to volunteer immediately, and we only needed eight. I chose those eight men personally and alas, sadly, one, a corporal, namely John Hamer, lost his life. I do not dwell on the life that was lost, but his name will be in my mind until the day I die. I don't have to explain to you, Steve, that this is the camaraderie that is instilled into not only the armed forces not only into the SAS, but all of the British people throughout the country. It's a British thing, and we must not forget that. Now just think, Steve: I carry John Hamer's name on my mind. Imagine carrying a thousand names on your mind, maybe a million; who knows? I struggle with one name. How many names could you carry, Steve?"

The room went deathly silent again. No one moved one iota. Everyone was waiting for someone else to make a move, to bring about the centre point of the meeting.

I was about to open my mouth to speak, when Vee's hand squeezed my wrist. She stood up, and, placing her left hand on my shoulder, she shook her head, and her beautiful black hair sparkled and shimmered from the lights in the room.

"Steve and I," – she spoke in a low but very precise voice – "have listened intently to everything that has been said, and what has been shown to us. I must admit I was shocked by the total resemblance of the photographs to both Steve and I, but due to the time that we have before anything can be initiated, I do not feel that it is necessary for us to give you an answer immediately, although we both do understand the severity of the whole situation, and also the urgency of the timeline."

Vee turned her head towards me, and squeezed my shoulder tightly.

"Both Steve and I, gentlemen," she said squeezing my shoulder again, "are very much aware of the seriousness of the situation, and also of the principles and the shocking parameters that the whole world has to deal with in this deteriorating present day and age; but I have two requirements at this moment. One is a time period of twenty-four hours for both Steve and I to discuss the programme as a whole alone, and in our own environment. At this moment in time, all I can say, looking at your situation in its entirety, is that both of us can perceive the necessity for Steve and I to be an integral part in your scheme, to try, with you, to eliminate what could be a catastrophic disaster; but, due to the magnitude of the situation, I feel that you cannot expect the two of us to make an instant decision, without conferring with each other in the privacy of our own home."

I glanced sideways at Vee. At first, I was quite shocked at what she had just expressed; but I had to admit that she is very much her own person, and that was just how Vee's mind worked. She had a very open mind, and never jumped to conclusions; she was always the one who weighed all of the evidence, worked out all the pro's and con's, taking into account both sides of any story, and only then would she ever think of coming to a conclusion. I could never contest what she had said, because that was one of the principles that I most admired in her.

"That's not a problem, Vee." Mel burst in, looking around the room to see whether it was a unanimous decision. "Not a problem at all," he said, considering that all, including myself, were nodding in conformity.

Mel, with his elbows on the table, pointed his left index finger towards Vee. "Vee, and your other requirement; you did articulate two, didn't you?"

Vee had a sort of half-smile on her face. "Yes, Melvin, I did; I would love a cup of very sweet and very strong black coffee; my nerves are shot at this moment."

With that, the room erupted into nervous laughter again, and even Franks laughed.

Margaret stood up, and walked towards the door behind us.

"Judy," I heard her saying. "Please bring in coffee and a few biscuits, thank you."

I looked at Vee, and I must have had disbelief on my face; she put her thumb and index finger on either side of my chin and gave me a friendly kiss on the lips. "OK with you, my love?" She raised her eyebrows, making it a question.

"Yes Vee," I said, "OK with me, I guess; as always, you're the boss. Twenty-four hours will give us adequate time to debate this whole scenario, and give them all a resounding 'No'."

I then stood up and looked at every person around the table individually; they had all seemed to be very nervous before Vee had spoken, but now they have seemed to have relaxed to some extent.

"Twenty-four hours" I said, "and we will give you our answer; but I would just like to stipulate at this moment, that it must be accepted by each and every one of you, without condition, or proviso. And if it comes to a definite 'No', and, at the moment, I assume it will, you must all just walk away." I waited a few seconds, then added looking directly at Franks. "Is that in conformity with everyone in the room?"

Margaret stood up at the head of the table; she had a smile on her face, but also, I could see, a definite look of some relief.

"Gentlemen," she said, slapping her hands together, "This has been a meeting that I could never have thought I would ever have

115

to address. I am sure that everyone around the table will agree with me, when I say 'thanks,' wholeheartedly, to both Vee and Steve, for giving us the time to enlighten them on the very seriousness of the situation in which we have found ourselves. I would also like to say, to all concerned, that this must not be discussed again with Steve or Vee; and we will all, and I repeat all, honour and respect the privacy of both of them for the next twenty-four hours, and, most importantly, their decision as to whether or not they will be participating with us in this operation."

Margaret looked to her right, and straight into Franks's eyes.

"Gentlemen, are we all in agreement that, if their answer is in the negative," she was still looking directly at Franks, "we just walk away?"

She then looked at everyone around the table, individually. "Gentlemen, are we all in agreement?" She paused, and once again looked directly at Franks. I could see that she had Franks taped. Franks nodded in agreement, but seemed very reluctant, and never raised his hand or his eyes from the table.

Everyone else around the table, other than Franks, all acknowledged, by nodding or raising their hands.

"Thank you all for your input." Margaret then looked directly at Vee with a smile on her face. "I've got to admit that I also need coffee, Vee. It must be a feminine thing, don't you think?"

Everyone laughed a strained sort of laugh. I think everyone in the room was so very relieved and thankful to Vee for eliminating the disparity that everyone had had, and that the meeting was coming to fruition with both Vee and I still in the room.

"Steve, Vee, and everyone present." Although Margaret was speaking to everyone in the room she was looking directly towards Vee and I. "I have got to reiterate once more that this meeting is of the highest national security importance, and nobody must discuss anything at all with any other person outside this room. I am sorry that I have had to say that, but I am sure that you are all fully aware of the national regulations regarding security."

With that, the door opened behind me, and I presumed it was Judy who wheeled in a trolley, with coffee and biscuits on it. The coffee smelt great, and it went through my mind that I didn't think it was a feminine thing at all.

We all stood around drinking coffee, and nibbling biscuits. All of a sudden, the atmosphere had changed completely; they were now the type of everyday people whom you would expect to meet at a school function, or in your local supermarket, or even at a church meeting, except for Franks and the two ministers of course; those three were Westminster and MI6 up to the hilt.

On finishing our coffee, Vee and I went through all the preliminaries with everyone, and then we were escorted down to the parking level by Paul.

As we exited the lift, Paul said to me. "I've got to say that, personally, I have missed working with you, Steve. I always remember how you would bring a serious situation into a sort of calmness, and yet it was you that was in theatre, and you that had the problem; I always admired you immensely for that."

"Thanks Paul," I said smiling at him. "But you must understand that being in theatre is very intense work, and, as you well know, you are always living on a knife edge. If there was any panic at all in HQ, then my situation would have been severely hampered, and the dangers around me enhanced tremendously. So calming you people was the best thing I could do to keep my sanity, and, obviously stay alive."

As we came to our car, I turned and shook hands with Paul while I was opening the door for Vee to get in the passenger side door; as Vee slipped into her seat, I closed her door, and made my way back round to the driver's side door.

"Thanks a lot, Paul." Then, as if just making conversation, I asked, "What are you doing over here now? You always seemed to be part of the furniture at MI6."

"Being part of the furniture was probably the whole reason for me moving here, Steve. I was in counter-intelligence with MI6 until the end of last year, but probably, as you say, I became part of the furniture. Then I found that it had become rather boring, and very repetitive; also, I've got to say, a little too much of government intrusion if you know what I mean. So I asked to be moved to the antiterrorism unit with MI5; then, three months ago I moved to the Infiltration Unit. Now I feel that I am part of MI5, as everything is hands on, and moving very fast. No time to get bored at all!" He smiled at me with a 'why is he asking that' look on his face.

"That's good, Paul, that's good," I said, shaking his hand again. "Speak to you soon." I gave him a wink as I turned away.

I got into the car, and as I reversed out of the parking, I glanced back at Paul in the rear view mirror. He was still standing there, with one hand in his trouser pocket and a sort of bemused look on his face. He knew there was something in the offing, I'm sure. I put the car into first gear, and headed for the exit.

I gave Albert a wave, as he raised the boom for me. "Lovely seeing you again, Mr. Taylor," he said. "Drive safely, and have a nice day."

Chapter Eight

It was raining steadily as we pulled out onto the Thames Embankment, but there was still time to get home before the rush hour traffic hit the streets. I had to get to Tudor's place first, to exchange cars and thank him for all his help over the past day or two.

As we pulled into the parking at Tudor's place, he was standing in a yellow raincoat outside the delivery door, checking some beer crates that were being delivered. On seeing us, he walked over, waving and wiping the rain drops off his face, and grinning broadly.

"The usual crap weather, eh, Steve? Stay in the car," he said. "I'll get your keys out of the office, no need for both of us to get bloody wet." Then he glanced across at Vee. "Hi, Vee! Long time no see. You must come round and see us some time soon; it's not often we get a beautiful woman in this den of iniquity," he said, running away laughing.

We parked Tudor's car in his garage, and then hit the road for home. As usual, the rain was still falling steadily. Vee sat quietly beside me, with her right hand on my thigh. I had noticed that she had never mentioned the night in the restaurant, but I've always said that people all have their different ways of dealing with personal post-traumatic stress, so I kept quiet as I knew she would come around to discuss it in her own time; and, at the moment, we both had enough on our minds.

"Steve," she spoke very quietly. "How about when we get home, we put the central heating on; then I will cook you a nice spicy lamb curry, open a nice bottle of red wine and we can play with Basil on the carpet. I bet he has missed us tremendously over the past few days."

"Yes, love, that sounds great," I replied, stopping at a traffic light.

"Funny you just mentioned Basil, Vee; I went home today to bath and change clothes when I left Tudor's, and he was nowhere in sight. I never thought about it until now. Is he with the Smiths?"

"Yes, love, you don't have to worry about Basil; I phoned from the hospital, and asked Mrs. Smith to look after him for us," Vee laughed. "If I hadn't phoned Mrs Smith, you can bet your life that he would have dug a hole under the fence, and would have been begging for his food from them, anyway."

We came into our street, and the first thing I noticed was that there was no spooks car parked at the kerb. Maybe they were still in Spain following the truck; you never know.

I got out of the car and rushed to open the front door; turning, I then called for Vee to get out of the car. She ran to the door, with both hands protecting her hair from the rain.

"Wow Steve is it bloody cold tonight, or is it me coming down with something?" she asked, as she swept past me and through the door. I initiated the alarm on the car, and went inside. I could hear Vee in the kitchen already opening and closing the cupboard doors, banging pans and lids around and humming some tune to herself. She sounded really happy; but I knew that, deep down, her mind was definitely not on the food that she was cooking, that was for sure.

I switched on the central heating, and put it on high to warm up the house quickly; and then I went through to the study, and pulled out one of Vee's favourite red wines from the rack. As I entered the kitchen, the food aroma was mouth watering; Vee was moving pans around the stove, stirring this and stirring that, putting lids on the pans and talking on the phone, all at the same time. You know that the feminine side of humanity can do multi-tasking without a whim, and we, as males, can't even think of more than one thing at a time.

"OK, lovely, thank you so much, Mrs. Smith; we'll pick him up now," she was saying, replacing the phone on the hook with a clatter.

Then, looking over to me and lifting her eyebrows high, she said, "Honey, do you want to go next door and pick Basil up?"

"Not on your bloody life, sweetheart; she will keep me there talking for at least an hour or more with my face looking the way it is. You know I can never get away from her, and I'm starving," I replied, taking the cork from the bottle, and putting it in the fridge. "Better you go, and I'll watch the stove for you."

"Do you know where it is?" Vee questioned.

"Do I know where what is?" I asked.

"The bloody stove, you buffoon," she iterated, slapping me on the backside, and laughing as she ran past me, heading for the front door.

I laid the table in the dining room, and played with Basil on the lounge floor, sipping on my glass of the red wine, while Vee finished off the dinner in the kitchen.

After a wonderful Indian curry, with all the trimmings, lovely red wine, and the best company any man could want, Vee's mood suddenly changed, and I knew that she now wanted to get something off her chest.

Vee was a very self controlled person, with a very calm disposition; she never initiated anything until she was good and ready, and I could see that the time was now right for her. I also knew that, while she was sitting quietly in the car and also scrambling around the kitchen cooking, she had been thoughtfully working behind the scenes, and I guess I was about to get all her thoughts laid out in front of me.

I was sitting on my chair, and Basil was fast asleep on the settee next to Vee. We had lowered the light to some degree, and the artificial fire was flickering light all around the room. Vee took her eyes off Basil, and looked across the room at me.

"Steve," she said in something of a sombre tone, "I listened very carefully to everything that was discussed this afternoon; and to some extent, as I presume you were, I was quite shocked at what I heard."

She was very lightly stroking Basil as she went on. "I've got to admit that at first I was a bit upset at what they were proposing; but afterwards, when I had taken everything into consideration, my mind was put back to my Punjab days with the Indian government." Basil had rolled on to his back now, and Vee was tickling his stomach.

"I have never," she went on, "told you this before, Steve, mainly because I had put it out of my mind for my own personal reasons. I remember that I had just made captain at the time; and being a female in a high-ranking position in India was not an easy task, as you were still not treated in accordance with your rank. You were, first and foremost, only a woman, and the captaincy was secondary. To many other officers, you should only have been in charge of the kitchen staff."

Vee was looking rather perplexed as she spoke, as if she was remembering memories that she had blocked out of her mind many years ago, and was very reluctant to bring them to the forefront, never mind to have to disclose them to anyone.

"I was contacted one day by a Pakistani female, who I had first met many years before, and she had, over time, developed into sort of an informant. She gave me information about an attack that was going to take place on a train line between the Punjab and New

Delhi. Obviously, I put in a report, and it was followed up by a meeting with a few high-ranking generals. In the meeting, I was made to look an absolute fool, and, as I walked out, I felt utterly degraded and stunned at the reaction of my so called superiors."

I thought I could see tears on Vee's face, but it could have been the light flickering from the firelight.

"To cut a long story short, Steve," she went on, "no one took the slightest notice of me; and seven days later, one hundred and forty men, women and children were killed, and many more seriously injured, in an horrific derailing of a train while it was passing another oncoming train from the opposite direction."

I could see that it was tears on her face now. I thought to move across to her, but I decided against it. Doing that might break her mood, and that was the last thing I wanted to do right now.

"Steve," she went on, "I cried for days afterwards. I also came very close to resigning my position with the Indian Intelligence, not because those innocent men, women and children died, no not at all, but because I never found the strength inside of me to stand up to those totally uninhibited, arrogant Indian men who had reached their status in life by being promoted to generals because their forefathers had been generals, or because they didn't have the guts to be out in the field. In my mind, they were not even men, because real men realise that females were not just born to cook their food and sleep in their beds; women have brains and feelings, just like men, and all they ask is to be recognised and accepted for that."

Vee wiped her face with a tissue, and Basil stirred next to her, looking first at Vee then across towards me. The look on his face said, 'What have you done to her?'

"But Steve," she went on, "if I had found that strength to stand up to those pathetic, demonstrative men that called themselves human beings, maybe all those people would be alive and well to this day."

I got up from the chair, taking my glass, and walked over to Vee to gather hers. Nothing was said until I returned from the kitchen, with both glasses replenished with deep red wine. She seemed to have consoled herself and took the wine from me with a sort of innocuous smile. I walked to my chair, sat down, had a sip of the wine, placed the glass on the side table beside me, raised my hand palm upwards and said. "OK, Vee. You still have the floor?"

"Thanks, my love," she replied smiling a half smile. "I'm sorry to show my feelings so deeply, Steve, but it's just that recollecting all those long-lost distasteful memories of that experience in my life is not easy. It's an episode that I must say I thought I had put to bed and out of my mind forever, and it hurts a little; no, to be honest, Steve, it hurts far more than a little."

Vee wiped yet another tear from her eyes. I could see she was struggling, deep down; just recalling those long-lost demoralising memories was hurting her very much.

"Are you sure you are OK, Vee," I asked, leaning forward and putting my elbows on my knees.

"Yes, yes, my love I'm fine, yes I'm fine; you know that I'm a very strong girl, deep down."

That was definitely no exaggeration. A strong girl she was, and she'd proved it to me many, many times over the years, both in the field, and as my partner here in the United Kingdom.

Vee gave a little cough, as if to grab my attention or get her mind back on the subject.

"That brings me back to today, Steve," she said, twirling the red wine in her glass and looking through it towards the fire. "I listened very intensively to what everyone had to say, and I can fully understand their apprehensions. I also very much understand your sentiments towards MI6. But Steve, this is not about you, nor about me; it's not even about MI6 or MI5. It's about all those very innocent people, men, women and children and that could be hundreds maybe even thousands – I dread to think of its being more than that – but what was being bantered about at Thames House was that it could possibly be in the millions, if it should be a dirty bomb attack."

Vee put her glass down, and pulled her feet up on to the settee, lifting her knees in front of her body and cuddled them with both arms. I could see that the whole event had really got to her, and it was quite understandable. To some extent, I felt the same way, but I was the one who knew MI6 inside out, and all Vee was seeing now was a catastrophic and devastating event that could, or would, or might never even take place. I understood her interpretation with respect to what had happened, but the event was obviously blocking out her reasoning, and she was not looking at the whole picture, so to speak. I let her continue, as I wanted to let her vent all her feelings and apparitions, so that I myself could really understand just where she logically stood in this matter.

"Steve," she went on. "This is far too much for me to even consider not acting in some way to alleviate the despair of such a tragic happening. I could never live with myself, even if the numerals were in hundreds, if I hadn't tried in even some small way to prevent the tragedy. If I tried and failed, at least I would know that I did my best to stop it happening. But to sit back and do nothing..." She put both hands over her face. "Steve, I just cannot envisage how I would feel, both mentally and physically, should this phenomenon take place, and I had just sat on the side lines doing nothing."

Vee stood up and came across towards me, picked up my empty glass and headed for the kitchen. Basil jumped off the settee and followed her. He knew where the food was, and he also knew who fed him.

Vee came walking back into the lounge with two replenished glasses of red wine, with Basil close behind, and a nice lamb bone between his teeth. She handed me my glass, and plonked herself on the settee, nearly spilling her wine. I could see the wine had taken some effect, but I knew she needed it to help her relax a little, as she'd had a rough time over the last couple of days, with one thing and another.

"Well," she said, "Now I think it's time you took the floor, Mr. Taylor." It was quite obvious that she had a little slur in her speech, and she had mellowed a little. I always enjoyed her when she was like this.

"Well, well, well," I said smiling across at her. "So I do get a say in this then?" She laughed, and mimicked zipping up her lips, as if to assure me that she was now going to keep quiet.

"Vee firstly I've got to say that I fully understand where you are coming from; also, I've got to admit that ninety nine per cent of human kind would be in your corner; but I want you to realise and fully understand that you are not looking at the picture as a whole. Let's go back just a few days. Basically, you could say, without a doubt, that you were kidnapped by Franks, and you were held until I came into them; and that, my dear, is tantamount to blackmail, in anyone's books."

"Oh Steve," she uttered. "Kidnapping is a bit too strong a word, isn't it? I can understand the blackmail side, to a small degree; but I can also see why they had to go to such lengths. It was the timeline, Steve; they had to move fast, whether it was with or without our help. Also, while I was with them, I was very well looked after and put under no duress whatsoever, other than not really knowing what was going on with you."

"Shush," I hissed, with my index finger across my lips.

"Vee, I gave you the floor without any interruptions whatsoever; now please give me the chance to give you my view of the picture. Then we can say that we are both reading from the same page, so to speak."

"Oh, I'm sorry, my love!" She had her hand up to her mouth once again. "I think it's a mixture of the wine and the prodigious stress that I have been under. I promise not to interrupt or make light of it any more."

"I thank you for that, my love," I said, with an understanding grin on my face.

"Now Vee, I want you fully to understand the situation that we are being forced into." I had a sip of my wine, and replaced the glass on the side table. "MI6 knew that they could never knock on my door and give me the story which they gave us; they knew that I would have laughed in their faces, they needed some kind of an edge, something that would sway me. You were the perfect acquisition. They knew that they would get to you with ease, and then that you, in turn, could, inadvertently, sway me. It's a game of good cop, bad cop, Vee, and they used you as the good cop. That's the way they work, Vee. You have got to understand that these people are total manipulators. They don't worry about who gets hurt; it's all about their own self-esteem, and getting the job done, and also getting the glory. Believe me, Vee, these people are not the nice, easy-going people that they showed themselves as to you over the last four or five days; as I said, they are the perfect manipulators. They have been doing it for nearly a hundred years, and have perfected it to a 'T'. That's where they got the name spooks from. They are not open and up-front people like you and I; they are very low, uncaring and conniving, get-the-job-done-at-any-cost kind of people, who have no feelings whatsoever for people like you or me. They are total movers and shakers, and I can see that they have done enough already to entice you."

I had moved forward to the edge of my chair, to try to elaborate what I was trying to get across to her.

"You have got to understand, love; we do not even know if they are telling the truth, now, do we? Maybe the whole damn charade is a lie; and there could be something far, far deeper and more sinister behind it all. They said that we would be required for about two days, but think about it: all they know, or all they told us that they know, is that Salim Rias and his wife Sharma are entering the country. And then it is pure presumption and speculation that Salim will be meeting up with any home grown terrorist cells, to oversee some kind of Jihadi terrorist act against the United Kingdom. To put it bluntly, they need you and me to infiltrate into unknown territory, at our own risk, in order for them to get to know what is really going on. It might sound stupid to you, Vee, but they don't have a clue what's going on, so how in hell can they put a time limit on it? I would also like to say that maybe, just maybe, they even know about what you have just said to me, about the train in the Punjab."

"Oh no Steve don't go down that road, please, how in hells name could they possibly know that?"

"Vee, please understand: we are dealing with MI6 and MI5, who are in cahoots with the good old CIA. They know everything they need to know, and more."

Vee reached for her glass of wine on the side table, but thought better of it and just twisted the glass between her finger and thumb. She was looking pretty calm now, but I knew that, deep down inside, she was having a hell of a time dealing with all this.

"All I am trying to do, Vee, is to give you some kind of guidance as to who you and I are dealing with, and what devious, conniving people they are. I have been in this situation more times than I care to remember; but then I was a young, enthusiastic MI6 agent who loved living on the edge. Since then, I have matured into a man of the world, who doesn't require that kind of adrenalin rush any more. I am quite happy with you, Basil, and the business; I don't need any more of this Kung Fu shit. Answer me a question, Vee, are you happy with what we have achieved together?"

"Yes, Steve." She was still twisting the glass on her side table. "I'm as happy as anyone could ever be. Ten years ago, I could never have envisaged being so happy; I love the business, the house, and, of course, not forgetting Basil." She moved her left hand down to Basil, and pulled him closer to her. Plus, she said, looking back to me, "I have the most wonderful, wonderful man in the world as a partner. Yes, Steve, I'm very happy indeed but this does not allow me to deviate from what I feel we should do in the situation that we are in right now. I cannot, Steve, under any circumstances forget what might happen if we do not at least try to alleviate the possibility of a terrorist attack against innocent men, women and children. I'm so sorry, Steve, but I cannot; and, to be more precise, I would never be able to live with even the thought of it."

Vee got up from the settee and walked over to the sideboard. She started moving things around, picking up the framed photographs, and brushing the tips of her fingers across the glass. I knew that she understood the whole predicament, but I also understood that her feminine intuitions were a very strong part of her personality.

I picked up my glass from the side table, drank the remainder of the wine, and took the empty glasses through to the kitchen. As I came back through the kitchen door, Vee was still standing with her back to me. What could I say? She had won; or, to be more precise, I should say that MI6 and MI5 had manipulated both of us into a situation, with their usual underhanded deviousness.

I walked over to Vee and turned her around, and, as I had thought, there were tears rolling down her face; I could see that she was taking it very hard. A thought crossed my mind. If I didn't agree to do what MI6 required, and some catastrophic event happened, would Vee and I ever be the same afterwards? Could this come between us in the future, and mar such a perfect relationship? I definitely couldn't take that chance.

"OK, my love," I said, kissing her lightly on the forehead. "I understand both you and your feelings. So let's say we both go to bed, have a good night's sleep, and if you are of the same mind tomorrow, we can phone Margaret and see what our next move will be. What do you say?"

Vee looked up at me, smiled a sort of sheepish smile, and kissed me on the chin.

"Yes, my love, I think that is the best idea I've heard all evening." She tried a half smile, and cuddled her head into my chest.

I took Basil out in the garden to do his thing. It wasn't raining now, but the pathway was wet and glistening from the light through the lounge window. Basil was running around the garden, his little tail wagging from left to right, smelling at every corner and bush. I stood calmly watching him for a couple of minutes, quietly summarising the discussions which Vee and I had had during the evening. I was left with a very ominous feeling deep down in my stomach, a feeling that I had never had before.

"Come on, Basil, it's time for bed; I think Mummy and Daddy have got one hell of a day tomorrow," I said quietly to myself.

As I turned for the door, I walked straight into Vee. She must have been standing right behind me all the time. She never said a word, just put her arm in mine, her head on my shoulder, and we headed back inside, with Basil, as always, very close on our heels.

I was up very early the next morning. I didn't get very much sleep at all. My mind had been twisting and turning over what the revelations were going to bring in the next few days; but after giving it a lot of thought, I had come to the conclusion that Vee had been somewhat right in her assumptions as a human being, and, furthermore, I understood how she was seeing things through her eyes; but this left me with the worries of how to do what we had to do and keep both of us, especially Vee, out of harm's way.

I had made scrambled eggs on toast, with a couple of slices of bacon, orange juice and very strong, rich-smelling coffee for breakfast. I laid the table and fed Basil in the kitchen. As I came back to the lounge, Vee walked through the door, still in her dressing gown. Her hair was all over the place. so I realised that she had probably had as little sleep as I had.

"Good morning, my love," she said, standing on her toes, bending my head forward and kissing my nose. "The smell of the coffee and bacon woke me; and, boy, do I need coffee."

We sat and had our breakfast, saying nothing of substance; but we both knew that our minds were very far from the breakfast table.

I broke the silence as Vee was picking up the plates and taking them through to the kitchen.

"I will give Margaret a ring at about nine p.m.; they will be very eager to see us so they will want us in there about one or two. That gives us enough time to get bathed and changed."

"That's more than enough time, Steve," she shouted from the kitchen.

"No it's not, my love; I want to take you over to see some very good friends of mine before we meet Margaret and her crowd, and that should take a couple of hours or so, now you go upstairs and try to make yourself more beautiful than you are now," I said, slapping her on the backside.

She giggled as she skipped through the door towards the bathroom.

I went to the study and picked up the telephone, but then decided that it was safer not to use the landline. I picked up Charles' mobile, and dialled his number, walking back into the lounge.

"Hi, Steve!" Charles's voice was very hyped for this time in a morning; but, I must say, he always said that it's the early bird that gets all the worms. "I thought maybe they'd locked you up or something."

"No, Charles," I laughed into the mobile. "They didn't lock me up, they just bushwhacked me into doing something that I didn't under any circumstances want to do; and you know the usual conniving MI6." I could imagine that he had that, 'I told you so,' smirk on his face.

"Charles, I want to come over and have an hour or so with you; but I have got to tell you that this is very confidential, and, even more, very highly classified at government top level. I can be there in about an hour or so; I'm bringing Vee over with me to introduce her to you, and to let her thank both of you personally for everything you did for us over the last couple of days. Is that OK?"

"Not a problem Steve we are both dying to meet your mysterious lady, anyway; we'll both be here waiting, with hot coffee and bated breath." With that, the phone went dead.

We jumped into the Cooper and headed for Charles's place. The streets were dry for a change, but it was still cloudy, with little chance of any sun; and it was still very cold. I explained to Vee on the way over, giving her an indication as to who Charles was, where I had met him, and how he had helped us both over the past two days.

As we drove past the place where the spooks car had been parked only two days before, I pointed out to Vee all their cigarette butts that were still lying in the street, even after all that rain.

Just as we pulled up outside Charles's place, the door was flung open, and out ran Carol; she must have been watching us through the window. She ran straight to the passenger door, and, excitedly she almost dragged Vee from the car.

"Wow!" she shouted, in her broad London accent, "You're a real stunner, girl; just what I'd expect Steve to have on his arm."

She gave Vee a cuddle and a kiss on each cheek. "No wonder you've been hiding her away! Come in, both of you, get out of the cold; Charles's in his office, and dying to see you both."

I didn't get a chance to introduce Vee to Charles. Carol grabbed her hand and rushed her through the reception and straight into Charles's office.

"Charles!" she almost shouted in her genuine excitement, "Steve's here, and look what he's brought with him. Vee, this is Charles Pierce. Charles, meet Vee; and wow, isn't she stunning, Charles?"

Charles moved forward, took hold of Vee's hands, and looked at her from top to bottom. He looked over her shoulder straight at me, saying "I hope you realise what you have got here, my boy; now I know why we haven't seen you for so long. You didn't want anyone to tell her the real truth about you, did you?"

He waved us both to a chair. "Sit down, sit down please. Carol: coffee, please, and maybe a few biscuits." Then his eyes glanced questioningly over towards me, with a smile on his face. "Maybe a little Chivas, Steve?"

"Not on your life, Charles; and when I tell you where we are going next, you will fully understand why," I said, sliding into the chair Charles had offered me.

"Well, well, well. I think you are about to tell me that you have been blackmailed, once again, by MI6." He raised his eyebrows and that 'I told you so' smirk came across his face.

"Not really, Charles, but you are close," I said grinning.

The door opened, and in came Carol, carrying a tray with an array of coffee, sugar, milk and coffee mugs, and, to top it all, creamed croissants on it. She placed it on the coffee table in front of us, and turned to leave the office.

"Carol," Charles said, smiling up at her. "You said you wanted some time to do a few personal things today; and, as Steve and I have a lot of quite delicate items to discuss, I thought that maybe you could take a couple of hours off now the rain has stopped, and things are pretty quiet. Take a couple of hours off, and get out there and do your thing."

"Thanks, Charles," Carol replied, with a bemused look on her face, probably wondering what she was going to be missing. "If you should need me, please phone me on my mobile; I will only be down the road in the shopping centre. Oh, and I'll also pick up your dry cleaning for you while I'm there."

As she walked through the door, she looked back towards Vee. "Lovely meeting you, Vee, and I hope to see more of you in the future. Thanks, Charles: see you in a couple of hours."

"Before you go," Charles said, "lock up at the front and put the phones on the answering machine, as we don't want to be disturbed for an hour or so."

"OK, will do!" Carol replied. With that, she went through the door, still with that bemused look on her face, and closed it quietly behind her.

"She seems a little upset, Charles," I said, as she shut the door.

"No, Steve," he replied, "she's not upset, she's just bloody nosy and wondering what she's bloody missing," he said, laughing. "She's worked for me for nearly three years now, and this is the first time that she hasn't been fully integrated into something that was occurring in my office. Don't worry about Carol, she'll get over it when I buy her one of her favourite bottles of wine."

Vee was already pouring the coffee into the mugs and passing them out to Charles and I.

"OK, Steve," he said, settling back into his chair, with his mug of coffee in hand, "the floor is all yours, my boy, the floor is all yours."

I sat for a while, wondering just where to start. I had full confidence in Charles and in his great faith in Queen and country; and I also knew that nobody outside this room would ever hear what we were about to discuss.

Charles butted into my train of thought with, "Steve, this is big, I can see it in your eyes; and you have never had this look in your eyes since we were both with MI6. Just spill it out, and let's see where it leads us."

I moved forward in my seat, coffee mug in hand, and let everything spill out. As I was talking, I could see Charles glancing towards Vee from time to time, and I could see that he wasn't very impressed to see that she would have such a large involvement in the whole procedure; but when I got to the discussions that Vee and I had last night, his eyebrows went up.

"Well, well, bloody well," he said, when I had at last succumbed to silence. He got up from his chair and walked round to his desk, picked up his pen, and did his usual thing, rubbing it between his palms. This, I remember, he always did when he had something on his mind.

"Steve," he said, walking back to his chair, "I could never have envisaged that it could be something as immense as this. The whole state of affairs is quite mind-blowing, and I have got to say that I, for once, fully understand HQ in contacting you; but I don't agree with the way they went about getting to you; nor do I agree that Vee should be implicated, as this could turn out to be a very, very dangerous situation. I myself have full confidence in you to be able to infiltrate them, and come out unscathed; but to have your pride and joy up front and behind enemy lines, so to speak? Steve, it's not on; no, Steve, it's not on; this is not right."

I mused over what Charles was saying for a minute or so, trying hard to come up with a conclusion that would not have Vee implicated. I looked at Vee from time to time but she gave no indication whatsoever of what she herself was thinking.

Then all of a sudden Vee chipped in. "Charles, I am fully aware of the danger, and feel that it's imperative that I must be there at Steve's side. Being Indian born and bred, I know these people inside out and I also know they are far more devious than Steve, yourself and even MI5 and MI6 put together. I have lived with them for years. I was brought up in the Punjab in India. When I woke up in a morning, the first thing I saw from my bedroom window was Pakistan. I'm fully trilingual in so far as Indian, Pakistani and English is concerned, and I am also fully conversant with their different dialects. I know their cultures, more so their adversities, and just about everything that these people are trying to influence throughout the world. Charles, I know that Steve was very good in the field, but you cannot expect him to fit in with these people, who are totally dissimilar even to the normal Muslim. I know how they think, I can read their eyes; and that is a very important element in understanding who you are dealing with. I'm sorry, Charles, but you are wrong in saying that I shouldn't be there. I have to be there, firstly for Steve's sake, and secondly for that of all the innocent men, women and children to whom these people mean to cause detriment."

I looked across at Charles, and pointed my finger towards him. I could see the astonishment on his face, and I don't think anyone has ever had such an influence on him. For once he was totally and utterly lost for words.

A smile came on his face. He looked across at me, rubbing his pen between his palms again.

"Steve, my boy; I have just found out who the boss is in your house." He laughed, and pointed his finger right back at me.

"Listen, both of you," Charles said, with a slight look of embarrassment on his face, "I have got to say that I owe you both an apology, especially you, Vee. I was wrong; I was looking at Vee as a house wife and partner and not as an operational person. But on listening to what you have just implied, I feel quite overwhelmed; and I have got to say that I now see that although you are very much a lady, you are also a very astute person, and I fully apologise unreservedly for not observing this before. Also, I think that you, Vee, are perfectly accurate in what you said. I take it all back, Steve; I hate to say this, but just listening to what Vee had to say has proved me very wrong in my assumption. I think she would be a great asset to you in this operation, and probably could be the key to making the operation a complete and utter success."

Charles stood up and walked slowly over to the window, still rolling his pen in his palms.

"Well, well," Charles said, smiling towards Vee, "You have come here and really embarrassed me. What more can I do but apologise, and say that, from now on, I will take a very different view of both you and of the overall situation? I can see now that Vee will be your missing link when it comes to the language, religious and, more important, the cultural side."

I could see that Charles was more than a little embarrassed as he took his seat again, mainly for not having seen the whole picture, and for not taking into consideration the Islamic cultural side, of which I myself had very little knowledge; but Vee knew it all backwards. She had grown up with these people for most of her life. I sat for a while, giving Charles time to take everything in, and lose his obvious embarrassment. Then I hit him with my big question, the question that I was there to ask.

I stood up and walked over to the window. The clouds had broken in places, and there was a little sunshine on the road outside, although the road was still very wet.

"How about you coming with us, Charles," I said, rubbing my now very well-bearded chin.

"Steve, you must be bloody joking! I'm too bloody old for this sort of thing; even Vee just made an absolute fool out of me."

"Charles," I said, quietly but firmly, sitting down across from him, "as you know, I am going into this operation with Vee by my side, and for that reason and that reason only, I will require someone that I can trust completely and who is outside HQ. All I will want you to do is to be in the close proximity of the operation, Charles. You are someone who knows and understands how my mind works, and, in addition, vice versa, someone whom I know and understand very well. It's a perfect match Charles."

I could see that Charles was rummaging through the situation as a whole, and trying to put all the facts together.

"Tell me, Charles," I went on, as I stood and walked over to the window again. I turned and leaned forward, pointing my finger at Charles, "Charles, if you were me, in this situation, who would you want to be there in your corner if the chips go down? You know as well as I do that HQ will have to have a two-hour meeting even if I only require more toilet paper?"

The tension in the room subsided as we all started laughing; Charles had just taken a swig of coffee and he burst into a coughing spasm. I thought he was going to have a bloody heart attack. Charles placed his coffee mug back down on the table and wiped his mouth with his handkerchief, then stared at the cup for quite some time. Then he looked straight at Vee and I with a very serious sort of ambiguous look on his face.

"Steve, my boy, it's not that I don't want to help you, you know that; it's more that I don't want to hinder you, or let you both down. I'm closing in on seventy now; I'm not the man I was down the years; and I could never live with the knowledge that I couldn't fulfil a request fully or fast enough to cover you in theatre."

I fully understood what was going through his mind, and I could see where the apprehensiveness was coming from; but I knew that I would feel far safer with him just being in the vicinity.

"Let me give you a little insight as to what I visualize, Charles. Firstly, I am going to make great demands of MI5 and MI6. I'm going to ask for Paul Lawson to be my inside man. You know him well, Charles; he is a very versatile guy, and he's worked with both

MI5 and MI6. He is, at the moment, working with MI5 in their antiterrorism and infiltration units; and I think he's the only guy in there that I know who would be fully prepared to bend the rules in an emergency, and stand up to the hierarchy in the aftermath. He's good, and he's solid, and he knows and respects both you and me."

Vee poured more coffee all round, and handed Charles and I our mugs.

"Charles," I went on. "All I will be asking of you is maybe another car, should I need one, or a tracking device, maybe; and, most importantly, for you to do the liaising with Paul, as I do not want to have any contact with HQ at all, or I will have Franks phoning me day and night. There also may be even a little surveillance on someone from time to time. It's all the simple things that, to HQ would need a mountain of paperwork and a week of discussions; and that, as you are well aware, I definitely will not have the time for."

Charles put down his coffee mug, picked up his favourite pen, and started to roll it between his palms again. He seemed to have a boyish grin on his face; and I'm sure he had just made up his mind to join us.

"Come on, Charles," I said, gesturing, holding both my arms out towards him, with both palms upwards. "It's simple, Charles; you just being there will give both Vee and myself a greater sense of safekeeping, plus a lot more time for me and Vee to concentrate on the job in hand. What do you say? Come on, Charles! It will be just like old times. You and I against the bad guys; and, even more important, it will be for the very last time."

"'The very last time,' you have said that how many times now, Steve?" He now had a smirk on his face, "Steve, you have been telling me that for bloody years now, and MI6 have always somehow managed to get you back in there, utilising their deviousness."

Charles leaned back in his chair and pointed a finger at me. "You know something, Steve Taylor," he said, grinning broadly, "I don't believe it, but I can see that some of their pretentious manipulating ways have definitely rubbed off on you over the years."

Charles leaned forward, picked up his mug of coffee, took a sip and glanced towards Vee, then back to me, raising his eyebrows.

"OK, Steve," he said. "Let's do it. But I must iterate strongly, and I want you to completely and irrevocably understand, that I am only undertaking this because Vee is out there in the field, and definitely not for you." He pointed across at me with his index finger, but he had a grin on his face, "And, Steve, I think you are just as much a manipulating old son of a bitch as Franks is."

"Hey, Charles, less of the bloody 'old'," I said, grinning from relief.

We all laughed, and a sense of respite went throughout the room; all three of us had a feeling of reprieve.

Vee and I left Charles with less than an hour to get to the meeting at Thames House; but it wasn't raining, and the heavy traffic had cleared hours ago. We made it with ten minutes to spare. Why I was worried about the time, I don't know; they would still have been waiting if we had been three hours late.

We took the lift up to reception, and walked across the foyer towards Claire. She was talking to two guys in suits, but, on seeing me, she picked up the phone and was saying to someone that Mr Taylor had arrived, without my uttering a word. I was dressed in a T shirt, jeans and a lumber jacket, with five days growth of beard, and I was getting better service than the suits standing in line. The suits looked me up and down, and probably presumed I was a plumber coming to fix the toilets.

It only took eleven seconds for Paul to appear at the top of the stairs; he threw two security cards down to me saying "OK, Steve you have clearance, come on up." The suits all waiting for clearance were just staring after us, as we went straight through the security barrier and hit the stairs.

Paul took us to the same room that we had been in initially. All of the individuals who had been there at the last meeting were all sitting in the same positions as they had occupied the previous day. The only difference was that there were quite a lot of files on the table, all marked Top Secret in red.

All the customary greetings were exchanged, and subsequently Vee and I slipped into the seats that we had vacated the previous day.

I poured water into both the glasses that were on the table in front of us, took a mouthful, and replaced the glass back on the table. I could see a smug smirk on Franks's face, and I knew it was only going to be a few minutes before it disappeared. Boy, was he in for a shock.

Mel took the lead, welcoming us, and all the bullshit that goes with it.

"Steve," Mel said, nervously moving a few files around that were on the table in front of him. "I was, no sorry," he said, very nervously, "we, we were all delighted and, I've got to say, very relieved when Margaret informed us of the decisions which you have both made to help us out in our predicament; nearly everyone here has spent most of the night getting more info and intelligence as to where we stand with Salim Rias. Up to now, we have ordered that his visa should be approved immediately, and we believe from the Intelligence that he will be arriving in the United Kingdom with his wife in approximately six weeks' time. This gives us, as a unit of MI5 and MI6, plenty of time to coordinate the situation. That will help us to delude both Salim Rias himself, and, moreover, the home-grown terrorists that he is to meet on his entry into the country."

"We have strategies in place already for, I suppose you could say, rehabilitating and indoctrinating you both into the infinite values of Islamism, which include cultures, activities and even very indiscriminate oddities across the board, and last but not least, the mannerisms of both Salim Rias and his wife Sharma. We have selected a team of five, which include a top psychiatrist, and a Muslim cleric and inspirational leader, who, I must say, has been acting as an informant to MI5, and has been for the last six years or so. We have full confidence in him. Also, you will meet a CIA agent who will be able to give you intelligence about Rias's voice, accent, dialect, mannerisms and habitual routines. You can both be completely assured that before you both go out into the field you will be fully conversant in every way possible with every Muslim way of life that will be required for you to infiltrate the inner circles of the Muslim world with total impunity."

Mel took his seat with a resolute look on his face, but I'm sure it was only because he was hiding his inner feelings, and was pleased that he had done his bit without much of an upheaval from either Vee or myself.

Margaret took the floor, with her mild, discreet manner. Looking straight towards Vee and I, she was just about the only person other than Vee and I who didn't seem to be nervous.

"Steve, Vee," she said, "I cannot even start to tell you how reassured we all were to get your telephone call this morning, and I personally can guarantee you both that everyone in MI5 and MI6 will give you our full backing and cooperation in every way possible, before you begin and when you are on your own in the field. We are classifying this assignment with the highest priority that has ever been given to any assignment since World War Two."

Margaret took a sip of her water, and came round the table to stand behind Vee and I.

"I know, Steve," she said, while placing both her hands on Vee's shoulder, "that Vee is not of this country and yet she is all set to stand with us against this adversity that now lies within our shores. And I want you both to know how proud we are that she is equally prepared to give her all in this venture. I can personally assure you that you will both be fully equipped, and have back up which is second to none whilst you are in the field."

"Obviously, Steve," Margaret said, walking back to her seat, "you, and also Vee for that matter, must have a lot of questions, requirements and even various permutations going on in your heads; and I would like you both to put them to us openly, so that, at the end of this day, we will all be singing from the same hymn sheet, so to speak. I want no abandonment of accountability for either of yourselves, and especially MI5 and MI6."

As she said that, she looked straight at Franks, her eyebrows raised, as if to say, "I am talking to you also." My oh my! She really had Franks taped. There was no doubt of that, and she didn't hide it from anyone, either.

I put both my arms on the table and looked around at everyone individually. I glanced at Vee and smiled, but it wasn't to reassure her; I think it was more to restore the much needed confidence in myself that I needed, in this delicate position in which I had found myself.

"Well, ladies and gentlemen," I started, "I have to say, first and foremost, that an enormous debt of gratitude should be shown to Vee by all of you, simply because she is the reason that we are both sitting here today. Last night, we had a long discussion as to the whys and wherefores of the situation, and whether or not to involve ourselves in your problem – and, I reiterate, 'your' problem. I myself did not under any circumstances want to go ahead with it. But Vee, very humanely, related a story to me about an incident in which a number of innocent people were killed by terrorists in the

143

Punjab in India; and for reasons that I will not disclose, she was unable to stop the incident happening, and one hundred and forty very innocent people, men, women and even children perished."

I glanced towards Vee once again, more for reassurance than anything else.

"Vee implied," I went on, after taking a sip of water, "That she felt she could never live with herself if something should happen, whether it be in the United Kingdom or anywhere else in the world for that matter, if she hadn't tried to alleviate the occurrence. To try and to fail, she said, she could live with, but to sit and do nothing, and to find there was a cost in lives lost, no matter how few; she felt that this would weigh profoundly on her mind for the rest of her life, and that she could never ever live with that."

I had another drink of water, and I felt Vee's hand squeeze my right thigh, in a sort of apology, I presume. I looked towards her, smiled, and gave her a wink, which must have meant "apology accepted." I glanced towards Franks, and I could see a demeaning smirk on his face. I'd seen that smirk so many times before; it was the smirk that said, "got you." Seeing him sitting there, so full of himself, made my blood pressure rise; I couldn't wait to bring him down to the real world. I had another sip of water, wishing that it was whisky, replaced the glass back on the table, and directed my eyes back to Margaret.

"Both Vee and I are prepared to go ahead and infiltrate this home-grown terrorist cell." I glanced towards Franks again; he was smirking even more now. "But it will be totally under our terms. Firstly, MI6 will take a complete back seat for the whole duration of the operation, and I mean the whole duration of the operation." I again glanced over towards Franks. His despicable sneer was no more; his mouth was wide open, and his eyes had become daggers.

"We will require," I said, looking directly at Franks, "Paul Lawson to be our HQ contact; and I will organise my own backup in the field. Over and above this I want everyone in this room, government personnel also included, to understand that there will be no interference with Paul from anyone, and he must be given your full permission to implement with impunity any requests that Vee or myself should make, instantly. I have worked with Paul many times over the years and I have nothing but admiration for his aptitude to be able to assess any given situation and the capability to act on his instincts instantly; and that will be a necessity in this situation."

I glanced towards Margaret and smiled, I could see she was not showing any apprehension at all by my forceful requests; in fact, the look on her face made me think that she had been fully expecting them.

"Margaret," I said, still smiling at her. "I think, before I go on, that at this point I have to request that Paul Lawson should be brought into this meeting, as he, in my mind, is going to have a very pivotal part in this operation, and I want to try, right from the start, to alleviate any chance of misrepresentation towards, and from anyone. I want everyone implicated in the operation to have full knowledge of who is who, what is what, and to be completely familiar with every aspect of the situation, and a full understanding of their authority and position. This, I'm sure, will eliminate any, and, I hope, all extenuating circumstances that could occur before, during, and also after the operation has come to an end, and hopefully to a successful result. There must be no 'need to know' basic situations, other than those for the people in the field. Vee and I will be working totally alone, and on our own cognisance."

I took the time to look directly at every individual that were sat around the table. "Now, is this totally understood by everyone around this table?"

Everyone around the table nodded in agreement, although I could see that Franks was not what one could call impressed with my declaration.

Without acknowledging what I had said, Margaret took out her mobile and dialled a number, and it was answered instantly. "Paul," she spoke into the phone, "Good morning to you. Paul, I need you to join in this meeting in room 417. Also, on your way through, can you get coffee and some biscuits sent up? Thank you, Paul." She ended the conversation, and the mobile disappeared back into her pocket. She looked across the table, directly at me. I think this was to assure me that she was definitely on my side and that I would have her total respect and, most importantly, her instantaneous backup.

Paul arrived in the room more or less instantly, looking a little bemused as to why he was there; then he saw me looking towards him. I gave him a wink. I'm sure that his mind had now started to understand the conversation we had had the previous day in the car park.

Margaret stood and offered Paul the seat open to the right of Vee; he gave both Vee and I a rather wry smile of acknowledgement, as he took his place at the table.

"Paul," Margaret was still standing. "I'm going to give Steve the floor, as it was he that requested that you join the meeting, and, on your approval, to join the operation. If you accept his proposal, then you will be here for the full extent of the meetings on the operation, and, of course, throughout the balance of the field operation."

It took me about five minutes to bring him up to speed on the situation, and during that time I watched his face go from an inconspicuous business-type look to a wide-eyed "when do we get started" look. He was fully accepting the position, without hearing what was to be expected of him, which took me back to my adrenaline rush days, and I could see that he was enthralled to be working with me, and also with the proposition as a whole.

The coffee and biscuits arrived, and we all stood around making small talk. Franks never even glanced over in my direction; he just stood looking out of the window. It showed on his ugly face that he was completely pissed off with the whole situation that had transpired over the last hour or so.

Margaret had Paul to one side, and I was sure she was reassuring him that this was his chance to really show his initiative and ability in MI5. Paul was just nodding his head, in full agreement with everything that Margaret was saying; his eyes never left her face.

After the coffee and biscuits had been consumed, we all drifted back to our seats to complete the ins and outs of the operation. Franks was the last to take his seat.

"Now," I said, looking once more at everyone individually around the table, "is there any person in this room who either doesn't understand, or disagrees with what I have said up to now? I must, at this point, also iterate that I am making these demands for one reason and one reason only; I have been in the field far, far too many times when I have been manipulated, and sometimes very much left to fend for myself, because of certain individuals who either didn't agree with my requests, or didn't have the guts or foresight to implement them without seeking higher authority; and, gentlemen, this must never ever happen under any circumstances in this operation while Vee is in the field."

I glanced down the table towards Franks. I could see that his face was now very pallid, and he looked like he was about to throw up.

"I want all of you," I went on, "to fully understand that this young lady sat by my side is my pride and joy; and should she be put into any kind of danger, because of any incompetence or any

147

ineffectiveness from HQ – well, gentlemen, you think you have got a problem with your home-grown Jihadi terrorist cells, let me tell you all up front: let me down, or put Vee in any danger whatsoever, and I will wreak havoc on you all, so much so that it will make your problems now look like an old ladies tea party on Sunday afternoon. I want everyone to fully understand that, in the face of adversity, I want all the stops pulled out, and immediately. There must be no, and, let me repeat, no questioning of my requirement. I want immediate reaction from MI5, with no questions asked. Years ago, when I was with the SAS, I learned that the best form of defence is attack, and I want you all to comprehend that; that is just how I am going to undertake this operation."

I got up from my chair and stood behind Vee with both my hands on her shoulders. I massaged her neck muscles with my thumbs. I could feel the knots in her muscles, and I fully understood why they were there.

"I want you all to know," I went on, "that I alone will make the decisions in the field, and I will require in writing that you all acknowledge and understand this. Whatever the outcome of the operation, I do not want anyone saying that I should not have done that, or I should have done this. You have got to understand that none of us at this moment have any idea what is going to happen, and only Vee and I will know when we get in the field. This could work out to be something small and fairly insignificant; but it could also be something catastrophic, and maybe I will have to make instant decisions from time to time. Ladies and gentlemen, you will have to accept any decisions that I find I have to make in the field, and I do not want any fingers pointed in my direction afterwards, after the operation has come to completion."

The meeting went on for about three hours, mainly getting the list of things not to do, and things to do, sorted out. Everyone in the room was fully behind me in the end, but I could see that Franks was not the smiling Franks any more, and I knew him well enough to know that he was keeping his inner thoughts very much to himself. He had almost certainly never been pushed aside like this before in his life, and, in all probability, was feeling very much embarrassed, and maybe a touch ineffective in the operation, to say the very least.

Chapter Nine

We were given two days to sort out the running of our own business, and to sort out our personal lives. From then on, we were given a list of various addresses to report to across London, to start our initiation into the world of Islamism, and the traits and implications of Salim and Sharma Rias.

We spent five weeks, from very early in the morning until sometimes very late in the evenings, going over and over and over again all the implications, ramifications and aspects of Salim and Sharma Rias: their habits, their caricatures, their mannerisms, even the way they walked, sat, stood and even coughed. It was probably like what an actor or actress would do, when taking on the character or personality of someone in a Hollywood movie.

We had some fun, also, as Vee had to be quite heavily pregnant, so a false stomach was made up and fitted so that if Vee pressed a button at the top of the of the inserted false stomach, the baby would kick, just like a real pregnant woman's baby would kick; this was done so that should anyone want to feel the baby kick, as some women love to do, Vee could switch it on and off, when a predicament arose. We had also made provision in her false stomach for a weapon. It was a Walther ppk 7.65, and, funnily enough, it was the same weapon that that was used by James bond in his films. It is a small weapon, very precise, and could easily be handled by either myself or Vee, should the necessity ever arrive.

One very important aspect of the initiation was learning about who Salim and Sharma were, and what they had done over the last twenty-odd years. We had to memorise dates, times and places, names of their families and friends, where they had lived, where they ate out, what their favourite foods were, where they had been over the last twenty odd years or so, and even the dates of distinctive activities in their lives. Both Vee and I used to question each other either in the car or at home until we had just about everything off to a tee.

On the Muslim side of our schooling, I personally had a hard time, but Vee seemed to take everything in her stride, although, in my defence, I've got to say she was far ahead of me, having been brought up in the Punjab, and the Punjab's having a very large Muslim society. As a matter of fact, her childhood friends were mainly Muslim, so, for her, it was just a matter of jogging her memory.

With regard to the learning of the mannerisms and traits of Salim and Sharma, it was quite easy – except for the names I was blasted with, quite a few times for calling Vee, Vee, instead of Sharma, and for not answering when I was called Salim. This amused Vee. We were told to use the names Sharma and Salim at all times, even when we were alone at home; this must have mixed up the thoughts of Basil a bit.

I had to go through quite a time with a Muslim cleric. His name was Kareem Mahmud. He was a real gentleman, with a patience that I had never seen in a man before. He taught me all the ins and outs of the Muslim prayer meetings. He was so expressive in everything he said that sometimes I got the impression that he was trying to get me into the Muslim faith.

My beard was now a full beard, that any Muslim would have been quite proud of. But somehow I had to get out of the habit of brushing it with my fingers. I was told that that was a no no.

Seemingly, people only play with their beards when they are new; and Salim had had his beard for as long as he had been old enough to grow one.

I had to have a wart put on my nose, which was done as a female would have her ears pierced. Then my skin, although it was quite dark, as I had some Portuguese blood in me from down the line, had to be darkened slightly. I then had to have a scar manufactured over my eye; a lot of various makeup artists tried all sorts of different ways to do it, but none worked; and time was running out. In the end I decided to have it done surgically. So, for the rest of my life, I would have Salim's scar staring right back at me from the bathroom mirror.

Things were coming to fruition now, and it was time for us to be Salim and Sharma Rias. Vee and I both thought we were ready for it, and all the people that had got us to this stage were very excited and much in agreement.

Chapter Ten

It was about the fourteenth of December when we were flown by helicopter from London to Manchester airport to do the initial take-over of the real Salim and Sharma Rias. The CIA had sent pictures of Salim and Sharma Rias as they were boarding the plane in Pakistan, and clothing had been hurriedly made up so that we would be dressed in a very similar way to them at the take-over. I was very happy to see that Salim was in a very European type of garb, because I could never see myself in one of those white night-shirts they wear. He was probably dressed that way because of the cold weather we were having in the UK, so that suited me down to the ground.

We were ushered through the back door into the massive luggage arrival area, up and down staircases, in and around passageways, finally coming out close to the International Arrivals. We were taken to a sort of lounge that was empty, except for three or four lounge chairs and a couple of chairs and tables, a coffee machine with a few biscuits. We were then told to settle down and wait.

We had five hours to wait before the plane was due to arrive, so we settled down reading magazines and drinking some, I must say, rather excellent coffee, for an airport; we had sandwiches delivered, and, now and again, Paul would pop in and update us on the plane's arrival time. He told us that the place was crawling with

MI5 and MI6 officers, and that they were scanning everyone who was waiting in the international arrivals area, to ensure that they would know who was meeting us – or, should I say, meeting Salim and Sharma Rias. The rest would now be up to how much information they could gather out of the real Salim and Sharma when they picked them up, on entry into the country. So much depended on the next few hours. Nothing must go wrong; everything must go like clockwork, or the whole operation would have to be cancelled – and that would be a total catastrophe, and not even worth thinking about.

Whoever it was who was about to meet Salim and Sharma Rias off the plane must be very quickly put into a position of total reassurance that we were the real Salim and Sharma Rias; there would be no second chances at this early stage. To make things even more convincing, we had our Muslim cleric Kareem Mahmud, who had spent so many, sometimes hilarious, hours, teaching us about Islam, and about the ways of life of Muslims in Pakistan, to walk up to us in the arrival lounge, and introduce himself as an old friend of mine from way back when. This would, without a doubt, secure and guarantee to them that we were the real Salim and Sharma Rias. But we must always remember that whoever it was who was meeting us, might have been born at night – but it definitely wasn't last night.

Paul swung the door open and walked into the room, with a beaming smile on his face.

"Great," he said. "The plane is on the ground and we have found the person meeting you, or should I say them. The stupid buggers showed us who they were, they have a sign board with Salim Rias on it, so we definitely know they have never met you in person, which is a good sign. We are now taking you to a room that looks down on the arrivals lounge. This will give you the initiative, as you will know them, and they obviously do not know you. Also,

Kareem has a friend that is going to try to make conversation with them, to see if we can get a little more info, this should result in getting their names, and perhaps which part of the UK they are living in, all this info will put you in like Flynn, Steve. It couldn't have worked out better if we had tried harder."

Paul had a big grin on his face, and I could see he was thoroughly enjoying the whole state of affairs; and this gave me a greater sense of security for both Vee and myself.

Paul ushered us out of the room, round a few corners, and up and down a couple of passageways and staircases, until we came to an office, overlooking the arrivals lounge; it had slightly darkened windows, and the lights were out in the room, so we could not be observed clearly from below. Paul indicated a man and a woman, obviously Muslims, who were standing very close to the exit into the arrivals lounge. Also, about three metres from them, was Kareem, in his full Muslim regalia, waiting to do his part in the initiation ceremony of Salim and Sharma Rias.

We were then taken by Paul to the airport security section; this was quite a shock to the system for both Vee and I. We entered a rather small room that had no windows and no furniture in the room at all, just a curtain down one wall. Paul walked across to the curtained wall, and turned to face Vee and myself with a sort of smug look on his face.

"Steve, Vee," Paul said with pride. "Let me introduce you to the real Salim and Sharma Rias." With that, he pulled a cord that opened the curtain. It wasn't a window: it was obviously a one way mirror. In the room, there were two MI5 or MI6 agents sitting with their backs to us, but across the table, and facing us, were the real Salim and Sharma Rias. Both Vee and I were totally shocked, as we were nearly their exact doubles. Paul pressed a button on the wall, and all of a sudden we could hear their voices.

The agents were questioning them both very strongly about why they had entered the UK, where they were going to stay, and who was at the airport to meet them. Sharma was in full flow with tears, and Salim Rias was slamming his hand hard on the table, demanding to see the officials from the Pakistan embassy, and threatening to sue the pants off the British government if they didn't let him through.

The agent with the bald head seemed to change his assault on them into being the good policeman.

"Mr Rias," he said in a very calm voice, "you have friends out there who are waiting to meet you; please give me their names, and then we can inform them that you have arrived but are stuck up here with Customs. If you don't, then they are not going to know whether you have arrived or not, and they will probably leave the airport, and then you will be stranded; now, come on, Mr Rias, just give us their names. It's to your advantage, isn't it?"

"It's Malik, Mohammed Malik; his wife is Mari," Salim said in a much calmer voice. "He lives in Leeds but I do not know where in Leeds. I have known him for years, his mobile number is in my mobile that you already have in your possession; anything more, I cannot tell you."

Paul switched off the sound and drew the curtain. "Well, Steve, what do you think? It's eerie isn't it?"

Vee looked from me to Paul. "Yes, Paul," she said. "It's quite uncanny, I've got to admit; I'm really struggling to get my mind round it."

"And you, Steve, what do you think?" Paul said, with a grin on his face.

"Eerie, uncanny," I said in a low whisper. "In fact, this is more paranormal to me than anything else Paul, it's totally and utterly unbelievable. I've got to say, I'm absolutely gobsmacked: we know who he is meeting, and we know we are going to be in Leeds. The

Leeds part I was not expecting at all: I was always under the impression that we would be in Manchester, Birmingham or maybe back in London. Leeds doesn't seem to fit into the picture, but I suppose there are going to be a lot more surprises before this situation gets resolved."

Paul stuck out his hand to Vee, then to me; his hand shake was rock-solid and he looked me straight in the eyes, with a very serious look on his face.

"This Steve, is about as far as we go together; from now on you are on your own. But I want you both to fully understand that you will have the best back-up that you have ever had in the field, Steve, even if it means me losing my position with MI5. You are both my personal priority, and I will never let you down," he said, with immense emotion written across his face.

"I have got to take you to the Director now, as she said she wanted a few words with you both before you leave. Then, for you both, it's the long walk into Islamism, and the very unknown."

"Thanks, Paul," I said, letting go of his hand. "Vee and I both fully appreciate that, and we both know that you will give it your absolute everything; but always keep in mind, Paul, that that's the one reason that I chose you. There's one thing that we have not spoken about, Paul, and this must be kept between you, me and Vee, not even Margaret must know; do you understand, Paul?"

"Sure. What is it, Steve?" he said, with raised eyebrows.

"While you were with MI6, I doubt that you ever met my HQ contact, Charles Pierce, as he retired a few years before you arrived."

"No," Paul replied. "But everyone still, to this day, talks about 'Old Charlie.' Seemingly, he was one of the best in the business."

"That's right, Paul," I replied. "He was definitely the best, and now you must step up into his shoes as Charles, unbeknown to anyone but the three of us, will also be in the field with Vee and I.

But I reiterate, Paul, that Vee, myself and yourself will be the only ones who know it; he will be in contact with you more than I will, but, please remember, this must be kept completely between ourselves. Don't even tell your dog, do you understand?"

"You know that you will always get the best from me, Steve," Paul said, very enthusiastically. "Whether I can fit into Charlie's shoes or not, I don't know; from what I have heard, Steve, they are big shoes to fill. But please, both of you, be assured that I will never let you down. As I said before, Steve, yourself and Vee and now Charlie are my priority, and I will never let you down. If you want a Sherman tank up there in Leeds, it might take a while to get it there, but it will be there, even if I have to drive the bloody thing myself."

"One more thing, Paul," I said putting my hand on his shoulder to ease the pain. "Never, ever call Charles, Charlie. He hates it with a passion and, with no hesitation, he will jump on you from a great height – and you already said that you know how big his shoes are, didn't you?"

Paul grinned back at both of us, looking a little bit embarrassed. "Thanks for letting me in on that, Steve, I can assure you that Charlie will be Charles from now on."

Paul's mobile started to vibrate; he took it out of his shirt pocket, switched it on, listened for a second, and then said, "Give us three minutes. We're on our way."

"That's the Director, Steve; she's waiting for us on the next level."

Paul walked over and opened the door, looked back at Vee and myself, and said, "That's it guys; looks like the show's really on the road now."

Paul ushered us down a couple of passageways, down a couple of flights of stairs, and there we were, looking down on the arrivals area. We were met there by a couple of obvious MI5 guys, who ushered all three of us into an office close to the customs area.

"Good day Steve, Vee." It was Margaret, standing in the far corner. "Just thought I would like to be here to see you both off on your adventure. I'm sure that you are both fully aware that everything is all systems go, with no problems other than the bloody weather, and I'm afraid that that needs a far higher authority than mine."

She smiled and walked towards me, both arms raised, and gave me a cuddle. "You look after that girl in the field, Steve Taylor. Remember: she is not doing this for Queen and country; she's doing it because her conscience says she has to. Any problems that come up, you must get her out of there, chop chop, and bugger the consequences." She stood back, and the smile was gone. She pointed her index finger straight in my face, and said, "You hear me, Taylor?"

"I hear you loud and clear Margaret, loud and clear." Somehow I felt I had a lump in my throat, probably because of the true emotion she was showing. I had never known anyone at the top in MI5 or MI6 show any emotion at all to any one, unless it was done to deceive or connive.

Margaret walked over to Vee and gave her a long, very meaningful hug. "The best of luck, Sharma. I hope soon to get to know you more as Vee. You've got a lot of guts, my girl, and, on top of that, you have a conscience too, and that makes you a rare breed in this world, a very rare breed indeed."

Margaret looked across towards Paul. "OK, Paul, get them out of here before I embarrass myself and start crying; and Paul, I don't need to stress to you to make sure that Salim and Sharma Rias get everything that they want immediately, and to give them the very best back-up that any one could ever wish for."

As we walked through the door, Paul looked back at Margaret smiling, and said, "Suppose they want a Sherman tank, Ma'am?"

"Paul, if they want a Sherman tank, get them two. Better to be safe than sorry, eh?" She replied whole-heartedly, and with a sort of motherly-love look.

Paul winked at me. "Just checking, Ma'am." He closed the door behind us.

We were then ushered by Paul towards the arrivals lounge, as we came to a corner in the passageway. Paul stopped and put his hand on my chest, "By the way, Steve, we have Salim's mobile in our possession; it's already gone to H.Q. for analysis. As soon as we get all the info together, all the relevant information will be redirected to you or Charles, with all the info of who is who and what is what."

"Thanks, Paul, thanks for everything you've done so far. I know it's going to be great working with you, and I look forward very much to having a drink together when this is all over."

Paul held out his hand, and, as I grasped it, he said, "I can't go any further with you both. I'm afraid you are on your very own from here on. Just follow this passageway through the doors, and you are into the arrivals lounge. Here is your luggage," he said, pointing to our two cases that we had packed the previous day. Someone had put them in an airport trolley with Pakistani airport tags on them.

"Here are your passports, Steve, stamped by immigration, and, of course, your return tickets; somehow I'm sure you won't be using them. And if all goes well, probably, they won't even be used by the real Salim and Sharma Rias, you never know."

He held his hand out to Vee. "Best of luck to both of you, and remember, if you need a Sherman tank, I have permission right from the top to get you two." This broke the ice a bit, and we all laughed.

Paul walked back up the passageway, not looking back, we watched him go through the glass doors and turn right down the passage. Then we knew we were definitely on our own. I glanced at Vee, not saying a word. I could see trepidation in her eyes. I grabbed hold of the trolley, as Vee reached to put her hand on mine. Her hand was very warm, and a little damp. I looked down at her and gave her a wink trying to console her a little.

"OK, Sharma, let's get this show on the bloody road." Vee gave my hand a little squeeze, in some sort of show of commitment, and then we started down the passageway, pushing the trolley before us.

Chapter Eleven

As we came into the arrivals hall, it was quite full, and very noisy, with the public address system giving travellers information on arrivals and departures, and also people waving and shouting excitedly to long-lost relatives and friends coming through the arrivals door. We followed the line of passengers, all heading around the barriers. I first saw Kareem dressed in his very Muslim regalia, as our eyes met he looked away, and spoke to someone next to him, and then I saw the guy holding up a board with Salim Rias written in red. I waved to him, trying to look excited at our meeting; we made our way to the opening in the barrier, and I could see Mohammed and his partner Mari pushing their way through the crowd towards us.

I let go of the trolley, letting Vee take over; the man with the board came straight over to me, and, as customary, he grabbed hold of me and kissed me on both cheeks.

"Good to meet you at long last, Salim," he said, standing directly in front of me. He stuck out his hand, "Mohammed Malik, I welcome you both to the United Kingdom; this is my wife Mari," he said, standing aside and beckoning to her to come forward. Both Sharma and I shook hands with Mari. She was quite short, like Vee, probably around five foot three or four, and very pretty indeed, although slightly overweight.

Mohammed was quite good-looking, and also quite short, probably around five foot seven or eight, but very stocky; he looked like he spent quite a bit of time in the gym. He had one of those beards that looked as if he just hadn't shaved for a couple of days or so. Straight away I was drawn to his eyes, they were very dark and deep-set. His pupils were half hidden by his eyelids, and they gave me a very creepy feeling.

I introduced him to Sharma, and noticed that his eyes went straight down to her enlarged stomach; but he had the good manners not to make any comment.

Just then Kareem came rushing over, all excited, with his arms waving furiously high in the air.

"Salim, Salim Rias," he was almost shouting. "God is good to me today, I cannot believe it; what, it must be fifteen years since I last saw you, do you remember me?" His arms went around my neck, and I got another kiss on each cheek.

"Wow, it's Kareem, yes, Kareem! Sorry, but it's been a long time, and what a surprise," I blurted out in my best knocked-for-a-six voice, "Wow, are you here to meet me also, Kareem?" I questioned.

"No, no, Salim; I am here to meet my son. What a surprise I got, seeing you come through those doors." He looked towards Sharma, who was standing behind me. "Sharma," he cried, taking her hand and kissing it. "It's been so long, so long. God is especially good to me today. I just cannot believe meeting you both after all these years, praise be to Allah!"

I introduced Kareem to Mohammed and Mari, and I could see that, straight away, they showed great respect for Kareem, since he was a man of God; and I knew we had just encrusted the fact with Mohammed that we were Salim and Sharma Rias. So, once again, another hurdle had been crossed.

"Are you both staying in Manchester, Salim?" Kareem questioned, turning to me and grabbing my shoulders with both hands.

"No, Kareem." It was Mohammed who replied. "He's staying in Leeds, with us."

Kareem sort of gasped out. "Leeds! That's where I live, Salim! You must take some time and come to my mosque and pray with us. While you are there I will be very honoured, really," he said, while scribbling on a notepad that he had taken from his pocket. "Let me give you my mobile number; you must come! A lot of my friends would love to meet you, and we can talk about the old times we had in God's country. I really can't believe this. I really can't."

With that, Kareem turned and walked closer to the arrivals door, as if waiting for his son to arrive.

As he walked away, I looked back at Mohammed, shaking my head, "Who would have thought that possible? After fifteen years, I walk into him at Manchester airport. It must be a sign from God, Mohammed; yes, a sign from God. I think everything is going to run like clockwork, I really do."

I saw Mohammed's face light up at what I had just said, and I knew that we had been fully accepted, which gave both Vee and I great relief.

"You can be certain that everything will go like clockwork, Salim," Mohammed said, looking straight into my eyes. "I am a perfectionist, and I know that you will be very pleased with what I have organised; and I thank God every day for the help that your people in God's country have given me over the last couple of years. I will always be grateful to them, for as long as I live."

I think it took about two hours to get from Manchester to Leeds. Mohammed drove, and I was in the front passenger seat, while Sharma and Mari were making small talk in the rear of the car. Mohammed didn't say much, other than pointing out a range of inconsequential sights that he thought would maybe interest me, this being supposedly my first visit to the United Kingdom. The weather had been cloudy but dry for the whole drive from Manchester to Leeds, which was quite unanticipated for this time of year. We came to the edge of Leeds, and drove through a couple of small middle-class suburban towns, until we then stopped at a small but very clean and neat-looking house.

Mohammed pointed to the house. "This," he said, "is the house of a very dear cousin and friend, who has gone out to Somalia for the winter months, and he has offered it to you for your stay in the United Kingdom."

He opened the car door and stepped out. I climbed out of the passenger door, and followed him up the driveway, with Sharma and Mari in hot pursuit. Mohammed opened the door with a set of keys that he took from his pocket, and we both entered into a lounge that was very sparsely furnished, although very adequate.

Mohammed showed Vee and I around the house, pointing out the two bedrooms, bathroom and kitchen, as if he was an estate agent trying to sell me the place. I could see that it was very clean and well kept, and very cosy, so to speak, if you liked that sort of thing.

"It's very nice, Mohammed," I said as we arrived back in the lounge, "and I am truly honoured that your cousin has put his trust in me by letting us stay here, when he has never even met me. He must be a really true friend of yours, Mohammed."

"Yes, Salim; he is a cousin of mine who has lived in the United Kingdom for some thirty-five years, but has never liked the winters. So, every winter, he migrates to the sun. You can't really blame him, can you?" he said, smiling broadly. He pointed towards the door. "Let's get your cases out of the car, then you will feel more at home." With that, we walked out into the driveway.

165

As we were extracting the suitcases from the car, Mohammed said that Mari would stay with Sharma and help her to unpack, and he would take me out to the farmhouse, where we could talk more freely. This, I understood, was to be an interrogation period for both Sharma and myself, so we would both have to be very much on our toes for the next hour or so.

We left the ladies at the house, and drove for about twenty five minutes. Mohammed said very little on the way. We were well out of town now, and the scenery looked very bleak, with very few trees; in fact, it looked very much like the moors, as I could see patches of heather here and there. At a fork in the road, we took the right fork and came on to a dirt road that was very narrow, and could only take one vehicle at a time. I noticed that, about a mile ahead, there was a two-storey building in stone, with a sort of barn alongside it.

"That's the place," Mohammed said, proudly pointing his index finger to the two-storey building. "I bought it about five years ago, with a little help from some friends in Pakistan. It's very solid, and far away from prying eyes. Sometimes I think it's a little too solitary living out here, but you can't have it both ways, can you, Salim?"

We drove through the open farm gates, and Mohammed parked the car inside the barn. The building was built out of carved stone, and must have been over a hundred years old. As we went into the farmhouse, I noticed that the door was at least three inches thick of solid wood, with a really old-fashioned door knob, bolts and locking system.

"Salim, welcome to my most humble abode," Mohammed said, as he stepped aside for me to enter first. There was a small vestibule that led to a large lounge, that had typical farmhouse furniture, and a large brick fireplace that was already filled with dried wood. A staircase led off from the lounge, and I could see a large kitchen off from the back of the lounge.

"I was going to let you stay here with Mari and me, but there isn't enough room really; and, anyway, I am sure that you will be far more comfortable on your own at my cousin's house. And I don't care who you are, but everyone enjoys a little privacy, don't you think?"

Mohammed moved to the centre of the lounge, with his arms outspread. "Well, Salim, what do you think?"

"Wow, this is great, Mohammed!" I said, slipping into a chair by the fireplace. "This place must be at least a hundred years old."

"It's a lot more than that, Salim," Mohammed said, with some enthusiasm. "It dates back over two hundred and forty years; it used to be a farm, but I'm told that, over time the moors took over the land, and it was never farmed again. The old couple who lived here died, and their daughter lived here for a number of years, but then decided to sell. I was very much in the right place at the right time, and jumped at it; and, with a little help from some very dear friends in God's country, I had it transferred into my name."

I could see that he was very proud of his farmhouse. His eyes shone as he spoke; and I've got to admit that it was very nice indeed, although sparsely furnished. Everything was neat, and looked very comfortable.

Mohammed walked over to the fireplace, and put a match to the wood. All of a sudden, the fames flickered dancing lights across the room. "Gas," he said. "We use gas to light it; it's far quicker than paper and wood, and, in a country with weather as bad as we have here, Salim, you need instant heat, eh?"

"Yes, Mohammed. Sharma and I got one hell of a shock with the cold when we got off the plane; but I suppose we should have expected it."

"What's the weather like in Pakistan, Salim?" Mohammed asked, walking through to the kitchen.

"Beautiful, Mohammed: blue skies, not a cloud in sight, and a temperature of around twenty-eight or twenty-nine degrees," I replied, thankful that I had been given that information earlier by Paul.

Mohammed came back into the lounge with two mugs of steaming coffee.

"Here, get your hands around that," he said, handing me a large mug. "The place will warm up in a couple of minutes, and you will feel much more comfortable, Salim. You must be really feeling the cold, coming from a warm climate to a cold winter climate."

Mohammed slouched down into the chair opposite, and put his mug on the table, beside his chair. I noticed his eyes again; when he looked at me, he seemed to be looking right inside me, and his eyes definitely had a sort of very sinister look.

"Well, Salim," Mohammed said, crossing his right leg over his left leg. "What do you know about our operation? Did anyone over there tell you what we are proposing to do to the infidels, here in the United Kingdom?"

"No, Mohammed," I replied. "No one said anything as to what you were proposing to do. All that was said was that it was a very big operation, and they wanted me to help, oversee and maybe advise on the operation. Whether they didn't know or they were reluctant to say, I don't know. Obviously, I didn't ask too many questions; when something as big as this is going to happen, people do not want it traced back to Pakistan, for political reasons. And anyway, I knew you would fill me in as soon as I got here. I am sure that my being here will give your disciples a great boost to their morale; and, as you must realise, in an operation of this nature, that can be an incredible influence for everyone concerned, don't you think?"

Mohammed never showed any reaction, so I had to presume that I had said the right things. I had to be very careful in what I said in this initial meeting; one word out of context, and I could blow the whole programme into the air. I have got to admit that I was pretty nervous, and had to hide it, so I decided that I would take the initiative, and put a few pertinent questions directly to him, and see if I could raise some reaction.

"Well, Mohammed," I said, putting my empty coffee mug on the side table. "I'm sure you are not going to keep me in suspense any longer. What is it you are planning to do with these bloody British infidels? You have got me quaking in my shoes with curiosity. We are both on the side of Allah and we all expect adversity in every move we make in bringing these infidels down, although we are all very sure that we will prevail valiantly in the end, we all know that it will be a long and hard fought battle of attrition for the sons of Allah."

I knew that I had said the right thing when Mohammed shouted very loudly, with both arms high in the air, "God is great, praise be to Allah!"

"God is great, praise be to Allah!" I retorted abruptly, also throwing my own arms high in the air. I was quite embarrassed, shouting like that, but I had learned that this was the general reaction that was expected of any Jihadist Muslim terrorist.

"So, Mohammed," I went on, "all I have been told is that the operation you have in mind is considerably large; but I'm afraid that is all I know, so now I am here, and we are alone. This would be a good time for you to fill me in on what you are proposing to inflict on these pathetic infidels. I would be very interested indeed to know where, and obviously how, and also if possible maybe even some indication as to your time-frame, as to when the mighty power of Islam will once again be perpetrated on these infidels, and once again show the world that there is no stopping the power and pure determination of Allah's disciples to bring down Christianity."

Mohammed smiled across at me, and took a sip of his coffee; I could see instantly that he was very proud of his plan and was dying to tell someone just what he had in mind, especially someone of authority like Salim Rias, who was admired and held high in esteem by the top people of Al-Qaida.

"Sure, Salim; let me fill you in from the beginning," he said. His face had now changed, and I could see hate in his eyes. "It all started near enough two years ago to the day. Mari and I were out shopping, about the twentieth of December, and some hate-mongering infidel, in one of the shops we were in, totally embarrassed both Mari and myself by serving someone first who was behind us. When I objected to this, he called for the security, and we were instantly ejected, not only from the shop, but from the shopping centre itself. After thinking about the whole situation, I thought about getting even with the infidels, just to show them how powerful and devastating Allah can be when one of his disciples is abused and demoralised, as both Mari and myself felt we were that day. I remembered thinking back on how packed it was, with infidels doing their Christmas shopping; and the idea came into my head that a bomb in a shopping centre, if large enough, would be devastating, and could kill thousands of the infidels just before their most important family holiday of the year."

I sat listening with a look of nonchalance on my face, but deep down, I was flabbergasted that someone could sit as calmly as Mohammed was, and could depict such a story of utter destruction and devastation, which he wanted to inflict upon hundreds, if not thousands, of innocent men, women, and children, just because he had been embarrassed by some shopkeeper and a couple of security guards. I could feel the hairs on the back of my neck stand up. What sort of a man was he, to be so demonstrative over a diminutive, embarrassing moment in his life? An old Chinese proverb came to mind. "When you seek vengeance, always dig two graves."

"Last year, I took a plane back to Pakistan," Mohammed continued, with a very proud look in his deep-set eyes. "I stayed there for nearly four months, where I learned to make bombs; and I also took the time to find people who would help me to implement the desire I had in mind, and that was not very difficult in Pakistan, as you can well imagine. I then went to Iran, Jordan, Syria and Lebanon, to organise to get explosives imported into the United Kingdom. I had drawings of various bombs and devices imprinted deep in my mind, so all I had to do was get the necessary materials required over here, and put them together. I was contacted last month by Al-Qaida, and told you would be coming here, to help me in the initiation of getting the whole operation implemented. To me, this was the greatest day of my life. I could not believe that they would send someone as high as you to help me; I was totally overwhelmed. Praise be to Allah, Salim; yes, praise be to Allah!"

"Yes, praise be to Allah, Mohammed, praise be to Allah!" I said, pointing my index finger in the air. "Your idea is excellent, and it will definitely shock not only the United Kingdom, but the world as a whole, if you are able to kill hundreds of infidels in one fell swoop. I am sure that our principal back home will be very, very appreciative, and also very proud of you and your courage as an individual. I am sure that your name will be shouted from the roof tops, as was that of the great Bin Laden."

This made Mohammed swell with pride. His eyes were no longer dull; they were shining with pride and enthusiasm; but still he had that dark depth that worried me.

"I'm glad you think so, Salim," Mohammed said, coming back to earth. "But this is far, far bigger than even you yourself or anyone even in Pakistan could ever anticipate. I envisage using fifteen bombs, with half a kilo of explosives in each bomb, being placed in

171

various shopping centres throughout the United Kingdom. I want every one of them to detonate within minutes of each other, and I can assure you that not hundreds, but thousands of infidels will die, because of the way I have designed my bombs. Salim, the best thing of all is that no one will know who did it; and, even better still, I have planned it so that no Muslim brothers in the operation will have to become martyrs or even suffer for the cause. Salim, at this very moment I have eleven pure fundamentalists, who are all very keen to take part in this operation; but I need at least another two, to make things go like clockwork. I have a meeting with a couple of guys tomorrow. Maybe you should come with me, Salim; this will show them how keen the people in Pakistan are on my plan, and also it will show you just how radical the home-grown Muslim extremists are in the United Kingdom, and how keen they are in bringing down these infidels of Christianity.

"God is great, praise be to Allah!" Mohammed screamed, jumping to his feet, and throwing his arms wildly up in the air.

"God is great, praise be to Allah!" I shouted loudly in reply, still feeling rather embarrassed doing so.

It was so hard for me to listen to this brand of utterance coming from any kind of human being. For me even to think that there were these types of inhumane people living in and amongst the human race, with such horrendous and contemptible mindsets, and, even worse, living amongst us in the United Kingdom – they were born and bred here; they had British accents, British education – it was just far too much even for me to grasp. I was very surprised when Mohammed said that he was using half a kilogram of explosives in each bomb. That was enough to bring down a very large building in itself, and would cause a great catastrophe in any shopping mall full of people doing their Christmas shopping.

Mohammed had just come back from the kitchen with another mug of steaming hot coffee. He placed my cup on the table, and flopped back into his chair. He had a very weird look in his eyes that made him, in my eyes, a contemptible person of unimaginable proportions.

"Mohammed," I said, "where are you going to implement this attack against the infidels from? Surely not here on the farm? This place is wide open to scrutiny, and can be kept under surveillance from all sides very easily."

"That's the whole point, Salim, of utilising this place. Neither the police nor MI5 would ever expect anything to come from the countryside; they expect everything to be in the cities. Take Leeds, for example. Some of my friends have been taken in for questioning, and grilled for hours, not because they had done anything wrong, but because they were Muslims; and as far as surveillance is concerned, there is only one road in and one road out, so I would be able to see any incursions towards the farm quite easily. Also, I have a security beam a mile down the road, and if a car or person should cut the beam, it activates an alarm in the house, and we would be able to take any evasive action necessary very quickly, to alleviate any intrusion."

"Mohammed, I can see that you have put a great deal of thought into this plan of yours, and I can only admire you for it; but are you telling me that you have got seven kilograms of explosives on this farm?"

"Yes, Salim," he said, smiling broadly. "It's been here for about three months now. At first I kept it in a well, about a hundred and fifty yards away, but now it is here in the farmhouse. I have already started building the bombs now, and all fifteen of them should be completed and prepared for implementation within the next few days."

"Come with me, Salim," he beckoned with his hand as he jumped from his seat. "Let me show you how far I have got with the bombs, or IEDs, as they call them back in God's country."

I followed Mohammed up the stairs, and into one of the front bedrooms. Mohammed switched on the light and walked in. There was a large dining room table in the centre of the room; the curtains were closed, and lots of cardboard boxes were piled up against the side wall. On the table was a pile of black-box-type briefcases. I counted around fifteen in all.

"These are the IEDs," Mohammed said, placing his hand on one of the briefcases. They can be detonated by mobile phone, miles away from the detonation position. Look, Salim! I have almost finished a couple of them. When you see them, you will better understand."

He opened one of the briefcases and I could see instantly that Mohammed was a very neat and very precise person. There were three colours of wires – red, green and blue – and in the centre was a mobile phone. On either side I could see two plastic packets, and I knew from experience that it was semtex. The wiring was very neat indeed. In fact the whole bloody IED itself was far neater than my own grandmother's knitting. I then knew that Mohammed wasn't playing any games. He was as serious as any man could get, and was determined to wreak mass destruction on the United Kingdom.

"Wow, this is beautiful, Mohammed! They taught you well back home. This is very neat indeed, it's well-compacted, and can be carried openly, without any chance of suspicion. Mohammed, I can only compliment you on your stunning workmanship."

When I said that, I have got to say that I meant every word of it, because these IEDs were just that, stunning in every sense of the word. They were very neatly prepared, and also very dangerous in his or anyone else's hands, for that matter, who had destruction in mind.

"In a couple of days," Mohammed went on, "when we have everyone together, I will show you everything; and I am sure that you will be even more impressed, because I am going to include anthrax spores in all the bombs. Here, let me show you."

He bent down and opened a box, and came up with a plastic envelope, approximately the size of the briefcases, that was full of a sort of white powder. I had never seen anthrax spores before, but I could see from the way he was carefully handling it, that he wasn't bullshitting me, and that this was the real McCoy.

"Salim, all will be revealed soon, and I am very sure that you are going to be exceptionally impressed, indeed."

He had a ghoulish sort of look in his dark eyes that gave me goose bumps. I don't think that I have ever met a man who held so much revulsion towards humanity. I was quite overwhelmed.

"But now," he said, looking at his watch, "I must get you back to your beautiful wife, so that you can settle in for the night. Both of you need a good rest after your long flight. You must both be very tired."

With that, he turned and headed back down the stairs, with me following close behind.

We left the farm at around three p.m., and headed back towards Leeds. Mohammed showed me the electronic beams as we drove past it. They were just about a mile or so from the farm gates. I kept very quiet, and just let Mohammed keep reiterating his decimating plans of destruction. This was showing me how overconfident he was about the whole deed, and I was already assessing ways of destroying his plans.

The clouds were low, and it was very cold, but there was no rain, so we did the trip in no time at all. Mohammed just kept repeating to himself how brilliant he thought his strategy was, and how he was going to shock the world with his plan of utter destruction to the infidels.

As we pulled up outside the house, Sharma and Mari came to the front door to welcome us. They were both smiling broadly, so I could see that they had got on very well together.

"Salim," Mohammed said, as we climbed out of the car, "I have to get back to the farm straight away. You have seen that I still have a lot of work to do, and time is getting short. I will pick you up tomorrow at around nine; then you can come with me and meet a few of my new comrades in arms, so to speak. I feel sure that your meeting them will definitely add to their commitment to the plight of the Muslim people."

He left more or less straight away, and Sharma and myself had something to eat, and settled down to a quiet evening with a bottle of wine. I gave her the lowdown on what had been shown to me by Mohammed at the farm, and watched her eyes grow bigger and bigger.

"Salim! Then this is not a small attack; this sounds like a very well-planned attack that has the intention of causing total and utter devastation. I never ever envisaged anything this immense. It's going to be a catastrophic time in the history of the world, should they be able to implement it; and on top of that, supposing they have a nuclear additive! Oh my God, my mind cannot envisage what these bastards can be up to."

I could see that Vee was as shocked as I was when Mohammed had shown me the fifteen IEDs; but at least we were now in the position of now knowing what they were going to try to accomplish, and our job was merely to eliminate their advantage, little by little.

"Sharma," I said, in a very calm voice. "What is really the high point of this situation is that we now know who they are, and we now know what they are going to try to accomplish; and our job is only to stop it happening, one way or another. If we didn't know the whos and the whats of the operation, then the whole thing could be even more catastrophic; but you must fully understand that we are well ahead of them at this moment in time, and all we have to do is stay ahead of them. Also, I am pretty sure that there is no nuclear additive to the IEDs, because Mohammed was bragging to me today, and saying that he was including anthrax spores in the IEDs; and I can only guess that, probably, he will include nails. Anyway, Vee, let's wait until we get the whole picture before we make any assumptions as to how we go about eliminating the whole show. At this moment in time, everything is on our side. Also, Sharma, I found that Mohammed is, very much, a very narcissistic sort of person, which is on our side; because, if he really loves himself so much, then that, more likely than not, will help to blind his vision to the reality that is going on around him."

"Anthrax? Oh my God, Steve, that's deadly, isn't it?" She had her hand over her mouth, and her eyes were very large and round.

I stood up and took her face in my hands, smiling down at her. "Sweetheart, go to bed and rest. We must stay very alert over the next few weeks or so. I will be there in a moment. I want to phone Charles and get him up to speed, as we need him here in Leeds as soon as possible, because, as Sherlock Holmes would have said, time is of the essence."

Sharma quickly cleared up in the kitchen, and went up the passage to the bedroom. I rang Charles, and, as usual, it was answered immediately.

"Yes, Steve, good to hear your voice. How's it going on the sharp end?" he questioned.

I gave him a quick rundown about what had happened that day, and I could hear that he was as shocked as both Sharma and I had been.

"Shit, Steve! I can't believe these bastards; they must have rocks in their bloody heads. Thank God MI5 got on to it so quickly; and, even more, thank God that they've got you in place to sort it all out. What in this world is humanity coming to, Steve? It's unbelievable."

"Look, Charles: to get to the point, I need you here in Leeds as soon as possible. So you will have to leave very early tomorrow morning. I'll get our address to you, so that you can fix yourself up with a place very close to where we are."

Charles came over the phone with a little snigger, "Steve, my boy, I'm here in Leeds, and about two miles from you, in a Bed and Breakfast. Do you think I just loafed around when I was with MI6? I was at Manchester airport early this morning, when you had your introduction to these bastards; and when I spoke to Paul on his mobile he said that you were being taken to Leeds. So all I had to do was just to follow you, and, abracadabra, here I am! Although I look young, I wasn't born yesterday, Steve," he said, laughing whole-heartedly.

"That's great, you old codger. Now I know why MI6 thought I was so bloody good. It was really because I always had you there in the background, backing me up."

Then something came into my head. "Charles, get on to Paul and ask him for fifteen mobile sim cards that can only be activated from one number. These I probably won't need, unless the shit hits the fan, but it's better to be safe than sorry."

"What in hell are you going to do, Steve, detonate the bloody bombs yourself?"

"No, Charles; at the moment I just want to alleviate the possibility of them doing the detonations. But if push comes to shove, and I have to do it myself, yes I will. It would be far better than them being detonated by the terrorists in large shopping malls. All we must do, Charles, is stay a few steps ahead of them; and I'm glad to say that, at this moment, we are well ahead of them, and that's where we must stay. OK, Charles, see what you can do; and don't let Paul in on any of the implications of the matter. I'm sure he will be very inquisitive. Just play dumb. See you soon, Charles, I'll keep you in the loop."

With that, I headed off to bed; but I knew I wasn't going to get very much sleep. In fact. I was pretty sure I wasn't going to get much sleep until this whole bloody episode was over and done with.

I was awake every hour on the hour, and at five a.m., I'd had enough. I got up and went through to the lounge. I made a steaming hot mug of coffee, and sat deep in thought for about an hour. I wasn't sure how I was going to implement the fall of Mohammed and his crew. All I knew was that it had to be done quickly, and with total precision, and all his radical Muslims must be taken out with him. With all my years of experience in the SAS and MI6, I had never ever come across such brazen killers as this bunch, and I felt that they should feel the wrath of the innocent men, women and children whom they were so deviously aiming to destroy.

I could hear Sharma in the shower, so I rushed to the kitchen and managed quickly to put some scrambled eggs on toast together. We sat and ate breakfast, drank a couple of cups of coffee, and never said one word to each other, except good morning greetings. I think this whole debacle was just too much for both of us to fully comprehend at this moment in time; and I myself was, in a way, worried as to what the day would bring.

I got into the shower and did my thing, dried myself off and dressed as warmly as I could. It felt a lot colder than the previous day had. I saw that the roads outside were covered in a beautiful sheen of frost, which told me that it hadn't rained at all during the night; but it was still going to be a very cold day.

At about nine fifteen, we both heard Mohammed's car pull into the driveway. Sharma looked across at me, and I could see a shade of worry in her eyes. I walked over, put both my arms around her, and gave her a very tight squeeze to try to calm her down a bit.

179

"Don't look so worried, sweetheart; just remember, we are ahead of them already, and we also have Charles on our side." I gave her a big smile, and she returned one to me that seemed a little questioning.

I opened the door, and found Mohammed and two other (obviously, from their dress, Muslim guys), standing in front of me. Mohammed introduced them to me as Aizaz and Elijah. They had just driven up from Birmingham, and had been anxious to be introduced to me. They seemed like very demonstrative sorts of guys, and not the type of people that I would have expected to be in on such a pathway of destruction and murder.

I invited them into the house, where we chatted for a few minutes, and then I introduced them both to Sharma. We all chatted for a few minutes, drinking a cup of coffee. I could see that Aizaz and Elijah were quite enthused to be in our company.

Mohammed then said that they were going to take me to meet a couple of guys who lived in Leeds, and were very keen to join us in on our Jihad operation against the infidels, and we must leave as soon as possible. I gave Sharma a kiss goodbye, and the four of us got into Mohammed's car; and my second day living with the Jihadist extremists got underway.

I took about twenty minutes to get to a kind of very old but small cottage, on the outskirts of Leeds. It seemed like a very broken down place, and in very bad disrepair. As we entered the yard area, two Muslim men appeared from the rear of the building. Both were quite stocky guys and wore the white taqiyah hats, and white gowns with black waistcoats. They were dressed like twins, but were definitely not. They both had beards that were sort of scruffy and unkempt; both of them had very dark, deep and close-set eyes. I have got to say that I instantly took a dislike to both of them. These two were definitely the type of men whom I would have expected to be in on an anti-Christian Jihad.

We were all introduced by Elijah. One was introduced as Mahmood, and the other was Ahmed; and both had very broad Yorkshire accents. I personally found that this was hard to contend with. Mahmood then invited us all into the cottage, and we were all given a mug of hot chocolate. The inside of the cottage was very small; it had very low ceilings and the door frames were all askew. The furniture was very sparse, and the whole place needed a good cleaning, but you couldn't really expect anything more, considering that Ahmed and Mahmood were approximately twenty-three-year-old university students, and lived here entirely on their own.

Mohammed started to explain to both of them what he had in mind, and why he wanted to carry it through. I was quite surprised, really, because he said very little about the actual operation itself, except that he had been planning it for a couple of years, and that Al-Qaida based in Pakistan were totally satisfied and were in full compliance with his plan; that they had sent Sharma and myself from Pakistan to oversee the implementation of the operation, which would bring the Christian world of infidels to rethink the power of Allah.

When Mohammed got to the size of the operation, and threw around the number of infidels that he anticipated would die in such a devastating way, and, over and above that, that no one on the Jihadi operation would have to martyr themselves, both Mahmood's and Ahmed's eyes lit up, and they said straight away that they were keen to join. I was quite surprised, really, because he hadn't said very much at all about the whys and wherefores of the procedure; he had only defined the very basic information, and, when I thought about it, he had not explained very much more to me either, I suppose. I could only put it down to the fact that either he was being very secretive, or he was on an ego trip, and waiting for that very special moment in time when he would reveal everything to everybody, in a hail of glory, which would promote him, in their eyes, to be one of the greatest leaders of the Jihad against Christianity that had ever lived. I was sure that he was aiming to overthrow Bin Laden from his seat of immortality.

We left two cups of hot chocolate later, leaving Mahmood and Ahmed looking as if they had just won the lottery. I was very surprised indeed at how gullible these people were when it came to indoctrination into the defeat of Christianity. Outside, by the car, we were all hugged and kissed, and Mohammed said that he would arrange to get them both out to the farm in the very near future, possibly in the afternoon, if time permitted, and they could then see the complete supremacy of his master plan.

"Allah is great!" Mohammed shouted from the car, as we drove away. "Allah is great!" both Mahmood and Ahmed shouted in harmony, as we pulled out on to the road, with the wheels squealing and burning rubber. This showed me how vulnerable Mohammed was, and my intellect told me that he wouldn't bend in the wind, should things change; he would definitely snap into pieces.

We drove into Leeds, but Mohammed never said where we were going; so I sat quietly, and watched the drizzle that had started running down the windscreen. We came to a garage on a main street; Mohammed pulled the car into the parking area, and got out.

"OK, Salim," he said, beckoning me to get out of the car, "let's see if we can get you a set of wheels."

"Oh," I said. "I was going ask you to take me to a place to hire one."

"No need, Salim! My cousin, who loaned you his house, said that he would be more than happy for you to use his car; and he always leaves it here when he goes away over the winter period."

He walked over to the garage, with a much-gaited step, and I followed in close proximity. We walked across the garage's oil-covered floor towards a small office in the back corner. Mohammed went into the office, and spoke to a fellow Muslim who sported a very long white beard and a taqiyah hat, and was dressed in the full Muslim regalia. I was standing at the office doorway, a metre or so behind Mohammed. Then I heard them speaking in Urdu, I quickly did an about-turn, and walked deeper on to the garage floor. I pretended to be looking at the cars that were parked around the place. I had no idea what they were saying, but I knew that if they spoke to me in Urdu, the game would be over. Out of the corner of my eye, I saw the owner reach for a set of keys from a key board on the wall, and hand them over to Mohammed.

Mohammed came out of the office, holding the keys up in his hand to show me, and pointed to a black Mercedes, parked just outside the door on the garage forecourt. "It's ten years old, Salim, but very comfortable; and you can be sure it's very reliable. This is one of the best maintenance garages in Leeds, and they have been servicing that car for my cousins since the car was just a baby; so you can be sure that it's in excellent condition."

We walked outside into the drizzling rain and cold wind of the forecourt. Mohammed turned to me, laughing. He threw me the keys, and I jumped into the Mercedes.

Mohammed walked over to me, and opened the car door. "Follow me, Salim. I will take you back to the house, and there you will be able to spend some time with Sharma. I will pick up Mahmood and Ahmed on the way back, and take them with me out to the farmhouse, to give them more of a rundown on the operation. Then Elijah and Aizaz are going to help me to get everything finalised over the next few days. God be with you, Salim!" With that, he walked over to his car, got in, and gunned the engine into life.

I followed Mohammed out of town, struggling a bit with the car, as I had never liked driving an automatic. I was struck with a thought, and a big worry had come to mind. When I had heard Mohammed speak Urdu to the garage owner, it made me worry, because Mohammed was born in this country and had a very broad Yorkshire accent; and, I have got to admit, I was more than surprised to hear him speaking in Urdu, if he spoke in Urdu to me I would be fucked, and so would the whole operation. I must be very careful, and try to have Vee along with me for all or as much of the time as possible. I was sure that she would be a great asset, should that kind of circumstance ever arise again.

I stopped the car behind Mohammed at Mahmood's and Ahmed's cottage. They both came running out of the house, and both jumped into the back seat of Mohammed's car. I was not surprised to see how eager they both were, and I must say it was quite an eye-opener to see how easily these Muslims were indoctrinated into a jihadist movement that would bring an end to the infidels Christianity.

I followed Mohammed closely, and about twenty minutes later I was back at the house. I drove the car up the driveway and parked it around the back. I got out of the Mercedes and walked back down to the front gate.

Mohammed leaned out of the car window and shouted, "Will you be able to find your way to the farmhouse by yourself tomorrow, Salim?"

"Yes, sure, Mohammed; if I get lost, as I said before, I'll phone you," I replied, laughing and waving my hand.

"That's great, Salim! You can go and get yourselves some shopping with Sharma this afternoon, and I will see you tomorrow at the farm, around nine." With that, he gunned the engine, and was soon round the corner and out of sight.

I stood in the garden for a few minutes, summing up how close it had been to blowing the whole operation out of the window. I came to the conclusion that I must have Sharma there at my side as much as possible, if not all the time. That was for sure.

I went into the house, and surprisingly I couldn't find Vee anywhere; I went through to the bedroom, and there she was, laid in the bed, fully covered up, and in a very deep sleep. I was starting to realise that the pressure was definitely getting to her. So I closed the bedroom door and went back to the lounge, leaving her to get the rest she no doubt needed.

I walked outside and did a very thorough check on the car, to see that there were no bugs or listening devices in it. After about fifteen minutes of doing a physical check, I was pretty sure that the car was clean, but I made a mental note to get Charles to check it out with his monitor, to be on the safe side. Also, it would be a good idea to check the house while he was at it, too.

I went back into the house and saw that Vee was still sound asleep on the bed. I went back through to the lounge, and sat pondering as to ways of removing her from the operation. But after the scare I had got from hearing Mohammed speaking in Urdu, I knew that I could not do without her by my side; and I also knew that I definitely couldn't keep quiet about what I knew about how serious this whole situation was becoming, even though I knew it was really getting to her. I guess it must have been getting to me also, as I soon fell into a deep sleep in the chair.

I woke about two hours later, with Sharma shaking my shoulder. "Steve, how long have you been home?" she said, in a very worried tone.

I glanced across at the clock on the wall and realised that I had been sleeping for just over two hours. I sat up and put my head between my knees, and ran my hands through my hair.

"Get me some coffee, please, Vee; my mouth feels as rough as a dog's arse."

I drank my coffee, and ate a slice of toast, while I filled Vee in on my day out with Mohammed. I also illustrated my worry over her, and asked her if the stress was taking too much out of her. She replied in the negative and gave me a bollocking for even thinking that she should pull out.

"Salim, you have just said that you heard Mohammed speaking Urdu, and it worried you. If I were there, it would be easy for me to reply to them in Urdu, and that could get us out of a very delicate situation that could have blown the whole operation out of the water."

I had to agree with her, as I now understood that there was no other way around it; and I knew that I could never get away with this conspiracy without her by my side. I must accept the circumstances as they were, and carry on regardless. I recognised that, with Vee being with me the whole time, I would have to be more ultra-alert every second of the time that we were in the neighbourhood of this damned terrorist cell.

We went out and got a bit of shopping from a small grocery store; then I got into the shower while Sharma knocked together a meal. We ate the meal, and drank a bottle of wine between us, and then my mobile rang. It was Mohammed.

"Salim, Mohammed," he said. "Sorry to worry you, but I just had Mahmood on the phone, and he doesn't seem to know how to get to the farm. I was wondering if it was possible for them to come to your place, as you are just up the road, and you can lead them here. What do you think?

"Sure, Mohammed," I replied. "Not problem at all, tell them to get here around eight thirty. Oh, and I need to ask you, Mohammed, can I bring Sharma with me? Then Mari can keep her company. I don't want to leave her alone here; she will only get miserable and take it out on me when I get home."

"Yes, of course, Salim, you must bring her, Mari is looking forward to seeing her again, and I think they will be great company for each other. Also, Salim, remember: the more cooks the better the food, don't you think?" he said, with laughter in his voice.

"OK, Mohammed," I said, "We'll look forward to seeing you both tomorrow, around nine."

I couldn't believe it when we got up the following morning. The bloody sun was shining. It was still cold, with a bit of frost on the windows, but at least the day looked liveable, and that always gave you a shot in the arm to get the day going.

We heard Mahmood and Ahmed's car pull up outside just after eight thirty. Sharma and I walked out and waved as we got into the Mercedes. We pulled out of the driveway, and they pulled in behind us, as we took off towards the farmhouse.

It took over half an hour to get to the farm, as I missed the right turn at the fork and had to double back. The sun had now gone back behind the clouds, and the moor seemed very drab indeed. As we drove up the driveway, the gravel stones hit the underside of the mudguards, making a rattling sound. I parked the Mercedes inside the barn area, next to where Mohammed's car had been parked, and Mahmood parked directly behind Mohammed's car.

We all jumped out of our cars, and rushed into the farmhouse to get out of the cold. When all the introductions and preliminaries were finished, we all settled down in the lounge, and were given some lovely hot spicy soup and a fresh crispy roll. That was just about the best thing to have in weather like this.

I counted ten people, without including Sharma and Mari. Mohammed did the introductions all round, but I found that I was struggling to get all these foreign names into my mind. We now had Mohammed, of course, Kamran, Kahn, Mahmood, Ahmed, Abdul, Elijah, Ishmael, Ajmal, and not forgetting Akram, whom I had never met as yet; but I was told that he would be arriving later in the day.

When we had all finished our soup, we were all asked to follow Mohammed upstairs. Everyone crowded into the front bedroom. Mohammed indicated to me to stand at the back of the table alongside him. I think this was to give him a bit of a lift, standing alongside the great Salim Rias.

Mohammed started by describing very proudly his IEDs, and the parameters of the devastation they would cause to the infidels. I could see the faces on the congregation in front of me, and they all had a mixed look of pride and excitement on their faces. After he had completed his abhorrent dialogue, he came to the part that I was most interested in: that was where they would be used, and, most importantly, when this devastating attack would be implemented.

Mohammed looked around the room at all his disciples. He had a very power-crazed look on his face as he went into the story of his humiliating visit to the shopping mall, which he had related to me the previous day, and of how he intended to reap havoc on all the infidels as they did their Christmas shopping. He had chosen ten of the largest and most used shopping malls in the United Kingdom. He read out the names of the people and gave them their targets. Most of them just nodded when they were given their targets; some rubbed their hands and smiled in a very appreciative manner, almost as if they were being picked as players in a youth football team. No consideration at all was shown for the hundreds, maybe thousands of people, men, women and children, who could be maimed or killed on that day of destruction.

After about three hours of his demonic rhetoric, we were all reassembled down stairs in the lounge once again, all finding seats or sitting on tables, or even the floor.

Mohammed never stopped talking about his plan, and the devastation that he was about to reap on the infidels, that would be remembered throughout the world as the best-planned and best-implemented demonstration of the power of Islam.

I broke into his diabolical babbling because, due to the insurmountable following that was erupting from everyone in the room, I was beginning to really believe every word he was saying myself.

"Mohammed." I was speaking in a very low and yet very determined voice, so as not to bring any of the focus away from Mohammed. "Can I ask when we are going to implement our plan? We are well into December now, and these shopping malls are in far-reaching parts of the United Kingdom. You did mention London, Birmingham, Manchester, Leeds, Nottingham, Leicester and even as far down as Portsmouth. Everyone will have to get to their targets, organise everything and be ready to detonate their IEDs at approximately the same time. This seems a little too close in the timeline, and we do not want our disciples having to rush into anything, because a mistake at this time would be devastating to both yourself and all the people back in God's country."

"Yes, Salim, I understand your concern and uncertainty; and I can assure both yourself and everyone here that we will all be ready and in place well before the attack." He didn't turn to me with his reply; he just kept facing his disciples, "we are going to hit the infidels hard, and on their biggest shopping day, before Christmas." He stopped for a moment, staring round at his disciples, then went on. "We attack on the twenty-fourth of December. 'Why?' you might ask. Well, on that day, they will all be buying their last-minute Christmas presents, and will all be in light-hearted and high spirited moods, looking forward to their holiday, and also, and most important, there is the fact that the police and the Mall's security guards will also be just as relaxed; and gentlemen, let me also tell you that that is when all their thoughts will be on just having a Merry Christmas, and will never have an inkling of the horror that is going to obliterate them."

He looked over to me, probably looking for my approval. His eyes were wide and totally demonic, as he threw his hands wildly into the air.

189

"I still have a lot to do yet on the IEDs," he went on. "But I can assure you that they will be ready on time, and you will all have more than ample time to get to your targets and seek the glory of Allah."

"God is great, praise be to Allah!" Mohammed shouted at the top of his voice, raising both of his clenched fists in the air once again.

"God is great, praise be to Allah!" we all shouted back loudly and in total unison.

Akram arrived about an hour later; he was a very small man, probably around five foot four. I would say that he was in his early twenties, and sporting a moustache with a little goatee beard about three inches long. He seemed to me to be a little hyped up, as he was always moving around. Maybe it was something to do with what they were intending to do in the near future; or maybe he was just a very hyperactive person. It was quite something to watch him, as he never ever stood still. We were all introduced to him, and I got the impression that he was staying at the farm and helping Mohammed upstairs in building the IEDs.

Around four p.m. or so, Mari came to me and said that Sharma was feeling very tired, and she thought I should take her home. It was the best thing I'd heard in days. I couldn't wait to get out of this madhouse, and a few of them, especially Mahmood and Ahmed, had started to speak in Urdu. Although I had had a few lessons, I struggled to even understand it; and if I had had to speak it, I would have sounded like a two-year-old. I rushed into the kitchen to Sharma. She was sitting on a stool with a bowed head, and her hands on her stomach.

"Are you OK, Sharma?" I asked, kneeling on one knee next to her.

"Yes Salim, I'm OK; but I think the long flight has caught up with me. I feel quite tired and a little dizzy. Maybe I need to have a sleep for a few hours."

"OK, wait there. I will tell Mohammed that we are leaving now." With that, I turned and walked towards the lounge, and almost bumped into Mohammed as he was coming into the kitchen.

"Mari says Sharma is sick, Salim." He spoke quietly, and with a very concerned voice.

"Yes, Mohammed. It could be that the flight has caught up with her, being pregnant and all that. Maybe I should have left her at home today."

"No, Salim, if you had left her at home today, she would have been totally alone," Mohammed said, with very real concern. "I'm sure she will be fine. Just get her to the house; she probably just needs a good night's sleep to get rid of the jet lag."

We left the farm within three minutes, and I don't think I have ever been so relieved. As we drove out of the yard, Sharma burst out laughing, grabbing hold of my thigh and shaking it.

After she had calmed down a bit, she said, "Oh, Salim, I was so bloody scared when I heard some of them speaking in Urdu. I knew we had a problem and I knew you could easily get caught out should they have directed a question straight to you; so I just pretended to be sick. It was the first thing that I could think of."

I threw my head back and joined Sharma in her laughter. "Good girl, Sharma! That was bloody quick thinking. I was getting very nervous in there myself. It was Mahmood and Ahmed that were speaking in Pakistani, and somehow I am sure that they did it for a reason. What would I do without you, sweetheart? You were bloody brilliant, if I may say so."

I put my arm around her, pulled her over towards me, and we cuddled all the way back to the house.

191

We had dinner that night, followed by a glass or two of a lovely dry white wine. We didn't talk very much, as I'm sure we were both in our own separate worlds, thinking how this was going to turn out. I myself could not get Mahmood and Ahmed off my mind. There was something about these two that I instantly disliked, even when I met them for the first time yesterday; call it intuition, call it what you like, but these two were bad news, and I would have to tread very carefully when they were around. At around ten p.m., Sharma went off to bed. I sat for a few minutes, then I phoned Charles, to give him an update on what had happened today.

Charles was quite shocked. "Steve," he said in his very fatherly manner, "we've got the full rundown now on the operation. Don't you think it's now time to call in the spooks, and let them take over?"

"No, Charles, not just yet; there are still a couple of these bastards that I haven't met yet, and we need to get the whole bunch, or there will always be a couple of them loose on our streets. Let's give it a couple of days. The operation isn't going to come to fruition until the twenty-fourth of December, so we have at least until the twenty-second. By then, I will have the whole mob on my list. It's no good going off half-cocked, and letting some of them get off scot-free. Also, there are a lot of other permutations that I need to know, like how in hell's name did they get around seven kilos of semtex, and thirty packets of anthrax into the country, and who brought it in for them? If we stop it now, then all I can see is a waiting game, until it starts all over again, using another set of home-grown terrorists, and maybe I would have to be involved again; or, worse still, we might not find out about it until it happens. No, Charles, we must be a little bit patient for a few days, and tread very carefully; we must ensure that this will never ever happen again in the United Kingdom."

"Well, yes, Steve; I suppose you're right," Charles said, with a bit of hesitation. "But be bloody careful out there, and don't ever let it leave your mind that Vee is there alongside you; we must keep her first and foremost in our minds. But I must say, Steve, I think you would be deep in the shit if she hadn't been there with you today."

"That's for sure, Charles; she's very quick-thinking, and also a first-class asset to have in the field with you. And she is also very good in the kitchen, Charles," I said, laughing.

"I bet she is. You must get me around for dinner, some time when all this shit is sorted out." He was laughing loudly into the mobile, and, I presume, he was trying to alleviate the seriousness of the ongoing situation.

"One more thing, Charles," I said, changing the subject a little, "I have been loaned a car. It's a Merc, old but very comfortable. I have checked it physically for bugs and listening devices, but I thought maybe you could give it a once over yourself? Also. it might be a good idea to go through the house as well; did you bring your bug detector with you?"

"Yes, Steve, I've got it with me; and it will give us a reading should there be any kind of device at all in the car or the house."

"OK, Charles, that's great. I'm off to get some sleep now. It's my big day tomorrow, and I need to be at my best. Then, maybe, we can hand the whole thing over to the spooks. Good night, Charles; I'll contact you tomorrow." I switched off the mobile, and threw it on the side table beside me.

Chapter Twelve

I suddenly came awake. I had to take my mind back a good five seconds or so. Something had awakened me. It was glass: yes, like a wine glass breaking. I grabbed the nearest weapon I could find. It was Vee's magazine on the bedside table. I rolled it up very tight. (This, by the way, is a perfect weapon in hand-to-hand fighting.) I knelt by the bedroom door and looked through the keyhole, to see if I could see any torchlight down in the lounge. It was dark, and very quiet, and I was beginning to think that I had imagined the whole thing.

"Steve," Vee's voice came over very sleepily. I must have woken her. I went to the bottom of the bed with my index finger across my lips and gave her a very low, "Shhhhh, grab the Walther, get in the bathroom and close the door behind you," I whispered.

The house was in silence now. I opened the bedroom door very slowly, ensuring that it wouldn't creak. I moved into the passageway and closed the bedroom door behind me, very slowly and quietly. I moved down the passageway fast and crouching very low. At the entrance to the lounge I stopped, but stayed crouched. No sound at all. I gave it a full thirty seconds: nothing. I started to raise my body, then I heard someone bump into something, and saying "shit" in a very low whisper. I entered the lounge, closed the passageway door behind me, and hid myself behind the lounge chair that was to the left of the passageway door. My bare feet made a squeaking sound on the wooden lounge floor. It seemed very loud to me, but I could see that the intruder had not heard it, as he came walking straight into the lounge through the kitchen door. He had a small torch glowing in front of him. Whoever it was, he was dressed in a jacket that had a hood, so I couldn't see his face. The beam from the torch moved around the lounge, and then fell on the briefcase, Vee's bag and a laptop computer that were laid on the coffee table by the far wall. He went straight over to them, he placed the torch in his mouth and did a systematic examination of the briefcase's contents, quickly and very professionally. So I knew that he was not doing this for first time. He seemed to be very professional, or he knew just what he was doing.

I saw him pick up something that looked like a business card. It had fallen out of some paperwork he had been scrutinising that was lying on the table next to the laptop computer, and he put it straight into the left hand pocket of his coat.

Quickly and quietly, he opened the laptop and switched it on. As the computer clicked in and lit up, my heart sank; from the light of the computer I could see that it was Ahmed. He messed around for a while, probably trying different passwords, then he took out the card from his pocket and tried again; but he gave up with a grunt, shut down the laptop, and put the card back in his pocket.

He was now looking across at the dining room table. There were quite a few papers on it, but I knew that there wasn't anything there that would be any use to anyone; but then I noticed the empty bottle of wine, and the two glasses from last night; and I knew that that would throw a spanner in the works. He would know that very few Muslims drink alcohol, especially the ones from Pakistan. After going through the papers, his torch came up and ran around the lounge. As it hit the side table, I could see the mobile that Charles had given me. Ahmed switched it on, and spent about five or ten seconds looking for any info it would hold. Then he slipped that into his left hand pocket also. His torch swung around the room, then on to the passageway door to the bedroom. I stayed crouched low behind the chair, but moved my left foot slightly forward. He came up to the door, and put his left hand out to reach for the door handle. This made him entirely vulnerable, because his frontal body was directly towards me, with his eyes looking down at the door handle. I knew that this was about time for me to introduce myself.

I changed position very fast, raising my body and moving my left foot forward, giving me full balance, I hit him with the end of the rolled magazine hard into his bread basket. All I heard was the air expelled from his mouth. He was down on his knees, facing the passage door, I grabbed his hair, pulled his head back, and drove the magazine hard into his temple. I knew straight away that he wouldn't be waking up for quite a while.

I checked all his pockets, and found the business card he had picked up. It was Vee's business card, and it had her name and photograph on it. How it had got in there I do not know, but what I did know was that we had a very serious situation on our hands, a very serious situation indeed. I took Charles's mobile from his pocket, and threw it on the settee.

Quickly I checked the kitchen; no one else was there. I went back to the sprawled body on the floor, and shone the torch in his face. Yes, I was right; it was Ahmed. This meant that they were definitely on to us, and both Vee and I could now be in a great deal of danger.

I rushed through to the bedroom, and opened the bathroom door. Vee was standing upright in her night dress, legs apart, and arms out stretched with the Walther PPK semi-automatic clutched in both hands and trained directly at my head. You know, I've got to say, she still looked beautiful.

"It's Ahmed, love; they're on to us. Get a couple of your scarves," I said, pointing to the wardrobe. I quickly jumped into a pair of trousers, and, pulling a heavy pullover over my head, I slipped into a pair of running shoes, and ran back down the passage with Vee close on my heels, Ahmed was still out cold, I felt his pulse to check if he was still with us. "He's alive, thank Christ," I said.

Vee started laughing. "Steve, I don't think our Ahmed would appreciate that sort of Christian sentiment, would he?" she said sarcastically.

I ran to the lounge window, and looked out into the half light. No car in view, which probably meant that he was not alone, and that the car was probably further down the street, with a driver in it, waiting for him.

Ahmed was wearing a black duffle coat with a hood. I took it off him, then tied his hands and feet as tight as was possible without cutting off his blood stream. I definitely didn't want to give him all those virgins for free. Vee had got a roll of masking tape from somewhere in the kitchen, and was busy taping up his mouth.

I put the duffle coat on, picked up the masking tape and put it into the duffle coat pocket. At the door, I turned to Vee. She was standing over Ahmed. "Any trouble, Vee, just shoot the bastard." I passed her a cushion from the settee. "Use this to smother the sound of the shot. We can't afford getting the bloody police from the local constabulary getting in on the action, can we? We have now got to look at this differently, as maybe, just maybe, we could be well and truly compromised, if we aren't already."

I went out of the back door, rolling the magazine up tightly again. I held it in my right hand, and put Ahmed's torch in my mouth. I ran down the driveway and out on to the road. The road was wet, and the street lights shimmered on the wet pavement. As I looked left, I saw a car's brake lights go on, so straight away I knew that that was the car he had come in; and, as I had guessed, someone was there waiting in it for him.

With the torch between my teeth, I ran down the road, as I wanted to get to the car on the driver's side. When I heard the car start up, I knew he had seen, or thought he had seen Ahmed running towards him. As I got to the car, I knocked on the driver's side window, while looking back down the street, as if I was looking for someone coming after me. That way I knew that Mahmood would not be able to see my face, just the duffle coat was identifiable.

He rolled down the window, and said something in Urdu. I hit him as hard as I could in the temple with the rolled-up magazine, as I reached for the door handle, and I hit him again, As I opened the car door, and, in the same movement, I dragged him out of the driver's seat and on to the wet road.

Yes, I was right; it was Mahmood. So they really were on to us. This was now going to very be tricky indeed. I put a strip of masking tape over his mouth, and my mind was now in very serious survival mode.

I taped up his hands as fast as I could with the masking tape, as I didn't want any of the neighbours getting an eyeful, and dialling nine, nine, nine. That would really put the cat among the pigeons, and I couldn't afford to have the metro police getting their nose into this. Mahmood was, although a bit dizzy, still able to walk back to the house with a little help from myself.

Vee opened the front door just as we arrived, I shouted "Lights, Vee," as I rushed Mahmood through the door and pushed him roughly on to the settee. In the light I could see that his face was covered in blood. I thought maybe his nose was broken.

I looked at the rolled-up magazine in my hand, and said cheekily to Vee, "Money well spent, my love; I'll buy you a new one tomorrow," and threw the magazine on to the coffee table.

We taped up Mahmood's feet tightly with the masking tape, rolled him on to the floor, and re-taped his hands, but this time at the back. His dark skin was now very pallid and covered in blood, and his eyes were as big as bloody saucers.

I asked Vee to get Charles's mobile from the settee for me. I was a bit mesmerised, to say the least, and not sure what I was going to say to Charles, really; I had to think fast now as to how we were going to clear this mess up, and still keep the operation ongoing – that is, if we had not been fully compromised already. I didn't want us to have to get out now, when the operation was so close to completion. I needed to talk with Charles, to get a different perspective on the situation.

Vee handed me the phone. "It's ringing, love, but I'm sure Charles will be fast asleep; it's two a.m. in the morning, you know."

Charles answered the phone as if he was wide awake, but I could tell we had got him out of a deep sleep, because I never heard him have a pull on his cigarette. "Yes, Steve," he said abruptly.

"Got a bit of a predicament here, Charles, and I think that maybe we could have been compromised; I need your help immediately. A couple of these home grown terrorists broke into the house about an hour ago. I don't know what they were after, but I know for sure that at least these two are on to Vee and I. Get here as soon as possible, and make sure you are not seen; drive round to the back of the house. I'll leave the back door unlocked. Oh, and bring the bug detector; I'm pretty sure there's a listening device in the car or the house, or how the hell could they know we are not who we said we were."

"Ok Steve, I'm on my way; just give me time to put some trousers on. We don't want the neighbours talking, do we?" With that, the phone went dead.

"Make some coffee, Vee; Charles will be here in about ten minutes, and I need to get things straight in my head before he arrives. This is moving fast now, and we don't even know the primary cause, or who was behind it; somewhere, we messed up, Vee, but where? That is the million-dollar question."

While Vee was making the coffee, I manhandled Mahmood and Ahmed through to the second bedroom, and threw them both roughly on to the floor, checking that both their strappings were still tight and in place.

I left the bedroom, locking the door behind me and headed into the lounge. I slumped on to the settee, with my mind spinning like a top. It was just question after question, without any feasible answers.

Now I would have to get hold of Paul. MI5 were going to have to hold these bastards for me, as I needed them off the streets, and out of my hair immediately.

"Paul, Steve," I said.

"Yes Steve," he replied, sounding wide awake, "what's in the mix?" I was surprised to find he was wide awake at this time of the morning.

"Are you still at Thames House, Paul?" I questioned.

"Yes we've got something on the go at the moment, so things are a bit hectic here. Obviously you are in the same position there, or you wouldn't be phoning me at this hour. What do you need, Steve? Surely not Sherman tanks already?"

That was the Paul I used to know; straight down to business.

"I am pretty sure that we have been infiltrated, Paul. Two of the bastards broke into the house I'm staying at about an hour ago. I've got both of them trussed up here; Charles is on his way over to collect them. What I need from you is a place to deliver them to as I have to have them kept in a place that is well under the radar, immediately, or the whole bloody operation will be blown wide open. That's if it hasn't been done already."

"I'm on it Steve, I'll get right back to Charles as soon as I've worked out a plan. Don't worry, and keep your head down."

With that, the phone went dead. Vee was standing in front of me with a mug of hot steaming coffee, and boy, did I need it.

"What are we going to do, Steve?" Vee asked, looking rather worried, I must say. "Do you think we should hand it all back to Margaret?"

"I only know what you are going to do at the moment Vee." I said taking a sip of the coffee.

"What am I going to do, Steve?" Her face was looking quite bamboozled, to say the least.

"You, Vee, you are going to see a prenatal Doctor about the pregnancy pains you have had all night. Sorry, Vee, but I cannot allow you out at the farmhouse today. They are surely on to us, and it could get very dangerous for you to be there."

Vee tried to interrupt, but I held up my hand palm towards her. "Sorry my love, no compromise. This is too susceptible to big trouble tomorrow, and I just cannot and will not under any circumstances put you in harm's way. That's too much for me to bear, and I know Charles will be of the same mind." I said it firmly, shaking my head and looking straight at her.

And talking of the devil, the back door opened, and in rushed Charles. He walked straight over to Vee and gave her a cuddle.

"You OK, my love?" he said, holding Vee's cheeks between his hands. Vee nodded, smiling a half smile. "And you, Steve?" he asked glancing across towards me.

"Sure Charles, I'm fine; just a little shocked at what has happened." I smiled, and beckoned to him to follow me. I opened the bedroom door, and pointed down to Mahmood and Ahmed, tied up, gagged and sprawled together on the bedroom floor.

"I've been on to Paul at HQ, and he said that he would contact you as to where we should put these bastards."

"He already contacted me while I was driving over. You were right about Paul, Steve. That guy's good; he doesn't stand around, he buys a round. And I agree with you, he's a good lad to have in your corner, especially when the chips are down. He's sending a car at this very moment with a couple of spooks, to make sure these two sleazes disappear somewhere, till the operation is completed. He said they will phone me as soon as they are in the neighbourhood, to make a time and place for us to hand them over. I didn't think it was a good idea to do it here, and also, I didn't think it too healthy to let the spooks know where we are working from. Paul, bless his cotton socks, suggested it would be best to hand them over in a police station yard, somewhere as close to here as possible, what do you think?"

"Sorry, Charles," I said. "That is what I had in mind earlier, but I've had a rethink. We must do this alone, and not involve the spooks. If they make a fuck-up, Vee and I will be in deep, deep shit. No, Charles, we must do this the hard way, and do it ourselves."

I could hear Vee running water in the kitchen, so I presumed that she was washing up or making more coffee. I indicated to Charles to follow me, and walked up the passageway to the main bedroom. As we both entered, I closed the door behind us, and walked across to the window.

"Charles, I need a couple of things done urgently, as soon as we've got those two little shits in the bedroom out of the way."

I glanced over to Charles; he was looking at me with that formidable cheeky smile on his face. "You know me, Steve, just name them and consider them done. What are we looking at?"

I walked over to the window and stared out into the garden; I could see a few drops of rain rolling down the window but nothing much to worry about. My mind was moving fast now but to tell the truth I wasn't sure it was moving in the right direction.

"There's a few small things I want you to do. Firstly, I want you to check the car and the house for bugs. Somehow they got on to us, and we must find out how they did it. Then, in the morning,

Charles, I need that broken window in the kitchen fixed; and it must look like it was never broken. You know: old putty, and the painting must look just like the original. And then, Charles, we come to the tricky bit. I need a synthetic all-in-one environmental suit, with shoes, gloves and a fitted respirator. It needs to be dark green or brown, not one of these bloody bright yellow or phosphorescent things they wear in the labs. If I need to use it, I will be out on the moor, and I don't want to stick out like a sore thumb."

Charles was nodding his head all through my list of requirements. I knew he didn't have to write anything down: I knew that he had the memory of a bloody elephant and then some.

"Charles, I am very worried that some of the bastards may leave earlier than anticipated. I am more or less guessing that they will leave the farmhouse about the twenty-second or twenty-third of December. This will then give them time to get to their targets, and do reconnaissance on their various shopping centres. But some could leave earlier. It's all rather worrying, really, and mainly because Mohammed always seems to be holding back on a lot of very relevant points; that could be for a number of reasons that I haven't fathomed out yet."

"Another thing, Charles," I went on. "Because Mohammed seems to be keeping an awful lot up his bloody sleeve, and we don't know if this is an ego thing or not, I don't think we can take any chances, and we must not under any circumstances underestimate him. He is far from a fool, but I feel his ultra-egotism will be his downfall. We must seriously take into consideration that someone could leave and be driving to their target at a much earlier date. If this happens, all the Malls throughout England would be in a very unfavourable position, and we won't know which ones they will be; so we will need some contingency planning. I am going to need at least fifteen magnetic bugs, one for each vehicle. I'll place one externally on each car over the next few days, so that if anyone should leave early, we will know exactly where they are, at any given time day or night. We had better have three tracking devices also, one for each of us, so that any one of us at least will be able keep track of them, in case the other two are unavailable at the time."

I stood and walked over to the window; my mind was very busy now. Everything was moving so fast, and I didn't have enough information at hand to make solid solutions; I also knew that if I was to make any wrong decisions at this stage in the operation, it would be fatal.

"Another thing, and also very important, Charles. You must pay for the suit in cash. I don't want it to be traced back to you or me. And last but, not least, Charles: I cannot take Vee out to the farm today. If they are on to us, it could get very dangerous; and, in those situations, it's better that I only have myself to worry about. So I want you to be here with her tomorrow."

"Sure, kid," he nodded. "Anything else?"

"Yes, Charles. Did you get any word on the fifteen sim cards I mentioned?"

"Yes. I put it through to HQ, and Paul said he would speak to the technical guys and come back to me as soon as possible; as of yet, I haven't heard anything."

"When Paul comes back to you on the sim cards, Charles, get him on to getting the bugs and trackers to us as soon as possible; they have to be in place within the next two days at the latest."

I turned and walked back over to Charles. I looked down at him as he sat on the bed. I was wondering how a man of his age never seemed to get overwrought in situations like this. He was always this very mild-mannered man, no matter what ensued around him.

"Well, Charles, that's about it for now; unless, maybe, you've got a lucky rabbit's-foot in your pocket for me tomorrow."

We both laughed, and I made to walk out of the bedroom, but Charles put his hand firmly on my shoulder.

"Why am I getting the feeling that you're not telling me everything, Steve?" he said, with concern in his eyes.

"Well, Charles," I said with a grin, "maybe it's because I'm not telling you everything. No disrespect, Charles, but at the moment, I don't know everything myself. I'm living on the edge at the moment, guessing and counter-guessing. All I can say is, the less both you and Vee know about how I'm going to end this matter, the better it will be for both of you."

We walked back into the lounge, and Charles was looking at my mug of coffee on the table with a "gee, that smells great" look on his face. Then, just in time, Vee came up behind him, and handed him a mug of coffee and a nice hot bagel on a side plate.

"Here, Charles," she said in a quiet voice. "You need to get some sustenance into your stomach. You too, Steve," she said, handing me a bagel and giving me a peck on the cheek.

"OK, Charles," I said, speaking through a mouthful of bagel, "I've got it. Phone Paul now and tell him to halt the spooks arrival, tell him we have sorted it out ourselves, and thank him for his instantaneous response."

"What the fuck have you got in mind, Steve?" Charles said looking, very worried.

"I'll let you know as soon as I've worked it out Charles; but you can be assured that it's much safer not to implicate the spooks in this. Too much now hangs on the outcome, both for the country and, let's not forget, for both Vee and myself. I know now that no matter what the cost, I have got to do this my way. Then I'll know that everything will turn out in everyone's favour – that's not including the terrorists, of course."

I walked through to the second bedroom where Ahmed and Mahmood were, and indicated for Charles to follow me. Both

Mahmood and Ahmed were very much awake now, with big wide eyes and looking very much like rats caught in a trap.

"OK, Charles, let me introduce you. This is Mahmood, and this is Ahmed. Mahmood and Ahmed, please meet my friend Charles." Mahmood and Ahmed just stared back. I could see that their eyes were filled with fear.

"OK, Charles; let's go through all their pockets. I want their mobiles, wallets, keys and anything else that they could be carrying."

Both Mahmood and Ahmed had a look of fear in their eyes now. I checked out Ahmed's facial injuries; it wasn't as bad as it seemed earlier. All of the blood had come from a nose bleed, and that had now healed.

I sat on the bed with their two mobiles, and checked who they had been in contact with over the last twenty-four hours. Most of the calls had been between themselves but Mahmood had been in contact with Mohammed three times, and Mohammed had contacted him about seven hours before they broke into the house, so I was sure there was the possibility that they were under his orders to do the break-in, and this obviously meant that we could have been compromised somehow. I cleared all the calls to and from Mohammed. There was also a call made to Pakistan at three p.m. in the afternoon. All this made me feel sick in my stomach. It meant that Mohammed could be on to us or at least that he was not convinced enough as to who we were. My mind rolled back over the last few days, looking for something, maybe something very small that could have given us away, but I couldn't come up with anything at all. I knew for sure now that I couldn't under any circumstances allow Vee to go back to the farm with me tomorrow; that was for sure.

I walked out of the bedroom and headed up the passageway towards the main bedroom, indicating that Charles should follow me.

"Look at this, Charles," I said, handing him the business card that Ahmed had picked up.

"Where the fuck did the card come from, Steve?" Charles said looking at me wide eyed.

"It fell out of some papers that were in Vee's briefcase when Ahmed was going through them; somehow Vee must have unknowingly left it amongst the papers in her briefcase. It gives them her real name, and even a photograph to go with it; also, Charles, they saw last night's empty wine bottle and glasses, which would be a dead giveaway. Salim never drank any alcohol at all. This gives them everything they need to be certain that we are not who we are supposed to be. No, Charles, these guys have got to be kept well under the radar until the operation is fully completed. And Charles, please don't say anything to Vee about them finding the business card. I don't want to worry her unduly. She has got enough worries on her bloody plate as it is."

Charles was sitting on the bed going through their wallets, which he had brought through, "Nothing here to worry about, Steve; just driving licences, a couple of pounds and a few pictures, probably of family; also, an entry card to Leeds University. There are two bunches of keys, but no car keys that I could find."

"Don't worry about the car keys," I said, taking them out of my pocket. "I grabbed them when I ejected Mahmood from the car." I smiled and held them up, to show Charles.

We walked out of the bedroom and back to the lounge. I slumped into a chair, and rechecked the overseas number that had been made from Mahmood's mobile.

"Charles," I said, handing the mobile to him. "Phone Paul and give him this number; maybe HQ will be able to find out who it was that he called. You never know, it might just be his family; if it's not, then we've got even more trouble – and more trouble I can do without, just now. Oh, and don't say anything with regard to these two little shits. If he asks you, just say you don't know, but you think that I have sorted it all out."

I went out of the back door and brought their car up the driveway and round to the back of the house. It was very cold now, and raining again, a very light drizzle; but there was no wind at all to speak of.

As I entered the back door into the kitchen, Charles was standing by the stove, holding another cup of coffee in both hands.

"I've checked the house for bugs, Steve," Charles said as I came into the kitchen. "It all came up negative, if you don't include the two Muslim bugs on the bedroom floor. I'll check the car now, and let's see what comes up there."

"OK, Charles; but drink your coffee first. It's bloody cold out there, and raining a bit."

"I phoned Paul, by the way," Charles said, taking a sip of his coffee. "He was still at HQ. He didn't ask any questions, and said he would get back to me as soon as he gets an answer from their technical department on the mobile number; also he said that he did manage to halt the spooks who were coming to pick up Ahmed and Mahmood. I also asked for the bugs and trackers to be sent with the sim cards, and told him they must be in my hands by early tomorrow. He also said something peculiar, he said, 'This is pea-knuckle, Charles; when will he' (meaning you of course) 'want the Sherman tank?' I hope that's a joke between you and Paul, Steve, or maybe I should I start to worry a bit."

I grabbed him by the shoulders laughingly, and explained the little joke which Paul, Margaret and I had had. When I explained, I'm sure I saw a look of relief on his face.

Vee handed me a cup of coffee, and gave me a peck on the cheek, she was fully dressed now in a light blue polo neck sweater, light grey trousers and a pair of black knee high boots. She looked up at me; her eyes were very questioning, but she said nothing. I gestured towards the lounge, and both Charles and Vee followed me through.

I glanced at my watch. It was nearly three p.m., so we didn't really have very much time to do what had to be done; and it looked like I wasn't going to get any more sleep tonight.

"Charles," I said, sliding into a chair. "We can check the car for bugs and listening devices later. I need you with me, but due to the new circumstances, I don't want to leave Vee here alone; so I want Vee to follow me, in Mahmood's car, and you can drive your car in at the rear. I'll take the little shits in the boot of the Mercedes. They both stay in a little cottage north of here on the edge of the moors; it's about ten, maybe fifteen minutes' drive from here. When we get there, I want you to help me get them into the cottage. Then I want you both to high-tail it back here in your car, and I'll be about an hour or so behind you."

"Vee," I said, glancing in her direction. "Wear gloves. I don't want any fingerprints left in their car," I held up the car keys. Here are the keys. You stay right behind me and in front of Charles."

Charles just nodded as he rose from his chair. That's what I liked about Charles: he trusted and understood me, and never ever questioned my reasoning.

"OK, Steve," he said, putting his coffee cup on the table and putting on his coat. "What are we waiting for? Let's get this bloody show on the road then."

As I walked through to the kitchen, I grabbed Vee's rubber gloves from the sink, and stuffed them into Ahmed's duffle coat pocket, that I was still wearing.

Charles and I put their wallets and mobiles back into Mahmood and Ahmed's pockets, after cleaning them of prints. Then I checked again, to make sure that their bonds were still secured.

"Vee," I said, pointing down at her hands. "Gloves love, gloves, you must wear gloves. I told you: I don't want your fingerprints left in their car."

"Sorry, Steve, "I'll get them now," she said, running down the passageway and coming back out seconds later, with a pair of black leather gloves on her hands.

Charles looked knowingly across to me, as if to say, "I recognize what you are going to do," but he never said a word.

Charles and I carried Mahmood and Ahmed out and put them both into the boot of the Mercedes. As I was closing the boot lid, I just saw Ahmed's eyes. They were as big as saucers and showed only deep, deep fear. I gave him a very wry smile, and slammed the boot lid closed. I jumped into the Merc and started the engine, while Charles and Vee walked towards the other two cars. As I turned right out of the driveway, I saw Vee pull in right behind me in Mahmood's car, and Charles pulling out and settled in right behind Vee.

We arrived at the cottage well within fifteen minutes, as the roads were very quiet at that time of the morning; in fact, we never saw even one car. The cottage was at least a mile away from any other buildings in the surrounding area, and I presumed that it must originally have been built as a sort of holiday home or something, or maybe even as a farm labourer's cottage. I drove up the driveway, got out of the car, and opened the boot. I reached into Mahmood's duffle coat pocket for the keys to the cottage, and walked to the front door. As I entered the main lounge, I switched on the light and went straight through to the kitchen. There was a gas meter on the wall by the fridge. It was one of those prepaid ones. I checked the reading. It seemed OK; it had enough in it.

I went back out to the Mercedes. Charles was already standing by the open boot. It only took a couple of minutes to carry Mahmood and Ahmed, kicking and squirming, into the lounge area. There were two two-seater corduroy settees on either side of the television. We threw Mahmood roughly on one, and Ahmed on the other. They were even more wide-eyed now and I could see the stark trepidation in their eyes. Their faces were a deathly pale, and both of them were breathing very heavily.

I quickly ushered Vee and Charles out into the driveway. I gave Vee a kiss on the cheek as I opened the passenger side door of Charles's car for her, and she more or less just slumped down into the low seat. I smiled and touched the end of her nose with my index finger; Charles climbed into the driver's seat, neither of them uttering a word.

"OK, Charles get straight back to the house. I'll be there in about an hour or so." With that, I closed the passenger side door and stood back. Charles unquestioningly gunned the car engine, pulled out into the road, and set off back to the house.

I took Vee's rubber gloves from the car, put them on and rushed back into the house. First, I checked that Mahmood and Ahmed were still fully secured. I opened the fridge; there was a pan of cold stew or curry on the shelf, with a dish of rice alongside it. I took the stew out, and put it on the gas stove, turning the heat up high. The rice I put into the microwave oven.

It took about five minutes for the stew to burn and boil over, and make one hell of a bloody mess, all over the gas stove top. I switched off the gas tap and took out two plates and two spoons from the drawer, and set them down on the table. Next, I checked that all the windows and doors were firmly closed.

I spent about five minutes going through drawers and cupboards in the lounge and the bed rooms, there were two briefcases in the main bedroom full of papers. I had no time to take a good look at them now, so I took them into the lounge and put them by the front door; also, I took the flash light that was hanging on the side of the fridge, and put it on top of the briefcases.

I took all the knives and sharp instruments; also a dish cloth that I had soaked in water from the tap, and put them in a Tesco plastic bag and placed them also by the door, with the two briefcases.

I took a couple of dish cloths from the sink and went through to the lounge. Mahmood and Ahmed were now getting very restless indeed, and I could now see the absolute pure terror on their faces. Well, they should know all about terror; they were terrorists, weren't they. I dragged them both from the settees and on to the floor, checking that their bonds were still secure. It was a bit of a struggle to hold them back to back, as they were both struggling quite a lot, and I didn't want to be too heavy-handed, as it could leave too much bruising. It took me about five minutes to complete the job, but I had managed to secure Mahmood and Ahmed's hands and feet together with the dish cloths. So they were now tied up back to back, and they didn't stand much of a chance of getting free for a while.

I looked around the lounge to check that everything was in place, and then went back through to the kitchen.

Switching on the gas tap, I lit the flame, and with a wooden spoon I had taken from the kitchen drawer, I poured a couple of spoons of the stew onto the gas stove, until it dowsed the flame. Switching off the electricity at the mains, I then turned up the gas under the stew, and headed out of the front door, picking up the two briefcases, the Tesco bag and the flash light on my way. After locking the house door, I put the keys in my pocket and walked over to Mahmood and Ahmed's car, I quickly rubbed down everywhere that I could have left fingerprints, with the damp kitchen towel. Then, locking their car doors, I got into my car and took off up the road, heading towards Leeds. I was looking for some kind of wooded area that I could pull into for a while that would put me out of sight of the road. About half a mile further up the road, I came across a farm gate that was open. The wall was a little higher than the car, so it would give me the cover I needed for a while. Getting out of the car, I first checked that the ground wasn't too muddy, and that there weren't any obstructions in the way. Hell, all I needed at that moment was to get the bloody car stuck in a muddy ditch.

I reversed the car cautiously behind the wall, switched off the lights, and adjusted the inside light so that it wouldn't come on when I opened and closed the door. Then I just sat and listened to the silence for a few moments. I was tired, as I hadn't had very much sleep, really; and it's at times like this that a person makes stupid mistakes. I took a couple of minutes just to go over the last hour or so, looking for an odd mistake that I could have made. Afterwards, thinking it all through, I felt quite confident that I had pretty much covered just about everything, and I was in the clear.

I put the radio on low and had to change stations abruptly, as Mohammed's cousin had it tuned in to some bloody Arabic or Muslim station. I found a classical music station, and listened to it for about twenty minutes or so.

I had left the car engine running and the heater on low, so I wasn't cold. It was just nice and comfortable but not too comfortable, as I didn't want to fall asleep. I took the wet towel out of the plastic bag, and wiped my face from time to time. Then I had a look through their two briefcases, that I had taken from the house. But they were just full of university papers and books, and nothing that would give me insight as to what had encouraged them both to break into my house.

Time seemed to be standing still. I must have looked at my bloody watch twenty times at least in the previous ten minutes or so. As soon as the forty-five minutes were up, I drove out on to the road, and set off back to the cottage. It had stopped raining now, but there was a strong breeze blowing. I presume that it had blown away the rain clouds, as I could see a few stars in the sky from time to time.

Everything was quiet, and the cottage was in total darkness. I quickly walked up to the door, listening for any movement inside. Just to ensure that all was as it should be, I went round to the rear of the house, and looked through the window. Both Ahmed and Mahmood were still lying prone on the floor, and both were still tied up back to back, although I noticed that they had moved their position, to some extent.

Placing the wet towel over my mouth, and putting the rubber gloves on, I picked up the torch and entered the cottage through the front door. First shutting off the gas tap on the stove, I then quickly went round, opening all the other doors and windows as I passed them. The smell of the gas was sickeningly strong. I rushed outside, and gasped in a big lungful of fresh air. My eyes were burning, and my skin was tingling everywhere. I stood for a while and took a few very deep convulsive breaths, I knew that with this steady breeze blowing and all the doors and windows wide open it shouldn't take long to bring the area down to a less lethal level, so I sat in the Mercedes car seat for a while, taking in deep breaths of air.

I soaked the towel again at the tap in the garden and rubbed it vigorously over my face and eyes, then tied it back around my neck, and lifting it over my mouth and nose, I went back into the lounge. I checked both Ahmed and Mahmood's pulse. There wasn't any; both were quite dead. I quickly took off the masking tape and the rest of the strappings from their hands and feet, and quickly rushed outside again, to gasp in some more very much needed fresh air.

I placed all the masking tape and strappings into a plastic bag, and put them on the back seat of the car. I was feeling pretty groggy now from the gas inhalation that I had had, so I sat on the car seat for a while, and took a few very deep breaths of very needed air for a few minutes. My head was sort of pounding right behind my eyes. I pushed the seat back and laid down, to try to get more air into my lungs. It took about five minutes before I felt ready to re-enter the cottage.

As I entered the cottage again, I could feel that the gas had dissipated quite a lot; but I still used the wet towel. I lifted Ahmed on to one of the settees and Mahmood up on to the opposite one, so that they were both facing the television. I tried to make them look very casual and homely. It took about five minutes looking around the place to make sure that I had not missed anything or left anything behind that would make the job look like anything other than accidental death. Everything seemed fine, so I put both their cell phones on a side table, and their house keys on the dining room table. I switched on the electricity and the lights in the lounge and kitchen, and turned on the television to the Sky News programme. I checked the gas meter reading, and it was very low indeed, making everything perfect, if that's the right thing to say.

I closed all the windows and doors again, and went back out to the car, grabbing their two briefcases and the knives and sharp instruments that I had removed earlier, putting the knives in the kitchen drawer, and the briefcases in the bedrooms where I had found them. I went around, closing all the windows that I had opened, and lastly I switched on the gas tap on the stove to low, and left hurriedly, closing the door behind me, and checking that the Yale lock was in the locked position.

It took me about fifteen minutes or so to get back to the house. There was no rain and there wasn't any traffic at all on the roads again. As I pulled up into the driveway the front door opened, and Charles came running out to the car and opened my door before I had come to a standstill. Now I could really see that the heat was also getting to him.

"Everything go all right, Steve?" he asked excitedly, taking the plastic bag from me. I could see in his eyes that all this had taken its toll, even on him.

"Yes, sure, Charles," I replied. "All I need now is a couple of hours sleep before I go back to the farm and find out how much music I have to face."

I walked into the house. Vee gave me a kiss and a big hug. Neither Vee nor Charles had asked any questions. Vee did mention the fact that I smelt; it must have been the gas that was on my clothes that she could smell.

I got about two hours sleep, waking to the smell of coffee and toast. I ate the toast, drank the coffee, and jumped into the shower. All I could think about was what was going to happen when I reached the farm. I had no idea what would be said, or whether Mohammed even knew about them breaking into the house. Maybe they had done it on their own initiative and suspicions, and Mohammed knew nothing about it at all; but somehow I just couldn't believe that. Anyway, I was sure that all would be revealed one way or the other today, and very soon.

Chapter Thirteen

After organising Charles and Vee for the day, I was all ready to leave, when Charles's mobile rang. I listened to Charles's part of the conversation, and gathered that it was Paul.

"Seems everything is OK, Steve," Charles said, smiling. "That overseas number we found was to his mother or Grandmother. So that should ease your mind a bit, eh? He also said that the sim cards, the bugs and trackers are on their way, and will be delivered directly to me as early as late this morning."

I nodded, and smiled at both of them. "OK, you guys; I've got to go. I'll be back early this evening. I'll use the excuse of being tired, and worried about Vee. You, Vee, can phone me sometime during the day, as if you are giving me a report on what the prenatal doctor had to say. If I say to you that I cannot get away early, then you know I have a problem; but if I put Mohammed or Mari on the mobile to talk with you, then you will know that everything is fine and you don't have to worry. That OK with both of you?"

Both of them just nodded, and I must say that they looked a little spooked.

Vee came over, and gave me a big hug. "I think you should take this as a just-in-case, Steve." It was the Walther PPK, in an ankle strap holster.

"Yes, good idea; maybe I should." I knelt down and quickly strapped it to my right ankle, and covered it with my trousers.

Then, on thinking about it, I realised that none of them would be armed; and should anyone at all see the Walther, the whole bloody programme would be blown. I took the weapon off again, handed it back to Vee, and gave her a hug. "Sorry, but on second thoughts I think it's better if I don't take it, Vee. If any one should see it, it would blow the whole programme out of the window; they are not armed, so I think it safer this way."

With that, I got in the car, gunned the engine, and began the twenty minute trip to the farm. There wasn't much traffic on the way; there was a bit of sleet falling, but nothing at all to worry about. I must admit that I was a bit more than apprehensive as to what to expect when I got out to the farmhouse, but I thought I could live with that.

As I pulled into the driveway at the farm, the loose stones rattled again, as they hit the underside of the car. I pulled the car over by the barn area, and reversed it around to position the car to face the gate, just in case I had to make a quick exit. I didn't lock the car, either; and I left the keys dangling there in the ignition.

Mohammed came rushing out to greet me, and I could see Mari standing just inside the door out of the cold.

"Hi, Salim! I expected you earlier," he said. Then he looked into the car, and saw that Vee wasn't there. "Where's Sharma?" he said, opening the car door for me.

"Oh" I replied, "We had a bit of a scare last night. We were up half the night, as Sharma was having pains in her stomach. I thought it best that she went to the Prenatal Clinic and have a check-up. It's not worth taking chances as this is our first child. She said she would phone me as soon as she leaves the clinic, and let me know if there is a problem or not, but I'm pretty sure she will be fine, I think most of this is from the flight, and the shock of the bloody cold weather that we were faced with on our arrival into the country."

"Oh my dear God!" It was Mari speaking. She had overheard our conversation. "When did she go to the clinic, Steve? You should have phoned us, and maybe I could have gone to the clinic with her."

"She went about an hour ago," I replied, "She took a taxi. I don't think it's anything to worry about, Mari but I thought it was better to be safe than sorry. It's probably the long flight that has caught up with her; flying is always stressful for everyone isn't it? Then, also, there's the cold weather that could have something to do with it. Anyway, we will know in a couple of hours, I'm sure; Sharma said she would phone as soon as she had seen the doctor."

We all walked into the lounge. There was a big fire going, with the flames gushing up the chimney, making the room warm, and very comfortable indeed.

Ishmael and Elijah were sitting on the settee by the wall; Mohammed sank into his chair, and I followed suit, sitting on the chair opposite him. Mohammed related what had happened to Sharma to Ishmael and Elijah.

"With the grace of God, she will be fine, I'm sure," Ishmael said with, funnily enough, a great deal of meaning. This gave me a great deal of confidence, as I was now pretty sure that Mahmood and Ahmed had not been in touch with Mohammed about breaking into the house. So maybe they had done the break-in on their own initiative? Only time would tell.

With that, Mari came into the lounge with a tray of food and four cups of coffee. She placed the tray on the coffee table, and handed out a cup of coffee and a plate of food to everyone in the room; then she went straight back into the kitchen.

"Well, Salim," Mohammed said, "I have very good news for you." He had that 'aren't I the greatest' egotistical look on his face again.

"We have nearly finished all the IEDs, and they look great. I will show you a finished one today, and I know you will be very pleased with what I have achieved."

He glanced over his shoulder, and pointed towards Ishmael. "Ishmael, by the way," he went on, "was the one whom we must all thank, as he organised to get the semtex and the anthrax spores into the country; so without him, we would not be in the position that we are now. I always like to pay tribute to people when it's deserved."

I sat looking at Ishmael for a second or two, wondering how I was going to get Ishmael to tell me how on earth he accomplished it. But I didn't have to ask, as he was so confident, and proud of his achievement, that he just blurted it out.

"I have lots of connections with some of the Chinese that are smuggling Chinks into the country up in County Durham, for slave labour and prostitution. All I had to do was to ask them to meet a boat out at sea, and take the boxes on board their yacht, and bring them into the country. They know all the angles these bloody Chinese. We had to pay them a lot of cash, though; I think it was three thousand pounds. But it is only a small price to pay for the big bangs that they are going to give us in a few days' time. Praise be to Allah, God is great!" he shouted loudly.

We all replied in unison, "Praise be to Allah, God is great!"

I could even hear Mari's outcry from the kitchen.

"Friends, friends, from the bottom of my heart," I said, getting up from my chair. I was feeling fully relaxed now knowing that no one had any inkling as to who we really were. "I," I said, "and all the people not only the people of Pakistan, but all Muslims throughout the world, who are the disciples of the Jihad against the infidels of the Christian world, will be very, very proud of you all; and I can assure every last one of you that I will personally make sure that you will be given the respect and admiration that you all very much deserve. I have got to say that what I have seen so far has given me a great boost, knowing that the people of the Muslim world still have the moral fibre and aptitude to keep the Jihad of our people ongoing, and with such vigour, tenacity and determination, as is necessary to achieve our goal."

Everyone clapped their hands together vigorously after my speech; all this was helping to instigate a feeling of security and relief in my mind.

Mohammed rose to his feet. "Salim," he said, with that proud egotistical look on his face. "You do not know what it means to all of us to hear such words from the top people of the Jihad; and I can assure you that, after this, our first attempt, and I repeat first attempt, there will be many, many more, and even more sophisticated attacks that will be carried out by ourselves, until the infidels are brought to the reality that there is but one God, Allah. God is great, Praise be to Allah!"

Everyone in the room jumped to their feet and shouted loudly, "God is great, Praise be to Allah!"

Their eyes were shining with excitement, and I could see that my revelation had put them all on a high second to none; and it had also helped me with my insecurity feeling, after the previous night's debacle.

After everyone had calmed down a few degrees or so, Mohammed, looking at his watch, glanced across the room towards me.

"Mahmood and Ahmed should have been here over an hour ago. Where the hell can they be, Salim?"

He picked up his mobile and dialled a number, waited for a while then switched it off. "I just get voice mail. Shit, where the bloody hell are they?"

"Maybe they got lost, Mohammed" I said, "Even I had some difficulty getting here yesterday; it's not the best position in town you know."

With that everyone burst out laughing, and the subject was, thankfully, changed.

"Ok Salim," Mohammed said. "We cannot wait any longer for them. Let's go upstairs, and I can show you my finished product. I think you will be very pleased with what you see. I will show it to everyone else tomorrow, when the whole bunch is here, but you, Salim, shall be the first person to observe our beautiful devices of destruction. Come, please, upstairs!"

I followed behind Mohammed, up the stairs and into the front bedroom. As we entered the bedroom, I was quite surprised to see Akram sitting in a chair at the table, putting the sim cards into the mobile phones; he didn't seem as hyperactive as he had been the previous day; maybe he was on some kind of medication now. His head didn't move, only his eyelids, as he looked up at us; then, just as quickly, his eyes went back down to the mobile that he had in his hand. He was quite freaky, I thought; and somehow he gave me the willies.

"Akram," Mohammed said, placing both his hands on Akram's shoulder, "has been helping me with some of the technical components, such as the mobiles and the wiring; at the moment, he is putting all the sim cards into the mobiles. Then all I have to do tonight and tomorrow is to put everything together, and make them into the devices that are going to help to bring about the start to the purification of all Muslims around the world, and the demise and downfall of the Christian world as we know it now."

"It's good that you have help, Mohammed," I said, walking around the table. "When you get too much pressure you are far more predisposed to making mistakes, and we don't want mistakes, especially at this point of time in the operation, do we?"

"You are right there, Salim, I have worked too hard to implement this operation, and I want it to be perfect when it comes to fruition. Let me show you how I am going to put them together. Then, maybe, you can give your opinion, and maybe some necessary advice," he said, moving one of the box briefcases on to the end of the table.

I knew he wasn't looking for advice, as he had that 'I'm the greatest' expression in his deep set eyes again, as he always had, when about to demonstrate his ill-begotten genius to someone.

He opened the briefcase, showing me with great pride the inner workings of his masterpiece. The mobiles were central, as before, with the semtex laid on either side; the wiring was very neatly laid out, with the detonators just hanging loose from the wiring. Altogether, it was one of the most beautiful exhibitions of engineering that I had ever seen.

"Now, Salim, let me show you the most important parts, the parts that are going to wreak the devastation that I described to you yesterday."

He bent down, opened a box, and took out a plastic folder that seemed to have metal objects in some sort of bubble wrap. It was just about the size of the briefcase, and looked quite heavy.

"This," he said very proudly, "Is full of ten millimetre ball bearings: one thousand three hundred per packet, in all. There will be two in every briefcase: one at the top and one in the bottom, meaning that when the semtex blows, two thousand six hundred ten millimetre ball bearings will rip into everyone within a hundred yards of the detonation point. That will cause far more devastation than two martyrs with AK 47s on automatic fire. Well, Salim, what do you think so far?"

"Brilliant, just brilliant, Mohammed; I know of very few people who could organise such an operation of this stature, and, on top of that, to organise how to implement it without the loss of life to our Muslim brotherhood. You have done exceptionally well, Mohammed, and I cannot fault you on anything at all."

What I had said was reasonable even in my eyes; the implementation, the makeup and the ideas for detonation were close to perfection, and I knew that his only problem was me, and my only problem was to make sure that this devastating act of terrorism was never ever to come to fruition.

"Now, Salim." His eyes were now gleaming; he reached down to another box and took out the plastic packet of anthrax, about the same size as the ball bearings packet. "This is the cherry on top; in these packets, Salim, we have anthrax spores, as I showed you yesterday. Can you imagine the havoc this will wreak on the infidels? There will also be two packets in each briefcase, one at the very bottom and one at the top."

Mohammed was outwardly beaming with pride; as he demonstrated his unbelievable plan of destruction I felt quite sick in my stomach just listening to him. But I had to show him my full support and try to invigorate him in his passion. The more I did, the more trust Mohammed would have in me, and the more chance I would have to disrupt the operation before it came to fruition.

We went back down to the lounge, and Mari brought us all a mug of very hot, very spicy soup, and a very large crispy bread roll.

Mari stood in front of me, looking rather worried, as she asked, "Have you heard from Sharma, Salim?"

"No, Mari, not as yet; but I'm sure I will hear from her, very soon."

As I spoke, my mobile rang; I looked at the face, and saw Sharma's name.

"Talk of the devil: it's Sharma," I said, switching the mobile on.

"Hi, Sharma! What did the doctor say? Yes, well that's perfect, I'm really pleased. Yes, I will be there soon; would you like to speak to Mari? Both she and Mohammed have been quite worried about you."

I handed my mobile over to Mari and they both had a quick chat on her pregnancy and health things.

Mohammed was sitting in his chair, breaking his roll and dipping it into his soup.

"Good to hear that she is well, Salim," he said, through a mouthful of bread roll. "She must be very careful with the first child, Salim; I think you should get back to her now, and give her a bit of support."

"Yes, sure, Mohammed; I'm sure you are right," I said, trying to look relieved at the news. "I think maybe a little moral support would be a blessing to her. This morning, she was very worried indeed. Females are always in need of support at times like this, and we are in a foreign country, with no family or close friends to call on. Yes, Mohammed," I said, standing up, "I think you are right. I should get back to her as soon as possible."

As I got to the door, Mohammed put both his hands on my shoulders; he had that pompous look on his face again.

"Tomorrow morning, Salim," he sort of whispered, "everyone will be here, and I will, by then, have completed all the IEDs. I will be able to describe to them the entire project, showing everyone the full operation, and also the finished product; and on top of that, I will be able to give them all their final instructions on their final individual assignments and locations. I will need you to stand beside me; this will give me support, and it will also give my disciples a shot in the arm, in the understanding that we are not alone in this war of attrition that we are implementing against the infidels. What do you think, Salim?"

"Yes, Mohammed, you are right; last night I was going through your plan, and your ideas on the execution of it, and I have got to say that from when you started showing me the details of the operation that you have come up with, I found that everything that you had related to me was exemplary in every way, and I never once thought that you should change anything. I can only commend you in every way, and I can assure you that everyone back in Pakistan will hear about it from me; your name will be on everyone's lips, and your operation will stay in everyone's minds and hearts throughout the Muslim world; and it will be even more remembered by those bloody Christian infidels for many, many years to come."

Mohammed stood there, reaping in the praise that I was heaping on his ego, with that nauseating "I'm the greatest" look on his face again.

"Thank you, thank you, Salim; with such praise coming from you, you just don't know what it means to me, and it gives me hope and the strength to carry the Jihad for the Muslim people all around the world to an overwhelming and incomprehensible victory here in the United Kingdom."

"That is good for the Muslim people, Mohammed," I said, putting on my "you're the greatest" look.

"Oh, I don't think I told you, Mohammed; I am going to mosque today to prey with Kareem – remember, the Imam whom we met at the airport – I promised I would go before I go back, and seeing that everything is now coming to a head, I thought it would be better to go today. We will be sleeping over at his place, so I may be a little late tomorrow morning, not knowing the roads too well."

"OK, Salim, that's fine; please give Sharma, and also Kareem, our best regards; and tell him that I will also go and pray with him some time in the very near future."

"I will do just that, Mohammed," I replied, stepping out into the yard and the cold wind.

I waved goodbye to Mari, who was standing by the door as Mohammed walked me out to the car. It was absolutely freezing outside, so I just jumped in the car, gunned the engine, waved at

Mohammed, and set off on my way back to the house. I must say that I was very relieved indeed that my day was finished and that it had gone so well. I was very surprised to find that they were not on to me; and I was totally at a loss as to what Mahmood and Ahmed had been doing breaking into the house. Furthermore, now they had left us for greener pastures, I supposed I would never ever know. I could only assume that they had done it on their own initiative, for reasons unknown.

I was in high spirits, driving back, and there was very little traffic, so I drove quite fast, since I was dying to give Vee and Charles the rundown on my day of trepidation out at the farmhouse.

On my arrival, I was whisked into the house, and given a cup of much needed strong, sweet coffee. Both Sharma and Charles had very questioning, and somewhat apprehensive, looks on their faces; and I knew that they were waiting with bated breath, to hear how everything had gone at the farmhouse.

I sat drinking my coffee, and related the day's incidents to them. I could see the immense relief on their faces when I told them that I was sure Mahmood and Ahmed had acted, for some unknown reason, alone; and I was sure that there was no need to worry that the mission was blown.

After Charles and I had had a few very strong whiskies, all three of us sat down to dinner. Sharma had made a lovely chicken curry, and from the way Charles gulped it down and asked for seconds, I could see that he had been eating from takeaways far too much while he had been up here in Leeds.

"By the way, Steve," he said, wiping his mouth on a napkin, "I have received the sim cards from HQ; they delivered fifteen in all, and they are all set on one number. Is that OK with you?"

"Yes, Charles, that's just great. I will need them tomorrow, and I will just have to devise a way of getting them into the mobiles over the next couple of days. What about the bugs and trackers? Are they exactly what you asked them for?" I asked.

"Got them, too," he said, smiling, "All of fifteen bugs and three trackers; top of the range, with about a two and a half mile radius on the ground. I cannot believe this guy, Paul; sometimes I get to thinking he's better than I was in the old days."

"No way, Charles!" I said, grinning, "But in a couple of years, I can see him moving up in MI5 very quickly, to being very near to the top of the totem pole; yes, I agree, he's been very impressive indeed."

I glanced across at Vee, who was standing at the kitchen door. "Don't forget: somehow, tomorrow, you must help in getting me upstairs on my own. I will need at least five to seven minutes; that should give me enough time to deposit the new sims into the mobiles of the IEDs. I'm going to make the excuse that I have the bloody runs; this could give me some time alone upstairs. We are going to have to play it by ear, I'm afraid; I can still do it on Thursday if we don't get the chance tomorrow, but I think the sooner the better, as the main aim of this whole operation is to eliminate any chance of these IEDs being detonated, and thousands of men, women and children being killed or maimed."

"OK, Steve," Vee said, "I'll see what I can do; maybe I could fake stomach pains or sickness. But I think that if I did that, Mari would want to comfort me; let us, as you said, play it by ear. I'm sure we will come right."

With that, Vee walked back into the kitchen, and I could hear her banging the pots and pans around. I followed her into the kitchen, gave her a big cuddle and told her, as I always did, how nice the food had been. I've got to admit that she too had that look of apprehension on her face again, and I fully understood why.

As I walked back into the lounge, Charles was standing by the front door, his hand on the handle; he coughed slightly, with his hand to his mouth, "I have that environmental suit in the boot of my car, Steve; do you want me to leave it there, or bring it inside?"

"I think it would be better if it was in the boot of my car, Charles," I replied. "Everything is coming together now, and we don't know what the time implementations are at the moment. The suit will be crucial should any radical changes be made that we haven't envisaged. I've noticed that Mohammed only tells everyone bits and pieces at a time; whether this is for his ego-trips or not, I don't know. But I still do not trust this man at all; so we will have to skate on thin ice over the next two or three days, and stay well ahead of them."

We walked out to the cars, and moved the suit into my boot. As we moved it, Charles gave me a full run down on it, as if he was a salesman selling it to me.

"I got the most expensive one," he said. "It has a built in oxygen bottle that will give you a good hour and a half of oxygen under normal activity; the shoes, gloves and body suit are all in one piece. Just the head portion is sectional, and I got it in a sort of sharky colour; you know, half way between shit and khaki. So you won't be able to wear it on your wedding day, I'm afraid."

We both burst into a fit of laughter, but I could still see that questions were still there deep in his eyes. He had not even asked about Mahmood and Ahmed, but that was Charles. He knew very well that if I didn't tell him something, I had very good reason not to.

"Here are the sim cards, trackers and bugs." He handed me a small cardboard box.

I gave him two of the trackers back, and asked him to keep one with him at all times, and to give the other to Vee; she must do the same.

"I don't want any chance of anything going wrong at this stage of the game, Charles; we haven't got any leeway at all, and if the shit hits the fan, we must be attentive at all times, and ready for any change in circumstances that could possibly, and probably will, arise."

We went out at around eight p.m., and went to the movies on the other side of Leeds, as we didn't want the possibility of walking into any of Mohammed's gang. The movie was an old classic comedy, and I knew it would help to take away the apprehension and anxiety that I had seen on Vee's face earlier; and I've got to admit that it also did both Charles and I a lot of good to relax and laugh for an hour or so.

Going to a comedy movie was a great idea; we ate popcorn, and laughed from start to finish, even more so when Charles threw up his hands, and covered Vee in popcorn. Afterwards we drank a few glasses of wine in the movies lounge; we were all still laughing and giggling like young teenagers, and doing everything that would help to alleviate what was always there in the forefront of all three of our minds.

I drove slowly back to the house; I wanted the evening to last as long as possible. The longer it lasted, the more comfortable we would all be, and I could see that we were all showing signs of relaxation; and that, at the moment, was a very good sign indeed.

Chapter Fourteen

Next morning, when Vee and I arrived at the farm, it was around nine thirty. As usual, it was raining, but a sort of sleet-type rain that hung on the windscreen, before melting and running down. The lights were still on in the house, and the curtains were all closed; I noticed shadows moving behind the curtains, and, on the upper level in a darkened room, I saw a curtain move to one side; obviously someone was checking to see who had arrived. There were a number of new cars that were parked in front of the house, and I asked Vee to take down the model, colour, and number plate of as many of the new cars as she could, during the next couple of days. The mud and stones made the usual clattering sound as we drove up the muddy driveway. I parked next to the Toyota that was parked with the front end into the barn. I noticed that there were even more cars parked at the back of the barn; it was an absolute full house now, that was for sure. Most of the cars I had never seen before, so obviously we were going to have the full membership of the jihad here today, and I felt a twinge of nervousness in my stomach.

"OK, Sharma," I said, extricating myself from the car seat. "Remember, I will require at least five to seven minutes alone upstairs, some time during the day. Don't rattle any cages; when I'm gone, just try to keep them interested in something that will keep their minds off me. Also, as soon as we know that all the vehicles are here, I will need time to put the bugs on them all; that's going to be quite tricky, but it's got to be done, and it must be done today."

I was looking at her as I spoke, and I realised that she was very anxious indeed. She was busy scribbling car numbers on a piece of paper, and I could see that her hand writing was very shaky indeed. I'd never seen her like this. I could see the apprehension on her face, and the scar above her eye sort of glistened in the half light.

"Don't worry, Salim," she said with a grim smile, as she lifted her headscarf into place, and lifted herself out on the passenger side. "I'm up for it, and running on high octane; let's get the show on the road."

I think she was trying very hard to reassure herself, more than reassuring me, but she was a strong girl, and I knew she would cope. She was smiling, but I knew that it was all getting to her, and there was nothing I could do except bring the whole episode to a final conclusion one way or another, and as soon as possible.

We both ran from the car, and headed for the front door; Mohammed opened the door just as we got there. He greeted us heartily, in his best Yorkshire accent.

"Come in, come in," he shouted, giving me an over-enthusiastic big hug. "Come on in, out of the rain and cold; Mari is in the kitchen, making some lovely chicken soup that will really warm the cockles of your hearts."

I was quite surprised at his big hug, and got the impression that he was giving my body a shake down. His hands seemed to feel all over my upper body. Was something going on that I was not aware of, or was I jumping to bloody conclusions again?

He glanced towards Vee. "Good to see you again, Sharma, we have all been worrying about you. I hope everything is fine with the baby now, and that you are feeling more like yourself again."

Mohammed was still slapping me on the back while taking the raincoat from my shoulders; he shook off the rain vigorously and hung it on the hook on the wall, alongside the front door.

Just then Mari came rushing up to Sharma and gave her a great big hug.

"We have been so worried about you, Sharma, come on in, out of the cold. I've got some hot coffee and soup in the kitchen, so let's go through and leave these men to their own things."

As I walked into the lounge, I saw Ishmael, dressed in a pair of very worn out jeans and a blue T-shirt; he was getting up off the settee and rubbing his eyes, he looked like he had slept there and just woken up.

"Hi, Ishmael," I said, grinning. "You look like you had a pretty rough night."

"No, Salim, I went to see my kids last night, and I didn't get back until the early hours." With that, he jumped up, and headed towards the stairs, never even glancing back in my direction.

Elijah was just sitting quietly in the corner, playing on his mobile; he just greeted me with a nod. He was definitely not what you would call a conversationalist; in fact it was rare that he spoke at all. I would put his age down to about twenty-three or twenty-four, not much more than that. He had a very shy sort of nature, and was the last person who you would ever think would be in on an operation like this.

Mohammed introduced me to three guys whom he had mentioned to me, but whom I had never met. Funnily enough, they were basically just like most of the others, sort of run of the mill Pakistani guys; and you would never ever have thought they would have got into this sort of contemptible operation. The whole thing was quite mesmerising, to say the least. All these guys had very strong British accents from various parts of the country; all had been born and schooled here, and yet they wanted to wreak such unadulterated devastation on the people with whom they had grown up. I was having one hell of a job trying to understand how their minds worked; it just didn't seem at all human. And to think that this had all come about because Mohammed had been embarrassed by a shopkeeper in a shopping mall! I just couldn't get my head around it at all.

Sharma interrupted my thoughts, as she came into the lounge with a cup of steaming hot coffee for me.

"Here you are, sweetheart," she said, with a big smile on her face, "Drink this. Mari is making you a sandwich; maybe that will help to settle your stomach," She winked at me and pouted her lips.

"Settle your stomach?" Mohammed said, entering the lounge, and overhearing what Sharma had said. "What's wrong with your gut, Salim?"

I looked over towards Mohammed. "Oh, we spent last night just outside Leeds, on the road to Skipton, and had to eat at a local take-away. I had a couple of pies with chips and they must have been off or something. I woke up at three this morning at Kareem's home running from both ends; that's why we got here so late. We left at four, and I had to stop twice *en route* to discharge, from both ends as well, may I add. Then we had to go back to the house and get bathed and changed before coming over here."

Elijah and Ahmed had come into the room during my narrative about my bad stomach; they were all in stitches, laughing gleefully at my predicament.

Ahmed was also laughing, as he threw himself down on the settee.

"You should know by now, Salim: stick to Halal food only in the UK." He was struggling to get his words out, he was laughing so much. "You are not in Pakistan now; you know, with Halal food you grow up to being a big boy, and you don't need to have a strong stomach." He made a farting noise with his lips and rolled around the settee, holding his stomach, laughing and pointing at me.

Mari walked into the room with a sandwich on a plate and handed it to me,

"That will settle your stomach, Salim, good old spicy Pakistani food," she smiled, and sat on the settee next to Ishmael, adjusting her headscarf.

Everyone was sitting around, drinking coffee, eating sandwiches, and discussing the weather, and other small talk subjects. Ishmael came over towards the table. He was a very short man, but stocky, with a light skin, but very dark around the eyes; his eyes seemed very deep in his face, but I think that that was because he had such a large, Roman-type nose. He had changed into a dark green track suit and a pair of grey slippers. He picked up a sandwich and a cup of coffee from the table, and strolled across the room to the chair in the corner.

I don't know why, but I had a gut feel that something was going on that I didn't know about. I handed my empty cup to Sharma, and, like any good Pakistani woman would do, she took it to the kitchen for a refill.

As she left the room, I patted my pockets and said, "Shit my mobile is still in the car," With that I stood up and walked to the door. As I opened the door, I noticed that it had stopped raining; but it was still quite cloudy, and very cold. I quickly walked to my car. I was out of sight from anyone in the house, so I grabbed a few bugs and put them in my pocket. I walked to the front of the Toyota and felt the bonnet; yes, as I had thought, the bonnet was still warm. So Ishmael had been driving the car within the last hour and a half, and hadn't been sleeping on the settee. "Mmm, interesting," I thought to myself. I walked around the back of the Toyota and placed a bug on it; then, keeping out of sight of the house, I placed another seven bugs on the various cars that were behind the barn.

I entered the lounge, brandishing and waving my mobile in my hand.

"Anyone got a charger? My battery is very low," I said, glancing around the room at everyone.

Mohammed pointed to the small coffee table by the kitchen door. "Over there, Salim; just plug it in."

My mind was racing, wondering where the hell Ishmael had been during the night. It was worrying me because I had said that we were at the mosque with Kareem, and if we had been followed, they would know that we hadn't been. Sharma and Charles were always checking to see if we were being followed. A couple of times we had an inkling that we were, but the cars always turned off after a while; but with the weather being so bad, it was very hard to determine either way.

"Mohammed," I said, slipping into my seat. "Have you heard anything from the other Ahmed, and his friend Mahmood?"

It was a straight question. I thought the best way to get everything into the open was to bring it up myself. I was feeling a bit worried, especially with Sharma being here.

"You wouldn't believe it, Salim; I must have phoned and texted him twenty times with no reply at all, just voice mail. I have no idea why; maybe they have had second thoughts or something. I've got to say, though, that I felt a little despondent when we met them the other day. There was something about them that I didn't like."

"I fully agree with you Mohammed, straight away I took an instant dislike to both of them myself, especially Ahmed; they seemed to be a little insipid to me, what do you think, Mohammed?"

"We must think very much alike, Salim. I don't think we could both be wrong. But maybe they both got cold feet; anyway, I have redesigned the operation, so we don't really need them. A couple of guys said they would take two of the IEDs."

To change the subject, I looked towards Ishmael. "How are the kids, Ishmael?" I asked, in my most appeasing voice, as I slumped into my seat next to Sharma.

"Great," he said, "Thanks be to Allah!"

"God is great!" Mari said lifting her hands in the air.

"God is great!" we all acknowledged in perfect unison.

"Praise be to Allah!" said Mohammed, hitting the air with a clenched fist and closed eyes, "And death to the bloody infidels." With that, everyone burst into laughter.

I took a bite of my sandwich so that they couldn't see the smirk on my face. It was very hard for me, not being a religious man at all, to fit into this kind of religious anarchism. It was hard for me to believe that they could even think in this way.

Mohammed put his cup on the floor by his feet, and sprang into the air. "OK," he said, in a dark sort of tone, "There's work to be done, because in four days' time, Allah will be proud of us all and the British infidels will be reeling from the wrath of Allah as no one has ever felt it. God is great, praise be to Allah!"

"God is Great, praise be to Allah!" we all repeated once again, in unison.

With that emission from Mohammed, the men all stood and walked towards the stairs. I could hear Sharma's voice making small talk with Mari, as they went through to the kitchen, I presume to wash up and start something for lunch.

As we entered the front bedroom, I could see that everything was just as it had been yesterday. All the fifteen IEDs were sitting in their briefcases, as neat as could be, the plastic packets of semtex (C4), that were at least half a kilo each (it made me cringe just thinking about the power that would be unleashed) were laid on the inside of each briefcase, with the wiring hooked to the timer, and a mobile placed in the centre.

C4, or semtex, as it is sometimes known, has been used by terrorists all around the world. In October 2000, terrorists used it to attack the USS Cole, blowing a gaping hole in the side of the ship and killing seventeen crew members, so you can imagine how devastating it can be. It was also used way back in 1996, to blow up the Khobar Towers, a US military housing complex in Saudi Arabia. It is a pliable substance that could easily be mistaken for plasticine or putty, but is a deadly explosive that was always used by the military, but now, somehow, gets into terrorist hands very easily, by some means or other.

I have got to admit that Mohammed really knew his job. Everything was laid out to perfection: just about the neatest job I had ever seen. We hear people say that the terrorists are not sophisticated or technically inclined enough to become too powerful; but let me tell you, from what I was looking at here in front of me, I can assure you that those people are definitely wrong.

"Shit," I said, "being the operative word. I have got to let loose again. Talk about the ring of fire!"

I turned and made my way to the bathroom, while everyone smiled and giggled. As I entered the bathroom I locked the door and looked around for a place to hide the other sim cards that I had hidden in my sock. In the cupboard under the sink, there was a piece of wood nailed to the wall at the top right hand side, that was just wide enough to hold them. To see them, anyone would have to go down on his hands and knees and look up; I didn't think anyone would do that. I placed them on the ledge and quietly closed the cupboard door.

I stood for a few minutes looking at myself in the mirror; I couldn't get over myself with a beard. It was getting quite long now – about three inches – and I have got to admit that Franks was right; I did look a lot like Salim Rias. I played with the wart on the side of my nose, rubbed the scar above my eye, and gave a little giggle to myself. I flushed the toilet and ran the tap, washed my hands and face, and made a few relieving sighs for everyone in hearing distance to hear.

As I walked into the bedroom Mohammed was speaking in a very low whisper, and as I entered the room, he abruptly stopped, and turned to pick up a couple of cardboard boxes from the floor. Was I being over-sensitive again, or was it my gut feeling? Once again I was getting the impression that they were somehow on to us. It was making me worry, not for myself but for Sharma; she had never been in this sort of position ever before. But I was sure that she would cope as well as myself, if not better, if something should necessitate that some kind of action should become necessary.

Mohammed beckoned for me to come round the table and stand next to him. He opened the two boxes, and placed them next to the briefcases; he motioned for me to stand at the end of the table, probably to give himself room to do one of his egotistical demonstrations. He opened the box, and very carefully pulled out the two rectangular polythene bags that he had showed me yesterday. They were filled with the fine white powder. It could have been baby powder, to any man in the street, but I knew that it was far more sinister than that.

Mohamed laid his flat palm on the packet of anthrax. He was staring dramatically at each and every one of his disciples individually, and sticking out his chest. I could see that he was very proud of his workmanship and, I've got to admit, he had every right to be. "These are anthrax spores, and I am sure you that you all know that this is a very highly poisonous element. Breathing this into the lungs will kill anyone within twenty-four hours. We will be placing two packets: one at the bottom and one at the top of each briefcase. When the briefcase explodes, on detonation, it will be blown into the air for at least a one hundred and fifty metre radius from the detonation point; it will be despatched into the air and will be blown by the wind to every corner of the Mall, and also into every air-conditioning unit. Everyone in the vicinity and beyond will have it in their hair, their eyes, their noses, and their lungs." He was smiling, and yet he had a diabolically sinister glare in his eyes, those deep dark eyes that always made me wince.

"Anyone who comes into that area," he went on, breathing heavily, and slapping his chest with his fist, "will breath the anthrax in; and let me tell you, there will be an abundance of them. There will be policemen, firemen, medics, doctors, nurses, and all the security guards, and obviously any other infidels who take it upon themselves to help the wounded. All will die, because no one will even have an inclination that there are anthrax spores in the I.E.D's until it is far too late; and, by that time, our Jihad will be a complete and utter success. One other thing I must mention is that the shopping centres that we hit will remain in ruins, for everyone to see for months, if not years, because of the anthrax implication."

Everybody in the room was absolutely mesmerised by Mohammed's volatile and very aggressive utterances. He leaned forward and put both his hands on the table, and, once again, looked at everyone individually with that dark sinister glow in those deep-set dark eyes.

"Yes, people," he said, almost shouting. "Thousands of the infidels will die with every bomb! It is going make the 9/11 incident in the USA massacre, totalling around three thousand dead, look like an insignificant tea party."

"God is great!" he shouted loudly, stepping back and throwing both of his hands high into the air. "Death to the infidels, praise be to Allah!"

"God is great, death to the infidels, praise be to Allah!" we all said in unison, throwing our clenched fists in the air.

I was shocked, and felt sick in my stomach, not at the thought of the devastation he had explicitly narrated to us, but from the pure volatile impact of his dialogue. My heart was beating so hard that I was scared that any one close to me would be able to hear it. I know that anthrax spores are a very dangerous poison, and when it enters your eyes, nose, ears, mouth, or even any open wounds, if not treated immediately, or at least within twelve hours, you are definitely on your way to your maker. I was now determined that this was the time to bring in the boys from HQ now or this catastrophe could get into a position where it would be unstoppable, and I could never ever let that happen.

I didn't have any experience at all with anthrax. All I knew was what I had read. I believe that letters have been despatched in the United States of America, and many other parts of the world, with anthrax spores inside them. When these letters have been opened, the person opening them can inhale the spores unknowingly, and it has a deadly affect. My mind was racing, thinking of the thousands of people who, although only injured, would, in the end, be poisoned by anthrax spores; and, on top of that, all the rescue authorities – doctors, nurses, firemen, police, paramedics, the list goes on. I could see that the proportion of this diabolical incident would have had no equivalent in the UK, since the Second World War.

Mohammed then picked up the other box that had the ball bearings in it; he opened the top, and produced another polythene bag of the same size, similar to the first one. This was the one with the ball bearings in, and it was very neat indeed, as was everything that Mohammed had shown me up until now.

"This," he said, looking at all his disciples, "holds ten millimetre ball bearings – in all, one thousand three hundred per packet – giving us two thousand six hundred per IED. Imagine two thousand six hundred bullets flying in both directions at the same time; each ball will have the same velocity as an AK-47 bullet."

Mohammed laid it carefully on the table, and ran his hand backwards and forwards across it, slowly, from left to right, as if he was caressing his own new-born child.

"This is the interim killer that will draw the infidels into the honey pot," he went on, smiling. "These ten-millimetre ball bearings are held in position by the plastic, and two of these packages will go into each briefcase, between the anthrax bags and the semtex. These ball bearings, once the semtex has been detonated, will rip apart the anthrax bags in the briefcase, sending the anthrax into the air; the ball bearings will kill everyone within a radius of fifty to one hundred metres of the explosion, depending on the density of the people in the immediate detonation area."

Mohammed was now really running on high octane. This was the definitive moment of his ego trip, and I could see that he was devouring it into his body, mind and soul, like a hungry lion.

"This," he went on, running his hand over the anthrax packets again, "will kill thousands of infidels in a slow and painful way over the days that follow. The people, not only of Britain, but of the entire world, will realise that the power of Islam is totally and irrevocably unstoppable."

I had to admit that Mohammed, and probably quite a few unknowns, had put a lot of time and thought into this operation; if the operation were to be successful, I thought that it would start a world war, with the magnitude of the first and second world wars put together. The devastation would be unbelievable, and the aftermath would take a long, long time for people to forget, if they ever could.

Mohammed walked around the table towards the window. He stood staring out into the cloud-strewn damp fields, not saying a word; he was running his fingers through his hair, and he seemed to be in a trance, after his sweeping interpretation of the devastation that the twenty-fourth of December would bring to Britain and the rest of the world, not to mention the changes to the future of the world as we now know it.

He stood at the window for at least a minute, turning slowly to face us all; his eyes fell on me, and I stared straight back at him, as I knew that if I looked away, it would be a dead giveaway.

"Mohammed," I said, holding both my arms out towards him with both my palms facing upwards, "You were given your name by your father, and I can see why he gave you that name. Mohammed, you are a great leader, and I know that, in the future, you will have the recognition that you deserve. God is great!" I shouted at the top of my voice, "Death to the infidels!"

Everyone in the room shouted together, "God is great! Death to the infidels!" Then Mohammed screamed at the top of his voice, "This will show the world that the power of Islam is unstoppable!"

"The power of Islam is unstoppable!" we all shouted.

Mohammed walked up to me, with his arms outstretched, and gave me a very strong embrace, patting me feverishly on my back, and kissing me on both cheeks. "You are a good man, Salim, and men of your stature are a necessity to the plight of Islam. God is great!" he shouted, throwing both his arms with clenched fists into the air.

At that moment Mari and Sharma walked into the room with a pot of coffee, and a few Pakistani titbits on a tray. We all looked a little bedazzled at each other after the very, very high emotional temperature that Mohammed had infused into the room, lowered by Mari saying, "Here's some coffee and snacks for you," in her very quiet female tone.

We all looked at each other, and started laughing; I think we all felt a little stupid, or at least I did, having got so absorbed in the operation, and then being brought down to reality by a calm feminine voice.

"Thanks, Mari; thanks, Sharma," I said, taking the tray and putting it down on the dresser behind the door. "Just what the doctor ordered; and I think the timing couldn't have been better."

Sharma stood beside me, and poured the coffee into the cups. She looked up into my eyes from under her scarf, and I could see the sentiment in her eyes saying that she fully understood the position I was in. She gave me a peck on the cheek, and then both Mari and Sharma headed for the stairs.

I sat on a stool, sipping my hot coffee; I had a great sense of relief in my heart, not only from the calmness that the girls had brought into the room with the coffee, but more so from Mohammed's praise for me. It wasn't much, but it allayed my theories that I thought, maybe, someone was on to us. I thought it must be my age that was giving me these feelings of insecurity.

After we had all drunk our coffee, Mohammed started to put the ball bearings and the anthrax spores into the briefcases, closing each briefcase as he had finished, and piled them into five separate piles of three. He did it all so carefully, as if every one of the briefcases was his own child.

Ahmed spoke for the first time with a grin on his face. "Mohammed, you are treating them as if they were your own children." Everyone laughed and put their hands over their mouths.

"Well, everyone, let me show you all why I am treating them like my own babies," Mohammed said, with that glowing egotistical look back on his face again.

Mohammed walked out of the room, and we all followed like sheep along the passageway to another bedroom. He turned to face us all, with his hand on the door knob.

"This is the best of all, my friends. This is how we will get the IEDs into the shopping centres, without causing even the slightest suspicion to either security or the police."

With that, he threw open the bedroom door and stood to one side, so that everyone could walk into the bedroom.

I've got to say it again: this guy was bloody good. He never stopped surprising everyone. Inside the room were all of fifteen prams; they were all the very modern, bulky type, with hoods and covers.

"Well, folks," he went on, proudly. "All the IEDs will be hidden in these prams, seventeen inches from the ground, and covered with hoods and pram covers. They will be securely hidden away from any prying eyes, alleviating any suspicion at all from security, or from any one else, for that matter. All that is needed is for you to wheel the prams into the malls, placing them in very strategic places where the most devastation will occur, then to leave the Mall and drive away to a distance of maybe two miles or so. All you have to do then is to make your mobile call with your mobile number, which I will give to you, and the rest will go down in history as the most devastating attack to ever be perpetrated in the western world. From that day on, the whole world will realise that the power of Islam is a power that is totally unstoppable.

Ahmed spoke next, very softly, and looking directly at Mohammed and myself. "Supposing someone steals the pram?"

I jumped in with both feet saying, "Then they are in for one hell of a bloody shock, Ahmed, one hell of a shock, that's for sure."

With that, everyone burst into hysterical laughter that did much to alleviate the tension that had been building up during the last hour or so.

We all went down to the lounge, and spent a good four hours going over and over the operation, all of them repeating and repeating the individual tasks which they had been given in order to perpetrate this astronomical and diabolical devastation of the British people, which was about to take place within seventy-two hours. I knew that I was the only one who could stop it; and I have got to be honest, I was feeling a little bit inept in the situation. If I messed it up, thousands upon thousands of innocent people were going to die, and it would be all my fault, and my fault alone; there was no room for even the slightest oversight, and I must never waver in my role: to stop this destruction from ever happening.

We were all sitting in the lounge, drinking hot soup with fresh bread rolls, and passing the time of day; the girls were in the kitchen, making food, and I've got to admit that it smelt great.

I turned to Mohammed, pointing with the hand that held my bread roll. "Mohammed," I looked straight at him with a very sombre face. "You seem to have everything worked out perfectly: positions, timing and who is doing what and where. I don't want you to take this personally, as I have seen your workmanship upstairs, and I can only say that you have made the most beautifully designed IEDs of destruction that I have ever seen."

I had to be careful with my words now, as I did not want to upset or irritate Mohammed. "Although they look great, how can we be sure that they are not going to malfunction? Has this type of bomb been tested before?"

Mohammed smiled and rubbed his hand through his hair. That egotistical look came into his eyes again and I knew that I was going to be in for another big surprise; but I was not ready for this shocking surprise, by a long chalk.

"Good question Salim, and I can understand where you are coming from. Also, I know that you put the car bomb outside the British Embassy in Egypt, and it failed. It must have been very heart-rending for you. And I sympathise very much with you."

I was flabbergasted to hear him say that. Was he trying to show me up in front of everyone, or was he just on another alter ego trip again?

"That," he went on, "must have hurt your morale very badly, Salim. To alleviate any fears that anyone may have about the IEDs:

I can assure you all that my system is as faultless as it can be. I myself tested one of these personally. We did not use the anthrax or the ball bearings, and we used far, far less semtex. I am sure that you all know about the bomb that went off about three and a half months ago in the restaurant in Central London. Obviously, Salim, you will not know about it, as you were in Pakistan at the time."

"No, I did know about it, Mohammed." I was speaking slowly, trying to hide my true feelings. "It was reported all across the world, but nobody admitted to it, so nobody knew who had perpetrated the deed."

"Well, I can assure you all that Mari and I did it; and we ignited the semtex from as much as three miles away, using my mobile." He had his mobile in his right hand and was waving it wildly in the air; his eyes and face were glowing with pride.

My hair stood on end; my blood pressure was rising at the speed of light. I had to hold myself back from attacking him. Surely not, I thought. I was standing in front of the man that had killed and wounded so many people in such a devious and cowardly way, and he was so proud of the devious escapade. He could also have ended the lives of Vee and myself, had we sat at a different table. All that Vee and I had been through, and this man was now standing in front of me and bragging about it! I was totally devastated. There and then, I knew that I was going to somehow send him to his Allah; all of a sudden this had now become very severe and very, very personal.

"I did this personally," Mohammed went on, "to test my system, because I didn't want any of our IEDs to fail. Mari and I went into the restaurant, with my briefcase, of course, and Mari had a second empty briefcase under Islamic dress that she wore. We did this so that if anyone saw us walking in with a briefcase, and walking out without a briefcase, it would not look too suspicious and draw attention to us."

He slapped his chest hard with the flat of his hand, just to elaborate the intensity of the feeling in the room. "We picked a lousy table against the wall," he went on. "You know, the table that nobody would pick if there was anything else available. We ate our meal and left, leaving the briefcase with the IED under the table, hidden by the table cloth. We sat outside in the car for about an hour, waiting for the place to fill up; then we drove off for about three miles. One call from my mobile, and the place was full of death and destruction; we could hear the explosion from where we were standing." He looked all around the room, taking in every expression on everyone's face, and I was having a very hard time trying to cover my inner feelings. Then, to put the cherry on top, he said, with an astounding look of pure pride on his face, "A perfect end to a very nice meal, I must say."

While he had been speaking, or bragging, you might say, he was gesturing with his hands; and when he came to the explosion, he jumped up and both his arms went round in circles, to elaborate the ferocity of the explosion.

I remember everyone laughing and clapping their hands. I hope that I did, rather than showing my true feelings, but I've got to admit that I really don't remember. I had gone as cold as ice; my mind went back to that night Vee and I had dinner. Seeing again the utter destruction that this man had caused, a word came into my head, and that word was RETRIBUTION.

"Yes, Salim," Mohammed was saying. "You can be assured that they will all detonate perfectly. One thing you must all understand: I pride myself in my work, and I am a total perfectionist in my war against the infidels. I had the best teacher that Al Qaeda had. I was with him for about three and a half months in Pakistan, and two months in the Gaza strip. He taught me everything he knew; also, over and above that, and most importantly, he taught me how to put pride into everything you do."

My eye was caught by movement at the kitchen door, and I caught a glimpse of Sharma, moving back into the kitchen, I was pretty sure that she had heard every word that Mohammed had said.

Just then the alarm went off so we all knew that someone was coming down the road towards the farmhouse, Ishmael was up and at the window in seconds.

"It looks like Abdul El Dimar and his cronies; they are late, for some reason or other," he said, with a smile on his face. With that, we all went outside into the damp, cool driveway. It was snowing hard outside now, with a slightly strong northerly wind, and the clouds seemed very low overhead.

Greetings and introductions were exchanged all round, and we all ran back into the entrance hall out of the cold. We were all brushing snow off our heads and shoulders, and laughing like schoolkids. We ushered them into the lounge, and the girls came through with more steaming hot soup and bread rolls for the new arrivals; Sharma and Mari handed them out to everyone.

"We are all bloody freezing," Abdul chirped, in a very broad London accent, walking straight over to the fire. "The bloody heaters packed up on the car, and the windscreen wipers aren't working very well. It was a bloody nightmare getting here." Then as an afterthought Abdul added, "We brought some food and clothing with us. It's in the boot of the car; can I bring it in, Mohammed?"

I was still standing with my back to the door so I said. "Sit still Abdul, and get warm; I'll get them for you. Is the boot open?" I questioned.

"Yes, it's open, Salim, but be careful with the blue bag. It's got cream cakes and croissants in it, and we don't want them crushed, do we?"

"OK, Abdul, I'll be very careful," I replied, trying to smile, and turning quickly towards the door.

I went down into the driveway. It was very cold, but I felt that it would help me to cool and control my temper, and would also give me a few minutes to place some of the bugs on the cars. I placed several very quickly on the underside of the cars; they had magnetic fixtures so it was uncomplicated, and very quick to do.

It was snowing hard now, and you could see that it was settling on the ground and on the branches of the trees by the gate. The clouds were low, and had a sort of mystic dark and light grey colour about them. It entered my head that, if it kept snowing like this, we could all be all snowed in, and the job would have to be put back a couple of days; that, I definitely didn't want, I wanted this to be over as soon as possible. I wanted my revenge soon, if not sooner; then I would be able to return once again to the normality that I had been enjoying in my world for the last five or six years.

I was still struggling, and trying to get my head around the ramifications that Mohammed had explained about the bomb in the restaurant. This was something that I had never ever expected, but it gave me even more incentive to play out the plan that had been manifesting in my head for the past couple of days.

While out alone, I rushed around the back of the barn and placed a few more bugs on a few more cars; there were still a couple to do, but I couldn't stay out here too long, or someone might get suspicious.

I went back to Abdul's car, placed a bug, and grabbed the three bags out of the boot, being careful with the blue bag as I had been told, and headed back for the warmth of the living room.

I think I now had my temper more or less under control, but I was never going to forget how Mohammed had stipulated with so much pride that he had placed that bomb in the restaurant, that killed and maimed all those very innocent people.

I went back into the house, placed Abdul's bags in the lobby, and took the cream cakes through to the kitchen, giving Vee a kiss and a smile, and then moved back into the lounge. The warmth inside felt great; I sat in the chair across from Mohammed. He was embellished in yet another ego trip speech to Abdul, and loving it. I watched him for a while; but looking at him now, I saw him in a very different light, and I was now very anxious to reap my revenge on him personally.

Mohammed had us all back in the bedroom again, going over and over and over the plan, ensuring that everyone had every move written deep in their brains. All the briefcases were now ready to be fully armed.

"OK." Mohammed spoke softly, but still had that sickly smile on his face. "Now the easy bit. Each briefcase has a mobile and sim card, with its own particular number; each one of you must put the number into your mobiles now, and I will personally check that you have the correct mobile number and the correct briefcase. We will mark each briefcase with your own particular name, making sure that tomorrow you have the correct briefcase." He smiled and glanced round once again at everyone individually; this was something that he did often, and it always got the full attention of everyone in the room. "We don't want to blow each other up, do we, gentlemen?"

Everyone burst into a sort of very nervous laughter. It was easy to see that they were all very, very nervous indeed about the circumstances, and could not wait for the twenty-fourth of December to be over.

"Mohammed," I said, "Sorry, but you mentioned tomorrow; but tomorrow is only the twentieth, isn't it?"

"Yes, Salim." Mohammed had a very mischievous grin on his face. "I did say tomorrow, and I meant tomorrow. I have got to say that I have brought the operation forward to the twenty-second of December at twelve fifteen. I have done this for two reasons, one being the snow – it could get very heavy and we could all be snowed in here or even worse stuck on a bloody highway on the trip to their destination – but the most important reason is that Mahmood and Ahmed have, perhaps, chickened out. But who is to know whether they might have informed on us and spilt the beans, or something? We cannot take any chances at this point in time; the operation must go ahead as soon as possible and without fault."

"Today, Salim," Mohammed said, "all of my disciples are here. I have given them all a last rundown, to make sure that everyone is fully aware of what their part in the operation is. Then, early tomorrow morning, they can all leave for their designated targets, and be there on site in plenty of time to inflict their wrath on the infidels on the twenty-second of December, at twelve fifteen."

I looked across towards Mohammed; he was standing at the window, running his hands roughly through his hair and staring out into space again.

"But Mohammed, you must not forget that you are now two men short, aren't you?" I asked.

"That doesn't matter, Salim, as one person can place two bombs quite easily. Take the Trafford Shopping centre. It's very big, and we are placing three bombs in there, and that can be easily done by only two people. So I don't really think that the shortage of disciples will be a hindrance at all, Salim."

We all moved back to the lounge, and were handed more hot soup with French bread, and the largest croissants that I had ever seen in my life; they were filled with cream and jam.

"That should settle your stomach, Salim," Mohammed said laughingly, as he dipped his French bread into the soup, and took a bite of it.

"Yes, I'm sure it will, Mohammed," I said, laughing through a mouthful of bread and soup.

As we were sitting eating, Mohammed switched on the television and put it on the news channel. They were discussing the

English cricket team that had left for Australia about three weeks previously.

All of a sudden, there was a big red "breaking news" sign running across the screen, and the news reader came back, saying that two Muslim engineering students had been found dead in a cottage just outside Leeds. Both men had died of gas asphyxiation. The police were there on the scene, but thought that the deaths were purely accidental, and were not looking for anyone else in connection with the incident.

"Wow!" Mohammed shouted, "That could be Mahmood and Ahmed! No wonder they didn't come today. They have passed, oh dear." He looked across to me and said, very seriously, "Salim, I have just been calling them chickens, and informants. Oh, Allah, please forgive me! Forgive me, and take care of their souls!"

I have got to say that I had never seen Mohammed show such sentiment, and I could see on his face that he was totally sincere in his revelation.

Sharma walked over to me, and wiped my face with a paper towel. I was still not used to having a beard, and I suppose I had soup or crumbs all over it. I could see in her eyes that she had seen what had been on the television, and she had heard everything that Mohammed had said; her dark eyes did not have the usual sparkle that I was used to seeing, but I could see that she knew I had only done what I had to do with Mahmood and Ahmed, and a kiss on my forehead told me that she understood, and was still in total control.

We all sat around laughing and joking nervously for a good two hours. You could feel the tension in the air, and see the apprehension on all their faces, and deep in their eyes. I knew just what they were going through. It reminded me of going into theatre when I was with the SAS. Laughing and joking in the plane sort of broke down the tension in the initial period, waiting for what was coming up; but when you get into theatre, then the adrenaline takes over, and you find that your nervousness has gone, and you just get on with the job in hand.

Everything had been cleared away, and the girls were in the kitchen, cooking again. We could all smell a very spicy curry being resurrected out there; and with the weather being what it was, I was sure that it would be welcomed by everyone.

Sharma walked into the room from the kitchen, with a dish cloth over her shoulder. "What time are we leaving, Salim? Dinner looks too good to turn down, and it will be too late to cook by the time we get to the house." She had her head on one side, and a look that said "please" on her face.

"OK," I said. "Sounds great to me, and I agree with you, it smells too good to turn down. Yes, we can stay to eat, but we must get on the road soon, as it's still snowing very hard outside, and if it carries on, the road will be quite slippery." I pointed to the window, and you could see snow flakes still falling, although, I must say, the snowfall was not as heavy as it had been earlier.

I still had to have a few minutes alone upstairs before we departed, and I would have to find some sort of excuse to get up there on my own. Mohammed, by changing the timeline, had really put a spanner in the works.

About ten or so minutes later, the girls came into the lounge with pans of steaming rice, and a lovely chicken curry. I must admit that it smelt wonderful, or, as Sharma said, too good to turn down. The girls stood by the table, filled the plates, and walked around, handing them out to us where we were sitting.

Sharma filled a plate for me, and, as she turned, I could see a crease of a smile on her face and then a wink; but I was not ready for what she was about to do. She tripped, and put the whole bloody plate of chicken curry upside down on my lap. The heat went straight through to my legs, and my you-know-whats. I was shocked, because Sharma just wasn't a clumsy person at all, and it was the last thing I would have expected of her.

"Oh Salim," she shrieked. "I'm so sorry, my love," She was down on her knees, brushing my trousers with a dish cloth.

"Let me get you to the bathroom, and get it cleaned up; oh, Salim, I'm so sorry, so sorry," she pleaded.

It struck me straight away that she had done it purposely. She was down on her knees in front of me. I struck her across the head with my open hand. "You bloody fool of a woman! How could you ever embarrass me like this in front of all my friends?" I slapped her once more; she was still on her knees, but now looking at me with a look of horror on her face.

"Get upstairs to the bathroom now, woman, and let's get this bloody mess you made cleaned up!" I shouted, trying to look as angry as I could.

With that Vee struggled to her feet, held her head in her hands and ran for the stairs.

I stopped at the door, turned and looked at everyone in the room. "Sorry about that, people, really sorry, just give me time to clean up, and then maybe your wife, Mohammed, can get me another plate of food and serve it as it should be served." There was silence in the lounge, and everyone was staring at me with shock on their faces.

"No problem, Salim," Mohammed uttered. "Just get yourself cleaned up; you don't have to worry, there's plenty more food in the kitchen."

I followed Sharma upstairs and followed her into the bathroom; she was grinning from ear to ear. "Hope I didn't hurt your old man," she said. We were both ready to burst into a fit of laughter, but knew that that was the one thing we couldn't do, nor did we even have time to do it. This was the seven minutes that I needed to complete the operation.

"Did you hear Mohammed bragging about the bomb in the restaurant?" I asked.

"Yes Salim, I heard most of it. I was totally devastated; it's a good thing that Mari was out of the kitchen at the time, as I was so shocked that I'm sure that it would have showed on my face, and that could have given us away for sure."

I gave her a peck on the lips, then bent down to get the sim cards from under the sink. I took off my trousers and threw them over the bath.

"While you are cleaning my trousers," I said, cracking open the door, to make sure nobody was close by, "I will try to get the sim cards changed; if anyone should come, try to delay them. I will only need a couple of minutes or so."

I walked across the landing toward the front bedroom in my underpants and T shirt. I could hear everyone down in the lounge talking loudly and laughing, probably about the incident that just happened to me, they all seemed well amused, so it would easily give me enough time to do the exchange, with a bit of the rub of the green.

The briefcases were still laid neatly on the table. They were three high and five wide, fifteen in all. I opened the top one closest to me. I once again had to admire Mohammed's work. I've got to admit that it was a genuine work of art. A pity he wasn't on our side! I could see straight away that they were all finished and ready for use. Both sets of bearings, and the anthrax packets, were in, top and bottom, and they all had their detonators fixed into the semtex. I would have to disconnect the detonators first, then change the sim cards in the mobile, as I didn't know how they were wired; and I didn't fancy going to my maker just yet. My heart was pounding, as I knew that I had only a few minutes to do the exchange, and I couldn't afford to have any problems. It was it, now or never.

I changed the first four very easily, but the fifth gave me problems. I couldn't get the original sim out. My hands were shaking. That was very unusual for me, but I guessed that it was one of those things that come with age, or maybe it was just a normal reaction to the pressure. You know that when you have three screws to undo, two always come out nicely, and then there is always the one that gives you shit. I had just got the sim card out, when I heard Mohammed's voice coming up from the stairwell, and my heart beat went sky high.

"Salim," he said. "Are you OK?"

Then I heard Sharma reply, "Yes, Mohammed, we're fine, we are just drying out the trousers, with Mari's hair dryer." I then heard the hair dryer being switched on. I grinned to myself. She was great. There was nobody in the world I would rather have by my side in the field. What a fast-thinking girl she was; it made me feel very proud.

"OK, Sharma! If you need anything, just shout." Mohammed replied.

"Will do, Mohammed; I just need to dry the trousers, and we'll be down there." I could imagine her sitting on the toilet with a grin on her face.

I changed the fifth sim card after a few tries, and managed another five with no problem. The next one was a bitch, as the sim card holder was damaged, and I knew that I had run out of time; so I quickly did the other four, closed all the brief cases, and reorganised them so that they were all in the same position as they had been in when I entered the room. I checked to see that everything was in place, and as they were before. I got to the door, and glanced back. There was a small flannel or cloth on the floor. I remembered that it was on the table when I came in. I picked it up, and placed it where it was before; then, gingerly, I opened the door and listened; all I could hear was cutlery and plates, being stacked

257

in the kitchen, and muffled voices and laughter, probably all at my expense, coming from the lounge. I swiftly crossed the landing and barged into the bathroom. Sharma was sitting on the loo drying my trousers with the hair dryer and grinning like a Cheshire cat.

"OK, sweetie, all done?" I asked, giving her a kiss on the cheek.

"Yes, Steve, everything's clean as a sixpence. Did you manage to change the sims?"

"I couldn't manage to change all of them, as a couple of the clips holding the sims in were damaged, and that took up too much time, I'm afraid; but I don't think it's anything to worry about. Time is still on our side."

"Damn it, woman, give me those bloody trousers! They are dry enough now." I said it in a loud voice, for everyone in the house to hear.

I took the trousers from Sharma, and had just put one leg in when the door burst open, and in came Mohammed.

He was laughing. Funnily enough, I think he was feeling sorry for Sharma, not me.

"Everything all right in here?" he said, looking straight at Sharma. He was not interested in how I was. It just goes to show that there must be a vast difference between the Pakistani Muslims' way of treating their women, and the home-grown Muslims' more orthodox way in which they treat their women.

"Salim!" he said with a smirk on his face. "Your balls OK?" He laughed out loud, and stepped backwards into the passageway.

I had just pulled up the zip on my trousers. "Yes, I'm fine, thanks, Mohammed, just a bit embarrassed more than anything, thanks to this bloody woman. I knew it was wrong to bring her over here with me." I glanced at Sharma and shouted, "Get downstairs, woman, and get me some food, and on the plate this time!"

Sharma ducked under my arm and ran through the door and down the stairs.

"Salim, Salim," Mohammed said in a quiet voice, "Calm down! It was only an accident. Sharma didn't do it on purpose, and there is plenty of food."

I was totally and utterly shocked at Mohammed's uttering those words, remembering that this was the man who was about to kill thousands of innocent men, women and children because he had been embarrassed by a bloody shopkeeper in a shopping centre. It made me wonder what he would do if a waitress had poured soup in his lap. Makes you think, doesn't it?

I looked Mohammed straight in the eye, and thought "if you only knew my boy, if you only bloody knew."

As we walked on to the landing, I looked at Mohammed and said, pointing at the bedroom door, "Everything OK with the I.E.D's?"

"Yes, all finished and ready to blow!" As he said "blow," his hand shot up in the air, with clenched fist; then, with a proud look on his face, he asked, "Want to see?" and, without an answer, he opened the door and walked into the bedroom.

He walked round the back of the table, and opened the top briefcase. "Just look at that, Salim. Have you ever seen such orderly and efficient equipment in your life?" He looked me straight in the eyes, and went on, "I hope, when you get back to God's country, you will give me a first-class testimonial about these beautiful, beautiful elements of destruction that I have manufactured. I want the heads of the Jihad all over the world to be proud of me, and, of course, of my disciples, when it is all over; I want everyone to remember that it was Mohammed Malik who created and enacted the most prevalent devastation known to man, against these unadulterated and despicable infidels of the United Kingdom."

"Mohammed," I said, placing both of my hands on his shoulders, and looking deep in his dark eyes, "You can be assured that everyone will be very proud of you indeed, and you can also be assured that I will hold your name high to everyone who are leaders in our Jihad against the Christians." I pulled him close to me, and kissed him on both cheeks.

Mohammed walked towards the other bedroom door, and indicated for me to follow him. "What do you think of my plan to use the prams?" he asked, opening the door to the next bedroom. He had one of the briefcases in his hand.

"These," he said, with a big grin on his face, "as I told you, Salim, are just as important as the IEDs, because they are the camouflage for the whole operation; everyone will allow these to pass into the shopping centres without a hint of suspicion."

He stood staring at me, with that disgusting ego trip look on his face, which was starting to really get to me.

"Look," he said, pulling back the hood of one of the prams. "When you place the IED in the pram, it is seventeen inches from the floor; and if the IED is upright, it will give maximum devastation to everything and everyone within a range of between one hundred and fifty to two hundred metres either side, when the detonation takes place." Mohammed stood back, and with that gleam in his eye, he shouted, "Vroom! Death to all the bloody infidels!"

Mohammed walked over to the nearest pram, placed the briefcase that he had carried from the other bedroom into it, and pulled the hood over the briefcase. I could see that no one would ever be able to see the briefcase, and there would be nothing suspicious or untoward to any one. It was just a person out shopping, pushing a pram through a shopping centre, a few days before the Christmas holidays; even the security or police patrols would not bat an eyelid. Yes, his plan was as near to perfection as anyone could get it; but he was not counting me in his equation, and, one way or another, I was fully determined to bring to an end it.

"Well, Salim, what do you think?" he was grinning from ear to ear. "No one will even see the IEDs, and with their being seventeen inches from the ground, it will give maximum velocity on detonation in every direction."

He was so proud of everything he had done that he kept repeating himself; or maybe, with his egotism, he just liked to hear himself talk.

I was nodding and smiling; but deep down inside, I could see that this man was just about the most dangerous, psychotic person that I had ever met in my life. His operation was planned so well, and with such total precision, to the very last detail, that I could not believe that this was what the world would have to fight in the future: not the knocked-together gas canister bombs, but totally sophisticated weapons of mass destruction. And maybe, one day, they would get around to using dirty bombs. That was just beyond any one's comprehension; the very thought of that made me shudder.

I stood there, looking straight back into Mohammed's eyes. "You are a real man of God, Mohammed; you have planned this procedure to perfection. I cannot think of anyone that I know anywhere in the world that could have planned it better. I can only compliment you on your achievements with the whole operation."

I walked over to him and gave him a big bear-hug; and I must admit, I was scared that he would feel my heart beat, because it was pounding ten to the dozen in my chest.

We both went down the stairs and entered the lounge. All went very quiet as we walked into the room. I went across to the table, and took a seat, not even glancing at anyone else in the room.

Mari walked in with a plate of food, and placed it in front of me. "Here, Salim, get this down you; then you will be ready for the drive to the house. Sharma is eating hers in the kitchen."

I ate my food very quickly, and, I've got to say, I fully enjoyed it. Mari took my plate away when I had finished. All the guys in the room had been laughing and joking about a few frivolous things while I had been eating; I suppose they were very nervous, and were somehow trying to alleviate the tension that must have been building up as the time got closer.

Mohammed walked over to me, and put his hand on my shoulder. "Salim, you definitely won't have a runny stomach tonight; that was real Halal food, intended to build men for the fight against the infidels of this world." Everyone burst into laughter, including me.

We left the farm just before three p.m., so it was still quite light. I drove the car very slowly, and I could feel that Vee was looking at me, and wondering why I was driving so slowly. As we got out of sight of the front of the farmhouse, I stopped the car, parked it, opened the door, and ran back to the farmhouse. There were still three bugs to place, and I had to do it now, and very quickly, as someone might start to wonder why it had taken me so long to get to the alarm on the road out. I placed the bugs on two of the cars, but the third one was right in front of all the other cars, and could be seen easily from the farmhouse window. It was an old maroon Audi. I had to crawl through a very muddy part of the yard to get to it. I quickly placed the last bug, but then the farmhouse door opened, and out came Abdul. I rolled quickly underneath the car, and there was a large puddle of water right in the centre; I could feel the freezing cold water come through my clothes and on to my skin. Abdul was messing about in the boot and muttering to himself in Urdu; it was only for about a minute and a half, but it seemed like an hour. I heard Abdul slam the boot and I saw his feet heading back to the farmhouse door. As soon as I heard the door close, I rolled from under the car, and high-tailed it back to Vee in the car. I climbed into the driver's seat, soaking wet and freezing. I put the car into gear, and lightly started to press the accelerator so as to make as little noise as possible. Then we were on our way back to the house, with a feeling of *fait accompli*.

I gave Vee my phone, and asked her to get Charles on the phone, and ask him to meet me at the house as soon as possible. It wasn't snowing now, but the clouds had darkened a lot. The traffic was very light, so we made good time. I needed to speak to Charles, more or less to bounce things off him that I knew had to be done; it is much easier to talk to someone than just to run something through your own head, and I could not really talk too much to Sharma, as I thought that maybe she would not agree with what I envisaged just had to be done. I knew that Charles would fully understand, and would also fully understand that time had now run out, and tonight was the night; and, most importantly, everything had to go like clockwork. Tick tock, Tick tock.

Chapter Fifteen

We had only been home five minutes when we heard Charles pull up outside. He came blustering into the lounge, complaining bitterly about the weather; but he soon calmed down when Vee put a cup of hot coffee into his hands. We gave him a rundown on what had occurred during the day. He was totally astounded when we told him about the bomb in the restaurant, and about its being Mohammed and Mari who had planned and carried it out. I must admit that when Vee told him about spilling curry into my lap, he laughed so much that he had tears rolling down his face, and a coughing spell so bad that Vee had to take the cup of coffee out of his hand before he spilt it. But his face changed when we told him that the date had been brought forward to the twenty-second.

"Steve!" Charles said, standing up and showing a very real expression of anger. I had never seen this temperament in his behaviour before. "This means that we don't have time to get the spooks into it. These bastards could be leaving the farm tonight, or, at the latest, first thing in the morning. Christ, Steve! What the fuck are we going to do?"

"Charles it's not a matter of what we are going to do. It's more appropriate to say what I am going to do?" I was stabbing my index finger into my chest. "This, Charles, is where I have to utilise the entire contingency planning that I have done over the past couple of two weeks."

"But supposing they all leave tonight, Steve?" Charles said, looking more than a little flummoxed. "Surely we cannot, under any circumstances, chase every one of them all around the country? Even with MI5 assistance, it would still be a total impossibility, and many innocent lives could be lost."

"Yes, Charles, you're right, to a point," I said, still staring out of the window. "But you have to take it into consideration that only four of the IEDs can be detonated from their mobiles. I admit that we are going to need a little, if not a lot, of luck tonight, and the one thing that is worrying me, Charles, is that, as you know, even just one of these IED's will kill and maim hundreds, maybe even thousands, of innocent people. Yes, Charles you are right; we don't have time to bring in the spooks, and it's all, figuratively, up to us now. I'm pretty sure that it can be done if we take action instantaneously. OK, as I said before, we will need a little good fortune; but we have no other option on the table as of now, do we?"

I could hear Vee in the kitchen, I presumed, putting some food together for Charles. This gave me a little space to have a chat with Charles, and see what he thought about what I felt had to be done to alleviate the devastation that was being planned out at the farmhouse. Charles just sat and listened to what I had in mind; he neither butted in or even showed any exhilaration or compunction as to my plan. In fact, the only thing that he did while I was speaking was to sip his coffee. Before he said anything to me, Vee walked into the lounge with a plateful of chicken curry. His eyes lit up when it was put in front of him.

"Enjoy, Charles; but I can assure you that it's not as good as the chicken curry I put in Steve's lap earlier today." She smiled and winked at him.

We all burst out laughing, and I think it was what we all needed at this time and place.

"Vee, you are a darling, and thank you for keeping mine on the plate, this time." We all laughed again, and I could hear that the laughter was whole-hearted, so I could see that the tension between us was back in a more composed juncture.

"Thanks, Vee, I'm starving, and I have promised myself never ever to eat another hamburger, toasted sandwich or piece of fried chicken ever again. In fact, to be very honest, I think that I'd rather eat your chicken curry from my lap than that fast-food shit."

A sort of feverish laughter went round the room once again; but in reality you could feel the tremendous tension that we all had deep down.

Vee gave him a kiss on the head, laughed, and went back out to the kitchen. Charles gobbled the food down like a starving lion, then, leaning back in his chair and wiping his mouth with his serviette, gave a burp second to none.

"Steve, just for your information, that's what the Arabs do, to say they appreciate the food they have been given," he said, laughing, and turning to face me. "You have got one hell of woman there. I do hope you realise that."

"After the last few days, Charles, I must say that I am beginning to acknowledge that fact more and more every minute. But I am a little apprehensive, because I'm not sure that she will condone what I am about to do; and I've got to say that I hope this will not hammer a wedge between us."

"Steve, whatever you do, we both know that it could never be done in any other way; if there was any other route, I am sure you would have taken it, and I want you to know that I personally am behind you in whatever you feel has got to be done, one hundred and ten per cent. I can't possibly speak for Vee, but I am damn sure that she would be of the same mind."

"Charles," I said, rubbing my beard. "I thank you for your back-up, and I am sure you are right about Vee also. But I am going to have to leave her in the dark a bit, as we are too close to the termination of this incident, and, to be honest, even I don't know how it's going to end at the moment. All I can tell you is that, in the SAS, we were all taught, and lived by, the rule that the only form of defence is attack. I still stand by that rule, and I have a gut feeling that this is the only way we can safely bring this situation to a satisfactory conclusion."

I stopped for a moment, still rubbing my beard, and letting my thoughts come to the forefront.

"Something that does worry me, Charles," I went on, pointing a finger towards him, "is that the western world as we know it has gone too far. Maybe they know it, but maybe they don't; either way, they have put the whole of the western world into one hell of a mess. But even then, I am sure that once this situation has been resolved, I don't think that the governments of the western world would agree with me as you do. They have got us into this catastrophic mess, that is now totally out of control. And most importantly, they are beyond knowing how to get us out of it. They will be pleased with the outcome of this situation, behind closed doors, but they will require a scapegoat to hang out to dry; and we both know that the scapegoat is going to be me. For that reason, Charles, I want both yourself and Vee to be on the outside of this, as much as possible."

"Steve," Charles said, lifting himself from the table. "I have never taken any interest in Muslims or Islam; I have selfishly just got on with my life, and left others to do the worrying; but over the last couple of months I have been reading, and looking at the internet, and I have got to say that I have been quite dumbfounded, to say the least, with some of the revelations that I have read and seen. You know, Steve, Islam destroyed the Christian Middle East and the Christian North Africa; and it is estimated that more than sixty million Christians were slaughtered during their conquest. Also, half the Hindu civilisations were annihilated, and nearly eighty million Hindus were murdered in the name of Allah. Islam's Jihad also destroyed over ten million Buddhists. This was all done by the "infiltrate, subjugate and devour" system that they more or less always use. Today it's the gun and the Quran, but, Steve, tomorrow it could be the nukes and the Quran. They talk loudly and openly of a total Islamic civilisation throughout this world. What oxymorons these people are, Steve! Since when has barbarism been called civilisation? Islam is purely an anti-civilisational cult *par excellence*. It has fully destroyed and mutilated every civilisation it has touched, and has brought misery, terrorism, poverty and war to every country into which it has moved. You know, Steve, ninety to ninety-five percent of all conflicts on this planet today involve Muslims fighting non-Muslims, or Muslims fighting each other. Yes, Steve, fighting each other! Because the Muslim people are the most disintegrated, sectarian people in the world. There are many, many trouble spots around the world, but as a general rule, it's easy to make an educated guess that one of the participants is a Muslim group of one kind or another. Muslim vs. Buddhist in Thailand, Muslim vs. Hindu in Kashmir, Muslim vs. Christian in Africa, Muslim vs. Russian in Caucasus: Steve, I could go on forever. The Muslims have a saying: "First destroy all the Saturday people," (this means the Jews), then come the Sunday people (this means the Christians); and when they tire of killing or converting non-Muslims, they will go after different sects in their own religion. You know, Steve, at this moment, one in every four humans is a Muslim. Islam is now the second-largest religious group in France, Great Britain, and the good old US of A. There is no point in beating about the bush, Steve, the facts speak for themselves; these militants are too intolerant to allow any other creed or religion to advocate in or around them. Whenever they have established their "critical mass" of about ten per cent of any given population, they then begin to encourage violence, revolt and jihad. In essence, Steve, it is a declaration of war on western civilisation and on Christianity, a kind of World War Three, so to speak. Their influence is growing steadily, and will continue to do so up until the Europeans and the western world wake up, stand up and be counted. Look how they treat the female section of their faith! To the males, the females are just bloody baby-making machines, to enhance the Muslim population for their takeover of the human race as we know it.

"Look at Belgium, Steve. It has now been nicknamed Belgistan. They have Muslim groups in Europe called Shariah4Belgium, Sharia4Holland. It is growing fast in Brussels, Amsterdam, Antwerp and Rotterdam, where there will be a Muslim majority in less than twenty years. The Belgian people are leaving Brussels at an incredible rate, and it will become the first major European city to become Muslim-orientated and ruled by Shariah law, purely because of Muslim pressure, and the total weakness of the western world. Steve, this will happen in only a few years time; of that I can assure you."

Charles stopped suddenly, as if to take cognisance of himself; he sat back down in the chair and put his elbows on his knees, looking down at his shoes.

"Steve, as I see it," Charles said, rubbing his hands together, "I cannot see the American and European governments waking up any time soon to stop this undercurrent of radical Islamism from creeping deep enough for them to be able to destabilise any other religions. In the last thirty years, the Muslim population in Great Britain has grown from eighty thousand to two million, and only seven per cent of them consider themselves British first, while ninety three per cent consider themselves Muslims first. Steve, a proselytizing religion like Islam cannot and will not stand still. Islam endeavours to expand in Britain, and aims to bring its message to all comers and by any means possible. Its hopes are to eradicate all other religions, so that one day the whole of humanity as we know it will be one Muslim community, 'The Umma'. See, they have even given it a name!"

Charles stopped talking and took a swig of his coffee. His eyes were now wide, and I could see that he meant every word he was uttering.

"Every single Muslim country on this planet was at one time ruled by a brutal dictatorship. That's why they were kept down in these countries. But the western world decided that they should eliminate the dictators, and free the poor Muslim people; and now we are looking at murder and mayhem throughout Northern Africa, to an extent that nobody could have ever envisaged."

He put his cup down on the table, looked directly at me, and went on. "And make no mistake, Steve: Islam is on the move, and is preparing a War of Attrition to extinguish any and all civilisations and religions that get in their way. Yes, Steve; Islam is showing us that it has no place in any democratic society, either in Europe or in the Americas. In fact, it has no place anywhere in the civilised world whatsoever. Also, what I found very worrying, Steve, is that they do not have a leader other than that of the prophet Mohammed, who has been dead for hundreds of years; but even more worrying, Steve, is maybe they do have a leader or even maybe a country that no one knows about, someone who is silently commanding and financing both Al-Qaida and the Taliban in their Jihad. I had to stop reading about it, Steve, because the more I read, the less I understood what was really going on. But I can tell you, Steve, it must be fought or it is going to impede the normal growth in Christianity and democracy. They believe that democracy is a fascist ideology."

Charles stopped his rambling and stood up, pointing his index finger straight at me. His face now looked very calm, and sort of tranquil.

"Steve," he went on, "I suppose that, in a very long winded and roundabout way, I am trying to tell you that I am with you all the way; and I also believe, although I cannot speak for her, that that is exactly where Vee would stand on this too."

I sat back, probably with a sort of surreal smile on my face, mainly because I had never heard Charles encapsulate his thinking so definitely on any one subject at all. He had really gone overboard on this Muslim thing, but I also knew that he was right in many aspects. I looked across at him; he was now sitting with his head sort of bowed, and gazing at his knees.

"I totally agree with you, Charles; and I can assure you that our Governments know that they have set up a time bomb with a very long fuse. But they can't, or will not, or, most likely, do not know how to correct it. Many of the European cities are already one-quarter Muslim. Just take a look at, say, Amsterdam, Marseille, Malmo, Denmark and most of Sweden for instance. In many of these cities the majority of the under-eighteen population are Muslim. Paris is now surrounded by a growing ring of Muslim neighborhoods, and to top it all, Mohammed is the most popular name amongst boys in many cities in Europe. And they are multiplying at a far greater rate than that of the Christians, or of any other religions put together. One day, even they may realize that the best form of defense is attack, but our western world governments, I'm afraid, will only attack if the word oil comes into the sentence, and this has been proven many times over recent years."

Vee walked back into the lounge, and I could see on her face that she had overheard the discussion that Charles and I had, had. She stood by the kitchen door looking down at both of us and spoke in her very low and calming voice.

"Gentlemen, I think it's a very old British saying that goes, 'It's not for us to reason why, but for us to do or die'. The world is a massive place, full of very distinctive people of varied religions, creeds and doctrines; there is no way that anyone person can, under any circumstances, change everything in one fell swoop. But we are in a position at this moment to save thousands of innocent men's, women's and children's lives; and I feel that that is what we should focus on at the present moment. We must not let ours or anyone else's feelings come into consideration."

Charles quickly jumped to his feet, clapping both his hands together enthusiastically; his eyes were now as big as saucers.

"That's my girl, that's my girl!" he almost shouted. "Yes, she is so right, Steve. We must focus on what we have in hand and at the moment. What we have in hand is to stop these bastards in any way possible from doing this despicable deed that they are hoping to inflict on innocent people throughout the United Kingdom."

Everyone just sat looking at each other, not knowing what to say. I looked at Vee and Charles, and decided it was time to be open and honest, and tell them both what I had in mind for tonight.

Vee came and sat at my side, and leaned her head on my shoulder. I suddenly got the impression that she knew what was coming.

"First and foremost, guys," I said, moving forward in my seat, "I want you both to fully understand that with Mohammed bringing the time frame closer there is no time at all for us to hand this over to the spooks; by morning, all or most of Mohammed's disciples will be on their way to their targets, and we know that at least four of them will be walking time bombs. We all know that only four of the IEDs can detonate, but we don't know where they will be sent to; we also know that should only one detonate, it could cause a thousand or more people to die. The only way to eliminate this disaster is to totally eliminate the source, and we all know that it must be done immediately."

Everyone went quiet, probably because we had all now realised the urgency of the situation, and the thought of what might happen should we not act immediately was totally unthinkable, and out of the question.

I sat back on my chair, and Vee's head came back on my shoulder. No one said a word for a full minute. Then Charles picked up his coffee, stood up, and walked across to the window. He stood with his back to us, looking out on to the street; he seemed to be lost in thought, and that was not like him. You could cut the tension in the room with a knife again.

Charles suddenly turned towards Vee and I, pointing at us with his index finger.

"Steve, Vee." He was talking in a very positive tone. "We all know what is about to happen and I think we are all being far too conventional in this matter. What we have got to do is to focus on what could happen if we don't do what we all know has to be done. Steve, we must put away our humanitarian thoughts and rules of engagement; we must think and act the same way as the Jihad thinks and acts from now on."

Vee then took the floor. She got up from the settee, brushing her hair behind her ears. She stood looking first at me, then over to Charles.

"I was in a very similar position many years ago, as you both know; and I was overridden by a stronger influence so I have got to say that anything you think you have to do, I fully recognize and understand. Also, I will be one hundred per cent behind both of you in your decisions. I am speaking from my heart, but I am also speaking with a full acknowledgement of the situation that we are in, and I recognize that there are no other options. We must go ahead, and immediately."

I sat for a while, quite pensive, as I knew what had to be done. I had earlier been unsure whether both Charles and Vee would agree with me; but listening to both their interpretations of the situation, I felt sure that they would both fall in with the strategy that I had already planned in my mind.

It was now my turn to stand up and convey to them what I had anticipated would have to be done, should the chips fall as they have. We had to alleviate this predicament that has risen before us, and there was no time to go into any type of justification or personal reasoning. Both Charles and Vee were now standing in front of me, waiting for me to take my turn.

I stayed seated on the settee, leaned back and looked up at both of them.

"Charles, Vee," I said, looking up at both of them. "I have spent many years in the field over time, and I have always given forethought to any predicament that could possibly occur at any given moment, but also and most importantly, to what could go wrong. It's probably that, that has kept me alive. Forethought and contingency planning is one of the most important dimensions in the field. Charles, I have asked you to get me quite a few odds and ends, so to speak, and you did exactly as I asked without questioning me; and that, Charles, I have got to say, I appreciated enormously. You got me the bugs and the trackers, the sim cards, and, of course, the suit. This was all contingency planning on my side, and I always hoped that I would never have to use them; but regrettably, things have changed dramatically, and we are now in a position where they must be used. There is no other way, and I need you both fully to understand that I would rather it had worked out differently; but we must accept the situation as it is, and get on with the job in hand. And please: I want you both to imagine what shit we would be in if I hadn't done that contingency planning."

"What shit we would be in, Steve!" Charles said, with a very serious look on his face. "What about all those innocent men, women and children that are out there?"

"What is this suit you're talking about, Steve?" Vee said looking very seriously at both Charles and I.

I jumped in to try to explain. "Vee, as you know, they are utilising anthrax spores in the IED's; so I had Charles get me this synthetic environmental suit, so that if I should have to detonate the IED's myself at the farm, I would be pretty sure that I was not going to be infected. Also, with the amount of Semtex they are using in each one of the IED's in the farmhouse, the explosion is going to be absolutely massive, to say the least. Even I cannot imagine what seven kilograms of semtex will do, and how far it will spread the anthrax. The farmhouse itself will encase some of the detonation, to some extent; but to what extent, I don't know. All I do know is that it's a building of carved stone that was built about a hundred and forty years ago, so I must take precautions. I don't want to do it from a distance because we need to know that everyone in the Jihad is at the farmhouse when all hell breaks loose. Should any of them have left and gone to their targets, we wouldn't know about it until all hell breaks loose on the innocent people out there just doing their Christmas shopping. You have both got to understand that should that happen in even one shopping mall, it will be a total and utter failure on our part, because in just one mall, thousands of people will die, and we cannot, under any circumstances, allow that to happen!"

I heard rain splattering on the window, and the sound of thunder not far away; and I knew that rain would help very much to achieve our goal.

"Look at the rain, guys," I said, getting up from the settee, and pointing to the window. "This will make it much easier, and maybe even keep the anthrax spores emissions to the very minimum. Look, there's even a heavy wind blowing. That will also help."

I walked over to the window. "We couldn't have asked for anything better than this weather, guys; maybe, just maybe both Gods are on our side today."

"Right," I said excitedly, clapping my hands together. "We are all in agreement, and we all know what has to be done. What's the time, Vee?" I asked.

"Twenty minutes to seven, Steve." It was Charles who answered, sounding just as excited and relieved as I was.

"Great, then; let's get this show on the bloody road. It can all be over by eight, and by tomorrow, we can all be back in London."

My mind had now moved up two gears. I sat on the settee again, grabbed a piece of paper and a pen from the coffee table, and started making a list of what I would require while out on the moors. I would have hated to get there and find that I couldn't finish the job.

"Charles, I want you to go and pack your things together at your place, and Vee, I want you to pack up everything here. Charles, as soon as you are finished there, get back here, and put all the luggage you can in your car; the rest, put in the boot of the Merc. One very important thing, also, is that I want both of you to spend half an hour going round the house and eliminating any fingerprints. By eight thirty, I want you both to be on the road, and heading for London. I will keep you both in the loop as to how everything is evolving out at the farmhouse, and if everything goes well, I should be hot on your heels by nine a.m., please make sure that you both have your trackers close to hand. Charles, I am hoping that you aren't going to need them; but you never know. As I said earlier: contingency planning!"

I clapped my hands, and all three of us jumped up from our seats at the same time. "Let's get this show on the road, guys!" I shouted, rather loudly.

Charles came running out to the car with me. We both checked out the suit and the oxygen cylinder. Everything was fine.

He gave me a big hug, and said, in a very concerned manner, "See you soon, Steve. Don't worry about Vee; I will look after her. You know that, but please, Steve, be very careful out there, and I'll see you in a couple of hours."

We were both soaked with the heavy rain that was falling now, but that was the least of our worries. Charles quickly turned, ran down the pathway, jumped into his car and took off like a bullet. I watched him driving down the road, and the thought came to mind: surely Charles wasn't getting all sentimental in his old age?

I ran back into the house. I was absolutely drenched. Vee was in the bedroom, packing the two cases. I jumped into the shower, dried myself off and got dressed in some dry clothes. Neither of us spoke even one word.

I took the Walther from the bedside table, and tucked it down the back of my trousers. There was our umbrella standing by the door; I picked it up. I knew that I had to say something to Vee, but I just didn't know what to say.

As I turned around, she was standing looking at me, with a little tear in her eyes. We both came together in the centre of the room. We just hugged for maybe a minute, neither of us saying a word. I pulled away, turned, and walked down the passageway.

I heard Vee shout from the bedroom, "See you in about two hours, Steve!"

I didn't reply, because I didn't want to lie. You never know, Maybe I wouldn't see her in two hours; maybe I wouldn't ever see her again. Who knows?

I took the environmental suit from the boot, threw it on to the back seat, climbed into my Mercedes, started the engine, and drove the car down the driveway. As I hit the road, I swung the car right, and gunned the engine. I knew that Vee would be watching me from the bedroom window, but I didn't look in that direction.

Chapter Sixteen

It took nearly half an hour to get to the farm in the heavy rain and wind. As I came to the fork that was just about one hundred yards before their electronic beam stanchion, I took the left fork, and parked about fifty yards down the road, under the trees. Anyone coming or going to or from the farm would not see the car. I switched off the engine and closed the air intake, so that no air could come into the car from the outside. Then I had to spend about fifteen or twenty minutes swearing and cursing, trying to put the bloody suit on inside the car. Good job I wasn't in my Cooper! That would have been the height of impossibility, and I could never ever have managed it, even with someone helping me.

I climbed out of the Merc, and was hit by the very hard rain with a very strong wind. The rain sounded really loud from inside the suit. I walked through the trees until I came to the road that led to the farm. I now had to find the electronic beam stanchion, and make sure that I didn't set the alarm off by mistake, and make my arrival into a grand entrance. It was hard for me to see, due to the rain that was running down the face of the suit like a bloody waterfall. My vision was grossly impaired, so I would have to be very careful; if it hadn't been such a serious manoeuvre, it would have been quite laughable.

When I came across the electronic beam stanchion, I was quite relieved. Now all I had do was make my way round the back of it, and then down to the farmhouse without being seen; and in this suit, it was not an easy undertaking, to say the least. The ground was very uneven, and my vision was very inadequate through the suit's visor; the rain was very heavy now, and the strong wind was pushing my limits to the hilt.

I could see the lights of the farmhouse, as it was now only about a mile away, only the downstairs lights were on. I could just make out the cars vaguely at the front, but not very clearly at all from this distance. The rain was not desisting at all. I was not happy with the rain and wind, but I knew it was a godsend to assist me in what I had to do, and also that it would eliminate a lot of the effects from the anthrax. The wind was blowing from my position towards the farmhouse. This was also very much in my favour, as it was very dense moor for about ten miles behind the place, with no housing whatsoever over that way.

It took about fifteen to twenty minutes to reach the farm gate; then my heart started to race. I immediately saw that the old maroon Audi was not in sight. I tried to reach into my pocket for the mobile, but remembered that I was in the bloody suit, and that I couldn't get to my trouser pockets for it. I must be really getting old, to have made a stupid mistake like that. I was getting very worried now. Was everything starting to go wide of the mark? I didn't have time to go back to the car, and I had to get in touch with Charles and Vee, and immediately.

I glanced around the ground, looking for something sharp. By the gate, there was a small piece of rusty barbed wire hanging from the fence pole. I wiggled it up and down until it broke loose. I took the wire clumsily in my gloved hand, and, using the barbs, tried to cut through the suit level where my trousers pocket was. It was a real struggle to get even a small rupture in the material, but as soon as I got a small tear, I was able to rip the suit a couple of inches, giving me enough space to insert a couple of fingers in, and retrieve my mobile. That wasn't the last of it, though. I then had to try to use the mobile with these bloody gloves on. Then I fell on my backside, and burst out laughing, because I then realised that I would have to take off the hood of the suit to be able to talk on the mobile. This took another five minutes of sweating and swearing. After about three tries on the mobile, I got through to Charles.

"Steve, is everything OK?" he said instantly but calmly.

"No," I replied. "I'm at the farmhouse, but the bloody old maroon Audi has gone. Both of you switch on your trackers and find the bloody thing; but don't get too close, because when I make my call, there is a twenty-five per cent chance that it will detonate and go up in smoke with the farmhouse, and that is not good odds, Charles. I can't detonate the farmhouse until you find the Audi. You will have to tell me when it's in a clear area. Quick, Charles find the bloody thing, and fast! I don't know when they left; all I know is that they could be heading for the Trafford shopping mall on the border of Manchester and Salford. But that is just a guess. Other than that, I can't help you, I'm afraid."

"I'm on it, Steve." He didn't sound at all frustrated. "At the moment, we are now on the M1 from Leeds down to London; but I think if we take a right in about a mile or so we will be able to cut across country, and maybe we will be close enough for the tracker to pick up the bug up when we reach the M62 from Leeds to Manchester. I'll let you know as soon as we get a signal. Sit tight for a while, and Steve: try to relax!"

With that the mobile went dead, but I did hear him laughing before he shut off the phone, and I knew he was really enjoying the whole debacle. I could imagine him gunning that MG as if he was a twenty year old with six beers in him.

I sat on the ground in the pouring rain, and I was now feeling the cold, even through the suit. I had to gather my wits now, as I needed to work out a time frame. I knew that, should any more of these bastards leave the farmhouse during the night, we were deep in the shit. I suddenly came to the conclusion that we had to bring in the spooks now, as to many lives were at stake to take any chances, and too much could go wrong very quickly that could not be predicted at a time like this. All I could do at the moment was to cross my fingers, and hope for the best.

I phoned Charles again. "Hi, Steve!" he said. "I am handing over the mobile to Vee."

I assumed that he was driving like a madman, and needed all his concentration on the road.

"Hi, Steve; we are closing in on the M62 to Manchester but we still have no signal from the bug as yet. All we can do is to keep going and cross our fingers, really." I could hear the tension in her voice.

"OK, sweetheart; this is what you must do. Phone Paul and tell him to get a chopper in the air. Explain the seriousness of the situation, and give him the coordinates of your position; then the chopper will be able to get into position quickly. It will be much easier for a chopper, as they are much faster, and, being higher, they will be able to pick up the signal from the bug from much further away than you." I've got to admit that I was feeling a bit tense and breathless myself, but I did my best not to show it in my voice.

"OK, Steve, will do. Love you!" And the phone went dead.

I sat for maybe half an hour. Then my mobile started to vibrate again. I quickly put it under my hood and answered; it was Paul.

"Steve? Paul." I could hear that he was very nervous, "I have been trying to get a chopper in the air, but they say the weather is too bad, as we are having heavy rains and gale force winds with very low cloud and some mist. Is there anything else that can be done?"

"Yes, Paul." I replied, "MI5 can take the rap for maybe a thousand deaths of innocent men, women and children, or you can risk the lives of two pilots for maybe two hours." I was fuming. "Listen closely, Paul; if I cannot detonate that car within the next two hours, then there are going to be another fourteen cars out there full of semtex and targeting targets throughout the bloody country, and we will not be in any position to stop it. We cannot, under any circumstances, let a little bad weather hold up an operation of this size. Now, Paul, tell them to forget the bloody health and safety shit, and get that bloody chopper in the air immediately; any problems, get Margaret to phone me immediately. I, for one, don't want innocent people's deaths on my hands. Do you?"

"OK Steve, hear you loud and clear," Paul said, choking on his words. "I'll keep you both posted." Then, with a very apologetic voice, he said, "Sorry, Steve, really sorry." And then the mobile went dead.

My mobile vibrated again. It was Vee, "Steve, they can't get a chopper in the air, they say the weather's too bad." I could hear in her voice that she was panicking, and I didn't blame her. I was also panicking.

"Don't worry, Vee, Paul just phoned me, and I think I've sorted it out. Just keep going, and try to pick up that bloody signal. Where are you now?"

"We are on the M62 highway, leading to Manchester, but no sign of a signal as yet. We will let you know as soon as something changes. Love you lots." With that, the mobile went dead.

It took fifteen minutes before my mobile vibrated once again. It was Margaret.

"Hi, Steve," she said. "Just to let you know that the chopper you requested is taking to the air as we speak, and should be in your airspace within half an hour or so. Sorry for the hold up, but it's all sorted out now, and everyone is on to it."

"Thanks, Margaret, I was beginning to panic a bit. What we require the chopper to do is, first, to fly up the M62 from

Manchester to Leeds, pick up the signal from the bug that we put on the car, and then let me know when the car is in a position where there are no other cars around it. It must be at least half a kilometre from any towns, or close proximity to occupied housing. You will have to block all the road's exits and entrances, going north and south, so that nobody can accidentally drive into it. There could be two large bombs in the car with a half kilogram of semtex in each, plus ball bearings, and that is one hell of a bomb; and to top it all, would you believe it, there are anthrax spores embedded inside. Only I myself, and perhaps the people in the car, can detonate the bombs, Margaret. I am sure that we both want as little collateral damage as possible, so it's totally imperative that I be informed immediately the car is in clear space. I am hoping that the heavy rain will disperse the anthrax spores, but we cannot take that chance. After detonation, the area must be kept clear of all humans. Sorry, Margaret; there is no time to explain any more to you. You must just do as I ask, or plenty of innocent people are going to die."

"OK, Steve, we've given the chopper pilot all the details of the car, and I will relay your message to them personally; and I will also keep in constant contact with the chopper until things come to fruition."

With that, the line went dead. I could imagine her giving orders to all and sundry that were within hearing distance.

Then my mind went back to the cold. The rain was still falling heavily, and sounded so loud hitting the suit, but my fingers and feet were quite warm, considering the temperature. I knew that I would have to sit here for at least an hour before any news would come from the chopper and I didn't have a clue of the time, as my watch was on my wrist and inside the suit; so I spent a while trying to close the tear in the suit, but I couldn't. I would just have to take a chance. I was pretty sure that the rain would very much dampen the effects of the anthrax, but really, what the hell did I know?

I was feeling pretty low just then, as I realised that, all of a sudden, I was not in charge of the operation. Everything was in other people's hands, and the seriousness of the situation was getting more and more tense by the minute. I decided to find an area where I would be able to detonate the explosion from a secure position.

I got up and started walking away from the farmhouse, and to the left, keeping the wind blowing into my face. About a hundred or so yards away, I came across a rather large boulder, about four feet high, that had bushes to the front and side of it. This put me about a hundred and fifty yards away from the point of detonation. I wasn't sure how much of the explosion the farmhouse itself would eliminate of the initial intensity of the blast, and I kept thinking that six kilograms of semtex was one hell of an explosion. I had used semtex myself quite a few times, but then it was only a few grams at a time, and even a small amount like that made one hell of a bloody explosion.

I settled behind the boulder, and curled up on the ground with my back to the boulder, it seemed to give me pretty good cover from the blast; but there was going to be plenty of debris coming down from the air, as the roof of the farmhouse was going to be the weakest point.

I sat down behind the boulder; but after about five minutes, I made the decision that it was too close to the farmhouse, and didn't give me enough cover overhead. I picked myself up and, once again, headed further away from the farmhouse. The terrain was very rough, with a mixture of heather, grass and small bushes, and a mixture of different sized rocks; so it wasn't a walk in the park, so to speak. I covered about another hundred yards, and came to what seemed to be a small wall, about three foot high. I couldn't quite work out what it was, until I knocked a stone off the top and I heard it hit water. Then I realised that this must have been the well which

Mohammed had said he had used to hide the semtex in, initially. It seemed to have been built in the same carved stone as the farmhouse, so it was very solid. I dropped a few stones into it, to try to decipher the depth, and how much water there was in it, but it didn't help me. I reached into my pocket and took out my mobile; I would have to be very careful that I didn't drop the bloody thing in the well, or the whole mission would be ended. As the mobile lit up, I could see that there was water in the bottom, at about eight foot down, but there were two boards or planks across at around four foot six. This was too deep for me to get into in this suit, and definitely too deep to get out of.

I walked around the area, to see if there were any other places I could use for cover, when I caught my foot on something and fell to the ground. After a couple of violent expletives, I directed the light from my mobile on to what I had fallen over. It was a kind of roughly made wooden ladder, about seven or eight feet long, but with only about four or five rungs on it. This would probably help me to get in and out of the well. I picked it up, walked the few yards back to the well, and slowly lowered it in. It held fine on the two planks, and I was sure that I would be able to climb in and out quite easily. It would definitely give me the cover I required when the detonation took place. This gave me a little bit of relief to my woes.

I climbed into the well, and stood on the ladder. It felt better there, as I was out of the wind; luckily, the rain was still falling heavily. I wondered what the time was. At a guess, I would have said that it was about nine thirty or ten.

Then my mobile started to vibrate. It was Margaret.

"Hi, Steve!" she said, excitedly. "Just to let you know, we have picked up the signal from the chopper; they are about twenty-three miles outside the suburbs of Manchester, and moving very slowly, due to torrential rain in the area. We have closed all the inlets and exits to the M62, and they will be coming to an area that it very sparsely built up, with just two farm-type buildings. One is five hundred yards from the other side of the road, and the other is seven hundred yards from the side of the road our target is travelling on. To be safe, we have sent men from the Manchester constabulary to get the tenants out and to a distance of safety from the area."

"That's great, Margaret," I said, with a sigh of relief. "Now it's just the timing we have to get right. By the way, what is the bloody time, anyway? I don't have a watch."

"Three minutes short of ten, Steve," she replied, sounding a little bit bemused at my not knowing the time. "Steve, if you haven't got a watch, you've still got a mobile and that will give you the time, won't it?"

"Sorry, Margaret," I said laughing, "but I've got a lot on my mind at the moment, or maybe I'm to bloody old for this kind of work now."

I took a step up so that I could look over the top of the well. The lights were still on in the farmhouse.

"How much time to the place of detonation, Margaret?" I asked.

"About five miles, Steve. I'm tracking them from here on the PC as we speak."

"Minutes, Margaret, minutes." I shouted rather tersely.

"At a guess, Steve, seven to eight minutes." Then, "Bloody hell, Steve, they've stopped. Hold on."

I could hear her talking to someone who I could only presume was the pilot of the chopper.

"Steve." She was back with me. "Steve, are you there?"

"Yes, I'm here," I replied.

"He's stopped under a bridge, Steve. He must be taking a piss or something," Margaret said, very excitedly.

"Is it a clear area, Margaret," I said, just as excitedly.

"Hold on, Steve." She replied

I could hear her in the background, talking to the chopper again.

"Yes, Steve, he is having a piss; and yes, it's a pretty clear area. Plus, he is halfway under the underpass; so I would say it's as safe a place as we could ever hope for."

"Where are Vee and Charles located?" I shouted.

"I just checked with Paul, Steve, and he says they are about four miles behind."

"OK, Margaret; tell Paul to stop them immediately, and do a U turn, then to drive back in the opposite direction, as fast as they can."

"Will do, Steve." I could hear her talking to Paul, "OK, Steve, your message will be passed on immediately."

"Margaret, get the chopper out of the way now. I'm going to detonate in twenty seconds."

"Chopper is clearing the area as we speak. Steve, you are clear to detonate." Margaret was back to her more business-like voice.

"Ten, nine, eight, seven, six, five, four, three, two, one." With that, I shut off the mobile, and dialled the number for detonation.

It seemed like a lifetime waiting. I was beginning to think that that something had gone wrong. I was just about to lift my head over the perimeter of the well, when all hell broke loose.

The explosion was totally horrendous. Even my eardrums felt the power and strength of the blast. I was shocked at its intensity. The ground was shaking as if I was in a seven or eight magnitude earthquake. Debris was falling all around me. I even heard debris splashing into the water at the bottom of the well that I was in.

It took a good thirty to forty seconds before things quietened down. I lifted my head above the perimeter of the well. It was very dark, with lots of small fires here and there, and the whole area was covered in dense dust and smoke.

As I lifted myself up to get my head above the well wall, my mobile started to vibrate again. I very carefully lifted my arms over the well wall, as I didn't want to drop the bloody thing down the well.

It was Margaret. "Steve, are you OK?" she asked, in a very sincere but worried tone of voice.

"Yes Margaret, I'm fine," I answered. "What was it like at your end?"

"The pilot said that there was nothing there that even looked like a car, and there is a one and a half metre hole in the ground, and some slight damage to the overpass. What's it like at the farmhouse?"

"Haven't got a clue yet, Margaret," I replied. "I'm waiting for the dust and smoke to settle, but it was one hell of a bang, and being so close to the proximity I suppose you could compare it to a very small Hiroshima. I have got to say it shocked me no end. I have got to go now, Margaret, as I need to check out the site, and make sure everything went off OK, so to speak. Please excuse the pun! I will contact you just as soon as I have had time to do some reconnaissance in the surrounding area. It should take me about an hour. Please tell Paul that no one should come into this area unless they are in environmental suits, and tell him to have all roads blocked off for at least a three-mile radius around the farmhouse."

With that, I switched off the mobile, and very gingerly climbed out of the well. I adjusted the suit, and refastened the hood-piece; and then my luck changed, due to the suit gloves being so clumsy, the mobile slipped out of my hand and fell down the bloody well. I cursed as I heard it hit the water. I realised that now I had no contact at all with the outside world.

The dust and smoke had cleared a little, but it was still heavy in the air, and about ten or eleven fires were strewn all around me. Even through the suit I could smell the very strong smell of marzipan in the air from the Semtex.

I made my way gingerly towards the farmhouse. Although it was dark, the small fires here and there, with steam rising above them from the rain, made it quite easy to see my way as I plodded on, through the very rough terrain underfoot. There was nothing to give me any indication as to where the farmhouse was now, as, obviously, there were no lights on, and probably no wall either.

All of a sudden, I came to the rock that I had been going to hide behind initially. Thank God I hadn't. The whole rock was peppered with hundreds of white dots, presumably from the ball bearings, and the two bushes that had originally been alongside it, were no longer.

My hearing was very much hindered in the suit; just about all I could hear was my heavy breathing, as I laboured towards the farmhouse. The heavy rain was still pelting down. All of a sudden, I found myself sprawled on the ground. As I picked myself up, I could see that I had fallen over the roof of one of the cars that was lying upside down on the ground. This told me that some of the cars must have had the IEDs already in their cars, for an early start the next day.

I was quite shocked to find myself just outside the farmhouse fencing, and about twelve metres from the gate. I stood for a minute or so, to let my eyes adjust. There were a lot of small fires around the house, so I could see much better now. Most of the fencing was down, and the cars were strewn all over the bloody place in various states of demolition. There were two cars that only had external damage to them, and one of them had a car's chassis placed right on top of it. I had to be very careful, as the ground had some very large and very deep craters in about four or five different areas. I could now see the farmhouse, or, should I say what was left of the farmhouse. Most of the upper walls had fully disintegrated, and there was no indication of a roof at all. The chimney stack was still precariously standing, and looking very ghostly indeed, against the background.

I walked slowly around the yard, trying to make sure that all the cars were still there; it was impossible to tell, with all the carnage that had taken place. But I was sure that if any more of the cars had left, I would have certainly heard them. Anyway, it was too late now; if anyone had left early, their car would be in smithereens somewhere on the road. I could only hope that nobody would be hurt in the explosion that would have taken place.

I stopped suddenly and listened; the rain had subsided quite a lot now, so I was hearing much better through the suit, and I was sure I had heard something. I stopped again and listened. There was nothing. Then, just as I started to move again, I heard the noise once more, and it was definitely a moan or a whimper. I still couldn't tell where the noise was coming from, though, so I started to walk around the side of the house. I heard the noise again, but louder, this time, and I had an inclination that it was coming from quite close by, but further away from what was left of the farmhouse. There was a pile of rocks and stones that looked as if they were part of the farmhouse walls. As I passed them, I heard the noise again, and, yes, it was a whimper. I looked down to my left, and was shocked to see someone laid face down on his stomach. As I got closer, I could see that it was Mohammed, and he was very badly injured, and covered in blood from head to toe.

I knelt on one knee alongside him, and turned him over. His eyes were wide, and showing absolute fear. He tried to lift his arm, as if to reach for me. Maybe he thought that I was some kind of alien from outer space. I looked down at him for about twenty seconds. His eyes never left my face, although I knew that he couldn't see who I was through the suit.

It took about five seconds for me to recollect what had happened to Vee and I in the restaurant that evening in London, when this bastard had nearly killed us both, and once again, the word retribution came into my mind.

I leaned across him, took his nose between my thumb and the index finger of my left hand, and slowly put my right palm over his mouth. His eyes went like saucers. This time he did manage to lift his arm, and grabbed hold of my right wrist. I squeezed my thumb and index finger together, so I knew that he was unable to breathe and fully starved of oxygen. I looked deep into his dark, dark eyes.

"Give my love to Allah, Mohammed!" I shouted, loudly, "and enjoy your seventy-two virgins."

He died very quickly, and his eyes were wide open in death. My thoughts were that the whole world, both Christian and Muslim, or any religion for that matter, were far better off without this torrid, egotistical bastard, and his friends also.

I spent the next hour or so trudging around the farmhouse. I didn't find one body that was in one piece. There were limbs and torsos and heads all around the place. What a bloody mess for the government to clean up! But I suppose it was better to have to clean them up than the thousands of very innocent British people all around the UK, had they managed to pull off this catastrophic devastation which they had planned.

After I had done a full reconnaissance of the area, I started the long trek back to the car. The rain was easing a bit, and the wind had died down to a sort of strong breeze. It took me about twenty minutes to get to the electronic beam stanchion. I stood there and waved my hand in front of it, and shouted, "Hi, Mohammed, it's me! Give my love to Allah!"

I waved madly at what was left of the farmhouse. I guess I was feeling a little childish now that it was all over, and the pressure and adrenalin was starting to ease a little.

I got to the car, and started to extract myself from the suit. The rain felt good on my body, although cold. I opened the boot, threw the suit into it, and climbed into the car. I started the engine, reversed back up the road to the fork, did a three point turn, and headed up the road with my foot flat to the metal. I slowed up about a mile up the road, and realised that it was an adrenalin rush that was pushing me. I stopped the car, took a couple of deep breaths, closed my eyes, and tried to relax my body and mind. After about five or six minutes I felt that I had calmed down enough to carry on.

I was feeling very inept indeed now, as I had no contact whatsoever with anyone and I wouldn't have until I got home to London; and in this weather, that would be about three hours, if not more.

The rain had calmed down quite a bit now, and I could see from the clock on the dashboard that I had been driving now for about forty-five minutes. I could see a truck-stop about a mile ahead, so I decided to make a stop there and grab a cup of coffee, and maybe one of those famous bacon sandwiches that truck-stops always brag about. I could also use their phone, and try to contact Margaret or someone, to at least let them know I was alive and well. It made me realise that, in this modern day and age of mobiles, when you lost your mobile you lost all contact with everyone, because all your numbers were kept in your mobile, not in your head.

The parking area was packed with six, eight and even ten-wheeled trucks. I supposed that they all wanted to get off the road for a rest in weather like this. I found parking very close to the doors of the restaurant, jumped out of the car and ran inside. The place was packed with truckers, all laughing and joking with each other, and enjoying their tea and their sandwiches. I made my way to the counter, and a guy came over and asked if he could help me.

"You sure can, mate," I shouted over the noise in the room. "Give me a large black coffee, and a bacon sandwich please."

He repeated my order over his shoulder out into the kitchen behind him and came back to me, "Seven pound eighty, sir, it will be ready in about five minutes."

"Thanks," I said, giving him ten pounds. "Keep the change, pal. Oh, by the way, do you have a telephone here?" I asked.

"Sure, mate, over there in the corner," he replied, pointing to the back of the room.

I lifted my hand in a gesture of thanks, and made my way over to the phone. I dialled nine, nine, nine, the telephone was answered almost immediately.

A female voice answered, "Good Morning, this is the police emergency line, PC Jefferies speaking, how can I help you."

"Good morning to you," I said, looking at my watch, "I need to be patched through to MI5. I have to speak to the Director, Mrs. Margaret Pewter, or Paul Lawson. Please PC Jefferies, this is a dire emergency."

"What kind of dire emergency, sir?" she said her voice not wavering at all.

"I'm sorry, but I cannot divulge that, but please; I must speak to them as soon as possible. This is very urgent indeed."

"Why don't you dial them direct yourself, sir?" she said, and I could imagine that she must have had a great big smirk on her face.

"That's because I don't have their bloody telephone number. Can you give me their number, then?" I was starting to get irritated now.

"Sorry sir, but this is a police emergency line, not a telephone directory service," she said, in a rather irritated way.

"Please PC Jefferies, as I said this is a dire emergency and I meant it. If you can't put me through then, please, you phone them and tell them that Steve Taylor is at a truck stop on the highway about an hour out from Leeds, heading towards London, just after the Sheffield turn off." I was now biting at the bit. "Please do this for me. As I said, it's very urgent indeed."

"Sorry sir, but we can't do that." With that, the line went dead.

She probably thought it was a hoax; and I've got to say, I don't really blame her. If she could have seen me looking like a street bum she probably would have had me arrested.

I walked back over to the counter, just as the waiter put my bacon sandwich and a massive pot of hot steaming coffee down in front of me.

"There you are sir, enjoy!" he said, with a very wide toothy smile.

I pulled myself on to the stool, and started to get stuck into the bacon sandwich. Boy, it was good; so was the coffee. I didn't realise how hungry I had been. I just wolfed it down, with big swigs of coffee in between.

Fifteen minutes later, I jumped into the Mercedes, feeling very revived after the coffee and bacon sandwich, and ready, once again, to hit the road. Next stop, London! It should take me another two hours, as the roads were very clear at this time in the morning; maybe even less, if I managed to outrun the wind and rain.

The Mercedes was very comfortable, but with these automatic cars you only seemed to be riding them, not driving them. I've never liked automatics at all, so I just sat back and relaxed, and tried to enjoy the ride, listening to some nice relaxing music, and thinking of Vee.

About half an hour into the drive, I noticed that I had passed the Nottingham turn off, and I could see the signs for Leicester coming up. So I was well on my way, and doing better time than I expected. Maybe it was the adrenaline, but I wasn't feeling as tired as I should be feeling from having had no sleep in twenty or so hours. It wouldn't be long now before I was back in London. Then I would be really able to to relax with Vee and Basil in my own home. It seemed so long since I had been there, and I was really looking forward to it.

Chapter Seventeen

About twenty minutes later, I noticed that the weather had cleared nicely. The rain had almost stopped; the roads were drying up, but there was still a very strong wind blowing that was buffeting the Mercedes from the right hand side. Through some openings in the clouds, I had seen a few stars from time to time; but otherwise, the weather was not easing up all that much. I was about twenty miles down the road from the truck stop now, listening to a news report to find out whether the media had got hold of the story yet; but obviously, they hadn't. The road was empty now, except for the odd truck which I had to overtake from time to time. Other than that, everything was hunky dory, and I was on my way home, and very much looking forward to seeing Vee and Charles – oh, and not forgetting Basil.

All of a sudden, the Mercedes was surrounded by a number of police cars, with their blue lights flashing. I was quite startled for a moment, but then I heard the sound of the police sirens. I carried on driving, thinking that it was a police patrol that was probably looking for someone or something, and they would soon realise they had the wrong car, but funnily enough, they didn't pass. They just stayed there, and I could hear over the car engine noise that a loud speaker was blaring out from one of the cars. Maybe there was an accident somewhere up the road in front of me. I took my foot off the accelerator, softly touched the brake pedal, and changed into the inside lane. The loudspeaker was still blaring away so I opened the window a little to see if I could catch what was being said.

"Attention the black Mercedes." I could hear it plainly over the noise of the sirens. "This is the police, please pull over on to the left hard shoulder and stop your car immediately."

I didn't have a clue what was going on, so I slowly pulled over and stopped the car. I've got to say I was bit worried, though, because I now realised that I didn't have a driver's licence, or any other form of identification, I was driving a bloody stolen car, and, on top of that I must have looked like a bloody hobo or something.

I undid my seat belt and climbed out of the car, but all I could see was a very bright light shining straight into my eyes from one of the cars. The first police car moved in front of where I had parked the car, and two police officers jumped out from their car and came running towards me. Instinct then took over, and I reached inside the car for my Walther, and tucked it down the back of my trousers.

All of a sudden, I was surrounded by about five police men in their luminous yellow flak jackets; all the police cars blue lights were flashing all around me, and their torches were all directed into my bloody face. I moved both my hands in front of my face, to stop the glare; this was very daunting indeed.

"Sir, are you Mr Steve Taylor?" one of them said, now shining his torch at my chest, rather than directly into my eyes.

"Yes, I'm Steve Taylor," I replied, uncovering my eyes now that all the torches were not directed at my face. "What the bloody hell is all this about, officer?"

"I'm very sorry, sir," the policeman said, very apologetically. "But we have had orders to find you urgently. Could you please step over to my car? We need to patch you through to someone who needs to speak to you immediately?"

I followed the police sergeant over to the car that was parked about ten yards in front of mine. He opened the front passenger side door, and indicated for me to get inside. I had no sooner sat down than the other police officer was on his radio, speaking to another policeman and asking to be patched through to Charlie One. I was thinking of telling him that it was Charles, not Charlie, when I heard Margaret's voice come on the line.

"Have you found Mr. Taylor, Sergeant?" she enquired, her voice more personal than business-like.

"Yes Ma'am, he's here, sitting right alongside me in my car." He glanced sideways towards me, and smiled as he spoke.

"Thank you, Sergeant," Margaret replied, "Now could you please step outside the car, as I need to speak to Mr Taylor privately." Her voice was very positive now, but also very mannerly.

"Yes Ma'am, right away Ma'am!" With that, he handed me the radio harness, and sort of looked at me as if to say "do you know how to use it?" I just nodded and smiled as I took it from him. With that, the sergeant got out of the car and closed the door behind him.

I could hear over the static that Margaret was obviously in a chopper of some kind.

"Yes, Margaret; Steve here."

"Steve! Thank God we have found you." She seemed very excited. "Please tell the sergeant to stop all traffic. We are going to land on the highway in about seven minutes, as I need to speak to you very urgently."

"OK will do, see you just now." With that, I shut off the radio, and laid it on the driver's seat next to me. I extricated myself from the police car, and relayed Margaret's message to the Police Sergeant, who instantly shouted orders to his troupes. Within seconds, there were blue lights flashing, sirens wailing and police cars rushing off in every direction.

I heard the rotor blades of the chopper before I could see it. Then the lights suddenly came into view. As the chopper hit the deck, I saw the rear doors open, and two people jumped to the ground and started running towards me. With the bright lights of the chopper shining in my eyes, I couldn't see who had ejected themselves from the chopper; but whoever it was, they were running very quickly towards me.

"Steve! It's Margaret and Paul." I heard her clearly above the noise of the chopper. "You switched off your bloody mobile, and we couldn't make any contact with you. I'm sorry but this was the only way to get to you, and we needed to speak to you urgently."

"I didn't switch off my mobile, Margaret, I dropped the thing down a bloody well, when I was climbing out. What the bloody hell's going on, Margaret? And how in hell's name did you find me?" I had to shout loudly over the noise of the chopper rotors.

Margaret was now standing directly in front of me; she bent over and put both her hands on her knees. I could see that she was definitely very short of breath from her hundred and fifty yards sprint. Paul was standing right behind Margaret, but not breathing quite so heavily. He did not say a word; he just nodded his head towards me in recognition and acknowledgement.

"We had a message from a PC Jeffries, to say that you had phoned nine, nine, nine. She gave us your location, so we put the cops out to find you, and here we are."

"PC Jeffries," I said, "She gave me the impression that she thought I was a bloody loony-tune when I spoke to her. She must have had second thoughts after she hung up on me."

"She did have second thoughts after she hung up. She phoned me and told me so, and very apologetically too; but at least she did her job in the long run, and now we've found you, that's the most important thing.

"Well, Steve," she said, as if looking for words. "Everything is going very well. Both MI5 and MI6 are at the moment on their way to the farm, to start clearing up and doing their analysis reports. We have put out to the media that the explosion could have been a terrorist cell that somehow accidently detonated a bomb that they were building for some kind of an attack on English soil. That should be sufficient for them to chew on for the time being."

"Margaret, I've done my job, although I did make a bloody mess doing it, but, please, you don't expect me to sweep up for you as well, do you? Just make sure that anyone who goes on site is wearing an environmental suit, as there could be anthrax all over the bloody place. I have no idea how anthrax spores act when in the atmosphere, but the way I understand it, it could have been washed away with the torrential rain and heavy winds that were blowing. But it's better to be safe than sorry."

"Yes, Steve," she shouted over the noise from the chopper. "That's all organised; we were informed by Charles earlier in the day."

Margaret had now found her breath, but she now had a very ominous look on her face that I did not understand at all. I glanced at Paul, but he just stared back at me, expressionless. I knew that something was very wrong. Margaret's composure just wasn't the Margaret Pewter composure that I knew.

"Steve, at the car explosion site we had a problem." She put both hands on my shoulders, and looked straight into my eyes. "Steve, we gave an order to Charles and Vee over his mobile phone, as that was the only way of communication that we had with them. They were, at that moment, one and a half miles behind the terrorist. We told them clearly to carry out a U-turn, and retreat from the area immediately."

Panic came across me, for once I was lost for words, and my legs went weak at the knees. I could feel my heart pounding in my chest.

Margaret squeezed my shoulders, "Steve, somehow they either misunderstood the order or never heard it, maybe due to the weather, or a bad signal; but, for some reason, they kept driving. When the explosion occurred, they were alongside the terrorist's car, but in the fast lane."

I couldn't speak, I couldn't even think; my mind was paralysed. I felt giddiness come over me. I moved towards the Mercedes and slapped both hands hard on the hood, then I hit it several times with my forehead. "No, no, no!" I heard myself screaming. To me it sounded very loud, but also so very far away.

"Steve, Steve!" Margaret was shouting excitedly over the noise of the chopper's rotor blades. "Steve, Vee is OK! She's OK Steve, but I'm afraid that Charles died instantly. I'm sorry Steve, so very, very sorry. I know you were both very close."

"Vee is OK?" I questioned after what she had said had sunk in. She's OK?" I questioned again, my voice begging for a positive reply.

"Yes, Steve; we flew her out in a chopper immediately after the crash. She is in a hospital in London as we speak. She was cut from flying glass, but nothing that will scar. She also broke her right arm as the car collided with the motorway barrier on the driver's side in the explosion. But other than being obviously traumatised and heartbroken with the whole experience, she is well, and asked me to tell you that she loves you, and you must be strong. It is an absolute miracle, Steve, because Vee, at the time of the explosion was driving the car, and, with her being so small and petite, she was shielded by Charles sat in the passenger seat. If she had been in the passenger seat at the time of the explosion, I would be telling you a very, very different story today, Steve."

Margaret turned me around from the car and cuddled me very resiliently. I could feel tears welling in my eyes, and I could feel the tears on Margaret's face. My mind was still paralyzed, and I knew that, for the first time in my life, I was very much losing control.

"Steve, Steve!" Margaret was shaking me very intensely. "Come on Steve, come on!" she was almost shouting, "Get into the bloody chopper; Paul will drive the car. Let's get you to Vee as soon as possible. You both need each other at a time like this."

Paul came over to us and put his hand on my shoulder, showing comfort. "So sorry, Steve," he said.

I don't remember much about the flight to the hospital, just that it was very bumpy. I sat leaning forward with my head between my knees, gripping and pulling at my beard, and sobbing inconsolably. Margaret was sitting next to me, with her left hand constantly rubbing my back between the shoulder blades. I do remember her removing the Walther semi-automatic from my waistband, which she probably put into her handbag.

The pilot and co-pilot never uttered a word on the trip, until they got on the radio, just before the landing at the London hospital. You have to take into consideration the way the chopper was throwing around in the wind; they had many other more serious things on their minds. The flight had taken about thirty-five minutes in all. Margaret had made a few calls on her mobile, probably to the hospital, to say we were coming, and I suppose to HQ, to keep them in the loop.

As soon as the chopper hit the deck on the helicopter pad, so did I. The wind was very strong, and blowing directly on my back; I could hear running feet behind me and I could only presume that it was Margaret.

As I went through the main doors, a uniformed police officer sort of grabbed me firmly by the shoulders. "OK, sir, please follow me. Down this way, sir."

He even set off at the run with me, while talking to someone on the police intercom that was strapped to his shoulder. We went down two passageways, then through some swing doors, and took a right turn; people in the passageways were kind of startled to see me looking like a street hobo, running with a police officer about three yards behind; they probably thought I was being chased.

The police officer stopped at the junction of the hallway and said, a little breathlessly, "Down to the bottom of this hallway sir. Police officer Duncan is on a chair right outside the door. It's room 109, sir." He did say something after that, but I wasn't listening; I was running again.

Just before I reached the policeman on the seat, he stood up from his chair and smartly opened the door of room 109 for me; I nodded to him briefly, and went straight into the ward.

Vee was asleep and lying on her back. She had a sort of peach coloured bedding; her long black hair was spread all over the pillows, and was glinting and shining as it always had. She had a few cuts here and there, but you could see that these were, just as Margaret had indicated, from flying glass. I sat on a chair that was on the left hand side of the bed; as I sat down, I glanced up and saw Margaret closing the door from the outside. I have got to say that this was a thousand times better ward than the one I had woken up in three months or so previously. I touched her hand with my index finger; she did not move. She looked so peaceful as she lay there sleeping; her right arm was strapped up in a sort of brace, and then held in a sling from around her neck. I could see her eyeball moving slightly behind her eye lids so I knew that she was dreaming. That meant that she was probably going to wake up any time now. I lightly gripped her hand in mine, and I could feel a response from her. Her eyelids started to flutter slightly; then they opened wide. She gripped my hand slightly, then turned her head towards me. A big smile came across her face, and I could see that wonderful gleam in those beautiful dark brown eyes. We did not speak for a full minute. We just hugged each other as though there was no tomorrow. You can be sure that we were both thinking of the great loss we had had, in the death of Charles.

"Oh, Steve," she said, as tears welled in her eyes. "I was so worried about you. Are you OK? No one could contact you, and we were all beginning to think the worst. Margaret has been so kind to me; she phoned me from a helicopter to let me know they had found you, and you were OK. Why weren't you answering your mobile? You had us all so very worried."

"Vee, I'll explain all that to you later; the most important thing is you." I could feel tears welling in my eyes. "I'm so sorry, Vee; when I made that call from my mobile, I had been assured that you were well out of the way, and moving in the opposite direction, but MI5, once again, screwed up."

"No, Steve, it's not like that. We were in full contact with MI5 all the time; but at that moment I was driving, and Charles was answering the mobile. But he dropped it in between the seats. We could hear someone's voice talking, but we couldn't make out what they were saying. The MG is so small, and with all the luggage all over the place, it was impossible to retrieve the mobile and we just kept driving. The next thing I remember was waking up in a helicopter with Margaret looking down at me."

We grabbed each other tightly, and both of us shed a lot of tears. We never spoke a word; we both knew that we were both thinking deeply of the loss of Charles.

She pulled away from me, and looked directly into my eyes. "No, it was nobody's fault, Steve," she said, shaking her head from side to side. "It was just a tragic, tragic happening. Nobody is to blame." She grabbed my beard and shook my head from side to side. "Steve, if I hadn't been driving I would be dead. Charles took the full force of the IED, and left me with only a few cuts and bruises. I'm so sorry about Charles, Steve; I know he was your mentor and a very dear friend to you. I also, over such a short period of time, had learned what a wonderful man he was, and I know that we are both going to miss him very deeply."

Just then the door opened, and in walked a doctor, with a nurse right behind him.

"How are we this morning?" he asked, looking at Vee.

"I'm feeling great now, doctor," Vee said, smiling broadly. "This, by the way, is Steve Taylor, and as long as he is alongside me, I will always be fine, of that I can assure you, doctor."

"Steve Taylor." He came round the bed and shook my hand. I could see a look of surprise on his face, but I would also have looked a little surprised, as I must have looked like a beach bum. "Doctor Bartley," he said, still with the curious look on his face, "We have heard a lot about you in the last six or seven hours, Steve, and I can't say how pleased I am for you to be here with her. She looks a different person already, and looking at her now, I am sure that we can have her out of here in a couple of days."

"A couple of days!" Vee retorted. "Doctor Bartley, I've only got a broken arm; I'm sure that there is no necessity for me to be laid up in a hospital bed for a couple of days."

"Yes, I agree, but you have also gone through a lot of trauma, and I would just like to keep an eye on you for a while."

"The trauma was because I didn't know whether Steve was alive or dead, not from the car accident. Doctor, underneath those scruffy clothes, and that disgusting beard, lies the love of my life, and let me assure you, that there is no better medicine in the world than just being with him, that anyone could give me."

"OK," he said, looking at me and smiling, "If Steve will leave the room for half an hour or so, then Sister Rose and I will give you a once over, and let's see what we find, shall we?"

"Thank you so much, Doctor Bartley, thank you so much," Vee said, with an appealing look on her face.

I squeezed Vee's hand, and smiled down at her. "OK, my love; see you in about half an hour then." I glanced towards the doctor, and winked as I walked towards the door.

As I came out into the passage, I saw Margaret sitting on a chair just down the corridor; she looked totally and utterly exhausted, and I could easily see that this whole episode had certainly taken its toll on her too. She looked tired, and didn't have that assertiveness that was always there in her composure.

"Steve," she said, getting up from the chair, and running towards me, "Oh, Steve, is Vee OK?" she put both her arms around my neck, and squeezed me tightly. I knew this was not MI5 talking; this was up close and very personal from Margaret.

"Vee's fine," I said. "Doctor Bartley said that I should be able to take her home after he's examined her."

"Thank God for that, Steve." Margaret said, holding me by the shoulders and gazing into my eyes.

"I think the trauma was not from the accident; it was from the death of Charles, and also from not knowing whether I was alive or dead."

"Steve," she said, hitting my chest with the palm of her hand, "Why the bloody hell didn't you phone us? We were all so very worried."

"Margaret, I told you: I accidentally dropped the bloody mobile down a well, right after the explosion, and that meant that I was totally out of communication with any of you, or anyone else for that matter. As you know, I did try to get in touch through nine, nine, nine; it was all I could do."

"Sorry, Steve," she said in a very quiet, meaningful voice, "My mind is in a total turmoil at the moment; it's been very hard on me also, and you've got to understand that I also have feelings, behind the façade of being MI5 Director. Even my children call me Mother, you know."

We both smiled at each other, but it was more a smile of relief than a smile of happiness.

"Talking about MI5, Steve," she said in a more business-like manner, "We want you to come in tomorrow morning just for a couple of hours, a sort of a verbal shakedown, so to speak."

"You must be bloody joking, Margaret," I must have said with slight venom in my voice. I just couldn't believe that they were really asking of me to go into Thames House tomorrow.

"But Steve, we need you to speak to the guys who cleared up the site at the farmhouse. They are all on their way back from Leeds as we speak. It's just a matter of dotting the I's and crossing the T's; just that, and nothing more."

I gripped her tightly by the shoulders and looked straight into her eyes. I could not believe what I had heard. "Margaret," I said in a very forceful voice, "I've done the job that I was asked to do, although as I told you before I did make a bloody mess doing it, and for that I'm sorry, but please: you really don't expect me to sweep up for you as well, do you?"

"Please Steve, they need to speak with you as soon as possible. They need to have a full verbal run down. The report can be done later, but they really need to speak to you." She sounded like she was pleading.

"Margaret you will have my full report on your desk within the next week. I have done more than MI5 and MI6 asked of me, and we were very lucky in saving thousands of lives, but you must recognize that it could have gone the other way very easily, and I wasn't left with any time to think the thing through. I just had to act on instinct, and act immediately."

I turned my back on her, looking down the passageway towards Vee's room, trying to keep my temper down.

"Sorry Margaret, I need to go home, to look after Vee, feed Basil, shave this bloody beard off my face and, most of all, relax for a while. What you must understand, Margaret, is that taking a life can be very easy in certain circumstances, when you are trained for it; but you must understand that it is never easy to live with it afterwards. This, nobody trains you for. You see those faces for the rest of your life, no matter who you are or who had to die. You must also take into consideration, Margaret, that one of the dead was my best friend and mentor; and I killed him. Over and above that, it could quite easily have been Vee on the slab. No, Margaret; we both need space for a while. Please respect that, and give us some time to clear our minds of the reality of what has occurred over the past few weeks."

I glanced down the passageway again, towards the constable sitting on his chair. He was well out of hearing, and seemed more interested in the magazine he was reading than in what was going on up here.

"Look, Margaret, I'm tired and very disturbed by the whole incident; but you have got to understand that I did everything that I could to make it a clean situation, and when you have read my report and fully comprehended the gravity of the situation at the time, you will understand that what I did was necessary, and there was no other way I could play it, other than taking chances with maybe thousands upon thousands of very, very innocent people's lives."

I could feel that I was tired now, and realised that I had had very little sleep over the last twenty-four hours, and everything was now really getting to me.

"Please, Margaret, listen to me," I said, trying to keep my temper down. "I'm very tired indeed, and I need to get Vee out of this hospital and home where she belongs, should there be any disconcertment on the Government's part about the way the operation was managed, they can do the same thing as they did with the Black Opps unit and Danny Bryce in the Oman War incident, where they had the SAS killing the SAS, even on the streets of London. Just hide it all for some thirty years under the government's Secrecy Act; then, after thirty years, everyone will have forgotten all about it. All I can say, Margaret, is that I did what I had to do; and, at that moment in time, there wasn't really an alternative. In fact, there was absolutely no alternative at all. Doing it any other way would have put many innocent people's lives, men, women and children, at stake and neither Vee, Charles nor myself could ever have allowed that to happen. Should I have done anything else, and had people had been killed, the Government, and both MI5 and MI6 would have said that we had failed. No Margaret, there definitely wasn't an alternative, no alternative whatsoever."

"We fully understand all that Steve, really we do, and all they are asking for is a verbal wash-up, to give everyone an understanding as to what happened out there. It's not a *fait accompli*, so that they can put the blame for anything on anyone; it's just a clearing of the air, so to speak."

Just then the ward door opened, and Doctor Bartley came walking over to us. He was smiling, so I knew that it was good news, and that was just what I needed at the present moment.

"Steve, I have just given your partner Vee a very thorough examination. Her blood pressure is back down to normal, and her heart rate is, although little high, nothing to worry about, as that is quite normal under the circumstances. So I think it will be OK for you to take her home; but, Steve, she must be totally supervised at all times, and relaxation is of the uppermost importance. I would like you to bring her in in a couple of weeks' time, so that I can see how her damaged arm is responding to the arm brace we have put on her."

He stood looking straight into my eyes. I could see that he was very serious, and he made me feel like a naughty schoolboy being reprimanded.

"You may go in and see her now. She may need some help getting dressed with that arm brace on her arm." With that, he stood to one side, and indicated with his right arm my clearance to go and see her.

"But Steve," Margaret started to say.

"You heard what the good Doctor said, Margaret. Vee must be supervised at all times, and that is what I fully intend to do. As I said before, you will have my report on your desk within a week; that's a promise."

"But Steve," she started to say something again.

"Margaret you are not assessing the situation as it should be. Firstly, Vee has to get well, and that is my first and foremost priority. Don't forget that over the next few days we have the stress of going to the funeral of Charles Pierce. Remember him, the man whom I killed? Margaret, there is nothing further to say on this subject." With that, I turned from her and headed toward Vee's ward. I didn't look back, my priority lay in ward 109; at the moment, nothing else in the world mattered to me.

Vee was up and already dressed when I entered the ward. She was smiling like a Cheshire cat, and her eyes were beaming with happiness.

"I can't wait to get home and see Basil, Steve; it's been a long time, hasn't it? He must be very heartsore, and missing us both terribly."

"Yes, sweetheart, it's been a long and very torrid time. Let's get the hell out of here, and get back to our home, and a breath of normality."

We left the hospital around six thirty, and caught a taxi home. It took a good half hour to get there. The weather had calmed down considerably, and it was just about becoming light when we reached the house. I sat Vee down on the settee, put the central heating up high, and went through to the kitchen to make some coffee. I had to ask the usual manly questions, such as "where's the coffee, Vee?

Where's the sugar, Vee?" (You must understand that the kitchen had never been my territory.)

As I gave Vee her coffee, there was a knock at the door. We both looked at each other questioningly, and simultaneously looked at the clock. It was only seven a.m. in the morning.

I answered the door to find Mr Smith standing there in his dressing gown; he was holding Basil in his arms. When Basil saw me, he started struggling excitedly to make a leap from Mr. Smith's arms into my arms.

"Hi Steve," he said, looking very surprised indeed, probably at the sight of me with a beard. "We saw you both getting out of the taxi, and somehow Basil also knew you were home; he was running around the house like a madman, or mad dog, should I say; so I thought I would bring him around. Is that OK?"

I grabbed Basil out of his arms; he was whimpering happily, and started licking me all over in his excitement.

"Thanks, Mr Smith," I said, struggling to contain Basil in my arms in his excitement. "We were waiting for a decent time to come and collect him. I can't thank you enough for looking after him for us; I will get Vee to invite you round for dinner, as soon as we get straight and settled in again."

"That would be nice, Steve, I'm sure Mrs Smith would love that too," he said. "Give Vee our love, now let's both of us get out of the bloody cold, eh?"

With that he turned and trundled off towards his door. Then he stopped for a moment and asked, "By the way, Steve, did you enjoy your holiday?"

"Yes it was great, Mr Smith; a nice change for both of us, but we are very grateful to be home at last," I lied.

As I closed the door, Basil jumped out of my arms and flew into the house, barking and whimpering. When I walked into the lounge, he was snuggled on Vee's lap as if he had been there for hours, and Vee had an "I'm home now" look on her face.

We spent the next few days just hanging out together with Basil. I spent a few hours a day doing my report for Margaret. We went to the shopping mall, bought a few groceries, and had a nice lunch together. While we were in the coffee bar in the shopping mall, a group of young teenagers were getting very boisterous and one of them banged against our table and spilt our coffees into our saucers. I jumped up, but Vee just looked at me, never saying a word. I could that see she was saying "please sit down."

As we walked back through the shopping mall towards our car, we could see shoppers shoulder to shoulder as far as our eyes could see. The mall was ringing out with Christmas Carols, and the Christmas trimmings and lights were in abundance; the people shopping were all smiling and chatting excitedly to each other, while happily going about their last-minute Christmas shopping. Everyone was enjoying themselves, and getting on with their normal lives and businesses. There was an electronic signboard overhead in the passageway, giving the time and date. We both saw it together. The time was twelve fifteen, and the date was the twenty second of December.

I looked at Vee, and I could see that her mind was on the same wavelength as mine. In my mind I was imagining the terrible death and destruction that would have come upon all these very innocent men, women and children, had we not alleviated that despicable and destructive plan that had raised its head under the flag of the Islamic Jihad.

"Looking round, Steve," she said, looking up at me, "look at all these smiling happy faces. I think it was well worth it, my love, don't you?"

I just smiled at her, put my arm around her, and we headed for the car park, with a feeling of a job well done.

The day that I was dreading soon came to fruition, and we had to go to Charles's funeral. I had to dress in a suit, and I always felt quite clumsy in a suit. There were about twenty people there. Most of them I didn't know. I recognised Carol, Charles's secretary, but no one else, really. As the Vicar stood to address the small congregation, I felt a hand on my shoulder. I looked around, and saw Margaret dressed all in black. Sitting alongside of her was Paul, and alongside Paul was Mel. Neither one of us uttered a word; our eyes said all that was necessary to be said.

We drove back from the service in silence, both of us deliberating deeply with our own thoughts. On glancing towards Vee from time to time, I saw her dabbing the odd tear away.

"Vee," I said, glancing over towards her. "Charles would not want us to be sad. What we must both keep strongly in our minds is the remarkable legacy that he has left behind for us all to hold in our hearts."

It took me eight days to complete my report, thirty-one pages, to be very precise. I shed a lot of tears while putting everything down in writing, because, as you can imagine, with Charles being a pivotal point in the operation, he was always foremost in my mind, I put forward all the details that were relevant to the operation, and remonstrated in depth as to why I had to bring things to the abrupt conclusion that I did in the end.

We went through Christmas alone at home with Basil, and I must say that Basil probably enjoyed it the most. We hadn't bought presents for each other, but we had our own very good company, with excellent food, and a few bottles of good wholesome red wine. Funnily enough, looking back, I think it was one of the best Christmases we had ever spent together.

I could obviously not email the data, so it had to be collected from their end. A lady and a gentleman from MI5 came to collect it. She had a briefcase manacled to her wrist. She opened the briefcase, and I placed the documents in an A4 envelope inside. She then closed and locked the briefcase, glanced up at me, and said "Thank you, sir," and abruptly turned and made her way towards the totally obvious government car, parked at the kerb.

It didn't take HQ very long to get on the bandwagon. The phone rang at nine thirty on the following morning of the second of January. It was Margaret.

"Hi, Steve, compliments of the season to both of you," she said, in a very unofficial voice. "I hope you both had a pleasant time; I know it must have been very hard for you after what you have both been through over the last few months. How is Vee, Steve? Is she coping OK?"

"Thank you, Margaret, and the same to you," I replied in a very nonchalant kind of voice. "We had a very quiet time, but we both enjoyed it, and Vee is more or less back to normal, that is, apart from her broken arm. of course. I suppose you are about to tell me that a meeting has been set up for the wash-up on the operation, or am I jumping to conclusions?"

"No; we thought we would let you pick a day that would be convenient to both of you; we will send a car to pick you both up."

"Margaret," I said rather sharply, "You have more chance of getting Charles Pierce there than Vee. I will be there alone at the meeting, and I will be coming in my own transport. There is no need at all for you to require that Vee be there, I think it would be too much for her at this early stage."

I moved the phone from my ear and gave it a bit of thought for a second or so.

"OK, Margaret," I said, rather formally, let's make it, say, ten a.m. tomorrow morning. How's that?"

I expected some kind of argument, but she answered "OK, Steve. Ten a.m. tomorrow morning it is. Oh, and Steve, you are not going to believe this, but I am really looking forward to it; and I want you to know that I will be in your corner every step of the way." With that, the phone went dead.

Chapter Eighteen

Funnily enough, I was quite nervous about the meeting the next day, as I knew that it was going to be a government inquisition, with them doing all the questioning, trying to do me down. Basically, they were a bunch of silver-spooned nondescript unadulterated paper pushers who had never even had a schoolyard fight as kids, but who carried the power to send young men into war zones, risking their lives, and making them stick to their pathetic rules of engagement.

I walked over to the settee and slumped myself down on it. I must have looked quite pensive and preoccupied, because Vee came over and slumped beside me on the settee. She never said a word; she just snuggled into my body and put her arm around me. Then up came Basil, to make it a threesome.

We were both up quite early the next morning. We had breakfast and a few cups of coffee. Very little was said between us. I guess that both our minds were on what the day held in store for us.

I ordered a taxi to pick me up at nine thirty, and gave Vee the keys to the Cooper. Before I left the house, I told Vee that I would give her a missed call from the meeting, when I knew it was coming to an end, and she must pick me up outside Thames House.

The taxi driver was as all London cabbies are, full of waffle, going on about the NHS, and its difficulties, and the government's great love of power. I didn't want to join in the conversation. I just listened; my mind was totally focused on what laid ahead of me in the meeting at MI5 Offices.

As I was paying my fare he asked, "You MI5, then, mate?"

"No," I replied, "They've got some blocked toilets, probably from all the bullshit in there, and I'm here to fix them."

"That's a real shit job you got there then mate," he shouted to me through the taxi's window, as he drove away.

I stood on the kerb in a fit of laughter; the cabbie had certainly made my day, that was for sure. What would we do without our London cabbies? I turned and faced the building, still with a broad grin on my face. It stood on the Milbank road Embankment, overlooking the Thames. and close to the Lambeth Bridge. I always saw it as a totally majestic and captivating building, and, overall, quite a pillar of power and discreet, although very diplomatic, concealed secrets.

I didn't have any trouble at the reception this time, as Margaret was standing there waiting for me, and I also looked far more decent than the last time. As we walked over to the security gates, Margaret grabbed my arm and stopped me.

"Steve, before we go in there, I want you to understand that while you are in there, I will be totally behind you. Just remember that you are not on your own; you will have my and Mel's complete support, and, what's more, and quite surprisingly, Steve, I am positive, judging from what he has said to me, that Donald Franks will also be very much in your corner too."

She moved in front of me, put her hands on my shoulders, and looked me straight in my eyes,

"OK, Steve: do you hear what I say?" Margaret said, smiling.

"Yes, Margaret, I understand, and I very much appreciate your support. Thank you." I smiled at her and gave her a peck on the forehead; not a done thing in the reception area of MI5, I suppose.

Margaret, not saying another word, led me to the same room that we had formally used for the last two meetings. All of the chairs, this time, were occupied and an extra chair, also occupied, had been placed at the head of the table, next to Margaret's chair. This time, though, everyone had folders full of papers in front of them, and I noticed that, in the middle of the table, there was a voice recorder. I was feeling very uneasy as I entered the room. It was like being called into the headmaster's office when you were a kid, not knowing whether you were going to get six of the best or to be made head boy.

I took my usual chair, and immediately filled my glass with water from the bottle in front of me. As everyone seemed to have found their places, Margaret stood up at the head of the table, and put both her hands tightly on the back of her chair. Her eyes were sort of gleaming, and I could see that she was very much at ease. This brought a definite sense of relief into my mind, and was going to help significantly with my awareness of the confidence that I was going to need over the next couple of hours.

"Gentlemen, we all know why we are here, but before we make a start, I would like first to inform Mr Steve Taylor of events which have occurred over the past week, so that he is fully aware and up to date with what we have achieved since the conclusion of this operation."

"Steve," she said looking directly at me, "we have cleared the site at the farmhouse, and completed all DNA tests on the human remains found there. I am sure that you are fully aware, from the television and newspaper reports over the last few days, that we have given the explanation that the explosions that occurred on the twentieth of December were probably an error in judgement made by the terrorists, which caused a number of bombs which they were manufacturing to detonate. We have also cleaned up the house you were using in Leeds, so there will be no evidence at all of yourself, or Vee, or anyone else, for that matter, ever having been there. We have also cleaned up the Mercedes that you were using, and delivered it back to the garage where you yourself took delivery. I must also add, Steve that the owner of the car is a Mr. Sheikh Habbid, who, at the moment, is holidaying in Somalia; both the CIA and MI6 are keeping very close tabs on him, and have uncovered quite a lot of information. Seemingly, he has had very close contact with Al Shebbab, the Islamic terrorist organisations in both Somalia and Northern Nigeria; and we are also pretty sure that for a number of years he has been organising the financial side of the group. By the time he returns to the United Kingdom we will have enough information on him to arrest and charge him with aiding and abetting terrorism, both overseas, and here on British soil."

Margaret then formally introduced everyone around the table. I didn't take much notice of the governmental names, as they were all Mr. Minister of this, and Mr. Deputy Minister of that. With all introductions done and out of the way, the bell rang for the start of round one; but the worrying thing was that there was no referee in the ring with me.

I was right in my thoughts earlier that this was going to be a Governmental inquisition. I could see it in their eyes and, as I had expected, they climbed in instantly, but I was more than ready for them. I would have to use my SAS training directive. The best form of defence is attack.

The first one to speak was a balding guy to my left. I couldn't remember who he was minister for, but he obviously came from a high-class family, and had had a top university education.

"Good morning. Firstly, let me say, from all of us here, a big thank you to you for being here with us today. We all know that both you and your partner Vee have had a tremendously stressful time over the past couple of months. Steve, may I call you Steve?"

he asked, dipping his head forward and looking at me over his reading glasses.

"No, I don't mind at all Mr. Minister," I said, leaning forward in my chair. "Not at all, what's your Christian name, Mr. Minister? That would place us all on more equal terms, so to speak." The air conditioning seemed to get very loud indeed at that moment. A number of people around the table were coughing, as if to clear their throats; but I knew that they were stifling laughter, with their hands over their mouths.

Without answering my question, the Minister went on, "Mr. Taylor, I see you are here today and I have got to say that I am very surprised to see that you do not have any papers whatsoever in front of you."

Mr Taylor! Wow, I liked that. I think I must come here more often.

"No Mr. Minister," I retorted abruptly. "If you have read the report in front of you, you will have realised two things. First and foremost, I wrote the paper; and secondly, I was there, leading the operation. Mr Minister I was there among fifteen home-grown Jihadi terrorists who were about to bring about the most horrific attack that has ever been known to man – even worse than the 9/11 attack – and, let us not forget, on British soil. The outcome of their attack would have been catastrophic to all of the Western World, to say the least. Mr Minister, I can assure you that I don't need to read it; it's embedded in my mind, and I can assure you it will never go away. Mr. Minister, I get very angry when I think that people like yourselves," I waved my hand, indicating all the Ministers, "have people trained to kill, but you never teach them how to forget; mainly because you don't damn care, as long as you have won your battle for oil. The post-traumatic stress situation in this country is making young men who haven't even reached the age of thirty commit suicide, simply because they can't cope with the memories of battle, seeing their close friends dead from IED explosions, and their bodies torn into three or four different blood soaked pieces. Only five years ago, you governmental people were in complete denial of its very existence; and we all know why. You had got your oil, and you didn't want the monetary expenditure that it would take to help these brave men, whom you had sent to the battlefield, to properly recuperate."

I was glaring at him, not because of what he had said, but because of the wretched attitude he had used in saying it.

"Mr Minister, I want you to understand something about governance, as we the people see it. Just before Vee and I went into this operation, we decided to take a weekend break at the coast, and due to the weather, we decided to go by bus. As the bus pulled in, the luggage compartment opened, and I put our suitcase inside. The next thing I knew, I had the bus driver run up to me, saying that I must not do that, because I might bang my head on the door. Then, the other day, I read that children playing conkers must wear protective goggles. And yet it is permitted for a six-foot man to wield a two and a half kilogramme bat at a very hard ball, and to hit it into a crowd of some seventeen thousand people who have no protection at all. And all this goes under the designation of government health and safety. Things like this, Mr. Minister, are what the real working people see in you people; and that is why fewer than thirty per cent of them vote. Yes, Minister, this is what governance is about; you are the most pathetic bunch of useless hypocritical people that could ever roam this planet. Everyone knows that you people just lie and lie again, and we always know when you are lying, because your mouths move. I don't think I can ever remember a government official answering a direct question. Is it because they don't know the answer? Or are they too scared, or even too ashamed, to tell the truth?

"Mr. Taylor," the minister said butting in, "these are very disparaging remarks that you are making, and very offensive to everyone in this room."

"Sorry Mr. Minister, but I have the floor and I am not by any means finished answering what I, personally, would call your impertinent and pathetic question."

The words of the cabbie who had brought me here came to mind. I got to my feet and put both hands on the table; I glanced briefly at everyone in the room.

"I want everyone in this room to understand that when the power of love overcomes the love of power, only then gentlemen, will we see peace in this misbegotten world which your people have blindly instigated over the years."

Nobody moved, not even an eyelid.

"Now ladies and gentlemen, I am asking, has anyone, anyone at all, got any pertinent or relevant questions about the operation? Or can I take it that I am done here?"

All the Ministers were shuffling papers around, as if they were going to deal a hand in a game of stud poker. People were pouring water into their glasses, and it seemed that no one wanted to take the floor.

The government official with the grey hair was the first to speak, although I could see a strong reluctance in his eyes to take the floor.

"Mr. Taylor," he said, looking quite nervous, "You said in your report that the date of the attack by the terrorist cell was brought forward by two days, and that you had less than seven hours to stop it happening. I have a question on this point, and my question is this: how can we be sure that it was the time schedule that made you initiate your attack? Or was it, rather, because you had found out earlier that day that Mohammed and his wife, what was her name," – he was scanning some of the papers in front of him – "ah, yes,

Mari, had detonated the bomb in the restaurant explosion in which you and your partner were caught up? Maybe you were just seeking retribution on a personal basis? Reading your report, you bought the environmental suit, unbeknown to MI5; the mobile sim cards and bug detectors which you ordered from MI5 were ordered well in advance."

"I do not believe this, Mr Minister, are you accusing me of bloody murder? I bought those items well in advance, yes, but that is known in any warfare situation as contingency planning, and it was used by Winston Churchill many times in the Second World War. Without the use of contingency planning all those years ago, we would all be sitting round here speaking bloody German." I was glaring at him now. "I know that, in Government circles, when you make a boob, you just do a bloody U-turn, apologise to your opposition in private, and then forget that it ever happened. Well let me tell you all, in the field, there is no room for mistakes at all. If you do make a mistake, it can easily lead to your death and the destruction of your mission."

"No, please," the Minister said, almost stuttering, "Nothing like that, Mr Taylor; I was not accusing you of anything, and I was just trying to get to the bottom line, with all the ducks in a row, so to speak."

"Then would you please define your question, so that we all know what you do mean, Mr. Minister?"

As it was said, I glanced up the table, and was very surprised to see that it was Franks who had made the statement.

"I also find that question very disturbing, and unpardonable myself, Mr Minister." It was Margaret now who was on her feet, with both palms laid firmly clamped on the table, "and I feel that an apology is in order here."

"I am not accusing anyone of murder; I am trying to get to the reason why the carnage took place when the whole of MI5 and MI6

321

were at Mr Taylor's disposal, yet he still chose to execute fifteen people on his own discretion. I am, in essence, asking if there is any proof that the date of the operation was brought forward."

I then again resurrected myself from my chair and stood for almost fifteen seconds just staring at everyone.

"I cannot believe what I am hearing in this room," I was almost shouting. "Are you asking me if I got it in writing from Mohammed? Because I cannot think of any other reason for the question, or for that matter, any other way that I could prove my statement."

"Ladies and Gentlemen," I went on loudly, "we must put some reality into the meeting. I am very perturbed at the questions that I'm getting, and I also feel that I wasted eight days putting the report together, as some of you don't seem to have even read it. Those of you who did read my report will know that one of the terrorists had already left the farmhouse by the time I got there, at around nineteen forty five, and that that caused the death of Charles Pierce, my mentor and a very dear friend of mine. Also, it could have caused the death of Vee, my partner, who, I may add, took part in this operation of her own free will. She didn't have to get involved in the operation at all. She did it because she thought it was the right thing to do. Now, gentlemen, let's look at another scenario. Supposing five of them had left the farmhouse when I got there? I had to fight like hell with MI5 to get one helicopter up in that bad weather; to get five up there would have been a total impossibility, if this scenario had come to fruition. I cannot even start to imagine the devastation that it would have brought about for the British public."

I took my seat again but made it known by facial expression that I was not impressed with what I was hearing.

"Mr. Taylor." It was the youngest of the parliamentarians in the meeting. "I have a question that I think is very pertinent to your operation, and, Mr Taylor I can assure you that I have read your report thoroughly not once, not twice, but three times, and in cross-referencing your report with other reports, I find that you seem to have omitted something that I consider very relevant to this enquiry, and to the operation as a whole."

He had a very smug look on his face, as he shuffled his papers around.

"Yes Mr. Taylor, here we are," he took off his glasses and placed them on the table. "On the eighteenth of December, Paul Lawson was contacted by yourselves and asked to dispatch MI5 agents to pick up two of the terrorists who seemingly had broken into the house that you were using in Leeds; but a few hours later Paul Lawson was contacted and told to hold off as the problem had been solved at your end. Is this correct, Mr. Taylor?"

"Yes, that is correct." I was shocked that this had been picked up, and knew that I had to tread very carefully in order to fully to explain myself on this issue.

"On the night in question, at around three a.m., I was awakened by the sound of breaking glass. I found that two of the terrorists had broken into the house. However I managed to restrain them both, but not before they had discovered very pertinent information that proved that we were not Salim and Sharma Rias. All of a sudden the whole bloody operation was in jeopardy. We still needed a lot of information about the operation; we had to find out how they had imported such a large amount of semtex and anthrax spores into the country, and also when and where they were going to implement their devastating plan. I've got to say at this point, and it is well known to most people around this table, that I have very little faith in either MI5 or MI6 at this moment in time. So I took it upon myself to eliminate the problem, and that as you all know is just what I did."

"Are you telling us you took the lives of these two men?"

His voice was very stern, and he had a very arrogant and yet hypocritical look on his face.

"That's correct," I said directly.

"But no matter who you are or what rank you hold, you cannot just go around taking the lives of people on a whim, Mr. Taylor."

"It wasn't a whim; it was a dire necessity at the time! It's strange that you say that, Mr Minister, because ever since I was a young man of seventeen, when I joined the services, I have been taught to kill. Every man and woman, on entering the British armed forces, whether it be the Army, the Navy or the Royal Air Force, is taught to kill, but now it seems that some paper pushers from the Government are telling me that it's wrong. What is it with you people? You should not be telling me; you should be telling the people who trained us.

"Also, Mr Minister, if you remember, about half an hour ago I asked the Minister here," I lifted my left hand, to indicate the guy on my left, "What his first name was. He never answered my question, and spent a full seven seconds before carrying on. Mr Minister let me tell you in theatre you have..." With that, I snapped my fingers loudly. "That is the amount of time you have to make your decision. Yes, Mr Minister, that is the time you have. Any longer, and you are the one dead."

I went very quiet for a few seconds. To say that I was perplexed with the level of questioning that I had had up to that point would be far from the truth. In fact, I was appalled and disgusted at their arrogance and ignorance.

"As far I can see, Mr Minister," I went on, "you people and governments throughout the Western World are a pathetic bunch of hypocrites, who are ruining whole countries, and also the lives of many of those countries citizens. You are the biggest bunch of two-faced hypocritical liars that has ever graced this earth. I am not a political person at all, but I am a realist, and I can assure you all here that, over the next ten or eleven years, the people of this country, and many other countries throughout the world for that matter, who have totally lost confidence in this pathetic kind of governmental dominance, will come together and turn on you, putting a far different kind of government into power, a very strong government, who will be there for the country and the people, and not for themselves, as is the case now. As I said earlier, gentlemen, when the power of love overcomes the love of power, which you people seem to get off on, we will then maybe find peace in this woe-begotten world which you governmental people have developed over the years."

I looked around the table with a look of disgust on my face.

"Gentlemen, not very long ago, I came across something on the internet that quite surprised me because it was written many, many years ago, in 55BC to be precise, by a Roman called Cicero. I myself had never heard of him, but I found it quite intriguing; and I can see that it has a total relevance to the circumstances of the governments of today. I brought a copy with me, and I would be very grateful if you would take the time to listen to it; and you never know, maybe some around this table could even learn a little from it."

I took a drink of water and raised myself to a standing position again, "Ladies and gentlemen, please keep in mind that this was written in the year 55BC."

I coughed and took the paper from my pocket, and started to relate the words to everyone in the room.

"The budget should be balanced," I read, "and the Treasury should be refilled, and all Governmental departments should be reduced. The arrogance of officialdom should be tempered and controlled, and assistance to foreign lands should be totally curtailed, lest Rome should become bankrupt. The people must again learn to work, instead of living on personal assistance."

I looked at all the ministerial guys around the table; their faces said nothing. "So evidently, gentlemen, it seems that in two thousand years you don't seem to have learned very much, have you?"

I took my seat again, took out my mobile, and gave Vee a missed call; I knew that she would be here in about ten to fifteen minutes.

"Well, gentlemen, if you have any relevant questions, and I mean relevant questions, to ask, you have about fifteen minutes of me, and then I'm out of here."

Everyone looked around the table at everyone else, but no one seemingly wanted to be taken to task.

"I was in a public toilet taking a leak a few months back," I spoke quietly, as if I was talking to myself. "Looking up on the wall, in front of me was some graffiti, and it said, 'Where are you now, Guy Fawkes, now that we need you?'"

I stood for a moment, staring hard at the ministerial guys around the table, "Many a true word is spoken in jest, don't you think, gentlemen?"

Then Franks stood up. He was smiling; this alone shocked me, never mind what he had to say.

"Steve," he said, "We have known each other for quite a number of years, and I know that, at times, we have come into conflict on a number of occasions; but I believe that this will always happen, due to the life-threatening way of life that we now have to live with. But I want you, and everyone around this table, to know that on every assigned commission that you have been given you have always come through with shining honours; and I can tell you right now, I will always be proud to have served with you. It has been a great honour Steve, a very great honour."

I sat unable to move. Franks had for the first time showed his inner feelings, and I could not believe my ears. I knew now that he really must have feelings deep down under, and maybe even blood flowing through his veins, although I'm not sure what colour it would be.

Margaret got to her feet and clapped her hands in applause; then Paul also rose to his feet, clapping his hands vigorously; and soon everyone around the table, except the Ministers of course, were applauding.

"Thanks for your time, gentlemen, I must leave now, as my partner will be out there waiting for me, and, to be honest and forthright, I can't, under any circumstances, put up with any more of this unadulterated crap."

With that I turned and, very proudly indeed, headed for the door.

Chapter Nineteen

Margaret almost ran towards the door, as if to stop Steve from leaving, but she only opened the door for him. Their eyes met very briefly for just a second; nothing was said verbally, but both their eyes spoke a thousand words. She would never ever forget those powerful words that Steve had used to end his rendition. 'When the power of love overcomes the love of power, only then will we find peace in this world.' Yes, powerful; so very powerful and so very appropriate, and also so very, very accurate, when looking at the carnage around the world and seeing it intensifying day by day, in every sector of the globe around us. Are we to understand that this is what we must acknowledge in this present day and age?

Steve then walked through the door, and entered the passageway, never looking back. Margaret heard him whistling a melody. It took a few seconds for her to recognise that it was 'God bless ye merry gentlemen.' She felt tears start to run down her face, and she knew that Steve would have the same on his face. She watched Steve step into the elevator, never turning or even glancing over his shoulder; she then slowly closed the door, and, for a moment, stood with her forehead pressed hard against it. She felt the tears running freely down her face, and then, turning, she proudly made her way back to her seat. She didn't sit down, nor did she wipe the tears from her face.

She stood proud and rigid behind her chair, with both hands tightly gripping the back of the chair, and the tears still rolling down her cheeks. She looked at everyone seated around the table individually, and, taking in the expressionless looks on each of their morbid faces, she seemed to be overawed with the situation.

"Well, gentlemen," Margaret said, then wiping the tears from her face for everyone to see. "Now you all definitely know what a real man is."

She looked quite anguished at what had happened that day, and she took no measures at all to cover it up. She stood at the head of the table, firm-faced, tall and very proud.

"Well, gentlemen," Margaret put both her arms out in front of her, to indicate everyone sitting around the table. "You know, gentlemen, today you have all been very fortunate, because you have just heard a very courageous and genuine man who has, for Queen and country, put his life on the line more times than I care to remember, speak from his heart, running both MI5's and MI6's top representatives – oh yes, and not forgetting the high ranking government officials from the Home Office – down into the ground. Personally, I have got to say that I fully agree with every bloody word that Mr Taylor had to say, and I think that deep down you must all agree with me when I say that this whole bloody country stinks to high heaven, and pathetically all in the name of oil and bad governance. Yes, gentlemen; as Steve said, it does make one think, doesn't it?"

Margaret walked over to the window, again wiping the tears from her face for everyone to see. Everyone in the room stayed silent. No one even looked towards any one else around the table. The room was so silent that you could have heard a pin drop. As she stared out of the window, she saw Vee, standing by the wall of the Embankment, looking out over the Thames, her dark shining hair blowing wildly in the wind. Vee turned her head to look back towards Thames House, she then saw Steve running across the road towards her. Vee turned abruptly, and they ran into each other's arms. They cuddled for a moment, a strong cuddle, as if there was no tomorrow. They then stood still, holding each other tightly, with their foreheads touching, and looking into each other's eyes. She knew that they were talking, but could only guess what they were saying. Margaret's tears started to roll again.

Steve and Vee then turned and started walking towards Lambeth Bridge. Steve had both arms around Vee, and Vee held on tightly with her left unhindered arm; both of their heads were to one side and touching in the middle. A very emotional smile came across Margaret's face, she had definitely never seen love and devotion between two people like that before; and it sadly crossed her mind that she would probably never ever see it again.